Kiss Your Strawberries Goodbye

Nina DeGraff

Copyright © 2023 by Nina C. DeGraff

First paperback edition September 2023

Book design by Nina C. DeGraff
Night Sky cover photo: Milosz_G/shutterstock.com
Berry photo, cover illustrations: Nina C. DeGraff

ISBN 979-8-9888-3690-2 (paperback)
ISBN 979-8-9888-3691-9 (ebook)

Round Pond Publishing, LLC
54 State Street, Suite 804 #9162
Albany, NY 12207

www.roundpondpublishing.com

For Joe

And for Sarah, Pepper, Iris, Max, Koki, Milo,
Woolberry, Gracie, Bubbah, Magnolia, Dot,
and all the other pets who've shared their unique
perspective and wisdom with us

1

According to one entry in my father's private journals, not one person has ever been murdered in the town of Gracious, Maine. Plenty of people had been shot, stabbed, or deliberately run over by cars in neighboring towns, but somehow, the residents of Gracious had stood tall above the fray for over two hundred and thirty years.

Then I came along. Rule breaker. Button pusher. Target of the gods whenever they felt the need to liven things up.

To be clear, I didn't do any murdering, and nobody ended up murdering me, although they did their best to pitch me into a shallow grave in the middle of the woods. My arrival in town had set a world of trouble into motion, which ultimately led to the disappointing news that my father's journal entry was not accurate after all. The deep forests and misty fields of Gracious, Maine had been a hidden stronghold of murderous deeds stretching back for who knew how many years.

My education into one of the darkest sides of human nature began at roughly 11:45 p.m. on a Saturday night. My father's hilltop strawberry and sheep farm was a thirty-acre world of its own, obscured from the winding, lightless road at the bottom of the hill by a stand of sixty-foot pine trees, with a spooky, ramshackle barn I didn't like to set foot in after dark. For three months I'd spent most nights feeling alone and out of my depth as I attempted to identify the rustlings and trills and sudden banging sounds that continuously unfolded outside in the pasture and strawberry field.

But on that night, I was not alone.

In all my twenty-eight years, I had never been inclined to let a near stranger walk in out of the blue and claim space on my couch for the night unless there was a solid reason behind the visit. My father's longtime farrier, Brumby Jones, had used an entire array of winning arguments as he'd tossed his Stetson on the kitchen table at 9:30 p.m.

"Dodge is due for his hoof trimming," he'd said of my father's Belgian draft horse. "I don't get down this way much. Busy as hell. Plus, you have questions about Raymond. I knew him better than just about anyone. Not the part about him having a secret love child, of course. Even his niece was shocked when you showed up. I assume you know to not drop your guard on that front for a good long while. Charlotte Bergley is mad as a cut snake over the fact that Raymond left his farm to you."

Admittedly, his handsome grin and Australian accent had a bit to do with why I'd dropped my guard and added a blanket to the couch for him to use. As for the stories he'd promised to tell, Brumby had put me off until morning. Farrier work was demanding, and he'd shared that it had been a particularly tough day. He needed his sleep.

Two hours after his arrival, I was upstairs lying on my back in bed, fully clothed after reading a worrisome assessment of Brumby's character in one of my father's journals. My neighbor at the bottom of the hill, Joan Dumas, was away for the night visiting an aunt, but she'd answered a text I'd sent faster than I could blink.

Brumby is there now? her text said.

I'd replied: *To shoe Dodge in the morning. He's only in town for tonight.*

Ding: *Sonny, he lives 10 miles away.*

10 miles? I wrote.

Ding: *I'm sorry I didn't clue you in about him before now. He's known for this kind of thing. Put him off if he makes a move.*

I assured Joan that I could handle Brumby just fine in that regard. My main concern was whether or not there were currently any jilted husbands who were looking to track Brumby down and "mess him up" for sparking the ugly collapse of a supposedly happy marriage.

Not that I know of, she'd texted.

I frowned in the darkness, still recalling his exact words, "I don't get down this way much." And if catching up on sleep was his first priority, why in the heck was he still clomping back and forth downstairs? The past two hours had been a marvel of exactly how loudly a man could sniff, gulp beer, clear his throat, splash water in the sink, rake the curtains aside to look out into the darkness, and loudest of all, rip open snack bags. I calculated that he'd managed to eat a month's worth of my food at the worst possible time. I was unemployed, and close to broke.

I groaned as a fresh round of heavy boot falls indicated he was crossing to the window again. The curtain hooks squeaked for the twentieth time. Clear as a bell, I heard Brumby say, *"Finally.* Took you long enough."

I sat up and stared toward the unlit hallway. A familiar whine of hinges downstairs indicated he'd opened the door of my father's bedroom. From the sound of it, he was rummaging around in a closet. I couldn't begin to guess why. For me, it had been too heartbreaking to enter the room where my father used to sleep. The scent of his cherry pipe tobacco was too vivid, his boots and clothes exactly where he'd left them on his last day on Earth. Brumby apparently didn't share the kind of sensibilities I had when it came to trespassing on the personal space of the dead.

I heard Brumby step out of the bedroom and cross back to the kitchen. Items spilled on the table and rolled around for a moment or two. There was a sniff, the thump of his cowboy boots crossing the old maple flooring, with its telltale creaks, then a series of clicks and snaps that sounded an awful lot like someone loading a shotgun.

I lurched from my bed and stumbled to the landing. Brumby stood at the bottom of the stairs in a T-shirt and jeans, his champion barrel racer buckle shining in the moonlight as if he'd just polished it.

And yes, he was carrying a shotgun.

"I was about to see if you were awake," he said. "Stay in the house for a while, all right? No matter what you hear."

"What in the heck are you doing?" I demanded.

"I heard the sheep running down the slope." He snugged on his Stetson. "I'm heading out in case it's a coyote. Like I said—"

"You don't need a gun. Just clap your hands and yell."

"Clap my hands ...?" In the darkness downstairs, Brumby fell into a laughing, chortling fit. "Lord almighty, you are a hoot."

Even in the dim light, I could see his movements had a tipsy quality, and I didn't like the shining look about his eyes.

"Have you been drinking?" I said.

I knew how many beers he'd consumed, but it seemed important to know if he'd also been helping himself to my father's whiskey.

"Of course I had a drink, you sleeping up there in your altogether."

"I am fully clothed," I pointed out.

"Not in my mind, that's for sure." Shaking his head, Brumby headed for the kitchen door. "Raymond's ghost would punch my lights out if he knew half of what I've been picturing."

"Brumby!"

Too late. He was out the door, and I would be stunned if he wasn't the kind of man who thought nothing of firing a warning shot into the air. Off the pellets would fly from my hilltop farm, past the stream at the bottom of the meadow to pepper somebody's roof along the lane of deep woods and scattered homes. The owners would piece together where the pellets had come from, and sue my pants off.

I grabbed a windbreaker, took the stairs two at a time, and found the flashlight I used every night to sweep the yard for signs of lunatics, no idea I would one day invite one to spend the night on my sofa. The floodlight stationed near the barn's peak had blown out long ago, and no ladder on Earth was long enough to reach the blasted thing.

I opened the kitchen door and stepped out onto the wooden porch, where a hammock and two rocking chairs faced east. Moonlight gleamed on the hillside, and a breeze stirred through the maples across the driveway. I crossed to the steps, and found the railing wet with dew. Brumby was walking carefully toward the barn some ten yards away on my right. Hearing my foot creak on the steps, he turned with an irritated hiss, then he motioned for me to stay quiet and keep back.

I spread my hands. *Why? What is it?*

The brim of his hat nodded toward the barn. At first all I saw was the black silhouette of the old building, then the beam of a flashlight flicked through the interior. Someone was prowling around in there. I heard my father's draft horse, Dodge, blowing and stirring in his stall. He didn't like the presence of the unauthorized visitor one bit. I took pains to silence my footfalls on my way over, though Brumby was not impressed.

"The hell are you doing?" he whispered.

"What if it's one of my cousins?"

"I'll handle it. Stay back."

"Wait until I get my camera."

"Your *camera?*"

"The Bergleys took valuables when I inherited the farm," I whispered. "If they're back for more, I want to catch them in the act."

"You've blown it anyhow, they've gone quiet," Brumby furiously hissed. "Just stay back, would you please?"

I fumed as he continued onward, no idea if I should stay put, run for my camera, or follow him to insist he not use the shotgun unless the prowler had a weapon and acted first. I hovered. Paced. Clenched my fists. As Brumby slid open the barn door, the sound of breaking glass signaled the prowler might be getting away through a window out back.

With a curse, Brumby launched into the dark interior at a dead run, and I crossed the distance to the barn in an all-out sprint. The sharp groan and tumbling noise of someone getting hit in the gut and collapsing to the floor came from inside. There was no time to worry if Brumby had been taken by surprise. Footfalls were running toward me.

I fumbled with the flashlight, a trembling, conflicted mess. Dodge added shrill whinnies and Godzilla-level noise to the night as he fought the confines of his stall inside the barn. I swept the interior with the light, illuminating hay bales, cobwebs, horse blankets, then a glimpse of a man with his arm covering his face. He hit me full-on, propelling me straight from the open doorway to the ground outside in a painful, sputtering tangle of swinging arms and kicking legs. A metal container he'd been holding slipped from his grasp and clattered to the ground.

I scrambled after him as he dove for the box, my fists pummeling his back. With greasy hair and stubble, he smelled of cigarettes and booze.

"Get *back*," he growled, shoving me aside. His hands were covered with latex gloves. He'd hoped to come and go without a trace.

Dizzy, gasping for air, I lay with my hands planted on the dewy grass near the barn and watched him roll and stagger to his feet. He limped at first, then he vaulted an old pile of firewood in sneakers and a jeans jacket with the sleeves torn off. Patches were sewn on the back. Sports teams, a flag, and other kinds of logos. All I could tell for certain was that he was not one of my cousins, or anyone else I'd ever seen.

"Sonny, look out!" Brumby hollered from inside the barn.

I climbed to my feet. "It's ok. He's gone."

"*Move!*"

A din of splintering wood said Dodge had won the battle with his stall door. I froze in place, mesmerized by the sound of such a large animal pounding toward me at top speed. It all but pushed air out of the barn into my face.

I whirled to one side in time to see the living, muscled hulk of Dodge's ton of weight clip the door frame with a thunderous rattle, then surge past me on hooves the size of cannon balls. Snorting and blowing, prancing with high steps, the horse whinnied into the night with his tail high and his eyes wild with fear. I realized the instant I reached out that it was the wrong thing to do. Dodge wheeled away with a frightened squeal and galloped down the driveway with a clattering of hooves.

Brumby strode out of the barn with the shotgun in one hand, his dusty hat and Dodge's halter in the other. He turned toward the sound of a car door slamming shut on the road at the bottom of the hill beyond the woods. A half-overgrown logging trail was down there, the perfect place to park in stealth. A vehicle gunned to life and sped away with a screech of spinning tires. The intruder, no doubt, in a hurry to put this chapter behind him and start planning his next criminal act.

"Why did you let Dodge out?" I demanded.

Letting a cross glare suffice for a response, Brumby issued a shrill whistle and called Dodge's name as he strode after the loose horse.

I dashed into the barn and reached for the light switch, adding the feeble, cobwebbed illumination of three bulbs to the central aisle and sections of the interior. Built of rough-hewn timber long ago, the building felt spooky at night, a place of shadows and strange wafts of air. It was the thickness of the old timbers that had saved Dodge's stall from destruction.

The damage appeared to be restricted to the sliding door, which now hung at a slight angle. It could be fixed. I grabbed an extra halter and a handful of sugar cubes, then I stepped back into the cool night air.

Hearing Dodge's whinny floating beneath the stars from an unseen place on the dark hillside, I swung in circles in a desperate attempt to identify the direction, then headed down the driveway toward the strawberry field. The jouncing beam of the flashlight illuminated divots and gullies into a featureless glare and my ankles kept turning as I slipped and tripped my way over the bigger stones. Abruptly Dodge surged past me out of the darkness, a flash of arched neck and galloping hooves.

He was heading uphill, darn it.

I swerved and dashed after him, only to see his haunches vanish into the black void beyond the feeble beam of my flashlight. This happened again and again, Dodge pausing to nip at grass or paw the ground just long enough for me to draw near, then galloping away with a frightened snort and swish of tail.

"Sonny!" Brumby hollered from down near the road. "You're not helping! Stay put at the barn in case Dodge loops back."

"Fine with me," I managed.

Arriving at the barn, I staggered to a halt with my hands on my knees, sweating and gasping for breath, and too spent to calm Bubbah, my father's old ram who lived in a pen by himself next to the barn. He blinked as the beam of my flashlight illuminated his eyes. Beyond the pasture fence, thirty ewes and lambs looked alarmed by all the hollering and running around. They stared at me, poised to flee.

Still a shaking, winded mess in danger of collapse, I continued onward, then I looked down as my foot landed on a piece of paper.

Unlike the grass, it was dry, no sign of dew, so I concluded it wasn't stray trash blown there by the wind. Guessing the burglar might have dropped the paper, I picked it up and illuminated its dusty surface with the flashlight. On it was a single sentence, very easy to read.

You didn't ask the right questions.

It had been written with a red crayon, the letters unevenly spaced and taking some wild tangents in terms of style. I pictured someone who couldn't make up his mind between cursive or print. It hit me that it was possible the guy hadn't come to steal anything after all. Maybe he'd meant to leave the note for me to find, a taunt alluding to the fact that I'd been blindsided when I'd inherited the farm. If so, Brumby had caught him in the act before he'd finished finding the right spot.

I turned to the round tin container he'd dropped. I picked it up and saw dust on the lid that felt chalky. It was a cookie tin of all things, showing a festive design that featured a snowman with a carrot nose, stick arms, and a top hat. I saw a length of pink satin and something else lying nearby in the grass. With a groan, I reached for the object, and was startled to find that it was an assemblage of small bones held together by glistening strands of fishing line. Turning them this way and that in the beam of the flashlight, I could make no sense of the arrangement, then as I shook the bones in an effort to untangle them, they unfurled into a skeleton hand.

I stared at it for a long moment. The bones were stained and grimy, and gave off the stink of decay as if they'd spent some time in a garbage dump or buried in the ground. The skeleton hand shivered as I held it there, brought to life by the pounding blood in my fingertips, then the smell of decay got to me.

I dropped the bones and backed away.

My father was dead. It seemed impossible when the thought hit me, but could the intruder have gone to Raymond's grave, and …?

No. It was animal bones. A cruel prank. The horrid man wanted me to *think* it was real. Scare me out of my wits. I had news for him, even a plastic hand would have done the trick. I couldn't believe anyone would hate me this much.

I swept the trembling beam of the flashlight toward the wood pile and the forest beyond. Mosquitoes whispered against my skin, and the trees appeared to be hovering in the moonlight with the blackest shadows imaginable beyond their trunks.

"Brumby?" I managed.

There was no reply, just the rushing noise of my own breaths. I closed my eyes, guessing how the sheriff's department would react if I dared to call. Her again, the giant pain. I pictured them rolling their eyes as I described what I'd found. A snowman cookie tin, a note, a skeleton hand fashioned out of animal bones. Maybe that was the intent behind the prank. Inspire me to call 911 in a state of panic and make a fool of myself. I would be the laughingstock of the county for the rest of my days.

So, what *was* the right thing to do?

Missing a step as I began pacing on wobbly legs, I flopped to my hands and knees, where the stench of the animal bones lingered in the air. My pulse thrummed in my ears and blackness seeped through my head. Lost in the cloying murk of finding myself in the crosshairs of angry people yet again, the horrid pranks and gossip I'd been weathering for three months, I rolled onto my back and blinked as the stars slipped from view. This was how prey animals died. Breathless. Wild-eyed. All because I'd traded my job, my friends, my comfortable, known world in Boston for the farm of a father I'd never known. It was reckless. Crazy.

You didn't ask the right questions.

The understatement of the year.

2

Air stirred through the dark trees with a rushing, circular cadence that left the dizzying impression of being swept heavenward. I rubbed my eyes, then I sat up and willed my head to clear, desperate to figure out how to handle the items the intruder had dropped.

"Sonny?" Brumby called out.

I held my breath and turned toward the clop of hooves.

"You up there?" he hollered.

"I'm here!"

I climbed to my wobbly legs. His voice sparked optimism, with a fresh kick of adrenaline to push me onward. I felt more grounded with every step as I headed past my father's house on the left. At the crest of the hill, I met Brumby leading Dodge up the driveway. All the spunk had drained from the horse. He looked tired, but not to the point where he seemed sweaty or in need of a blanket as he plodded toward me.

To be sure, I said, "Is he hot? He ran a lot."

"His chest is dry. He had a good rest in Joan's lily bed."

Perfect. Joan prided herself on her flower garden.

"I know it sounded like Dodge was busting up the barn, but he was mostly out of his stall when I went in," Brumby said. "The guy we tangled with unlatched the door, figuring we'd run after a loose horse instead of chasing him. I'll be darned if he wasn't right."

Whatever his flaws might be, Brumby's reputation as a horse expert was second to none. He patted Dodge's neck, speaking softly, then he carefully checked hooves, hocks, and all other parts for signs of injury. Minor scrapes, nothing more. Brumby led the horse to the pasture and set him loose with a stern remark that I shouldn't pamper Dodge in the barn. It was healthier for animals to be outside, mosquitoes or not.

"The breeze is better than repellent," he pointed out.

As I looked his way, Dodge softly nickered to me from the fence, as if to say, *Sorry for losing my cool.* Beside him thirty sheep were vying to see what was going on, squished into what looked like a seamless mass of wool, their faces staring at the crazy humans with fascination.

"Damn it," Brumby said as one of the lambs squeezed through the rails and darted onto the driveway. "We don't have time for this."

"Just stay calm. She'll probably go back to her mother."

Fifteen pounds of trouble, Gracie was covered from her ears to her tail in silken ringlets except for her brown face and kneecaps. She planted her little hooves and regarded us with a defiant look that said, *Yup, I've broken out again. What are you going to do about it?*

Too impatient to let the problem resolve itself, Brumby chased after the lamb and returned her to her mother. Once he'd rejoined me near the barn door, I pointed out the items the intruder had dropped.

"Giant pain in my butt," Brumby grumbled, using the toe of one of his cowboy boots to flip over the lid of the snowman cookie tin. He knelt and brushed dirt from the assemblage of bones. Turning them, as I had done, he watched them unfurl into a skeleton hand.

"What the hell?" Brumby said. "Somebody made this thing."

"With fishing line, do you think?"

"Looks like it."

"Was the guy looking for a place to put it?" I said.

"I was busy getting hit in the gut, so I can't say for sure. If you're right, I bet he lost his nerve. Stringing the bones took a lot of work. If he couldn't finish the job tonight, he figured he could try again later on."

"Instead, he ran into me and dropped it, so now we have evidence," I said. "What kind of animal bones, do you think?"

"Pig. Dog. I don't know. All I can say for sure is somebody went to great lengths to scare you. Maybe make you give up the farm."

"Charlotte has vowed to get rid of me," I said.

"Her son, Tyler, is more apt to come up with this kind of thing."

"Exactly."

On more than one dark night, Tyler Bergley had issued lunatic howls from the pasture, dumped trash all over the lawn, and dragged tin cans along the driveway. Stealthy, he was not. His teenaged giggles were enough to give him away, but I had also seen his plump, slinking silhouette from my bedroom window every time.

"It wasn't Tyler tonight," Brumby said. "But the Bergleys have money. Maybe they convinced some jackass to do their dirty work."

As Brumby returned the assemblage of bones to the ground outside the barn, I knelt and shined the flashlight on them, examining them from just about eye level. I had to admit the effort showed actual promise. The bones were assembled in such a convincing way, whoever had made it must have consulted diagrams in order to pull it off.

"There's this, too." Brumby handed me the note that had been hand-written in red crayon. "It's dry, no sign of dew, so he definitely brought it with him."

"There's enough here to nail them," I said. "I can rattle *their* cage for a change. Whoever that guy was, he must have left fingerprints."

"No, he had latex gloves on," Brumby said.

"You're right. I did see that."

Brumby was scowling, studying the items as he rubbed the stubble on his chin. He leaned down as I had done and shined the beam of the flashlight on the bones. He regarded the note next. I saw his lips moving as he silently read the words.

"Wait here," I said. "I need my camera."

"Why?"

"To photograph it all. It's evidence."

"Sonny, hang on."

"I'll be right back."

I took the porch steps two at a time, then flung open the door and turned on the kitchen lights. I winced at the radiant orange walls. This was no time to wonder if my father had been color blind, or if a particularly dark winter had inspired such a bold choice.

But I did pause as I passed the framed photo of my father that one of his friends had given to me. I picked it up and studied it for the umpteenth time. In his game warden's uniform, Raymond looked friendly and approachable, grinning at whatever had been said before the photo was taken. We had blue eyes and wavy hair in common. People at his memorial service had reacted by looking shocked and spooked when I'd stepped into the crowded room. It had been a snowy day in February, just three short months ago, when Raymond had taken his last breath. I would never forget the moment his attorney had called and delivered the news that had upended my life. I'd almost hung up, thinking it was a prank. I was raised in Newton, Massachusetts, hundreds of miles south of the town of Gracious, Maine. Why would a stranger named Raymond French have named me in his will, and made me his heir?

My mother still had a lot of explaining to do.

My phone rang in my jeans pocket as I grabbed my camera. I checked to see who was calling. It was my neighbor, Joan Dumas.

"Sonny?" she said. "I'm still at my aunt's house. A neighbor down the road called. She heard yelling up at your place. What's going on?"

I stepped outside, wondering which tiny light in the distance belonged to the busybody who'd reached out to Joan.

I related the bare minimum of what had gone on.

"The burglar knocked you down?" she said.

"I'm fine. The guy is long gone."

"I'm calling Stable," Joan said.

This pulled me up short. *"No."*

"I know he's been harsh with you—"

"Please don't call him, Joan. I'm fine."

Whatever she said next was lost in the confusion of hearing Brumby's truck door slam. The headlights flicked on, and the engine gunned to life.

"Hey," I hollered.

I banged on the fender as I crossed around the moving vehicle. The tires skidded to a stop. I confronted Brumby at his open window.

"You're not *leaving?"* I demanded.

13

"I just heard you talking to Joan." With his hair rumpled and his stubble shining in the glow of the dashboard, he shook his head. "Stable Bartlett and I don't get along."

"I told her not to call him."

"She'll call him. Trust me."

"All the more reason for you to stay."

"I'm sorry, this whole thing …" He motioned toward the barn. "It's beyond what I expected. To figure it out, I can't have Stable breathing down my neck. Don't tell him I was involved. I wasn't here."

"I can't *lie*."

"Of course you can."

"What about Dodge? You said you'd trim his hooves."

"I'll loop back in a few days."

"You can't leave me to handle this alone!"

"You're up to it. Just hang tough."

"Brumby. *Brumby*." I made feeble attempts to clutch at his truck as it started rolling forward. "This is wrong! You know it is!"

"I'm sorry, Sonny."

Once he'd passed me enough to pick up speed, he pressed the gas and did not pause until he'd reached the pines at the bottom of the hill. Only then did his brake lights flash, and only because of a deep pothole.

"You are a selfish *jackass*," I hollered after him.

"Remember, I wasn't here," he hollered back, then he was away down the winding road, leaving me to handle whatever was to come on my own.

Fuming, I crossed back to the barn and began documenting the evidence. I had never photographed a crime scene before, but I assumed the important thing was to be thorough. If Stable did show up and take me seriously for once, he would bring the cookie tin and other evidence with him when he left. Knowing my luck, the Earth would slowly turn innumerable times before his inquiries led anywhere. With photographs in hand, I could conduct my own investigation and show the police how it was supposed to be done.

"First the cookie tin," I said. "Then the fake skeleton hand. Make a grid of photos of the area. Plus, the pillow and the note."

I smoothed the note on the ground and took a few shots with the barn lights illuminating the paper, plus a few more using the flash. Folding the note and slipping it into my jeans pocket, I noticed a couple of footprints that had been made by a sneaker much larger than mine. Brumby was wearing boots. The footprint had been left by the intruder.

Poof. Poof.

"Got you," I said in triumph.

"Excuse me," a man said behind me.

I whirled, startled to see a blonde young man standing nearby, looking worried by the fact that I was talking to myself, and taking pictures in the dark of night. He made his living as a builder, by the look of his paint-splattered shirt and cement-speckled work boots.

"Sorry to just show up," he said. "I'm with the volunteer fire department. I heard there was trouble up here over the scanner."

"Yes, that was a while ago."

"What happened?" he said.

"There was a prowler. He's long gone."

I saw his truck parked down the driveway a bit. I'd been so absorbed that I hadn't heard him pull up. This told me I needed to wrap up my camera work and prepare myself in case Stable Bartlett did show up. I scanned the area and confirmed I'd captured every important element of the scene. The man looked puzzled. I crossed to him.

"I was testing the flash," I said, knowing any details I disclosed would fuel rumors and gossip. "It's part of my work."

"What's that?" He pointed to the snowman cookie tin.

"It's nothing, just some junk."

"That's the kind of thing can lame a horse."

"I'll pick it up," I said, shepherding him with one hand as I headed to the house. "I'm all set, really. Thank you for coming."

"Sure. I'm Everett."

"Nice to meet you. Call me Sonny."

He glanced at me shyly. "You've got nice eyes. Real blue, kind of like Raymond's." He paused. "I guess that makes sense!"

He was maybe in his early twenties and reminded me of some of the other young guys I'd met in the area, awkward when they spoke to women, having spent most of their time hunting and fishing and working at hard jobs from dawn until sunset instead of developing social skills. We both turned as a distant siren began closing in on my farm.

"That's the police," he said.

"I think it's Stable Bartlett."

"Stable? You're in for it, then."

"You know him?" I said.

"Enough to not get on his bad side."

With official help on the way, Everett crossed to the cab of his truck. There was a sharp rustling from the truck's open bed, then a blue tarp lifted abruptly, and a teenaged girl with wild blonde hair climbed out. She ran to me and engulfed me in a hug.

"Lily!" Everett exclaimed. "Not again!"

"You know her? She's …?" *Not your kidnapping victim trying to escape?* I thought.

"She's my neighbor."

"*Shh,*" the girl whispered, her breath smelling of cherry candy. She patted my back as if I needed to be soothed. "*Shh …*"

"Lily, Miss Littlefield doesn't know you. Come on, let go." With an effort, he released her grip on me. "You're supposed to be grown up. You need to quit this nonsense."

"Has she stowed away in your truck before?" I said.

"All the time. I barely have a life anymore."

The girl was smiling in triumph, her eyes a little on the wild side, but I suspected she might be as smart as a whip. She pawed the air as if to draw me closer as Everett led her away.

"Your name is Lily?" I said.

"She doesn't talk," Everett said. "It's one of those mind problems I can't pronounce."

"Well." I smiled. "It's nice to meet you."

"Don't encourage her," he said. "Come on, Lily." He opened the truck door. "One of these days you're going to fall out and hurt yourself."

"Thank you again," I said.

"No worries." He paused, then added, "Can you leave all this out when Stable comes? He's threatened to have Lily locked up."

"I don't see any need to tell him."

"Thank you, Sonny. I'll see you around."

As the truck eased away, I saw Everett continuing his stern lecture. Lily ignored him as she watched me intently through the window. When I waved to her, she smiled and clapped her hands.

Judging from the proximity of the siren, gaining volume as it rounded wooded bends, I had mere minutes to stow my camera inside the house. It was tough to fault Joan for calling Stable over my protests. She and her teenagers, Harry and Jess, had been kind and understanding to me from the start. Raymond had been like family to them. It was thanks to their help that I had a chance of pulling in cash from the strawberry field.

With my camera inside the house, I opened the kitchen door to the news that Stable had brought reinforcements. I groaned, seeing a familiar sheriff's deputy climb out of his car. The gods had delivered to the scene not just one, but *two* men who hated me to the core.

Buck up, I told myself, squaring my shoulders. *You are the victim of serious crimes. Trespassing. Harassment. Assault.*

They snugged on their hats, almost in unison as they approached. The deputy was an ordinary sort of self-important jerk. Stable Bartlett was the opposite of ordinary. Just shy of fifty, the same age my father would be if he were still alive, Stable always looked spotless and freshly shaved. Even at 12:15 a.m., he'd arrived in a crisply pressed game warden's uniform, with a sidearm gleaming at his hip and boots that spent their days murdering the woodland ferns of the area he patrolled. It would be apparent to even the most unobservant mind that Stable was a rigid, unsmiling man of the law with chiseled features, iron standards, and a withering stare that sparked the most primal of instincts. The urge to hide. The need to flee.

I met them at the bottom of the porch steps.

"I told Joan not to call you," I said. "I want to make that clear. But there was a prowler. We caught him in the act right over there." I indicated the barn. "He knocked me down, but I'm ok. He dropped some items that I think he'd planned to leave."

"Joan said it was a burglar."

"That's possible, but I think his main intent was to scare me."

"Here we go again," the deputy murmured.

Stable shot him a glance saying he would handle things. A quick nod further instructed the deputy to inspect the yard.

Stable turned back to me. "You need to be straight with me, understand?" he said. "Was this prowler somebody from Boston, maybe?"

"From Boston?"

"Some perp looking for drugs?"

"*Drugs?*" I flipped my hands. "Perfect. I knew it."

His irritated sigh said this was going to take more than the ten seconds he'd allotted for wrapping it up. "Let's start at square one."

"Fine," I said. "Great."

"Why is a shotgun propped by the fence down there?"

"What …?"

I stared in the direction he pointed. Brumby must have put the gun down in order to catch Dodge. He'd forgotten all about it. So had I.

"Well?" Stable prompted. "I recall you saying you're not familiar with firearms."

"I'm not."

"Yet you brought one out anyway. Is it loaded?"

"Well …"

"So, novice though you are, you grabbed it when you heard a sound."

"Wait." I motioned for him to stop. "Please just listen for a second. There are important facts you need to know."

It was not ideal, but I rushed through a rough sequence of events, then I sputtered a description of the items the deputy was now studying with a flashlight near the barn. Cookie tin. Pink fabric. Fake skeleton hand. It was all right there. Whoever had broken in had meant to scare me. And he might have succeeded if we hadn't stopped him.

"You keep saying 'we,'" Stable interrupted.

I focused on his steely glare. "What …?"

"You — keep — saying — *we*," Stable repeated with deliberation, the way he would do if he were addressing an inebriated moron.

"Joan didn't tell you?" I managed.

Stable sighed. "Who was here with you?"

My hands milled for a moment. I wasn't hesitating for Brumby's sake. It was pure self-interest that had me hovering in silence. In his journals,

Raymond had described the women who fell for the known womanizer's charms as "sadly blind" and "lacking in common sense."

"It was Brumby," I said.

"Brumby," Stable repeated. "Jake Jones."

I started to say that nobody called Brumby by his given name, then I thought better of it. "He was going to shoe Dodge in the morning."

"Even with his own bed ten miles away?"

"Nothing like that happened. I know better. He was on the couch. At least that was the plan. He never really fell asleep."

Just then, the deputy prompted, "Sir? Over here."

Stable's expression said he was not finished grinding what little remained of my self-respect into a paste on the order of engine grime.

He strode to the deputy's position and knelt with his own flashlight illuminating the cookie tin. The beam moved to the bones. He pulled out a pen and lifted the assemblage. Inspecting them with a scowl, he set them down and looked up at the deputy. I interpreted their silent exchange as an agreement that this was a bigger pain in the ass than they'd thought.

Stable strode back to me. "Tell me you didn't touch anything."

"Well ..."

"Jesus Christ, Alison."

"Excuse me for thinking I was on my own here."

"We're done for now. Go inside. You look a wreck."

I gaped. Dismissed, just like that, with a personal insult to boot. *And* as always, he refused to use my nickname, Sonny, since Alison offered an extra syllable for him to express his displeasure.

Stable stepped away before I could summon a retort.

I climbed the porch steps and slammed the kitchen door on my way in, then I furiously set both locks, the deadbolt as well as the one on the knob. Stable Bartlett would *never* cross my threshold again.

Truth be told, I had to pee so bad it was a miracle I hadn't let loose out there on the front lawn. With the light off in case they ended up searching outside the window, I closed my eyes in relief and reclaimed at least one essential element of my humanity.

Then I turned on the bathroom light.

"No ... oh no ..."

19

Stable's remark was a kind assessment.

My wavy hair was not inclined toward obedience even on a good day. The damp breezes and wild manifestations of country air had been a challenge from my first days of living on the farm, but that night, I had broken a personal record for frizz and fugitive curls. Add a sunburned nose, a glazed expression showing only dim intelligence, and streaks of dirt on my face. I had become a living, breathing wanted poster.

I splashed water on my face until the threat of tears subsided, scrubbed off the dirt, then raked a brush through my hair and secured it with a band. A fresh shirt and a blue hoodie were folded on the washing machine in the cramped bathroom. I put them on, zipped up the hoodie, and then with a series of karate-chop moves I shut off the lights in the kitchen and living room to make it clear I was not to be disturbed.

The plaid couch sat in hunched resignation along the far wall, as if it had crawled into the house for refuge at some point, gasped its last breath, and died there. Bookshelves were stacked with volumes about nautical history, fishing, and other sporting topics, and a sixteen-point trophy buck glared at me from the wall above the fieldstone fireplace and wood stove. Raymond's Canadian-born father had felled the deer during his youth. My grandfather, I reminded myself: a severe man who'd dropped dead from a heart attack at 52, so add heart disease to my list of future worries. From a background of distant wealthy relations and chilly great aunts in Newton, Massachusetts where I'd spent the bulk of my twenty-eight years, I had leaped into a new reality that included a collection of boisterous, French-speaking relatives in Quebec.

I crossed the living room and plopped down on my back on cushions that still smelled of Raymond's pipe tobacco. The couch had been my bed for three months because I had never mustered the proper frame of mind to think of the front bedroom upstairs as my own. Raymond had painted the room pink and added a pine vanity and matching chest of drawers in the hope that he would invite me to either stay for visits, or to live there one day. He'd written about it in one of his journals. I'd calculated that I was eleven years old, more or less, on vacation in Camden, Maine with my mother when Raymond had spotted her and remembered the steamy dates they'd gotten up to long ago at college basketball games.

Then his gaze had fixed on the young girl holding my mother's hand. Me. I was the spitting image of Raymond's sister, Olivia, when she was eleven years old. What a surprise that must have been.

Olivia had died during her early twenties, and Raymond's wife, Ella, had passed away seven years ago, which left me on my own to deal with the Bergley clan, who'd always imagined a clear path to inheriting the farm and turning it into cash. The rumors of their foiled plans were known far and wide: the forests would be gutted for wood, the barn dismantled for its timber, the house and all of its memories leveled to the ground, the land would be chopped into parcels and sold to the highest bidder, and most alarming of all, Woolberry, Bubbah, Daisy, Dot, and every other unique pet on the farm would be turned into cube steaks and kebabs.

Dizzy, my head spinning, I pulled Ella's frayed, hand-knitted quilt over my head. It had very large holes through which I could see the sturdy pine furniture, cast iron floor lamps, and rustic décor. It takes two words to describe how fast I fell asleep. Lights out.

3

With my face pressed against a plaid, pipe-smelling couch cushion, I groaned, dredged from the hypnotic clouds of a desperately needed deep state of sleep. There was a tapping sound. Then a banging sound.

My eyelids scraped open. Instead of the usual unnerving darkness outside the farmhouse windows at 1:15 a.m., there were lights. Blue police lights, I realized. And I heard men talking out in the yard.

I pushed up onto one elbow and squinted toward the kitchen door. The silhouette of an armed, uniformed man was framed in the glass, his fists planted on his hips in a show of impatience.

"*Alison*," Stable hollered.

I closed my eyes. When he'd said 'We're done for now,' I'd thought he'd meant he would call me in the morning. Or next week. Or never.

"Alison!"

"Yeah, I'm coming."

I dragged myself up onto shaky legs, realizing that I hadn't eaten a proper dinner. For three months, ever since I'd inherited the farm back in February, the demands of getting up to speed on how to pull the strawberry patch into shape and bring twenty newborn lambs into the world had left very little time for normal activities like shopping for food, let alone preparing anything resembling an official meal. That day's dinner had been a half-brick of cheese that I'd eaten straight from the package, and a bowl of strawberries that I'd found in the back of Raymond's freezer. God only knew how old they were.

Speaking of strawberries, I was supposed to be out in the berry field by 6 a.m. conducting a desperate battle against all the rodents, birds, and insects that were depleting my ripening crop all hours of the day. They were organized, and worked in shifts. Mother Nature was a formidable adversary, and unlike me, she was armed to the teeth.

I flipped the locks and opened the kitchen door. Now that his wood-penetrating voice had summoned me forth, Stable stepped aside, allowing an officer in plain clothes to fill the gap and shake my hand. He introduced himself as Detective Roy Allen, Maine State Police.

"May we come in?" he said.

Shaky and lightheaded, I waved off their forward movement toward me and said, "No, it's better outside. I need some air."

"Do you need paramedics?" the detective said.

"No, but thank you for the thought."

Stable's truck had been joined by a state police cruiser. The deputy's vehicle was parked further down the driveway. On the road beyond the pines at the bottom of the hill, I could hear a car slow down. I could just make out the deputy's voice firmly instructing the driver to proceed. The farm was a crime scene. No loitering allowed.

Detective Allen gripped my elbow as I almost missed my footing on my way down the porch steps. The night was gloriously cool, with a breeze stirring the scent of spring grass into the air. Seeing Dodge at the fence and hearing him softly nicker to me, I felt almost whole. Almost normal. It did wonders for clearing the haze in my head.

"Miss Littlefield?"

I indicated with a nod that all was well.

Detective Allen was a heavyset man with a stern face, but there were hints of sympathy, maybe even the capacity for humor in his eyes.

With a pen and notepad in hand, he said, "Let's start with the beginning of the evening, before the business in the barn."

After months of skirmishes with Stable, my father's enemies, and his embittered niece and her assorted entourage, I was finally in a position to show I was not a "drama queen," or a "flake," or any of the other labels I'd earned from the gossips in town, most of whom had never met me. I was like a machine as I launched into a precise account of every moment of the night. It was one of the most self-possessed moments of my life.

I did not spare Brumby as I added how annoying he'd been when he was supposed to be sleeping. The crumpled snack bags he'd left were in the house for the detective to see if he felt it was important. I described hollering at Brumby when he'd loaded the shotgun. How I'd demanded he not bring it outside. Everything afterward happened fast. I focused on the events in my mind's eye. Precise. Detailed. Like the exact window through which I'd seen the intruder's flashlight moving around. The detective nodded as I pointed to it. I described the shock of the stranger knocking me down. How he'd smelled. What he was wearing.

"Excellent," the detective said. "You mentioned the perpetrator had on a jeans jacket with ripped-off sleeves and logos on the back. Can you describe the logos in any detail?"

"We were caught off guard, so there was no time to turn on the barn lights. It was too dark to be certain of specifics, but I remember colors and shapes. A yellow circle. A red square. I think one logo was a baseball, and I'm almost certain there was a small American flag."

Subtle shifting sounds caused me to open my eyes. I'd closed them in order to focus. Detective Allen's expression said I'd hit a nerve.

"Where was the flag, exactly?" he asked.

"Right here." I indicated the back of my right shoulder. "The flag sort of gleamed. Or shimmered, if that makes sense."

"Did you get a sense of his age?"

"Early thirties. His neck, the side of his face. I didn't see wrinkles."

"That could indicate a teen."

I shook my head. "This guy had substantial stubble, and his hair was thinning a little. His voice was gravely. He wasn't a teen."

I brought the story up to the moment Joan called. How I'd asked her to not call Stable. My confusion when Brumby started leaving.

I spread my hands to indicate the tale was complete.

Detective Allen nodded, looking pensive as he studied what he'd written down. He tapped the notebook with his pen. "It's puzzling, you not wanting Joan to alert Stable."

Oh boy. Things had been going so well.

"Stable is ... rather difficult," I said.

"How so?"

To avoid stirring up stung feelings and trouble, I glanced around and saw that Stable was far enough away to not hear me.

"I don't think Raymond told Stable he had a daughter," I said in a near whisper to further contain the subject to just the two of us. "Imagine a good friend keeping a secret like that. How it would feel. I'm no psychologist, but in this instance, any anger and confusion Stable feels about it unfortunately ends up landing on me."

Detective Allen's expression said he understood the concept.

"But 911 was an option," he said.

"As a victim of vandalism in recent months, I was discouraged from resolving issues through official channels," I said carefully. "While we're paused here, Stable is the reason Brumby decided to cut loose instead of stay, and if I can reiterate for the sake of my good name, I'm not involved with Brumby. He showed up out of the blue."

"Hmm." Detective Allen studied me. "Brumby Jones returned my call a while ago, and his version of events is a bit different from yours. He said you invited him to spend the night, and further stated that you wanted him here because you were afraid to be alone."

I'm sure I looked the way people do when they're struck in the forehead with a large stick. This prompted Detective Allen to press on.

"You see our concern? It's one of those he said, she said situations. If you were afraid tonight, of all the nights you've lived here, it would suggest you had some prior knowledge of the events that took place."

"You believe Brumby's version?"

"I'm open on the subject." He paused as an officer signaled to him. "The Evidence Response Team will be here in a minute."

That sounded official. Finally, a break-in at my home was getting serious attention. Charlotte had better brace herself for rough going.

"Just focus on your account," he said. "Anything to add?"

"The guy took off that way." I pointed to the log pile. "I heard him running down the hill through the woods, then a vehicle sped away."

"Truck? Car?"

I shrugged. "It was an iffy engine. Like it needed work."

"Good detail." He scanned his notes with pursed lips as if there were an important element he'd expected to hear, and I'd come up short.

"That's everything," I insisted.

"You're sure."

"Positive," I said. "Once the guy fled, I found the cookie tin he'd dropped, the bones, the—" I paused. "Oh … uh oh …"

"And?" the detective prompted.

I glanced around the scene of police vehicles pulling up the driveway and officers standing around staring at me. The handwritten note. What had I done with it? Looking down, I reached into my sweatshirt pockets, and then searched my jeans. There it was in a front pocket.

"I found this too," I said. "A note."

I pulled it out and saw that during the confusing aftermath, I had folded it up multiple times. My hands moved to unfold it.

"*Aa-a-a*," the detective admonished.

My hands froze, one hovering in midair with nothing to do, the other gripping an edge of the note by my forefinger and thumb.

Without removing his judgmental gaze from my face, Detective Allen motioned for someone to give him a pair of Nitrile gloves. The entire scene was eerily quiet, everyone staring as if the two of us had joined forces to disarm a bomb. The gloves snapped into place, again with a very judgmental sound, then he gripped my hand and indicated I was to let go. The note, with all of its many folds, fell into his other gloved hand.

Nearby, Stable shook his head with a grim expression that said for the umpteenth time, my "flaky" ways had managed to disgrace Raymond's good name.

"I'm sorry," I said. "I didn't imagine this kind of police response."

Detective Allen looked baffled. "No?"

"I'm grateful you're taking the matter seriously, but wouldn't it be more useful to track down people with a motive to do this sort of thing?" He looked blank, but expectant. I pressed on. "Such as Raymond's niece, Charlotte Bergley. She's angry that I inherited the farm."

The detective said slowly, "You think Charlotte Bergley is capable of letting her feelings of resentment go this far? You think she would handle human remains?"

"All I can say is that ever since I moved here—" I stopped, feeling like I'd been struck in the forehead with a stick again. "Human ...?"

"Bones." He paused. "You didn't know?"

"It's animal bones. Made to look real."

"No."

"With fishing line," I insisted.

His expression said two things. The skeleton hand had belonged to a human being. And though I'd succinctly illustrated my level of stupidity on more than one occasion that night, he found it difficult to grasp why I hadn't seen the obvious myself.

"Stable talked to you, surely," he said. "Before he called us."

"No, he didn't."

Unless anyone wanted to count, *We're done for now. Go inside. You look a wreck.*

What kind of man would not think it useful to inform me that I'd found an actual skeleton hand outside my barn? I relived the past half hour with the proper context in place. No wonder the detective had looked at me as if I had a screw loose.

"It's going to be hectic from here on out," he said, signaling to a good-looking, brown-eyed man in a black T-shirt and leather jacket. Unlike the long beards that were often a favored style in rural Maine, his was trimmed, sleek, and smooth. No words passed between them. It was understood the job at hand was to help usher me into the house.

"But I have questions. I need to understand."

"You will in good time," Detective Allen said.

As long as I'd stood there in a braced stance, I'd lost sight of how tired, hungry, and woozy I'd become. They performed a gentle bum's rush on our way up the porch steps, my legs not quite responding to the task the way they normally did.

"I mean, where would someone find a human ...?"

"Again, all in good time." Detective Allen reached for the kitchen door, then paused. "One more important thing."

27

"Hmm …?"

"The note is in an evidence bag," he said. "We'll want to unfold it once it's in a proper setting, which means you're the only one here who has read the note. I need to know. Was it typed? Short? Long?"

"One sentence. Handwritten."

His gaze instructed me to relate what the note said. For a long moment I couldn't remember. *Think.* It had been written with red crayon, the letters odd.

"You didn't ask the right questions," I whispered.

"That's what it said? Can you write it down?"

A pen and notepad arrived in my hands. Slowly, I wrote the words in the off-kilter way I recalled seeing. *You didn't ask the right questions.*

The night blurred as it hit me where someone might find a human skeleton, and which skeleton might be employed to make the most dramatic point. I'd handled the bones. I still vividly remembered how they'd smelled: as if they'd been buried in the ground.

"No … no …"

Hands gripped my shoulders as I began to sink downward into swimming blackness. There were voices. Commands. A warm, solid wall served as a prop to lean my back against, and strong hands continued to firmly hold my upper arms so I didn't drop to the porch. I smelled leather and cocoa butter. Soap? Lotion? Impossible to say. It was delicious. I inhaled. Exhaled. Detective Allen's face emerged from the dark fog.

"Please," I whispered. "That thing. Tell me it wasn't …"

"Wasn't what?" he said.

I gulped air. "Raymond."

The detective looked confused, then he shook his head. "Your father was cremated. The bones—they're not his."

Cremated. I knew that. How stupid could I be?

"Thank God." I sagged in relief.

"I'm sorry if I came across as gruff, Miss Littlefield," Detective Allen said. "Get some rest if you can. And stay inside. Out here—"

"It's too dangerous," I murmured.

"Too chaotic. We appreciate your cooperation."

I suddenly realized I was not leaning back against a comfortable wall. I was reclining against the man in the leather jacket, and his gentle grip on my arms had propped me up for the past few minutes. I noticed that he'd taken pains to turn his face to one side, either to keep from breathing down my neck, or startling me with his beard. I wobbled as I straightened and balanced my weight on planet Earth again.

"I'm sorry about that."

"No problem," he said. "All set?"

"I think so."

I was gently propelled through the doorway. Detective Allen nodded to the man in plain clothes, indicating he was in charge of the situation, and then he stepped off the porch to join the throng of officers who were setting up a table and portable lights.

"Can you manage ok?" the bearded helper said.

"I think so."

"Here, I'll just …" He leaned forward to reach inside and flip on the light switch. "There you go. Give a holler if you need help."

I nodded. The door softly closed, and then I was alone.

Like an unstoppable gladiator who had been stabbed ten times but had managed to stay alive, I crossed to the couch for the second time that night. Brumby had left a potato chip bag and a can of cola on the coffee table. I ripped the bag open and started eating. For a while, my mind was consumed by three powerful things: the crunch of the chips in my skull, the fizz of the warm soda on my tongue, and the handwritten note.

You didn't ask the right questions.

A fourth thing arrived in my mind.

The skeleton hand.

Who in God's name had it belonged to?

4

In Gracious and surrounding towns, it was widely known that trouble had unfolded on my farm at around 11:45 p.m. What happened next, especially for local gossips, was an intolerable silence. Few details. No specifics. Nothing to give anyone bragging rights for being the authority on what had happened, or what could be expected in the days to come.

Even if I'd wanted to fall asleep, the shrill ringing of my father's old landline phone wouldn't allow it. Apparently, there was a point in recent history when people had wanted to be able to hear their phone ringing from the other side of town. The landline had been silent for most of my stay in Raymond's house. Tonight, even Joan Dumas, who lived with her two teenagers across the road, had resorted to using the landline because I wasn't answering my cell phone.

I was too frazzled to talk to anyone, so I let Raymond's old answering machine take the hits for me. The messages started piling up.

"We're home now," Joan's voice said. "It looks like chaos up there. If you can't sleep, you're welcome to spend the night here."

Not five minutes later, people I'd never met chimed in.

"Miss Littlefield? This is Nadine Gilbert. I'm … that is, I was a real good friend of Raymond's. If you need a place to stay, let me know."

"Hollis Oakes here. Volunteer firefighter. If not for my bad leg I'd be up at your place tonight. My young neighbor, Everett, feels awful about leaving you up there on your own. The police response is startling, to say the least. Don't hesitate to reach out if you need help."

"Alison," Charlotte Bergley's voice grated. "I am not finished contesting the ownership of the farm, so if the police presence damages any property up there on the hill, I will sue, do you hear?"

Actually, no. I plugged my ears until Raymond's niece hung up.

And finally, "It's Chuck Brewster. Friend of your dad's. Call me."

After twenty minutes of mostly cheering phone calls, and bolstered by the potato chips and cola, I had some belated revelations that stemmed from my interview with Detective Allen.

I popped up from the couch and lurched around the pine coffee table that weighed a ton. Not for the first time, I banged my knee on the corner because come what may, the blasted table never budged. All the rustic furniture in my father's house appeared to have been intended to last through a nuclear explosion, or an Ice Age, whichever came first.

I opened the door, and standing there in my way, with zero room to even glimpse the yard beyond, was the man Detective Allen had appointed to handle the doorway. I'd been too addled to properly assess him before. Now I did. He had the kind of smooth, trimmed beard I would call an asset, rather than a sign of a lazy streak. Jeans, black T-shirt, and dark, wavy hair that was a little windblown. His leather jacket looked as if it had encountered hail, landslides, and possibly lightning strikes for most of its existence. He seemed startled, apparently shocked to see me awake and alert. He reigned in his surprise, his brown eyes warm.

"Miss Littlefield—"

"I need to talk to the detective."

"You have questions," he said. "It's natural. But there are too many moving parts out here. I'm sorry. It's not possible right now."

"Detective Allen got it backwards," I pressed on. "I didn't have prior knowledge of an intruder coming here tonight, but I think it's possible that Brumby did. The way he behaved, showing up out of the blue and checking the window."

He nodded. "That's good information."

"I don't think Brumby is a bad guy, but he needs to explain himself."

"We're on it."

"Plus, Detective Allen reacted when I mentioned the flag logo on the perpetrator's jacket. I could tell it brought a suspect to mind."

"We will handle it."

"If I can just—"

"I'm sorry, it's too hectic out here."

"I have a right. It's my property."

"If I may …?"

He didn't shove his way in or anything overtly aggressive, but somewhat like my draft horse, he employed a kind of invisible force field that slowly, carefully took up space in front of me as I tried to push past him. From my side of the doorway, the scene outside got further and further away. Lift right foot, step back. Lift left foot, step back. It was so smooth. Almost like a dance. Within seconds, he was inside the house.

With one hand, he reached back and shut the door.

Thirty seconds. That was all the time it had taken to neutralize my escape. Admittedly, he displayed some valor in not flinching at the color my father had chosen for the kitchen walls: a sherbet sort of orange that stood the chance of bringing on seizures under the fluorescent lights. The quality I needed in him just then was instant understanding.

I drew myself up to my full height of five foot four. "Look—"

"I know it's frustrating," he said. "You've had a shock. Understand, it's not personal. We need to contain the area. I'm sorry. Truly."

"I need to know—"

"You will get answers in time. I promise you."

He relaxed, very calm, looking pleasant and entirely non-threatening as he looped his thumbs on his belt. *Nothing on God's green earth is going to budge me from my appointed task*, his demeanor said. *You can make any move you want, but it's not going to work.*

Well, if he was going to be inflexible, I needed a plan B. Some way to befriend him, maybe. Get him to relent and make an exception.

"I'll make coffee," I said, crossing to the kitchen countertop.

"There's no need."

"I insist. It's automatic," I said of the coffee maker. "Very modern."

Why I found this an important detail to share, I couldn't say. *You* cope with being locked in your home after finding a skeleton hand on your lawn.

"Are you fire department?" I said. "Volunteer rescue?"

"Trooper."

"Plain clothes. A detective, then?"

"No."

He remained silent as I installed a paper basket with trembling hands, then measured out who knew how many spoons of the coffee I'd brought back from Spain, probably the very last time in my life I would be able to afford to go anywhere. With the machine gurgling and sending a delicious aroma through the room, I turned and folded my arms, and then I clapped eyes on something alarming on the coffee table.

If Stable ever caught onto the kind of details that Raymond had disclosed in his journals, he would contrive a reason to confiscate them, and that night, he had back-up. Stiffly, I crossed to the leather-clad volume I'd left on the table. People knew that Raymond had kept track of farm-related business in his journals, but not much else. Even Raymond's niece had ignored them when she'd emptied the house of valuables shortly after Raymond's death. Dusty old volumes didn't have any value in Charlotte's eyes. She was looking for jewelry, silver, antiques. Anything that could benefit her, or more likely — anything that would *not* benefit me.

If so, she'd misjudged what I would hold dear. Raymond had written about ways to get around Charlotte's constant scheming, Stable's refusal to curb his temper, and a range of other topics, from the misdeeds of supposedly upstanding citizens to a startling range of local crimes like embezzlement, extortion, and robbery. Raymond had enjoyed musing on the awesome mysteries of nature, and every now and then, in the dark of night when he couldn't fall asleep, he'd written about me.

Hearing Stable's voice outside, alarmingly close, I pulled the volume behind my back as I faced the man in the doorway. Pulled it in front of myself to avoid suspicion. Brought it behind myself again.

The trooper wore the most neutral expression I'd ever seen on a man's face, but his brown eyes said he hadn't missed one thing for the past ten minutes.

"It's personal," I said. "My private—musings."

For once, my prayers for deliverance from an awkward moment were answered because Detective Allen opened the door and stepped in.

"Miss Littlefield, can you do me a favor?" he said.

I brightened. "Sure. Anything."

"Your neighbor, Joan Dumas, drove back from her aunt's place after she spoke with you. She's down on the road. Won't accept our assurance that you're ok, given the commotion up here. If you head down and spend the night, it's best for all, don't you think?"

The carrot approach, using the need to reassure a worried neighbor as a means of getting me out of his hair. Masterful, I had to admit.

"Ok," I said. "I'll pack a few things."

"Excellent. Thank you."

"I think all the activity will keep the sheep away from the fence, but there are a few lambs who like to escape for the fun of it. Can the officers keep an eye out, and return them to the pasture?"

"It's already happened. Any tips on catching them?"

"Grain. They won't stray too far from their mothers. Just make sure to look twice before backing up any vehicles, that sort of thing."

Detective Allen nodded, then stepped out.

Stable ruined the vibe by using that moment to come in. As if it would pain him to glance my way, he addressed the doorway guard.

"Everything good?"

"All set. She's packing a bag."

5

Once in my bedroom upstairs I didn't waste time second-guessing myself. I had my own crime scene photos to examine, but my main priority was getting to a stress-free location where I could process the events of the night, and it would be nice to finally get some sleep.

I heard Stable's distinctive, marrow-shriveling growl as he spoke with the bearded, plainclothes officer. He'd come that night because Joan had called him, but his role as a game warden would not include being present in my house. There was zero doubt in my mind that he would be tempted to look around once I was out the door. Boston, where I'd come from, was the epicenter of evil in his mind. He refused to believe I didn't have cocaine or some other kind of drug squirreled away. He would come up empty if he expected to find any signs of illegal activity. In fact, I welcomed him to look around if it helped him get over his ridiculous suspicions.

With the journal I'd fetched from the coffee table in hand, I realized there was a downside to consider. I pictured Stable fuming with outrage if he picked up one of the journals and happened on an entry where my father had ranted about Stable's harsh ways. The idea of *me* reading such criticism would send him over the edge. There was no time to find a secure hiding place for the journals. Every volume had to come with me.

I fetched a carry-on suitcase from the closet, dumped out the cosmetics I never had time to use anymore, and packed essentials first. Laptop, cables, backup drives. Underwear, hair blower, a few clothes.

Now came the hard part.

I pulled the journals from the drawer I kept them in and started arranging them around the equipment. *One, two, three, four …*

They took up a lot of space, so I put half in a second suitcase along with my camera and lenses. I counted the journals as I packed them until all eighteen volumes were safely stowed.

I squished down the lid of the first suitcase, but it was no good. The jeans took up too much room. A fresh pair was a luxury I couldn't afford. I hauled the suitcases off the bed and set them on the floor. A thousand pounds each, but no matter. I had no choice. Getting them to Joan's house would be a challenge. If anyone offered to help carry the bags, I would need to come up with a plausible reason to say no thank you because the weight of them was bound to spark curiosity and draw questions.

With my hands on my hips, I blew a stray curl from my eyes and surveyed the bedroom to be certain I hadn't missed any items because I doubted it would be possible to skulk past a dozen officers and fetch anything once I'd retreated down to Joan's house.

Earlier in the day, I had opened one of the windows facing the barn to keep the upstairs from getting stuffy. I stepped to the window and studied the activity in the yard. Detective Allen was near a table where some papers were being pointed to and discussed. I knelt next to the waft of cool air stirring the curtains, hoping to overhear anything that might explain the bizarre situation I'd gotten dragged into.

"… compare the DNA … must be out of state … back in the game … toy guns and all that business … grown adults playing dress-up … vendetta against officers … a lot of hate for our folks out there these days …"

For all I knew they were discussing another crime entirely, or what they were planning to do over the weekend.

Raymond had been a true man of the outdoors, which apparently included having at least one set of binoculars in every room. I pulled one from the shelf and knelt next to the window, slowly panning the yard of officers, vehicles, and equipment. A floodlight flared to life inside the barn.

The shadows of officers moved about beyond the window I'd pointed to when I'd described where I'd first seen the intruder.

Another group was talking next to a cruiser, lit up by the powerful portable lights they'd set up close to the barn. I honed in on Detective Allen again. With his arms folded, he gestured toward crime scene photos that were arranged side by side on the field table.

The binoculars bowed the window screen as I adjusted the focus ring and strained to see details in the photos. Below a frame of ruler marks was a human skull. The empty eye sockets and nose holes were chilling, the teeth yellowed, a grimace frozen in time. The view swam as I realized the skull had been posed inside a cookie tin with an elaborate flower design, and instead of pink, the color of the pillow was lime green.

Another photo showed a skeleton hand resting on a yellow pillow with the thumb missing. It *wasn't* the one I'd found.

Breathing fast, I focused on the other images being discussed, frustrated that the officers kept getting in the way. Finally, I caught sight of three photos of notes handwritten in red crayon, with familiar sloppy lettering that switched between cursive and print.

I quickly read them, in succession:

You didn't believe.

You didn't follow through.

You didn't care.

I stopped breathing as an epiphany obliterated what I'd assumed for the past few hours. I wasn't the lone target of a lunatic. I was the *latest* victim, and who knew how long his twisted errand of leaving unsettling notes with human remains had been going on.

"Alison!" Stable bellowed behind me.

I yelped and lost my balance, the binoculars tumbling from my hands. You would have imagined it was my first attempt at standing up, the way I lurched to my feet. Still shocked by what I'd seen, I clamped down on the impulse to defend my actions. I needed to exit as fast as possible. Only then could I process the jarring photos.

"What the hell are you doing?" Stable demanded.

"I ..."

"You've got everyone waiting, and here you are showing your priorities in life. Meddling, pushing your luck, being a pain in the ass." He strode closer, his angry, flushed face at odds with the frilly curtains, bedspread, and pink walls. "Where is your common sense?"

"I'm sorry," I said. "I thought I saw a vehicle parked over the septic tank." I waved toward the window. "Turns out it wasn't."

"Of course it wasn't," Stable said.

"While you're here I want to thank you for coming when Joan called. I know I came across as ungrateful. I was in shock, and I felt ashamed that I'd let Brumby pull the wool over my eyes. Also, I made coffee for the officers. Tell them I appreciate the response tonight."

Stable eyed me, as if thinking, *Who is this new agreeable woman?*

"I'm ready to head to Joan's," I went on. "I know it's best if I'm out of the way." I firmly held out a hand to stop him from helping with my suitcases. "If I am to make things work on the farm, I need to strengthen myself and toughen up. This is step number one."

This was nearly a direct quote of what Stable had been saying about me around town. When it came to neutralizing an argument in record time, I'd found that there was nothing more effective than using a man's own words to support what I was planning to do.

Stable indicated I should proceed.

I inhaled deeply, gripped the suitcase handles, and hauled upward. My shoulders instantly narrowed from the weight. I infused extra iron into my backbone, my fingers damp from anxiety and slowly losing their grip on the handles.

"I'm ready," I managed. "To go."

"It's only for one goddamned night."

"This is my work. My cameras."

Struggling, I walked unevenly through the door and made it to the landing. I paused, gulped in a breath, and thudded my way down the stairs.

The good-looking, brown-eyed man had been joined by another officer in my kitchen near the coffeemaker. They stood stock still with their eyebrows raised as they watched my progress. No one on planet Earth had ever come down a flight of stairs so loudly before. Not ever.

Eye contact was impossible as I heaved my way past them, my eyeballs suffering from the sudden demand for blood in my extremities.

"The door," I wheezed.

"Sure." The bearded guy in the leather jacket rushed to open it for me, then he reached for one of the suitcases. "Here, let me—"

"No. I've got it."

Imagine my words in tiny, tiny print. That's how they sounded.

"Are you sure?" he said.

"Mm hmm."

They'd no doubt heard Stable yelling at me upstairs. Hopefully, they would attribute my stiff behavior and ungainly movements to that. I whispered curses through my teeth on my way across the porch, then clenched my jaw as I navigated the creaking wooden steps. Trembling, almost spent, I turned to a nearby officer.

"My car …?"

"It's blocked. You'll have to walk."

I stared into the night.

Dear God. Joan's house was a thousand miles away.

The hated deputy who'd been rude to me in the past had apparently been pulled from road duty. He was standing nearby.

"She's expecting a cab," he murmured.

"That's enough, Pike," Stable growled, abruptly turning on the man. "Why aren't you manning the barricade on the road?"

"The road is covered. I came up because I have prior experience with the subject in residence here. I can shed light on—"

"You will man your post until instructed otherwise."

"Yes, sir."

There was no time to celebrate the deputy's sharp dressing down because I was now experiencing all the symptoms of a coronary event.

"Let me help," a man said softly behind me.

Resolute, come what may, I took a step forward.

Then a miracle happened. From behind me on my right came a leather-clad arm. A warm hand slipped over mine. The feat of transferring the suitcase meant securing the handle with two fingers at first, then as my hand retreated, he took the weight. In seconds flat, he secured the other bag the same way. The artistry of it was astonishing.

Even better, nobody had noticed. They'd all moved on.

I turned and looked up at the brown-eyed man standing there in the night, easily holding both suitcases as if they were filled with fluff. Instead of outing my secret, he used one bag to indicate we should proceed down the steep driveway toward Joan's house.

"After you. Watch your footing," he prompted.

I did so, tripping over loose stones and thinking to myself, if only I'd met him properly when my arms had been a normal length, as they had been ten minutes ago. The way my shoulders and arms felt now, all but ripped out of their sockets and seemingly as thin and ungainly as stork legs, I was no match for a man of this level of gallantry. I wasn't even a match for the odd loner who reportedly lived down the road.

On our right, at the bottom of the pasture, the churning torrent of Cold Stone Stream emerged from the pipe beneath the road, then flickered in and out of view before it disappeared into the surrounding forest. The sheep were grazing on the cool May grass, and their guardian, Dodge, stood nearby. I could picture his big lower lip twitching as he dozed.

"Beautiful place," my escort said.

"About the suitcases …"

"Let's leave it for another day."

"You aren't curious?"

"Sure, but I'm taking a leap of faith."

"Do you do that often? Take leaps of faith?"

"Never."

I studied the side of his face, the beard that fascinated me for reasons I didn't quite understand. "Can I ask your name?"

He cracked a smile. "Call me Porter."

"First name? Last?"

"Never mind for now. Detective Allen wanted me to stress the need to not disclose the particulars of what you found. Human remains."

"Won't it have been mentioned over the scanner?"

"Your neighbor told Stable you had a burglary. We kept a tight lid on chatter after that. The less you say, the more it helps us."

"Why?"

"Complicated case. You'll need to trust us."

"Ok. I guess I understand."

Who was this guy, with a leather jacket all beaten to hell, dark wavy hair, and neatly trimmed beard? The beard looked soft, rather than prickly, I decided. That's why I kept studying the shape of it. Not to mention I made a living photographing people. What could I capture when he was distracted? Just then, he had an unreadable look.

All troopers are masters at the deadpan thing, Raymond had written in one of his journals. *Stable has it, too. I've teased him about how many calories it must burn to stay so tightly wrapped up. I worry he'll die before his time.*

"Why did you write that?" I whispered. "Tempting fate."

"What?" Porter said.

"Nothing. Just ... things really suck."

"It will get better," he said softly. "Day by day."

Exhaustion was starting to weigh me down. I forced my legs to work, my eyes fixed on the ground so I wouldn't trip. We crossed the wooded road, passing the deputies manning the barricade. Arriving at Joan's yellow Cape, my escort climbed the steps. Joan opened the door for him, illuminated by the lamplight inside her house.

"My kids are finally asleep," she whispered.

He spoke softly to Joan, then stepped in with my suitcases.

I climbed the steps, then smiled at Joan, sadly out of breath.

"So sorry," I managed. "It's been a long night."

"Don't worry. Almost there."

Through the darkened kitchen and down the hallway, we entered a cozy room of antique bureaus and a poster bed with a thick, inviting comforter and piles of pillows. My escort was waiting there with my suitcases tucked out of the way along one wall. Seeming in a hurry, he crossed to me and knelt as I sat down on the bed. Leather and cocoa butter wafted into the air every time he moved, his eyes so kind.

"Can I see your phone?" he said. "Unlock it for me?"

Ok, this was kind of forward.

Squinting at my phone, I did as he instructed.

The trooper entered "Detective Roy Allen" into my contacts. He hit the call button, and then handed the phone to me.

"Good night," he said, standing up.

"Thank you. So much."

"Glad to help."

Detective Allen answered the call. "Miss Littlefield?"

"Yes, hello."

"I wanted my direct line in your contacts. If I reach out, please pick up or call back as soon as you can. It might be urgent."

"Ok."

"This next part is also for you Mrs. Dumas because I have an idea you're standing there. Miss Littlefield will need your help keeping curious folks at bay. The pressure will be awful. Friends. Gossips. Everybody will come at her with questions."

"Officer Porter already explained," I said.

"Officer Porter?" he said.

"The guy who escorted me down."

The detective snorted as if he found this hilarious, then he sighed in a way that said he'd needed a good laugh.

"I get it," Joan said. "A porter carries bags. But why—?"

"Are you about to ask a question?" Detective Allen demanded.

"No," Joan said.

"Good night, ladies," he said. "I'll be in touch."

Click.

"That was interesting," Joan said.

I could have fallen asleep in a matter of seconds, but my fortitude was further tested by two teenagers in flannel pajamas entering the room at top speed. Ignoring their mother's protests, they tumbled into the space the trooper had occupied next to the bed.

"Sonny!" Harry said. "We were so worried!"

"I'm fine."

"Was it one of the Bergleys?" Jess said, her blonde hair and freckled face downright angelic as the lamplight pooled in her eyes.

"The intruder? No."

"Intruder," Jess breathed. "That sounds so scary."

"Did Brumby tackle him?" Harry said.

"He tried to."

"We're scheduled to go to archery camp tomorrow," Jess complained. "We want to be here with you, but Mom won't let us cancel."

"We can catch up later," I assured them.

"You can come to camp with us," Harry said.

"Maybe next time."

"All right, off to bed the both of you," Joan said firmly.

She pulled them away and scooted them out the door.

Joan had been a kind, reliable neighbor — good with general advice, and willing to let her teens help with farm chores — but she'd tended to not look me in the eyes, and her exits from conversations with me were abrupt. There was always a pressing errand she needed to tackle, someplace she needed to be. I'd come to understand that my presence on the farm unsettled her. I was a reminder of Raymond's death.

Joan returned. "All set?"

"Sorry to impose," I murmured.

"*Shh*," she soothed. "Just sleep."

As my mind closed down, I pictured the skeleton hand I'd found, plus the one in the photo. The skull. The notes. How had a living, breathing person ended up becoming a plaything for a lunatic?

6

At 7:15 a.m., when I emerged from the murky haze of sleep, I heard Joan outside, helping to organize Harry and Jess as they climbed into a minivan bound for archery camp. Once she was back inside the house, Joan began sending wafts of delicious aromas from her kitchen. Fresh bread. Cinnamon buns. Sizzling onions and peppers. She was making one of the omelets she was known for far and wide. Thick. Fluffy. Perfect.

Now it was 8 a.m. Perched on one of the stools along the countertop island in her kitchen, I ate everything she put in front of me.

"I can't believe you're up," Joan was saying. "I'd still be conked out."

"Nervous energy. This is how I handle stress."

Sunlight poured in through the curtains, lighting up Joan's cozy furniture and cheering country décor. Whitewashed boards hanging on the walls were stenciled with uplifting sayings, like "Embrace kindness" and "Never say no to cake."

"You were saying?" Joan prompted.

I'd been filling her in on my early life in Newton, Massachusetts. My mother, whose maiden name was Evelyn Grand, had been born to the task of maintaining the brick mini-mansion that had been in the Littlefield family for generations. She did none of the work herself, of course. Only on dry summer days would she venture from one of the walkways onto the manicured lawn, and even then, it would only be to holler at anyone who was not performing a chore properly, or was behaving badly. Which of course tended to be me.

Every now and then, I'd suffered through bewildering audiences with chilly grandaunts in rooms full of fascinating artwork, pricey vases, and other items I was instructed to never touch. I was always afraid that my mother was trying to convince the chilly relatives to take me off her hands because she went to great lengths to sell my worthy attributes, using adult language like "excellent scholastic aptitude" and "facility with golf at an early age." She would instruct me to play the piano, and if I missed any notes, her lips grew tighter with every stumble.

"She plays flawlessly at home," she'd said. "Her instructor is absolute rubbish. A part of the art is mastering stage fright."

I'd known early on where the idea of getting rid of me had come from. Donald Littlefield, the man I'd been led to believe was my one and only father for twenty-eight years, could not endure even five minutes in my presence without directing barbed looks and harsh criticism my way. A stalwart figure in Boston's financial arena, he'd always carried himself with an air of importance, and put stock in keeping his emotions contained. Only two things in our home could put him in a boiling rage: my "lack of focus," and talk of tax hikes for the one percent.

In the dark of night, a more contained form of anger would unfold in their bedroom down the hallway. Hushed arguments, with occasional louder bursts of back and forth that I could hear, and once again, his dark mood seemed to revolve around me.

It's intolerable, Donald had said. *I feel cheated.*

Well, I'm sorry I haven't produced a son.

You know it's more than that. It's her. Where she came from.

You begged me to be with you. At any cost.

Always, the arguing would end with my mother stomping to a closet and saying she'd had enough. His tone would simmer down, then devolve into pleading. She would burst into tears and say she was sorry for not measuring up. Then I would hear them having sex.

At six years old, I would lie in bed with my ears plugged, figuring it was only a matter of time before all the arguing would end with my being cast out. I had to be smart. Excel in school. I had to build inner strength and learn skills that would help me get by once I was on my own. I helped the maids clean. I asked the gardeners how they knew when to trim the shrubs. I crouched next to the pool repair man to learn the intricacies of inflow and outflow. I told my best friend, Arlene, that if I did get cast out, I would live in the pool shed.

Arlene would giggle, thinking I was kidding.

"You met Arlene when she visited," I said. "You saw how close we are. I used to think my mother tried to steer us apart because Arlene's mother is Puerto Rican and her father is black. But I think she saw how our friendship gave me confidence in how I felt and thought. Arlene reinforced who I am on a basic level if that makes sense."

"It does, especially given your mother's secret," Joan said. "She was desperate for you to be a match for her world."

Donald had died suddenly when I was ten. My mother collapsed when one of his colleagues arrived to deliver the news, though she quickly recovered and began to thrive despite the loss. It seemed a weight had been lifted from her. She still chided me at every turn. I remained a frustration to her through high school, college, and beyond.

She'd figured Raymond's influence would worsen all the traits that made me a poor fit for a life in her precious highbrow world. Fate hadn't allowed for a soft landing for either one of us. I would never forget the phone call I'd received from an attorney from Maine.

This is insane, I'd said. *Why would a total stranger make me his heir?*

A few hours later, I'd stormed my mother's bridge party and said we needed to discuss her "friend," Raymond French.

"It's obvious I'm busy right now," she'd said, somehow remaining a poised pillar of ice. "We can talk tonight."

Did I think it was fair to out her secret in front of company? Oh yeah. To our mutual surprise, her friends had fussed over *her* with sympathy, while I'd stood there like a superfluous piece of décor in the room. I'd stormed back out. We hadn't spoken since.

"I'm stunned," Joan said, pulling me from my recollections.

"That I'm not a spoiled princess, as everyone in town thinks?"

"I knew you weren't."

"In hindsight, I'm certain Donald knew I wasn't his daughter," I said. "Possibly before they even got married."

"He did not handle it well," Joan said. "Not one bit."

"Don't tell anyone, ok? It's really private."

Sliding a piece of French toast onto my plate, she cast me a glance that said I was being ridiculous. She pushed maple syrup toward me, sat down on the adjacent stool, and pointed to a list she'd written on a pad.

"It's all here. Every nutty story Charlotte and her minions are spreading about you. After last night, who knows what kind of angles your cousins will come up with. I'm launching a campaign, and Sue and Kate are going to help put all the gossip to rest."

Sue and Kate owned the Corner Pocket, a small store that offered wonderful foods and a coffee bar in the heart of town.

"That is a long list," I said.

"Exactly. If I may?" Joan tapped the pad with a pen.

I shrugged. "Sure, go ahead."

Joan delivered her questions rapid fire, and I responded in kind. No, I did not have a trust fund. No, I did not have any involvement with drugs. No, I wasn't "faking" my affection for Dodge and the sheep. No, I wasn't a drama queen hoping to use the circumstances to become a social media star. No, I did not sleep with Brumby last night.

"Nor will I *ever*," I said emphatically.

"If cash is tight, why did you quit your job in Boston?" Joan said.

"I did not quit my job."

"No?"

I explained how a new boss had been selected to head the graphics department of the agency where I'd worked in Boston. Unqualified, no industry training. A bully. Imagine my surprise when he'd said yes to my request for bereavement time.

"He insisted I take off a few weeks," I told Joan. "Then he lied to management and said I was 'absent without leave.' His fiancé has a cousin who was out of work. They thought, digital photography isn't complicated. He can learn the ropes fast."

"Tell me they're going down in flames."

"Oh, yeah." I smiled. "Jerk boss is asking me to come back."

Joan looked stricken. "You won't say yes?'

"I might have to if the berry crop doesn't pan out. I won't sell the farm," I assured her. "I'd come back on weekends."

Still frowning, Joan checked her list. "That covers the gossip we can contain for now. Are you sure you don't mind me doing errands?"

"Positive."

"A soak in the tub might help after last night."

"Maybe later in the day. Showers are my morning routine."

"I'll lay out extra towels, so you're set either way."

"That would be great."

Joan had retreated into her brisk mode again, but I felt we'd made some positive strides in our friendship. Later, I would return the favor and gently pry out some details about her life. Such as, was her husband, who worked at sea as a merchant mariner, truly out of the picture for good, as people in town said? She still wore a wedding ring.

Following her to the guest room where I'd spent the night, I said, "I'm sorry, but I might need to borrow a change of clothes."

Her gaze took in the suitcases. "Really …?"

"It's mostly camera stuff. And my computer."

"Of course. I'll be right back."

Glancing through the window, I saw the police barricade blocking my driveway. What was taking so long up there?

"I'm afraid these are mom jeans," she said as she offered a stack of clothes, neatly folded and smelling of laundry soap.

"They're fine. Thank you."

"Stable wanted me to tell you he put Raymond's shotgun back in the safe last night. Also, he brought your car down to my driveway in case you need it," Joan added, putting my spare keys on the nightstand. "He must have found these in a drawer."

I nodded, thinking, *Yup, while he was taking a look around.*

"We don't tend to lock the front door, but you know where the spare key is in case you need it, right?"

"I'm all set. Thank you so much, Joan."

While I was in the shower, I heard her car reverse out of the driveway and surge away down the road. I toweled off and dressed, then I sat down on the bed and opened my computer. First, I typed out the handwritten note I'd found, plus the others I'd seen in the police photos.

You didn't ask the right questions.

You didn't believe.

You didn't follow through.

You didn't care.

If my assumption was correct that there were other victims who knew what I was going through, they might be frustrated if the case had dragged on for a period of time. I had to be prepared for them to reach out if they connected their experience to the hushed investigation unfolding on my farm. Detective Allen hadn't put the kibosh on my *listening* to anyone if they decided to vent. I hoped they would reach out.

Every note began with, "You didn't …"

I certainly hadn't asked the right questions. Not once had I imagined my blue eyes and curly hair were thanks to a stranger I'd never met. The antagonistic theme in the notes struck me as odd. Why would someone care whether or not I'd "asked the right questions" regarding my genetic origins, or any other aspect of my life?

Maybe a hidden theme linked all of the targets in the perpetrator's mind. Not that any sort of logic could be applied in leaving skeleton parts with cryptic handwritten notes. The act of stringing human bones together involved a mindset I couldn't begin to grasp.

I gratefully turned to the photos my best friend, Arlene, had sent from London, where she would be staying for the next month. Her husband was flying back and forth to work in Boston. She'd texted several times that I had a standing invitation to join them.

I sighed. Maybe next time.

It was a stroke of luck to have Arlene on vacation in a foreign land, chasing after her toddlers with her in-laws tagging along to offer unwanted advice. If she'd been home in Newton and had checked in with me first thing, she would zero in on any evasion I attempted. I would have confessed every detail I was not supposed to be talking about.

Hearing a fresh round of vehicles enter my driveway across the road, I pulled the bedroom curtain aside and was discouraged to see a new round of activity at the top of the hill near my house and barn. I didn't have to wonder what was going on for long. Detective Allen called and said the police would remain on the scene for the rest of the day.

"What we're dealing with up here is a new lead within a larger case," he said. "The perpetrator got a bit lost on his way up to the farm. We found signs of a snack he'd stopped to eat, plus a receipt. Hence, we're conducting a careful grid search in daylight."

"That makes sense," I said.

"You weren't kidding about the lambs escaping. There's a competition underway on who can catch them the fastest."

However calm I'd attempted to sound, I stood next to the window after we hung up and internally hollered at the police cars at the top of the hill. *Can't you work faster? I want my life back!*

Alone in the house, I made a succession of trips to the kitchen where Joan had set out an array of food in case I was still hungry after my ordeal. Granola. Muffins. Yummy banana bread with cream cheese and home-made strawberry jam. Fruit. Coffee. Orange Juice.

I definitely needed to live there.

With my cheeks full of banana bread, and crumbs cupped in one hand, I noticed that Joan had left a note on the counter near the door:

Sonny,
If you're worried about being peppered with questions, the farmer's market is a place you might want to avoid. A police announcement is scheduled for 10. A lot of people are bound to be there.

Good Lord, it was 9:45. I grabbed my keys.

7

In the late 1700s, a collection of settlers with first names like Eleazer, Persis, Blanche, and Phineas had established the town of Gracious, Maine. After clearing stumps from a central area for militia drills, they built a tavern, a cooper's shop, and other businesses, with an access road encircling the central common and four roads branching off in all directions. Some of the homes that had been built in the 1800s still stood along the connecting roads, with flags out front and flower boxes on the windows. Here and there were ancient weathered outbuildings that had been updated to hold anything from boats to seasonal antique shops.

On weekdays, traffic was always light in the center of town. Thanks to the farmer's market, cars and trucks were parked beneath the maples along all of the connecting roads. I pitied the soul who'd parked on the grass in front of my cousin's stately white colonial. Someone who hadn't heard about Charlotte's obsession with a flawless lawn.

Perched around the common were a brick post office, a firehouse, a wonderful yellow store called the Corner Pocket, a real estate office, and a B & B with fragrant rose hedges partially hidden by a white picket fence. I slipped my camera into the canvas bag I used when I planned to shoot casually as I conducted shopping, and stepped out into the heavenly scent of pancakes and bacon coming from the B & B.

There had to be a hundred people talking in groups or visiting the local vendors who offered an assortment of vegetables and handmade crafts. Every table was covered with a cheery umbrella or a collapsible tent. The police had already made their announcement. The main gist had been to enlist the eyes and ears of the community without offering information in return. People needed to stay alert, and so on.

On to studying the crowd on the chance the intruder had shown up to hear what the police had to say. I'd calculated that he was a bit taller than I was at 5'4". Average build, stubble on his chin, thirties, lanky hair. If he was careless enough to wear the same jeans jacket with torn-off sleeves and patches on the back, I would spot him in an instant.

No such luck. I paused as I caught sight of a man with dark, wavy hair talking to another man near the post office: none other than the officer who'd carried my suitcases to Joan's house. "Porter" was not wearing the leather jacket from last night, but judging from the T-shirt he had on that morning, black was his favorite color to wear.

I snugged on my sunglasses and drifted closer, then I paused to study the salad greens on display at one of the stalls in hopes of overhearing him if he happened to be talking about the case. Even without looking at him, I recognized his voice. He was speaking in fluent *French*.

I'd never mastered French in school. In fact, I'd mixed it all up into a language soup by overloading my brain with Spanish.

To my novice ear, what I heard him say was something like *bouahgee zhuablah bouf deuzzwha foubehhh* and so on. As always, spoken with a man's deep voice, every syllable had that sexy, foreign appeal one thinks of as so much more alluring than mundane, clunky English.

I began melting back into the crowd, using tree trunks, the pavilion, and people to serve as cover in case he looked toward me. Once I was well enough away, I paused to reassess "Porter" from afar.

He'd smiled when he'd told me that name. Maybe he'd used it as an inside joke of sorts, figuring what was the harm? I pulled out my camera. Zooming the lens to 200mm, I got up close and personal with the muscles beneath his T-shirt, and involuntarily hit the shutter release button a few times. He wasn't bulked out, weightlifter style. I decided he had more of a quarterback kind of physique. Strong, but agile.

Ok, settle down, I told myself.

Panning out again, I saw another familiar face in the crowd.

It was Everett, the young man who'd stopped by last night. In dusty work clothes, he was talking to an older man who was resting most of his weight on a wooden cane. Lily, the teen with the wild blonde hair, was sitting on the ground working intently on a drawing. As if picking up on someone gazing at her, she looked up at me, then smiled and tugged on Everett's pant leg to direct his attention my way.

I crossed to the three of them to say hello.

"Miss Littlefield," the older man said, extending his free hand to shake mine. "You're the last person I expected to see here."

"I love the market. It's such a nice day."

"I called and left a message last night," he said. "I'm Hollis Oakes."

I nodded. "Thank you for reaching out."

"I'm sorry for not stopping by after Raymond died. Nobody knows how to handle that sort of thing."

"Don't apologize. I get it."

"You met Everett, and Lily, my daughter."

"I almost turned around ten times," Everett said. "I felt bad for leaving you alone after the scanner kept going on about the need for the state police. I hope Stable wasn't his usual self."

"I survived. That's what's important."

"What the heck was it about?" Everett said.

"A prowler. I don't know specifics."

"The response doesn't surprise me," Hollis said. "The idea of somebody burgling Raymond's farm is causing outrage."

"Exactly," I said. "That must be it."

My gaze landed on a hard-luck sort of fiftyish man sitting in the shade next to a tree with his head bent and his hands laced over his knees. He gave every indication of having a bad hangover.

"That's Everett's father," Hollis said, then prompted encouragingly, "Come on, Earl. This is Raymond French's daughter."

Earl squinted up at me. "Didn't know he had a daughter."

"Nice to meet you," I said.

"Whatever." Earl motioned for us to leave him alone.

"I told you it was a mistake to bring him," Everett said crossly. "I'm sorry, Miss Littlefield. Pay him no mind."

"Everybody has a bad day now and then."

"He's a hard worker," Hollis quietly confided. "But come the weekend, it's tough to get him to leave the bottle alone. It's a disease, you know. Not his fault. He's our neighbor, so I'm not about to give up on him. I keep thinking fresh air will do him good."

Feeling a sharp tugging on my jeans, I looked down and saw that Lily appeared to be miffed that I hadn't acknowledged her yet.

"She's got something to show you," Hollis said.

Apparently, Lily was not going to stand up. With a groan, achy from last night, I knelt as she handed me her sketchbook.

"What's this?" I said, then I held my breath as I stared at a stunning, atmospheric, colored pencil drawing of Dodge tossing his mane in the moonlight with stars above him, and a glittering stream flickering in the background. "This is beautiful. Wow."

"She's got real talent," Hollis said proudly.

"Lily," I said. "You saw Dodge in the pasture last night?"

She nodded, looking pleased by my reaction.

"She's got a visual form of perfect pitch," Hollis said. "You've got a camera. Her snapshots are wired in her head."

"Her watercolors are even better," Everett said.

"You should stop by and see them," Hollis said. "For now, we've got to head out. 867 Quaker Lane Road. Come any time."

"I will."

"She'll most likely give that drawing to you," Hollis called back to me as they started heading away. "But she's a stickler for getting it right. One pencil stroke off, and it's not finished."

"I'd love to have it if she's willing."

It was with reluctance that I'd let Lily take the drawing from my hands. I wanted to study it longer, to savor the nuances of light, shadow, and color that made the drawing so real. I made a mental note of their address. This day was turning out so much better than I could possibly have anticipated. From darkness, a bright note had arrived.

"Sonny! My goodness, how are you?"

I turned and hesitated in confusion as a mid-thirtyish woman breezed toward me, her high heels clicking against the pavement and her smile suggesting we'd known each other for years. More than one man who happened to be passing by lost a step when they caught sight of her cleavage, lipstick, and clingy leotard.

I gulped in surprise as she enveloped me in an energetic, perfumed hug. "I'm sorry," I managed. "I think you've mistaken me for—"

"I'm Nadine," she whispered. "Pretend you know me. We're being watched so I need to be careful." She abruptly pulled back and held me at arm's length with a look of concern, then said loudly, "What are you doing here? You should be resting."

"I … needed some air?"

"I'll understand if you can't come to class!"

"Umm … class. Right. I am a bit …"

"Tired and rattled, of course you are. Listen, I have a zillion errands to run, so we'll have to catch up later." Nadine hugged me again and whispered close to my ear, "I'm putting a note in your bag, but don't read it until I'm well away. The undercover cop you took a picture of a few minutes ago is really bad news."

"You can't mean the guy with the—"

"*Shh.* Please be careful."

"I will." I attempted a smile. "Rest, that is."

"Bye, hon! See you soon!"

Nadine patted my cheek, which brought her extravagantly long and bedazzled fingernails a mere inch from my left eye, and then she waved to a few people as she treated the menfolk once again to her fluid, high-heeled progress down the sunny sidewalk. She slipped into a blue sedan, gunned the engine, and pulled away.

"Now *that* was entertaining," a man behind me said.

In faded jeans and a windbreaker of substantial wear and tear, he tossed a lit cigarette to the asphalt and crushed it under his boot, in no hurry to explain himself. In his fifties, maybe, and heavily tanned. However anxious I was to read Nadine's note, I was held in place by the twinkle in the stranger's eyes, his air of having things to disclose.

"This is quite a long pause," he said.

"I'm sorry. I can't quite place you."

"Chuck Brewster, one of the last race drivers to build his own cars from scratch, and steer clear of big corporate sponsorship," he said, enveloping my hand in a firm grip that promised to leave traces of motor oil. "You've met me just in time. I'm a dying breed."

"I'm Sonny Littlefield."

"Ray's daughter, right?" he said. "I helped your father keep an old tractor alive for years. A great man. I'm sorry he's gone."

"I hear that a lot."

"You looked surprised by Nadine."

"Do you know her?"

"Everybody knows Nadine. She and a couple of friends fancy themselves as crime stoppers. Nadine blogs about it from time to time."

"A blog on crime. I'll check it out."

Chuck stood in a relaxed slouch as he smiled at a passing man who tossed him a thumbs up. He showed no sign whatsoever that he craved a life of careening around a track at blinding speeds. He plucked a cigarette from his shirt pocket, set it ablaze with an old silver lighter, and then blew the smoke away from us.

"Your name," he said. "Short for sunshine?"

"Short for Alison."

"I heard you're a photographer."

"That's right."

"You any good?"

"I worked at a design firm in Boston, handling advertising campaigns. Lately, I'm building a portfolio of Maine portraits."

"As in, plunk people in a chair and say cheese?"

"No. I'm shooting people at work."

"Well, I'm told I need to ramp up my online presence. If you think you can deliver the right kind of shots, there's good money in it."

"Did you leave a message last night? On Raymond's landline?"

"Sure did."

I assessed his furrowed brow and confident gray eyes, the crooked nose and scarred lip that alluded to a tempestuous youth. I had the impression he had more to disclose, but it wouldn't arrive without the cagey dance he'd been conducting for the past few minutes. Now I did see the influence of swerving his way past growling race cars at blinding speeds. The rest of life must seem dull in comparison. Like an engine, it needed ramping up.

"Well?" he said.

"To be honest, you had me at 'dying breed.'"

Chuck smiled. "Then why not chronicle the whole deal? Get a picture of the car I'm working on before you attend a race. She's a beauty. Ford Mustang. I nicknamed her 'Wicked Pissah.'"

"That would be great," I said. "The sooner, the better. In a few weeks people will come to pick strawberries. I'll be tied to the farm."

"Here's my card. Give a holler."

"Chuck—" I touched his sleeve to keep him there. "I get the sense you had another reason for coming over to say hello. If I'm right, I'd love to hear ... anything you can share."

My stomach lurched as I toyed with pushing past the guidelines I'd been instructed to follow, but I reasoned that I was asking a general question. I didn't have to disclose information in return.

"Very forward. I like that." Chuck settled into a storytelling mode. "That cop you took a picture of a while ago came over when I got here and kept nudging around about a guy he'd seen at a race one time. Asked if I knew a guy in a jeans jacket with patches."

I scanned the crowd and didn't see the officer anymore. "The state trooper, you mean?" I said. "In a black T-shirt?"

"Didn't make note of what he had on," Chuck said. "But I had an idea his inquiry was related to your burglary last night."

"Do you know a guy with the jacket he described?"

"Dozens, more or less. You see, there's all kinds of patches." Chuck listed them with his fingers. "There's ones for car parts. Sports. There's a world of motorcycle patches. Triumph, Indian, Hogs. There's even police and fire department patches."

"Right, I should have realized."

"Do some homework before you stop by," he said. "I have crowd pictures with zillions of guys wearing jackets with patches."

"Maybe someone will already be in custody by then."

"An optimist. I like you more and more."

Chuck winked and moved on, smiling as he gripped the hands of race fans, and accepting congratulations all around. Looking past him toward the Corner Pocket, I groaned as I saw my cousin, Charlotte, tearfully describing her tribulations to a group of ladies who patted her shoulder as if she'd been the one who'd been "burglarized."

"And *there* she is," Charlotte said, pointing toward me the way someone might do if an ogre hunt was in progress.

With indignation as fuel, my cousin could funnel the combined energy of her stocky build, stout voice, and staid dress into a package of distinction. She could be a newscaster or a politician. Instead, she was bent on devoting her full attention to becoming my nemesis.

With her purse clutched under one arm, she marched over to intercept me, though I had already begun the journey to the store. Some weeks devolve into endless kicks in the pants. This was clearly one of them.

"What have you done now?" she demanded. "There has never, not *once* been a break-in on Raymond's farm. Not until last night."

"Because Raymond lived there," I said. "His presence was a deterrent."

"Save your sideways meanderings for less intelligent ears. You will soon know better than to stir the wrath of the Bergleys."

"Umm ..."

"Enjoy your last days of freedom," she said with her chin lifted to a dignified degree. "The hammer shall fall very soon."

With that, she stalked toward her Lincoln with an audible cadence of stout heels and swishing nylon. This was no woman to ditch pantyhose for the modern, barelegged look. Charlotte properly ensconced herself, even on a warm, spring day.

The door of the Corner Pocket creaked open, and Kate McKenna peeked out into a beam of flickering sunshine that set her red hair ablaze with highlights.

"Still standing, I see," she said.

"At least it was brief this time."

Kate giggled, then said with drama, "'The Wrath of the Bergleys: A Young Woman's Triumph Over Sideways Meanderings.'"

"As long as I do triumph in the end."

"She's been spinning theories all morning. You're running a meth lab, etcetera. Her bubble burst when Stable said that thanks to her efforts to drive you out of town, the police want her family to account for their whereabouts last night." Kate looked puzzled that I was still standing there. "Aren't you coming in?"

"I'll be there in a minute."

I crossed around to the side of the yellow building and pulled out the printed pink flyer that Nadine had shoved into my bag. In bold, feminine handwriting, she had scribbled a message on the back:

My name is Nadine Gilbert. Your father helped me out a time or two, so I naturally want to help you if I can. Please be aware that your break-in last night might be connected to an extremely bad situation, and the undercover cop you took a photo of is not to be trusted. The one with the big brown eyes? Call me. And be extra, extra careful.

Nadine included her phone number. I took a screenshot of the note so it would be saved to my cloud account.

I folded the note, seeing a giant problem if it was known that "Porter" had an undercover role. One would think that sort of information would be kept under tight control. But it might explain why he hadn't told me his name. Maybe all that mattered was keeping me in the dark: an unknown quantity from Boston with a reputation for asking questions. That made him cautious and smart. Did it make him dangerous? Just because he'd been kind last night didn't mean I should drop my guard. Trusting Brumby had been a mistake. I would never have predicted that he would turn tail and run in the face of trouble.

I pulled out my camera and studied the photos I'd taken of the mystery man. Detective Allen was a solid sort of cop. If he trusted the trooper, that seemed a significant endorsement. I deleted the first photo. It was of the trooper's chest, after all. No good for making an ID. Convinced it was the right thing to do, I deleted the other photos of him.

Turning to head to the store, I collided into the muscled chest of the very man whose images I'd just deleted from my camera. He scarcely moved from the impact, gently gripping my arms to steady me as I lost my footing. Once I'd recovered, he released me.

"What are you doing?" I said.

"Sorry, you turned too abruptly to stop," he said, studying me with his intense brown eyes. "What had you so absorbed?"

Maybe he'd found out that I'd taken his photo. To save time and avoid getting into a back-and-forth, I handed him my camera.

"You know how to scroll through the photos?" I said.

"You're saying I can?"

I waved him on. "Be my guest."

He looked surprised to have gotten there with no fuss. Holding the camera so the sunlight didn't put a glare on the LCD screen, he carefully scrolled through every photo on the digital card.

"I deleted the photos of you," I said, then further explained, "There I was, scanning the crowd when I got here, and I thought I saw the guy who carried my bags down the hill last night. I took a few shots to be sure. I deleted them because it didn't seem right."

"Because …?"

"You're a trooper. I figured—" I paused and assessed the puzzled twist of his eyebrows. "You had no idea I'd taken your photo."

"I might have been flattered, but I guess that's over with now."

I sighed. "Then why did you look through my shots?"

"I heard you have talent. I was curious." He handed my camera back to me, then he folded his arms in a way that brought supreme definition to his biceps and chest. "I was particularly moved by the photos of the snowman cookie tin and the skeleton hand."

I closed my eyes. Apparently, my role in the back and forth was to die inwardly a little bit after each and every reply.

"I took those when I thought it was a prank," I said.

"I was present during your statement," he said. "I saw you get up to speed in realtime. My sense of you is that you won't be posting them on-line, or sharing them with friends."

"Of course not."

"Glad to hear it."

"You're not going to demand that I delete them?"

"They'll be in the cloud by now. I'm stuck with having faith in you."

"Last night you said you never take leaps of faith."

"That's right."

"Now you've done it twice. First with my heavy suitcases."

"What suitcases?" he said with another appealing twist of his eyebrows, then he smiled. "Back to your photos. I pride myself on seeing things that other people don't. You're on a whole other level. Your photos of Champ will stick with me. They're priceless."

"Champ?" I said.

"The elderly man on the tractor. Bundled up, with his pipe clenched in his teeth. How you got him to grin I can't imagine."

"I liked how determined he looked as he drove down the road. I pulled over and waited for him. We talked for a half hour."

"Did he tell you he lost his driver's license from his bad eyesight? Cataracts. Made him mad as hell to be sidelined. It didn't last long because he figured he could use his tractor to come and go. Chalked it up to farm business. There's no seatbelt on the thing, and his eyesight made him a menace to himself and others, so my colleagues and I had to tangle with him every time we turned around. His grin in your photo says it all. He did what he wanted, right to the end."

"Oh no ..."

"He died last month. His family would love a copy of those photos. I can put you in touch with them if you don't mind sharing them."

"I'd be glad to."

He sighed. "I hate to change course, but I saw Nadine put a note in your bag. Was she pressuring you to talk about last night?"

"Not at all."

"So, the gist of what she gave you was ...?"

Without knowing more, I didn't want to land Nadine in trouble. I brushed a curl from my brow, looking toward the tree-lined sidewalk for an escape route, and then, a stroke of genius arrived.

"It's a flyer," I said. "We're taking a class together."

"A class with Nadine. Very nice."

His eyes were amused, instilling the impression of a lion who'd just watched a gazelle totter into his path. I knew I'd stepped into trouble in some way, but I was busy noticing how the reflected light around us brought warmth to his tanned face. He smelled of cocoa butter, of all things. Suntan lotion, or something to keep his skin smooth?

"What was the question?" I managed.

"I don't believe I asked anything. But now that you've invited a question, are you a part of Nadine's group activities as well?"

"Blogging about crime?" I said.

"Actually, I was talking about her sex toy parties. It's just a guess, if she put one of her flyers into your bag. You did say you're taking her pole dancing class?"

I lifted my chin. "You have a problem with that?"

"No, I think we could have a special relationship. Let's see, my favorite color is blue. My favorite sport is skiing. My favorite subject is safety … wait, that might be a deal breaker. Here you are, not twenty-four hours after your big shock—"

"I didn't say anything to anyone."

"Just being here is an unnecessary risk."

"Now that you mention it …" I looked around to be sure no one could overhear me. "Someone brought a human *skeleton* hand to my barn. I've been lectured about keeping my mouth shut, but there's been zero mention of what it means in terms of safety. I'm staying with Joan Dumas and her children. Am I putting them at risk?"

"That's one of the reasons I wanted to talk to you."

He paused and dragged a hand over his whiskered jawline, the way men do when they're weighing how much to disclose. It was fascinating to have the tables turned, him attempting to patch an answer together that rose to the level of the question I'd asked without compromising the veil of secrecy the police were determined to maintain.

"Ok." He held his hands apart as if he were holding an invisible bowl. "You had an intruder. He dropped items. The investigation is ongoing at your farm. That part will end soon. Picture this early phase here, within my hands. Once we release the scene, picture all of the above moving off-site with us." His hands shifted the invisible bowl to the side. "Contained, still in high gear, but not your concern anymore."

I paused for a long moment. "*What?*"

"Which part doesn't make sense?"

I spoke slowly, "I was targeted by a lunatic."

"I know it feels personal," he said. "And it is, in one sense. But we have leads. Solid leads that were in place before last night."

"Detective Allen said what happened on the farm was a possible new lead in a larger case."

"Exactly. The larger case … if a trail goes cold for a while, officers end up getting reassigned to different duties." He paused, then further disclosed, "That's what happened with me. I returned here, only for a day. Then last night happened. I stayed to help. Long story short, it's possible I won't be here to see it through."

"Unbelievable. You're breaking up with me."

He laughed, showing a smile that was a marvel of proper dental care. Even more important, he had a natural, spontaneous reaction to humor, which in my book had always been a must.

"I'm sorry," he said. "It's not you, it's me."

"Story of my life."

"I don't believe that for a minute. In fact, I'll put it out there that this region is my main work area. I'll be back before too long. Maybe I could check in when I get back. Take you to dinner. The coast is nice year-round. I know some good spots."

I hadn't expected my joke to lead anywhere, except in the dizzy confines of my own head, which was a given when I spoke with an attractive man. The joke was a one-off. Standard procedure.

A moment of silence elapsed. He waited. I waited.

Guess what happened next? My mother called.

I'd let her calls go to voicemail for three months, but I found motivation in wanting to escape, however briefly, the implication at hand.

"Excuse me, I need to take this."

"Sure. Go ahead."

I turned, took the call, and said to my mother, "Yes?"

"Alison? You finally answered. Rudely, I must say. But let's not start on a sour note. I'm making preparations for when you get here."

"When I get …?"

"Home. A very kind man called and explained you've gotten into some trouble up there. Stable, I think his name was."

"Stable was kind?" I said. "*Kind?*"

"Are you driving? I'm hearing an echo."

"That's shock you're hearing. And—" Seeing the trooper still standing there, I stepped away and hissed so as not to be overheard, "I am not coming to Newton, and it isn't home anymore. I've moved here. Why? Because I have to reconstruct my entire life."

"Honestly, Alison. You need to let this go."

"You're the one who needs to let go. Turns out there's a good reason why I never fit in at the country club."

"Alison, your anger with me has been so distressing that I did the unthinkable. I've been to a psychologist. And he said—"

"Oh, nice. I don't suppose it's the same psychologist you sent me to when I was ten? The one who said I had PTSD?"

"You told me yourself his notion was overblown."

"I said that because ... I don't know why, I was ten. To protect you, of all things. But I bet you took pains to find a shrink that accepts your side of the situation this time. I'm being stubborn, unreasonable, the rift between us is all my fault. Right?"

"If the shoe fits, darling."

"I'm wearing boots now, Mom. Barn boots."

I pressed the "end call" button. That's right. For the first time in my life, I hung up on my mother. Vowing to not make the same mistake of answering her calls for the foreseeable future, I turned and collided into the muscled awesomeness of the trooper all over again.

"Good god," I moaned.

"You forgot I was here?" he said.

"I kind of did."

"Wow. That's hurtful."

His smile was half-hearted. He looked concerned.

"I couldn't help but notice—"

"It was my mother," I said. "Surprise. We *really* get along."

"I was about to say your hands seem chilled. How you're even standing after last night ... have you eaten anything today?"

"Let's see, I had a ham and cheese omelet with peppers and onions, hash browns, four slices of French toast, bacon, coffee, orange juice, muffins, a half-pound of banana bread, and it's gone. I'm burning calories a mile a minute. So, if you will excuse me …"

I continued around him.

He snagged my arm. "Let me buy you lunch."

I paused, transfixed by his warm hand on my arm. My gaze traveled upward to his bicep, past his shoulder and his beard, then landed on his warm brown eyes. *You can trust me*, they appeared to be saying. *I was there for you last night. You know I was. I want to help if I can.*

I couldn't think of many times when I'd let an empathetic alpha male get this far with me. He'd done it in a matter of minutes. And right on cue, there I was conveying a mutual attraction might be at hand. It was a chemical thing, a signal beyond my control. His eyes looked hopeful, a little surprised. I reminded myself that men were always on the prowl, and good or bad, every one of them had their own agenda.

Given the circumstances, and the terrible luck I'd been having, I found myself picturing the worst: him putting in a supportive, flawless performance all the way up to the moment when he picked up a shovel, pointed to a hole in the ground, and said, "Sorry to disappoint, but you need to be a good girl and hop in. I'm the murderer."

I pulled away. "No thank you. I'm in a hurry."

"Did I hear correctly that you have PTSD?" he said. "Since you were ten?"

"I … *what?* Oh my God. If you spread that around, it will play right into the crap I'm getting from Stable and Charlotte."

"I won't tell anyone. You can trust me."

"They'd make it sound like a flaw. It was just a rough patch from getting kidnapped. Me and my best friend."

"Kidnapped?" he said. "Where …?"

"See, this is what happens when you butt in uninvited. Push the wrong button, and you'll hear stuff that's private. Well done."

"I didn't mean to overhear. I'm sorry."

"I don't even know your name."

65

"We need to reset. Here—" He pulled a business card from his wallet and handed it to me. "Let's start from scratch."

"I don't want to know. I just want to go home."

"Look, I'm seeing in hindsight that I should have—"

"No." I backed away from him. "I know you mean well. At least I think you do. I hope you do. But right now, I can't ... it's too ..."

With a sideways blast of my hands, as if that ever dispelled any trouble I was in, I continued past his furrowed eyebrows and out-turned palms, his indication that I was missing a golden opportunity to find out that he was a prince. My gut agreed, hollering in the back of my mind to turn back, he was totally hot. So what if he was a murderer, every relationship had obstacles to overcome. It was a shame to not give him a chance.

Shut up and keep moving, I told myself.

8

Not for the first time, I thanked Heaven there was a safe refuge to duck into after encountering trouble in the heart of town. In the space of ten minutes, I'd plunged from feeling relatively normal to a state of profound exhaustion. I hadn't been kidding when I'd said all the food I'd eaten had burned away in record time. I didn't merely need some quiet time and cookies. I needed to plug myself into a wall outlet.

The Corner Pocket was a former pool hall that Sue Black and Kate McKenna had painted canary yellow and converted into a space that was a significant upgrade from the usual convenience store. It served the needs of gourmands and ordinary palates alike, with a gas pump out front. A bell jingled as I stepped in, and I was greeted by the aroma of apple pie. Vintage photographs of pool-playing locals lined the walls that framed gleaming oak aisles of necessities and baked goods. With bright collectibles and a corner with tables where people could read and sip coffee or tea, the store was the one place in town that replicated the feel of my favorite shops and coffee bars back home in Newton, Massachusetts.

Today, I headed straight for the freezer aisle and opened one of the glass doors. Enveloped by billows of icy fog, I deliberated over flavors of ice cream and attempted to calculate how many gears my frazzled brain had cranked through since last night. Shock. Horror. Puzzlement. Anger. Curiosity. Denial. A split second of lust for a police officer who could quite possibly be more trouble than Brumby. No, not lust. Well, maybe. More shock, and last but not least, complete humiliation.

What a fine day it had been.

Why did you answer your mother's call? I demanded, in agony over how I'd blurted things that had been dormant for years.

Soon, a concerned committee of two arrived at the end of the aisle, where they paused to assess the situation.

"She was fine ten minutes ago," Kate said.

"What could have happened?" Sue said.

"My guess is, it has to do with a man."

"She's definitely pink, and it's not from the freezer." Sue's black, glossy hair spilled around her shoulders as she gave me a quick hug. Tall and dark-eyed, with features that reflected the Passamaquoddy side of her ancestry, she held me at arm's length and studied me for a moment. "You look frazzled. I'll open the brandy if it'll help."

"No booze. And no dates. Bad idea."

"She's babbling a little," Kate said.

"Come on, honey." Sue took my arm. "Let's sit down."

I steeled myself as I followed them to the café area, fully aware there were perils in coming to the store in a vulnerable state. Their combined minds were like a supercomputer as they processed the entirety of local gossip that unfolded in the store from day to day. After considering all the facts, theories, and provable details, their guesses were on the money more than not, so I had to proceed with the utmost care.

While Sue stepped away for a moment, Kate sat down at one of the round tables and smiled encouragingly, indicating I should join her. "We have a few thoughts. Want to hear them?"

"Thoughts about what?" I said.

"Last night."

"Umm. I don't know."

"Let's start with Nadine Gilbert."

I hesitantly sat down. "Why?"

"Because her son, Kyle, has a history of burgling." Wisps of Kate's red hair had escaped her ponytail to curl around her face. She sat forward and folded her hands. "Kyle is one of those difficult kids. Trouble in school, pushing his luck with drugs, and running with the wrong crowd. Raymond nabbed him for DUI in a boat when he was sixteen."

"In a boat?" I said.

Kate nodded.

"Here you go, hon," Sue said, placing a steaming mug of cocoa in front of me, plus a plate of cheesecake brownies.

"I shouldn't. I ate a lot at Joan's house."

"Sonny, you've lost weight since you moved to the farm. About ten pounds by our reckoning, so eat as much as you want." Sue indicated the business card clutched in my hand. "What's that?"

"Huh? Oh. I don't know."

Sue pulled it from me, read the information, and then handed it to Kate. They exchanged a long, pointed look with raised eyebrows and apparent agreement on something, then turned back to me.

"Where were we?" Sue said.

"I was telling her about Nadine's son," Kate said. "Raymond tried to be a mentor for Kyle, but the boating incident was the last straw. Kyle raced past a swimming area where children were playing in the water. It's a wonder one of them wasn't killed."

"Why are you telling me this?" I said.

"Here's a photo of Kyle."

Kate swiveled her laptop toward me. I studied the image of a grinning teen. With his scrawny chest and thin arms flexed in a muscleman pose, Nadine's son exuded mischief and optimism, as if to say, *I'll get bulked out. You wait and see.* He seemed high-energy, but likeable. It was sad to think he was throwing his life away on drugs.

I sipped the cocoa and savored the brownie. The texture was smooth, with swirls of melted chocolate in between the cheesecake filling.

"Interesting," Kate said.

"No reaction," Sue agreed. "I mean, none."

"To what?" I said.

"Kyle. His photo."

"It wasn't him last night, if that's what you were thinking." I paused. "Just to be sure, how old is Kyle now?"

"I think he just turned eighteen."

"Eighteen is too young," I said. "Plus, his hair is wavy and thick. My impression of the intruder was that his hair was thinning on top."

"Intruder," Sue mused. "That's an interesting word."

"I meant burglar."

"Did he get away with anything?"

"Not that I know of."

"You surprised the guy in the act?"

"I guess. It was dark. No lights."

"Why are the police still there?"

I shrugged. "Beats me."

"They didn't say?"

"Something about ties to a larger case."

"Oh," Sue said. "That makes sense."

It did? Hallelujah.

With her elbows on the table, Kate looked glum as she rested her chin in her freckled hands. "When I saw Nadine approach you out there at the farmer's market, I figured she was hoping to convince you to not press charges. I had it all worked out."

"It's Nadine's pattern," Sue said. "Kyle is always in trouble, and Nadine is always bailing him out and making excuses for him. If her version of events is to be believed, the police corrupted him all the more by using him as an informant."

"They use kids at such a young age?"

"Again, this is according to Nadine." Sue shrugged. "For all we know it's a lie Kyle cooked up. You know how kids can bend the truth."

"Informants are useful in undercover work, right?"

"I suppose so. Why?"

"I'm free associating. It came to mind."

We sat in silence for a moment with Kyle grinning at us from the laptop. The burden of not being able to share what the intruder had dropped was giving me a headache. It seemed to me the police hadn't accomplished much with all their secrecy, given the other crime scene photos I'd seen. Exactly how far back did this business extend?

"Ok, new train of thought." Kate munched on a brownie and pondered the situation for a moment. "Nadine knows something. I'd bet money on it, so maybe Kyle drove the guy there last night. Nadine at least fears he's involved for whatever reason. He might not admit it, even to her, so she comes up to you to gauge your reaction."

I waited for more. Kate sat back with a pleased expression.

"That's it?" I said.

"It's huge, considering how little you've told us."

I carefully ventured, "Is Kyle's father a local?"

"My sense is Nadine doesn't want to share who provided the DNA," Kate said. "She had to 'entertain' a lot of men to make ends meet. There'd be a negative connotation around who the father was."

"I get it," I said. "Does she still …?"

"Hook? I don't think so. At some point, she secured enough money to open a club. She's legit now. It's stripping, but legit."

"She gives pole dancing lessons?"

"We took the class ourselves. It's a hoot. You'd love it."

"It's possible Nadine simply wants to help you, Sonny," Sue said. "A lot of people feel guilty for not reaching out to you."

"True enough," Kate said. "Nadine has risen above a lot of awful stuff, and she's a supportive mom. I admire her for that."

"Me too," Sue said. "Nadine hasn't updated her crime blog for a while, but I bet last night will inspire her to revisit her favorite topics. Wrong arrests. Police incompetence. Excessive force."

"Did she ask you about last night?" Kate said.

"No."

"That's odd. I would have expected her to pry."

Their gazes invited me to share details, anything that would help put them on firmer ground in their deliberations. Using the mug of cocoa for cover, I looked away and thankfully found a compelling new topic hanging on the nearby wall: a vivid watercolor painting of a blue and yellow rowboat drifting on a pond under a sky of sunlit clouds. Using white space for spectral highlights on the water, the artist had created depth, drama, and a sense of warmth with minimalist strokes. Even the shadows shimmered, purple in one spot, deep blue in another. The effect was peaceful and serene. All achieved with pencil, paper, and paint.

"Beautiful, isn't it?" Sue said, following my gaze.

"Did Lily Oakes paint it?"

"Yes. You know her?" Kate said.

"She and her father were at the farmer's market today."

"It's terrible what happens to children who are different," Sue said. "I think all that creative energy in her mind made it difficult for her to focus in school. In my book, who cares about getting math and science across if someone has this kind of talent?"

"How old is she?" I said.

"Eighteen. Kyle's age. She behaves as if she never progressed past the toddler stage, but she's super smart."

"Tough to handle sometimes," Kate said in a confiding tone. "From what we've pieced together, one of her tantrums might be the reason Hollis 'sprained' his hip last year."

"Golly," I said. "I hope not."

"It's just speculation, so please don't take it as fact."

"I won't."

"When she was in school, she was accused of pushing other children down when they teased her," Kate said. "Hollis protects her, come what may. Doesn't want her to end up in a facility. But we picked up on things he's said. That's where the thought came from."

"He got worried about her hair getting more and more tangled," Sue added. "Tried to help her brush it. I guess it hurt."

"Honestly, I think Hollis is wrong in protecting her," Kate said with a frown. "I feel bad for not speaking up."

Sue shook her head. "We have a pact. No overt meddling."

"Have you ever seen her be violent?" I said.

"She's pure sunshine when she's here," Kate said, then with a wince indicating she was about to take the discussion into choppy waters, she added, "Have you met their neighbor, Earl?"

"Hollis introduced us," I said. "He looked …"

"It's the weekend so I bet he was hung over."

"Yeah."

"It's sad when people give up on life," Sue said. "His wife ended up with one of his buddies. It happens more than people realize. To Earl's credit, he made sure Everett went to school and put dinner on the table. But he's depressed a lot. A hopeless drunk."

"Hollis told me he's a hard worker," I said. "And his son seems to have dodged picking up the drinking problem."

"Everett is a really good kid," Kate said. "You could look to him for doing chores, like putting hay in the barn."

"Actually, I'm low on straw for the berry patch."

"We'll put the word out for you," Sue said.

Every pause felt worrisome, a chance for them to pose questions. The problem was, I wanted to pose questions myself. Was it sensible for the police to leave me in the dark? Did I need a bodyguard, for heaven's sake? I pictured a future of nights where I startled over every odd sound if the "larger case" continued to remain unsolved.

"What the hell," I murmured. "I mean, really."

"I know it's disappointing to not have answers," Sue said. "Come back in a few days. We'll have a better sense of things."

"Ok, I will."

I meant it. If the police didn't start gaining ground in a few days, I would need to take matters into my own hands.

9

My head was starting to whirl from fatigue, but I couldn't stop wondering why Nadine Gilbert had approached me. Her crime blog was zero help: there were no recent posts, and her main focus was on spinning threadbare, unrelated facts into a narrative of potential police misconduct. I'd promised to not talk about the case, but I could at least assure her that her son hadn't been the 'burglar,' if that was why she'd approached me.

I wanted an in-person meeting. Seeing how she reacted would give me a better sense of her. From there, I would see where things led.

An internet search revealed her address. Soon I reached a back road of tattered homes with an assortment of mutts chained to porches. Here and there were attempts to brighten front yards, like flowers growing in old tires. A pile of rusted metal in the yard of one home looked positively lethal. Scattered toys and a bicycle said a family lived there.

Nadine lived in a trailer with one of the neater yards. There was no car out front in the driveway, but I thought I saw the curtains shift as I pulled in. I stepped out and crossed the grass.

"Nadine?" As I knocked, the screen door rattled on its hinges.

Maybe the shift of the curtains had been a trick of the light playing against the window glass. After a moment of waiting, I dug through my bag and fished out a pen and a scrap of paper.

Nadine, I wrote. *I have some questions about your note. Give me a call. I'd love to chat.* I signed the note, then tucked it into the screen door.

Shirtless, as if to show off his pale, flabby gut, a neighbor stepped out and squinted at me through glasses that didn't appear to have a left lens. The remains of his thinning hair looked as if it had been pasted on with bacon grease and a spatula.

"Nadine's out," he said. "Left a half hour ago."

"I thought I saw someone in the window."

"Kyle, most likely. Her son. He comes and goes like the wind. Usually on a dirt bike that's not registered."

I nodded. "Well, nobody seems to be home, so—"

"You want a beer?"

"No, thanks."

"Come on, give a poor bachelor a chance."

I rolled my eyes and headed to my car.

"You one of her students?" he said.

"Just a friend."

"Bet you'd be good on a pole."

He made dramatic motions indicating the kind of pole he had in mind in case I didn't get it. Unless the town took up the cause of importing a wider assortment of single men to choose from, assuming I ever had the time, my love life would range from scary to doomed.

* * *

On my drive back to Joan's house, I opened the window and let the sweet May air thunder into the car, pulling with it a succession of scents. First, I detected the sweet smell of freshly cut clover and grass, then I inhaled the stirring warmth of pine and balsam fir trees as I passed the forest where the perpetrator had both entered and exited my hilltop property. At least he'd chosen a nice time of year to terrorize me.

Up ahead as I rounded a bend, I saw the dreaded police barricade at the end of my gravel lane that cut upward through the pines. I pulled into Joan's driveway directly across the road, leaving room for her car when she got home. It was 1 p.m. in the afternoon.

Seeing an updated note from Joan in the kitchen as I stepped into the house, I learned that she'd stopped in for a minute while I was out. She'd left again to complete other errands. She would be back in a few hours. Harry and Jess would be back around four.

Joan had suggested I might benefit from a hot bath. As always when it came to letting simple pleasures turn the corner on a rough day, she was right. I couldn't think of anything I wanted to do more.

I closed the bathroom door in case the family returned ahead of schedule. Soon the vanity mirror was opaque with steam.

"Oh boy," I said, slipping into the hot, bubbly water.

Why had I deprived myself of this simple pleasure for so long?

If Joan ever wanted to earn some extra cash, she would have a bright future as a B & B hostess. The best part of her bathtub arrangement was a nifty metal arm with a sturdy clamp for a phone so a person could check messages and surf the internet without any danger of their device dropping into the water. I checked online for any news stories that would explain how someone had come into possession of human remains.

Soon I was up to speed on funeral parlor practices to the point where I planned to live more carefully from now on, but there was no mention of bodies being stolen in the state of Maine. Acts of vandalism in cemeteries had to do with toppled headstones. People might kill each other over matters as trivial as not cooking a hamburger to the proper level of pinkness, but digging up the dead was a line not to be crossed.

This left me to wonder if the twisted individual behind last night's ordeal had murdered someone in order to hack off their body parts. In that case, my online searches would lead to some mention of the partial remains of a dismembered body being found, wouldn't it? Unless the rest of the remains were still hidden out there somewhere.

A quick search revealed that 90 percent of Maine was covered by forest: roughly 17.5 million acres of impenetrable gloom in which to carry out a murder. There were 6,000 lakes and ponds in which to hide a body, 5,100 rivers and streams to dump remains, plus the surging depths of the ocean where lobsters picked the bones of anything unfortunate enough to sink to their watery lair. Tie a cinder block to a victim ten miles off the coast, and their remains were not likely to come back.

Depending on the year, between 500,000 and 900,000 people were reported missing in the United States. For all I knew the skeleton parts connected to the case had belonged to multiple victims. Their death could have occurred anywhere on the continent.

I reminded myself that it had been less than twenty-four hours since the intruder had upended my life. Impatience, I had been told throughout the years, was a path to trouble and disillusionment. Understanding the concept, and gathering fresh examples left and right as I plowed through life, had not decreased my proclivity in the least.

I had to strike a balance. Slowly, and only through trusted sources like Sue and Kate, I would find out enough to feel safe living on the farm, but not to the point where I got dragged into further trouble.

All too soon the water in the tub cooled.

I sloshed out of the tub, dried off, snugged the towel around myself, and set my phone on a small table equipped with essentials like soap and cotton balls. Steam covered the vanity mirror. I wiped it clean with a tissue, then began systematically scrunching my wet curls.

The creak of Joan's front door opening stopped me in midmotion as I reached for the hairbrush on the sink top. I looked out the window. Joan wasn't back from town, and it was too early for Harry and Jess to be back from archery camp. Maybe stress was making me think the worst. The sound was the house settling, something like that.

Joan's kitchen door softly closed.

Any warmth I'd gained from the bath left me as I stared toward the sound of footsteps approaching down the hallway.

"Who is there?" I demanded.

No answer.

I held my breath, vibrating from shock and disbelief as the footfalls neared the door. I was naked, except for a towel.

I rushed forward to lock the knob but the parts were misaligned. The latch wouldn't catch. Putting my palms on the door, I braced myself to hold it in place, but a shoulder pushed from the other side with violent force. I pushed back, slipping on the wet floor, desperate to gain time enough to grab my phone and call for help.

"Who is it?" I demanded. "*Stop.*"

My arms gave way as the shoulder hit the door harder.

Stumbling to the sink, I secured the top edge of the towel and grabbed the ceramic soap dispenser from the countertop. A man's hand, wrist-watch, and arm came into view as he pushed the bathroom door open. Drawing it out, as if he knew it would make my heart clench and my head drain, and the feeble weapon shake in my hand.

I expected a stubbled face. A jeans jacket.

But the man who stepped into view was the deputy Stable had repri-manded last night. I'd forgotten all about him.

He'd clearly not forgotten about me.

"What the hell are you doing?" I demanded.

"I knocked. I heard you call for help."

"You didn't knock, and I did *not* call for help."

"Sure you did." He rested his right hand on the butt of his sidearm. "Maybe you thought I was Brumby, coming to help you wash up."

"Get *out*. Right now."

He stared at me coldly. "I don't know how you got Raymond to leave the farm to you, but me and some other people are onto how you twist things around to get your way. The gall of it. Boston-borne, high-brow. That wasn't enough, was it? You wanted more."

"You don't have a *clue*."

"Well, guess what?" he said. "I'm acting on a tip that says you made a false statement last night. That's a serious crime. How about you come clean the other way? Not with a sponge. Tell me your connection to the surprise you found. Come on, out with it."

"That's ridiculous. You're making it up."

"I got a tip. I can prove you lied."

"Then do it. For now, get *out*."

"You're bluffing," he said.

I put down the soap dispenser. It wobbled and almost fell to the floor. All I cared about was keeping the towel secured with both hands.

"If I were you, I'd start thinking about your future employment," I said. "Why not save time and put on your own handcuffs?"

"You like handcuffs, huh? You're friends with hookers."

"Jesus. You are sick."

He advanced toward me a few steps and hollered, "Tell me the truth before I get ugly! What are you hiding?"

"My statement was accurate."

"You had advance warning. Who broke in last night?"

"I don't have a clue."

"Bullshit. This is serious."

I inhaled to scream. It came out rough. I was new at screaming. It was impossible in a terrified state. I inhaled again.

"Stop!" He held up his hands. "Ok. I believe you."

"Get *out*," I managed.

He assessed me, then appeared to grasp that having his colleagues show up might go as bad for me as it would for him.

"You called out for help. Say it."

"I did not call out for help."

"*Say* it," he hollered.

I stared at my phone. He followed my gaze.

"You want to make a call?" He swept my phone onto the floor, then stepped on it hard with his boot heel. "Oops, sorry."

He picked it up and held it out, his angry eyes almost daring me to reach for it. Then what did he have in mind?

I gripped the towel with both hands, desperate to keep it in place. If it fell, slipped, revealed more of me …

"Please," I managed. "Just leave."

"Reach for it," he said. "Go ahead."

As he shoved the phone closer, right under my chin, I turned my face away, wanting to knee him in the groin.

Then what?

I caught a dizzy glimpse of Brumby suddenly standing in the doorway. The two men were opposites, one in a uniform and of an ordinary build, the other packed with the muscles that came from shoeing horses and hard work from sunup until sundown.

"Hey pal," Brumby said, then he held up a callused hand as the deputy started to move. "See this device here in my shirt pocket, with the lens aimed at you? It's called a *cell* phone," he said with drama. "I hit the video button when I saw you come in. You realize phone videos are how cops like you end up behind bars."

"I was answering her call for help."

"Sonny, you want to weigh in?" Brumby said.

Trembling, ashamed to have needed help, I snatched my phone from the deputy, then I said through my teeth, "I already told you to get out. I'll decide later what to do with the video."

Flushed in the face, he paused, apparently weighing some rash moves, and then he pushed past Brumby. For a breathless moment, I thought the blacksmith was planning to escalate the situation by landing a punch, but with a clenched jaw, Brumby lowered his fist.

The kitchen door opened, then closed. Even then I couldn't stop clutching the towel. My hands were numb from the effort.

"Are you ok?" Brumby said.

"Turn it off," I managed. "The recording."

"Sonny—"

"Give me a second. Please."

As Brumby stepped out to wait in the hallway, I gripped the sink and closed my eyes. I willed my hands to stop shaking, and my heart to return to a normal rhythm. Not in my wildest paranoid thoughts had I imagined the deputy hated me enough to antagonize me in such a brazen way. What would have happened if Brumby hadn't arrived?

I never wanted to find out.

10

"Sonny," Brumby kept prompting from the hallway, sounding more and more impatient. "Are you all right?"

By the fifth time he uttered this question, which anyone else on Earth would have had the sense to not ask, I felt a burst of annoyance and almost snapped at him, then I reversed into a feeling of gratitude so strong it burned away some of the numbness and fog.

I focused on getting dressed, then I returned to the task of blow-drying my hair. My cheeks were aflame, my eyes bright with emotion. I splashed water on my face until I started to cool down.

Finally, I drew in a breath and stepped out into the hallway.

"Good thing I was in the neighborhood," Brumby said.

"Thank you. It got very bad very fast."

"But you handled yourself." He reached out and gave my shoulder a bolstering squeeze. "You held fast until help arrived."

He was right. The fact that the deputy hadn't seen me naked felt like a major victory. I'd refused to respond to his baiting. That would have escalated the situation. However ashamed I'd felt in the moment, I'd done the best I could until help had arrived.

"Listen," Brumby said. "I know this won't make up for what happened last night. I was pure shit for taking off."

"I'll get to that in a minute." I indicated his phone. "When did you start the recording? I doubt I'll need it, but just in case—"

"I never hit the record button." Brumby gave a rueful shrug. "I just said that in hopes of ending it fast. Did he step on your phone? That's what it sounded like from down the hallway."

"He did, but hopefully it won't be a problem." I checked my phone's screen, relieved to confirm that the shatter-proof case had done its job. "It's filthy, of course. What a jerk."

"I straightened the record with Detective Allen," Brumby said. "I told him you didn't invite me. I'd hoped to get lucky."

I folded my arms. "When you were amending your statement, did you add that you knew about the prowler in advance?"

Brumby's eyebrows twisted. "I didn't know anything."

"Come on. You looked out the window twenty times like you were expecting trouble. Don't lie to me."

"I was admiring the night. I couldn't sleep."

"Brumby—" I paused, staring at his socks. "Where are your boots?"

"I flung them off on the porch. The last thing I need is Joan coming after me for making scuff marks on her floor."

"Did the jackass leave any marks?"

Brumby looked down. "A few."

"Get started, then."

"Huh?"

"They need to be cleaned up, and I'm still too shaken to do it. Call it the beginning of your penance."

"I just saved your ass," he said.

"I'm grateful, but you left me with a giant disaster last night. I still can't believe it. What would Raymond think?"

Brumby looked miserable. "Don't go bringing him up."

I pointed to the nearest boot print. "You'll need to be on your hands and knees to be sure every mark is gone."

"You're serious," he said.

"Very."

Ten minutes later I was finished cleaning the bathroom and standing over Brumby with my arms folded as he scrubbed at a mark.

Joan stepped in with a grocery bag under one arm. She opened her mouth to say hello, then her gaze landed on Brumby.

"This is surprising," she said.

"Sonny's got me doing penance."

"Well." Joan smiled. "How nice that it benefits me."

"It wasn't me who marked up the—"

"*Tsss.*" I tapped Brumby with my toe to indicate my ambivalence about reporting the deputy. I didn't want to muddle the investigation with a twist that might slow things down or put me on the defensive with the police. I'd come out of the encounter unscathed. The deputy thought we had a video. That ought to keep him in check.

"She just kicked me," Brumby said. "You're my witness, Joan."

"It was a tap," I said. "Big baby."

My cell phone rang. It was Detective Allen.

"You can head home to the farm," he reported. "We'll want you to stop by the barracks to be fingerprinted. You touched evidence, so we need to isolate your prints from any others."

"I'm sorry, I can't say yes to that."

The detective sighed. "Miss Littlefield—"

"It's something I decided a few years ago," I pushed on. "I did a photo shoot of a wrongly convicted man. I'll never forget him saying he wished he'd never agreed to be fingerprinted when the police asked."

"This is a different kind of situation."

"I won't change my mind. I'm sorry."

He grumbled under his breath, then said, "Brumby got his memory back. Your version of events stands."

"I told her already," Brumby hollered, sponge in hand. "She's got me on my hands and knees cleaning Joan's floor. She says it's penance for ducking out on her last night."

"I would like a picture of that," the detective said.

"Now that I can agree to." I lifted my phone and snapped a photo of Brumby looking darkly up at me. "I'm texting it to you."

"I'll be in touch," Detective Allen said in closing.

Once the photo loaded to his phone, he sent me a smiling face emoji.

"Did you have to do that?" Brumby demanded.

"I did." I pointed. "And you missed a spot."

As I helped Joan put away the groceries, she came up with a way to help put the "burglary" business behind me.

"I was planning to make chili tonight. Why don't I bring it up to your house? We'll turn the corner with a little party."

"You've already gone to so much trouble."

Joan took up a pose with an impatient expression and her fist planted on her hip, which she used to great effect on Harry and Jess when they were making pointless arguments.

I took the hint. "If you're sure …"

"To push the cobwebs away, we can make it a sleepover, like Raymond used to have when—" Joan stopped as if thinking it might be a sore subject, then she put on a smile again. "Never mind, we'll stick with dinner. Go on and make sure all is well with your animals, and take this pack of trouble with you." She indicated Brumby, who'd finished with the floor. "He can come for dinner too, I suppose."

"Is that a good idea?" I said.

"He's only irritating to people like us who've reached adulthood," Joan said. "Harry and Jess will be thrilled."

"I can help make the chili."

"No, I have a system. Cooking is my thing."

"Sonny," Brumby prompted from the hallway. "Stop pestering Joan and come get your things together."

"I'll be right back," I told Joan.

As I stepped into the bedroom, I found Brumby shaking his head and frowning as he studied something on his cell phone.

"Bad news?" I said.

"Just listening to that asshole, how he harassed you."

I paused. "The deputy?"

"It's all right here in the video."

I flipped my hands. "You told me you didn't make a video."

"I didn't lie, exactly. I delayed saying the truth."

"Send me a copy." It was a large file, but soon I was adding it to my library. "Brumby, you're a good guy, but this business of lying and making up your own rules is not a path to happiness."

"Look who's talking," he said.

"I don't lie."

"You sure as hell do when it suits you. It's a big thing to report a cop. Even with this video, they're apt to support his side. He could claim all sorts of things. He's not going down without a fight."

"Would they believe him?"

"Depends, really. It's a crap shoot."

I had to admit I was torn. "I should tell Joan, at least."

"The woman who called Stable last night over your protests? One, we've got the situation contained. Two, the police would swarm in and make a fuss. Three, I've had my fill of cops."

I closed my eyes and gripped my brow. "You're right, it's a big thing to report an officer. I need less drama, not more."

"Then keeping quiet makes sense. Here, this ought to brighten your mood. I ran into Chuck earlier."

Handed an envelope, I opened it and stared at a five-thousand-dollar check made out to me from Chuck Brewster.

"I haven't taken photos yet," I protested.

"Down payment. He means business getting your help."

"Wow." I paused. "Holy crap."

"This is the thing you need to know, Sonny. People who loved Raymond will do anything you ask of us. Other folks will hate you on sight, like the deputy. Pike is his last name, right? I'm pretty sure his uncle is the logger you kicked off the farm a few months back."

I paused, remembering all too well the man who'd shown up in his big truck with his arrogant attitude. Without even pausing to say hello, he'd insisted he had an agreement with Raymond to cut old-growth trees from the mixed-wood forest I now suddenly owned.

"He was lying," I said. "There was no agreement."

"You stood your ground. People like that guy don't think in terms of truth. They just want what they want."

"Maybe that's why the deputy has been rotten to me from the start."

"Most likely. Next point. Do you realize the last time the police were at the farm? The night Raymond died."

"Oh my God. I should have thought of that."

85

No wonder Joan had seemed brittle all day. Raymond had been like a father to Harry and Jess, and Joan had relied on him when her marriage had hit an extended rough patch. Her husband worked out to sea as a merchant mariner. He hadn't come home for over a year.

"Joan had serious feelings for Raymond," Brumby was saying. "I'd see her studying him, wondering if he was over losing Ella. Then the bottom dropped out. Maybe she thinks if she'd acted on her feelings, he wouldn't have been alone that awful night. He would still be alive, and—" Brumby paused. "Don't start crying, for Pete's sake."

"Why didn't she tell me?"

"*Shh.*" Brumby shook my arm to stop the waterworks. "Joan'll wonder why you're upset. You need to let her bring it up."

"I know …"

"Then cut it out. Come on."

I wiped my eyes and instructed myself to do as told. "Thank you for telling me. I've been stupid."

"You're right about that. Stupid as hell."

This helped rein in my feelings. I glared at him.

"That's more like it. Shall we go?" Brumby started to heft the cases, then stared at them. "What in God's name …?"

"No questions. Part of your penance."

"I saved your ass and cleaned the floor."

"Again, what would Raymond say?"

"I will draw the line at some point." With an irritated scowl, Brumby headed for the door. "I'll do this for you, then we're even."

"Not even close," I said.

"I'll trim Dodge. Then we're good."

"Nope."

Grumbling about how women make their own rules and get to lie all the time without any serious consequences, he carried the suitcases out.

11

Across the road from Joan's yellow house and trim, flower-decked yard, which always seemed to beam encouragement toward my entrance of overgrown weeds on the opposite side of the wooded lane, I stopped by my mailbox before heading up the hill to my house and examined the latest offers directed at Mr. Raymond French. No matter that I'd followed every step required to make his death known to all concerned parties. Credit card companies had no respect for the dead. They were determined to solicit him in the grave.

I crossed to my idling car, then I headed home. The bottom of my driveway cut through a stretch of tall pines, paper birches, and boulders with ancient lichen caps. I drove onward through the shade, then sunshine claimed my car as I headed upward toward the house and barn at the top of the hill. To my right, the golden paths of the strawberry field curved around the slope in neat rows. To my left, Dodge lifted his head with sprigs of grass in his muzzle and bellowed a resonant hello, then trotted beside my car along the gray fence with a dramatic thud of hooves, his neck arched and his mane aglow with sunlight.

On my first visit to the farm back in February, when deep snow was draped from the boughs of evergreens and sat in dollops on every fence post, the layout of the hill had seemed so round and well-proportioned that I felt as if I'd entered a magical snow globe.

Now it was May, the sky a wide expanse of bright, New England blue above the flickering greenness of it all. The house, alas, was green as well: a vibrant, food-color shade that had declared war on the purple lilacs and orange quince blossoms that flanked the porch.

I had chores to tackle and a crime to ponder, but for now, I wanted to hug my animals. A breeze stirred through the maple trees that shaded the yard as I slipped between the fence rails to pat Dodge's neck.

"Did you keep those officers in line? Good boy!"

With a barrel chest, hooves the size of dinner plates, and withers about level with the top of my head, he was the most impressive and powerful animal I'd ever met in person, aside from elephants at the zoo. As one of the lambs leaped and gamboled around his hooves, Dodge shook his head, but otherwise stayed still, seeming to take on an amused paternal air. I scooped up Daisy to hug her tightly and pat her pink, milk-filled tummy. On the ground again, Daisy bounced away like a wind-up toy on skinny, barely coordinated legs.

Looking like a gathering of ladies in their resplendent coats of ringlets, the ewes pressed toward me with *baahs* and insistent gazes, as if to say, *You do realize a bunch of guys took over the place last night?*

I don't know about any other sheep in the world, but my father's flock of individualists had obliterated any notion that sheep were unassuming little animals who led boring lives of placid innocence. Woolberry. Magnolia. Paisley. Dot. Ruby. I could identify each sheep by their markings, their unique habits, and even the sound of their voices.

From the start, the ewes had a way of planting their front hooves and looking up at me with an air of swagger, as if to say, *You think you're qualified to run things around here? Well, good luck to you because we are not an easy bunch to please. Now, hand over the grain.*

And then there was Bubbah, the ancient ram who stood vigil with his front hooves perched on the lowest rung of his pen next to the barn. As always, he looked hopefully toward the ewes as they grazed, only to watch them ignore him entirely. Robbed of the vigor of his youth, all he could do was stare mournfully at the loves he'd once known and spin tragic, sheep poetry about the sad arc of life with a low, gurgling *bah*.

Brumby was strapping on leather chaps over his jeans, an indication that he planned to follow through on trimming Dodge's hooves.

One minute of watching him stride around in his chaps was all it took to knock my chores to the bottom of my to-do list. I grabbed my bag and pulled out my camera. Brumby grinned, looking so pleased by my endorsement of how manly and colorful he looked, that it almost spoiled my plan of catching candid shots of him as he worked. We crossed to the pasture where Dodge was grazing and climbed between the fence rails.

"Cover your ears," Brumby said.

"Why?"

Without pause or further warning, he pursed his lips together and issued a shrill, air-shattering whistle. Dodge responded instantly, swerving in place and thundering toward us with ridiculously excited whinnies.

"How do you do that?" I said. "Teach me."

"Put your lips together like this." Brumby puckered his lips into a pre-kiss pose and leaned closer. "Come on. Don't be shy."

"Nice. After I was nearly assaulted today."

"Crap, I forgot."

Based on what I'd read in Raymond's journals, I had a hunch that Brumby's helpful attitude just then was more complicated than wanting to get back in my good graces. Brumby's mindset apparently included a strong belief in poltergeists, magic to a certain degree, and other mystical forces that secretly governed how things worked on planet Earth.

If ever there was a man to end up as an opinionated and touchy ghost, Raymond's spirit was a certainty. At least that was how Brumby might read any coincidence or unexplainable sound that happened on the farm. I had a feeling that if I ever shocked him by responding to his flirting, he wouldn't make it past a five-second kiss before he felt the full weight of Raymond's disapproval and ire glaring down on him.

Bending at the waist, facing backward toward Dodge's hindquarters, Brumby clucked to the horse and smoothly lifted an enormous front hoof until it rested between his knees. With my camera in hand, I zoomed in for a few close-ups, then zoomed out to catch pieces of hoof flying off as Brumby clipped them with metal nippers.

Other tools were within reach in his pockets. Flipping each one to position them properly, he used a knife to clean the frog area, and a rasp to smooth the outside edge of the hoof.

"One down," Brumby said.

He grinned and flexed for the camera.

Ok, time to let his ego cool off, I decided.

I climbed the wooden porch steps and returned to Raymond's vibrantly orange kitchen. The living room was a vivid blue reminiscent of a Caribbean sky at noon. How a straightforward, woodsy man like Raymond had endured such an arresting backdrop had yet to be explained. Love was one explanation since it was possible that his wife, Ella, had chosen the colors. If so, he'd left them in place long after she'd died.

Hearing a text alert, I dug out my phone.

Is everything ok? Arlene texted me from London. *No morning check-in.*

Just busy. How's London?

Fun. You would love it here.

I'm tied up right now. Let's catch up tomorrow.

I decided to leave Raymond's journals in the suitcases and stow them in the spare bedroom on the first floor. Next, I took a screenshot of the check Chuck had given to me for our upcoming photo shoots, then I used the bank app on my phone to deposit it into my account. After a moment, the process was completed. In a few days, I would make sure the money had cleared, but for now, it seemed I was gainfully employed.

I took a moment to copy Brumby's video of the deputy onto a thumb drive, then I hung it on a peg near the kitchen door so it would be easy to grab if the need arose. In my bag, I would come across it multiple times. My preference was to forget why I'd hung it near the door in the first place. Hopefully, I would get my way on a subject for once.

Brumby opened the kitchen door and leaned in with a grin.

"You've got company," he said. "Come and see."

With a sigh, I stowed my laptop, wondering if I was ever going to regain control over the trajectory of my life.

Outside, I was surprised to see a battered truck with a towering load of straw pulling up the driveway. Everett waved from the driver's seat, and I saw Earl beside him in the cab. Hollis and Lily emerged from a sedan.

Sue and Kate climbed out of their Jeep. Next, Chuck Brewster and Nadine arrived in a loud, yellow, vintage Corvette convertible. People I'd never met pulled in as well, parking end to end along the steep slope. Everyone waved hello, and then as if acting under prior instructions, they converged on Everett's truck and started unloading straw bales.

I jogged down the driveway. "This is a surprise."

"You mentioned this morning that you need straw," Kate said. "We figured while we're at it, you can use a burst of help."

"Thank you so much. This is amazing."

Everett crossed toward me, looking purposeful. In his hand was a bouquet of wildflowers. He offered it to me.

"This is sweet," I said.

"I've seen something along these lines in a movie, so I figure I can't be too far off," he said, "You have super pretty eyes and all kinds of other things I like. I don't mind at *all* that you're a little older than me. I'd be proud to have you on my arm going through life."

I looked toward the horizon. "Umm ..."

"Ask anyone. I'm a good guy. Handy with tools."

"The trouble is, I'm not looking for a relationship," I said gently. "It's not a good time. I'm very independent, so—"

"You're difficult, I've heard the rumors and such," he persisted. "I'm patient. You saw how good I am with Lily."

"It's not going to happen. I'm sorry."

"Everett, come on now," Hollis said, patting his shoulder and steering him away toward the other helpers on the slope. "Miss Littlefield has a lot on her plate, so how about you focus on getting the straw off the truck? It's getting late in the day."

"Bye, Miss Littlefield," Everett said. "We'll talk later."

I turned to Hollis with a desperate expression and whispered, "Where did that come from? He can't be serious."

"Everett's been feeling his age the past year or so," Hollis said. "He's fallen in love about eight times since Christmas. It'll pass, I assure you. Unless you're keen on him ..."

"No, he's way too young."

"He's twenty-four. You can't be much more than that."

91

"I'm twenty-eight."

"Oh, I didn't realize," Hollis said gravely, as if he took this to mean I was beyond hope and spoiling on the vine. "Well, I know things are different down in the city where you're from."

"Exactly," I said, figuring he could think what he wanted, as long as it was understood I did not see Everett as a love interest.

"You remember Earl, Everett's dad," Hollis said, indicating the sullen, disheveled man who'd climbed out of the truck. "We heard from Sue and Kate that your lawn mower is acting up."

"It's been stalling lately. It's in the barn."

"I'll take a look," Earl said.

"Thank you. That's really kind."

As he departed with his hands in his pockets, Hollis said, "This is doing him a favor. Sunshine will do him good."

Feeling a tug on my shirt, I turned to see Lily standing there with her wild hair in a ponytail, and a shy expression on her face as she handed me the atmospheric pencil drawing of Dodge. Hollis said Lily felt satisfied that it was finished, and it was mine to keep.

"It's wonderful," I said, hugging Lily. "Thank you."

I dashed to the house to put the drawing in a safe spot where it wouldn't blow away and get stepped on, then I returned to Hollis and Lily as they made their way to the pasture fence.

"Is it ok for her to pet the lambs?" he said.

"Sure."

"I'll check on Earl's progress. Can you mind Lily?"

"Absolutely."

Smiling, Lily reached for my hand. Her fingers were sticky, but I didn't care. She was like one of the lambs, skipping along beside me.

Before I could talk her through the trick of befriending the sheep, Lily clambered between the fence rails and sat down in the grass, as if knowing that sitting quietly as a new, curious element in the pasture would draw the animals to her. She giggled as Dodge clomped over and sniffed her hair, most likely because her blonde frizz smelled of candy. Soon she had a lamb tucked under each of her arms, and another pawing her leg. She was gentle with them as she petted and hugged them, closing her eyes as she brought their wriggling wooly bodies to her face.

"Well, I can see what's going to happen now," Hollis said, returning with a slight limp, then resting his weight on his cane as he stood beside me. "She'll be wanting sheep of her own."

"They make wonderful pets," I said. "If you don't have room at your place, you can bring Lily here for visits."

"The lambs will grow fast, of course," he said.

"I noticed you limping …"

"Don't mind that, just a sprain. I'm mending every day." He smiled. "I think you're needed in the berry field."

To say I was 'needed' was a stretch. As I arrived at the patch that wrapped around the hill on my left in a succession of neat rows as if it had been put in place with the aid of a giant comb, I found Sue in command of an ambitious weeding operation. The volunteers listened intently, including Harry and Jess, who'd returned from archery camp.

"Bindweed, thistle, burdock, dandelion," Sue said, pointing out each kind of plant that needed pulling. "Be careful where you kneel, and do *not* pull any weed at the expense of a strawberry plant! Dig straight down or at an angle so you don't disturb the berry roots."

"Then tuck in fresh straw as you go," Kate added.

Inspired by the sudden sense of being surrounded by a gathering of my father's friends, I ventured to the volunteers, "Hey, everyone. This is the week Raymond would start swimming in Horse Shoe Lake. Did anybody else ever meet him there to take a dip?"

"We usually never swim before June," Joan said. "To be honest, the water isn't super warm until July."

"June is just a few weeks away."

"Raymond was a tough dude," Sue said of the lack of interest I encountered. "Bear in mind, during the winter he usually wore a quilted flannel shirt instead of a jacket, even on freezing cold days."

"Well, I'm going to give it a try."

Kate smiled. "Color me surprised."

I grabbed one of the trowels someone had brought and dug into the work of rescuing the strawberry crop from weeds, bugs, and clumps of grass that had been there since the previous year. The most surprising volunteers on the work team were Chuck Brewster, who was bent over a stubborn weed thirty feet away, and Nadine Gilbert, who stepped to my side and knelt next to me with a waft of perfume.

"Sorry if I startled you at the farmer's market," she said.

"No problem," I said. "It wasn't a big deal."

"Listen, I need to be sure about a thing or two," Nadine said with a look of apology. Wearing pink gardening gloves that fit oddly because of the length of her fingernails, she swiveled her derriere my way. "Get my phone, would you? It's in my back pocket."

She gave me her passcode, then she prompted me through her photo library. I saw innumerable shots of men smiling behind beers and drinks at the "Starlight Lounge," the strip club she owned.

"Keep going, keep going," she said. "There! That one is good."

Pulling her phone closer, I found myself looking at a photograph of Kyle Gilbert's boyish, likeable face.

"Well?" Nadine said.

"Who is he?" I said, not wanting to tell her that Sue and Kate had already shown me his picture to see how I reacted.

"My son, Kyle." Nadine looked at me sideways. "I take it he wasn't your burglar? If he was, please tell me."

"It wasn't him. I'm positive."

"Thank you, Jesus." Nadine closed her eyes, then swiveled her butt toward me to indicate the phone should return to her pocket.

"Why would you think it was him?" I said.

"Oh, he's laying low this week to the point where he doesn't answer my calls, and I don't know why he would avoid me this time. Truthfully, Sonny, he's a good kid. I couldn't ask for a better son, but he runs with the wrong crowd sometimes."

"So, he's a typical teenaged boy," I said.

Nadine beamed. "Exactly."

"Do you have any pictures of his friends?" I said.

"I don't think so. Why?"

"You mentioned the wrong crowd. I wondered …"

"Oh, maybe his friends burgled you? I hope not. Kyle would feel bad about it and tell me. I'll check back with you on it."

"I've heard you're a devoted mother," I said. "Kids know that deep down. I'm sure he'll reach out when he's ready."

"Oh, honey, more of that and you'll ruin my makeup." Framed by false eyelashes, Nadine's eyes glistened with gratitude. "What a sweetheart you are. So much like Raymond."

"You knew him?"

"Oh, yes." Abruptly worried, she held up her gloved hands. "Don't go thinking he and I were involved. I swear."

"I wasn't thinking that ..."

She grinned and nudged me. "Imagine finding out you've got a little brother!"

"That would be surprising for sure."

Not impossible, I realized. I hoped to heaven that my mother was Raymond's one indiscretion along those lines. I decided it was time to plow through his journals at a faster speed.

"The shortlist for Kyle's father starts over there."

Nadine indicated Chuck, who had abandoned the weeding and now stood to one side, talking to Brumby and smoking a cigarette. The two men seemed to be arguing, Brumby making emphatic motions with one hand, and Chuck rolling his eyes as if his friend was talking nonsense. Brumby scowled. He didn't like losing an argument.

"That man has been good to me over the years," Nadine was saying, still gazing at Chuck. "Isn't he sweet for pitching in today? You wouldn't believe what I had to do to convince him to lend a hand with garden work," she added with a suggestive wink.

"Golly, you didn't need to ... I mean ..."

"Now, honey, don't tell me you're a prude."

"Kind of not. I don't think so."

"That's good because I had an idea. You know the cop I warned you about, the one with the nice big shoulders and brown eyes? I've been in the sex trade long enough to know a smoking hot pair when I see one. Have you jumped him yet?"

"Have I—? No! I don't even know his name."

"Oh, a mystery element. Even better." Nadine leaned close and said with a conspiratorial air, "You want answers. You'll get them lickety-split if you play your cards right. Picture it, your hands on his chest, his hands on your ass. He's kissing you, all passionate. In your bed. On the couch. Anywhere. You on top. That's the best way. It's going to take self-control, but just when things are totally heated up, *you* know what I mean—"

"Woah, Nelly!" I exclaimed. "We don't even—"

"That adds to it, not knowing him. Bear in mind, I don't want you to trust him. Just get him to say what he's holding back."

"I don't think … he's not …"

"Do you know who burgled you?" she said.

"No."

"Then he's holding back, which puts you at risk."

I looked desperately around, hoping Kate or Sue or anyone would come over and change the subject. Bugs. Weeds. *Anything*.

"You're hot for him, I can tell," Nadine said.

"I don't know him. So, you're wrong. Very wrong."

Nadine heaved a sigh. "I have seen this so many times. Sheltered life, raised to put your foot on the brake. Afraid of taking risks in the love arena to the point where you've blocked his name."

"I haven't … what are you saying?"

"You've blocked his name. A classic case."

I blinked as I knelt there in the sunshine amidst the berry plants. The last thing I needed after a string of jarring ordeals was to have a former prostitute weigh in on how fear of commitment had guided my love life for years. Even worse, her conclusion made *sense*.

Chuck's boots stirred the straw near the weed I'd been working on, and then his cigarette smoke and shadow claimed me.

"Nadine," he said. "What are you saying to this poor girl?"

"I'm enlightening her."

"Doesn't look like it. She's pink in the face."

"You ready to head out, hon?" Nadine said, looking up at him.

"Afraid so, got stuff to do." Chuck reached his hand down and did most of the work of getting me to my feet. "We set for a photo shoot?"

"Yes," I said. "Thank you for the advance payment."

"Let's name a time."

I followed them to Chuck's Corvette convertible, then came to my senses as I saw how the light was highlighting his face.

No mental meltdown I'd ever weathered had rendered me so far gone that I couldn't instantly recover my wits by reaching for a camera. Just then, I only had my phone handy, but it was the perfect tool for catching some crisp, breezy, informal shots that would be perfect for adding to whatever digital platforms Chuck had in place.

I captured him smiling at me as I knelt, his car in the background, and cigarette smoke drifting around him. Nadine leaned in, adding a flirty element to a few shots. I shot him with the door open, his boot resting on the runner, his thumb looped on his front pocket. In the driver's seat with the door closed and his arm draped out of the open window.

"Can I leave now?" he said.

"We're good," I said. "See you in a few days."

The Corvette growled to life, and with a noise level that deserved a ticket for unnecessary disturbance of the peace, Chuck pulled down the driveway, then zoomed away along the wooded road. Nadine smiled and waved to me from the passenger's seat.

In less time than I'd imagined the chore of weeding the strawberry patch would take, I saw people starting to stand up and brush dirt from their hands and pants. They high-fived each other and stowed tools and baling twine in Everett's truck.

Turning toward the drone of an engine, I saw Earl come into view on my father's green and yellow mower in the narrow orchard that began behind the house and ended along the forest's edge at the bottom of the slope. Raymond and Ella had planted most of the trees two decades ago. Other trees were so old their hollow trunks provided homes for birds. In one of those odd contrasts one notices, the apple, plum, and cherry trees, which were in bloom at that time of May, sent showers of white and pink petals around the dark-haired man as he hunched in the seat of the mower, seeming oblivious to the beautiful scene around him.

Harry and Jess gave me a quick hug. They smelled of fresh air and were grinning ear to ear as they took in the berry field.

"It's a great crop, Sonny," Harry said.

"The best ever," Jess agreed.

"Where's Brumby?" Harry asked.

I pointed. "Up there with a rake. What's he doing?"

"He's making a bonfire!" Jess said.

They ran toward him to help, and as I arrived, I saw that he had cleared some tall grass from a five-foot-wide ring of fieldstones. Once his raking was finished, he piled an armload of firewood in the center, shoved in some dry clippings, and held his lighter to it.

The chill that came to my arms wasn't just because the sun was setting behind the trees. I was glimpsing the kind of activity that had unfolded on the farm before Raymond had died. His friends, and even the unknown volunteers who'd shown up, knew every inch of the place, every chore that needed to be done. I watched them gather in high spirits around the yard, laughing, ribbing each other, and opening cans of soda from a cooler. I heard Raymond's name being mentioned as if he'd just made a joke. Everywhere I looked were exchanges that reflected known habits and long-time relationships, which made the scene seem like some past event that Raymond had organized. A time when I would have been living in Boston, completely unaware that he or any of his friends existed.

In that moment, I had the dizzying notion that he wasn't the ghost.

I was.

12

"I dug these out of the closet," Joan said, indicating the blankets loaded in her arms. She put them on the grass a safe distance from the campfire. "We'll need these once it's dark. I've got the chili inside on the stove, and bread warming in the oven."

"Thank you so much, Joan," I said. "While you're here, I want to ask about this business of Detective Allen telling me to not talk about the case. Would Raymond have agreed with the secrecy, or would he have encouraged me to speak up and demand answers?"

"He'd urge you to keep quiet if that's what the police wanted. There are times when a lot of harm can come from leaks."

I nodded. "Ok, good to know."

"Stop looking so lost. You're due for some fun."

Wouldn't that be nice for a change?

But hearing Brumby's voice, I all but clapped my hands to my face in alarm as I saw that he was in the midst of describing the break-in to the people who'd gathered around him outside the barn. It was obvious, the way he was making shoving motions, then landing a punch in the air. Sue and Kate were staring at the spot where the snowman cookie tin and skeleton hand had landed. Sue asked Brumby why the spot looked as if it had been gone over carefully by the police. Brumby shrugged dramatically, then caught sight of me staring at him with an alarmed gaze. He waved me off, indicating he wasn't going too far.

While I was looking toward the barn, my gaze fixed on the tack room window where I'd seen police lights for an extended time. Tomorrow, I would go in there and see if I could piece together any clues that would tell me what had caught their interest.

As dusk settled in, I alternated between eating chili and corn chips and using my phone to photograph my new friends and neighbors around the campfire.

Soon, as the air rapidly cooled and night mist descended over the hill, I needed one of the quilts Joan had brought out. Jess sat down on my right and snuggled close. Not to be outdone, Lily jammed in on my left. Her breathing was audible as she sat very still and watched everyone intently. Maybe she was drawing them in her mind.

I was thrilled when Everett had zero chance of joining me under the blanket. He knelt nearby and tapped Lily's shoulder.

"Shove over," he said. "Go sit with Hollis."

Lily clung to my side, and I patted her arm in thanks.

"Darn it," Everett said. "You are a constant pain."

"There's room over here," Brumby said from the other side of the campfire, appearing to catch on. "Leave the ladies alone."

Voices quieted as night fell. It was peaceful, but a little somber.

"Raymond had a matching Belgian, didn't he?" Hollis asked.

"Goldy, Dodge's brother," Brumby said. "He died some years back."

I recalled Raymond writing about the loss.

Colic is a terrible, cruel way to go. Dodge nearly went down too, sweating and shivering as his best friend in the world rolled in pain. It took the strength of Hercules to pull on the lead rope and halter enough to coax Goldy off the ground. The vet said to keep him moving, but toward the end, he would wobble along for a couple of strides and drop with a horrific, sudden thud that I felt through my boots. The vet said it was time. He gave Goldy the shot, and in a few seconds, the biggest presence in the world was gone.

No more tumbling bellow of a whinny to greet me in the morning, so reminiscent of a human laugh. There is nothing like the hard death of an animal that big. I never want to experience it again.

The tough side of owning animals had sunk in on the first day I'd visited the farm, just after Raymond's memorial service. Harry and Jess had come up the hill in their black mourning clothes, hesitantly at first, then in a rush when they saw my resemblance to Raymond. I could scarcely hear what they were telling me. Some kind of warning about the worst possible outcome waiting in the wings if I didn't act.

"Slow down," I'd said. "Call me Sonny."

"You have to stop Charlotte!" Harry had hollered with an air of desperation. "She's talking about bringing the sheep to the butcher, and Dodge will end up at the glue factory!"

I'd looked at the animals lined up along the fence on the snowy hillside. I would never forget their attentive gazes, as if they were aware of the dire possibility Harry had presented to me. Would I condemn them to death, or was I going to step in and protect them?

Now, three months later, I knew they'd probably lined up along the fence to complain about not getting treats on their expected schedule. Or they were reacting to the chaos that had unfolded when Joan had found Raymond lying in the snow without a pulse.

Pitched into sadness, I gazed at the campfire with the skeleton hand in mind. Somewhere out there must be a family suffering from the loss of a loved one, no idea their search for answers would lead to a barn in the middle of Maine. Would I ever learn the identity of the victim? Their history, their talents and habits and every other trait that made them unique? Or would the jarring mystery never be explained?

Looking up, I saw Kate and Sue whispering to each other with an air of concern as they studied me from the other side of the campfire. I managed a smile, hoping to convince them that I was fine, just drained and a little emotional after a tough couple of days.

As the fire began to die down, people fetched sticks and toasted marshmallows that sent the aroma of sizzling sugar into the night air. Joan provided the ingredients for making S'mores. Jess left my side multiple times to make the gooey treats.

It was nine p.m., and the sound of people slapping mosquitoes on their arms prompted me to step into the house to get some citronella candles.

I opened the door and reached for the light switch on my way in, then yelped as I collided into a man who'd been standing there. The sudden bright light illuminated Earl's stubbled face and rumpled clothes.

"Oh," I said. "I didn't see you."

He made no effort to move out of the way. I stepped around him, noticing that his breath smelled of whatever alcoholic beverage was contained in the bottle he was holding. I realized it was Raymond's blueberry cordial—the very last bottle he'd ever made.

"Where did you get that?" I said.

"Cabinet. Deli'shis," he slurred. "Might throw up from it, though."

"Maybe you should step outside."

"Jus' lookin' around. Everett's set t' propose," he said. "He's talked of nothin' else sn's last night. Got you flowers and all."

"I am not interested in dating your son," I said firmly. "I made that clear to him. Can you hand me that bottle?"

"Don't be grabbin' me, woman." Earl yanked his arm away.

"Let's head outside, ok?"

"Everett's right, thi's big place for a girl." His fist contained a belch. "Didn't know Raymond was gone. Must've mish'ed it."

The door opened, and Hollis ducked his head in. One glance at Earl, and he could see I needed help with a dire situation.

"Earl! What the hell are you doing?" Hollis turned and hollered into the night, "Everett, come get your father."

"Here he is, dad of the year." Earl tearfully clapped Hollis's shoulder. "You're good to me. I'm a failure. A rotten drunk."

"I'm sorry you're seeing him like this, Sonny," Hollis said.

"It's ok, I understand."

Staggering a little, Earl fixed his watery gaze on me, as if he'd only just noticed me standing there. He gripped my arm. "You need to be good to my boy, understand? He deserves to be happy."

Seeing the bottle starting to slip from his grasp, I lurched to catch it too late. It landed with a clunk, spilling the rest of the cordial in an expanding swath that claimed Earl's shoes. I crossed to the counter and tore off enough paper towels to clean up the mess.

In the meantime, Everett came in and gripped his father by the arm to keep the drunk on his feet. If necessary, I would bring Dodge in to haul him out. I needed him gone. Whatever it took.

"What have you done now?" Everett said. "I can't believe this."

"Can't believe," Earl crooned on his way through the door. "Can't wait no more ... no, tha's not it ... how's that song go?"

"Quiet, Dad. You're upsetting folks."

Finally, they were outside, and heading to their truck. There was no point in lighting the citronella candles anymore. The interruption had everyone climbing to their feet and saying goodnight. I shook the hands of the people I'd never met before, except maybe at Raymond's memorial service. I'd figure out their names at some point.

Everett returned from his truck with a glum frown. "I hope Dad's nonsense hasn't ruined our chances," he said.

"Everett, your father has nothing to do with why you and I don't have a future. For one thing, you're too young."

And golly, was he ever. His wide gaze showed zero understanding of how to turn life's challenges into learning moments. He was looking for an easy solution. It would take time, experience, and a healthy dose of self-awareness to know that growth comes from within.

He could learn a thing or two from the mystery trooper, with his intense brown eyes and air of having all kinds of complicated gears. There was nothing wide-eyed about him. I blinked away the tangent lest it devolve into Nadine's scenario for getting answers.

"I'm sorry, the answer is no," I continued. "But thank you for helping today. I'll pay you for the straw and gas for your truck."

"Sue and Kate said to bill them."

Once again, Hollis steered him away with a reminder that I had a lot on my plate. I hugged Lily, who blinked sleepily, then thanked Sue and Kate for arranging the rescue effort. Brumby and Joan joined me as I waved toward the last of the retreating tail lights.

"It's a shame Earl ruined the evening," Joan said.

"I should have been more supportive," I said. "I know it's a disease. He was talking about being a failure. I just wanted him gone."

"You don't need to sympathize with every person who comes along," Brumby said. "It's ok to not want a drunk in your house."

"Harry and Jess have tummy aches," Joan said, indicating her teens, who were slumped against each other. "I told them to stop eating S'mores a few hours ago. They never listen."

"I'll give you a lift," Brumby said. "Let me get the fire out, first."

Using a bucket of water and a stick, he put out the last of the embers. They sizzled dramatically and cast up fragrant wafts of blue wood smoke, then the embers died down to a soft hiss.

"We're good now, right?" he said.

"We're good. You're lucky I'm so agreeable."

Brumby grinned and kissed my cheek. I let him get away with it, too tired to argue or second-guess the moment. His chin was scratchy, and he smelled of wood smoke. A rough sort of guy who fit some of the elements of my rough new life. He was definitely not *the* guy I could count on for the rest of my days. That was an impossible dream.

Once Brumby had packed the Dumas clan into his truck, I waved as the last of my visitors departed down the hill. I didn't pause to clean up, other than to fetch the blankets from the grass so they didn't get ruined by dew. I tossed them in a heap inside the kitchen doorway to sort out tomorrow, then crossed directly to Raymond's plaid couch.

I closed my eyes, and almost instantly fell asleep.

13

At 2:05 a.m., I groaned as the jarring ringing of my father's old phone jerked me awake. I clapped my hands over my eyes, wondering what kind of jackass would call at such an hour. Maybe it was an emergency. I pushed up onto one elbow on the couch as the answering machine played the recording of my father's clipped instructions to leave a message.

There was a pause, a low hiss. I frowned, deciding the caller was taking a breath, then as if distorted by some kind of robotic means, a deep, warped voice began speaking, and it froze me to the bone.

"You didn't ask ... the right questions," the voice droned. "You didn't ... follow through. You didn't ... care. You didn't ... *believe*."

I lurched to my feet, horrified by the sound of breathing coming over the speaker again. Somewhere out there in the night, at the other end of the line, the lunatic was letting the moment play out.

Click.

I sagged and clasped my hands on my knees, winded from the sudden fright. With a shaking hand, I turned on the floor lamp and stared at the winking red light on the answering machine. I slowly approached the table where the machine sat, reached out to play the recording, then retracted my hand and backed away. If I never heard that distorted voice again, it would be too soon. How had the caller warped it that way?

Was he finished trying to rattle me? Unable to stand the idea of being seen from the dark yard, I shut off the lamp and sat in stiff silence on the couch. It was just my luck that Raymond had left an old clock that clicked every time the second hand moved from notch to notch. I'd never noticed it before. Now it seemed obnoxious and overly loud.

Falling back asleep was impossible.

In the darkness, I pulled my laptop from the cabinet and launched my photo library to study the shots I'd taken of the crime scene. I doubted the exercise would resolve any questions, but it helped bring some fire back into my limbs. I wasn't about to be somebody's plaything. If whoever had called intended to scare me, they'd won that battle. I vowed to not let them win the war. As the succession of photos appeared on the screen, one by one, I clicked through them with my right forefinger.

The snowman cookie tin. *Click*. The skeleton hand strung together with fishing line. *Click*. Another shot of the bones. *Click*. The note, which I would never read again without hearing the horrid, warped voice in the back of my mind. *Click*. The pink fabric that had apparently been used as a pillow inside the tin. *Click*. A wider shot of the box with the surrounding grass. *Click*. The perpetrator's shoe print. *Click*.

I paused, then backed up to the shot showing the surrounding grass. In the background, I'd seen a tiny glint amidst the shadows that I'd figured was dew. On the off chance the perpetrator had dropped a small item, I pulled up the image in Photoshop and added a succession of layers to bring the darkest shadows amidst the grass from near black to a level of gray. I leaned in and tweaked the resulting color noise and graininess to the point where I could see what in the heck had created the glint.

And what I saw was a woman's wedding ring.

"Oh my God … a clue!"

I figured there was little chance the police had missed it during their search, but I lurched from the couch, raced to the kitchen door, and then froze as I took in the dark night beyond the windows. It was 2:35 a.m., the very worst time in the world to be heading across the yard to my spooky barn. No matter how rational I tried to be, a cringing, primitive corner of my mind believed in the existence of aliens, and even worse things. After last night I knew beyond all doubt that one of the "worse things" was actually very real: a demented madman who was stringing together human bones and leaving them in cookie tins to shock and scare people.

It made sense to investigate the area near the barn in the light of day. Could I control my curiosity until then? I very much could not.

Raymond had outfitted the house with an assortment of flashlights. I'd used them so many times that most of them had begun to lose power. I spent a frantic couple of minutes putting fresh batteries into the biggest flashlight, which was made of metal, and would also serve as a weapon. Of course, using it to clock a madman would plunge me into darkness, I realized. I slipped two small flashlights into my pockets, took in a deep breath, and experimentally opened the door.

Except for a dog barking in the distance, the neighborhood of scattered porch lights beyond the hill was silent and dark. The sheep were peacefully grazing, and I could see Dodge dozing beyond the fence. It was another misty night. As I touched the railing on my way down the porch steps, I found that it was wet from dew, which brought back a vivid recollection of the same thing happening on Saturday night. With my heart thudding, I pushed onward toward the barn, casting worried glances in all directions. In the eerie quiet, my footsteps and breathing seemed overly loud, enclosed by the mist as I crossed the driveway.

I rushed the last few yards to the barn, slid open the huge door, and then reached for the light switch, adding the cobwebbed illumination of three bulbs to the central aisle and sections of the interior. As always, the building felt spooky at night, a place of shadows and warm wafts of air that carried the sweet scent of the timothy hay bales stored in the loft. Having the interior lit lessened my unease by a few degrees.

Kneeling next to the spot where I'd taken the photo of the ring, I carefully parted the grass, changing the angle of the flashlight beam in hopes of causing the object I sought to glint.

With a frustrated growl, I gave up after I'd covered every inch of the area, including the place where the cookie tin had fallen.

"The police have the ring," I said. "That's what matters."

I decided to tackle the question of why the crime scene techs had spent time in the tack room. The police had closed the rough-hewn door as if to remind me that I shouldn't snoop around. Sorry, guys. Attempts to curb me are more apt to spur me on. I switched on the light, then I studied the pulling harnesses, reins, and other old leather tack hanging on pegs along the walls. The small room smelled of saddle soap and oil.

It was obvious where the police had focused: the graphite powder they used to check surfaces for fingerprints was in specific places on the door, the old wooden workbench on the back wall, the bulletin board behind it, and even the light switch. I remembered reading a story about a family who'd had to hire a cleaning service to remove fingerprint powder from their home at their own expense after they had been burglarized.

Lucky me, I thought.

The workbench was covered with dust and hay chaff, except for a round void in the center that matched the dimensions of the snowman cookie tin. Behind and above it, a patch of the graphite powder was on the bulletin board. I stepped closer and saw a tiny hole where a thumb tack had been removed. I pictured the madman putting the tin down on the workbench, and then attaching the note to the bulletin board directly above the tin so it wouldn't be missed. When he'd heard Brumby and me outside the barn, he'd ripped the note down in his rush to leave.

I pulled out my phone to zoom in on my photo of the note with the crayon message. Along the top edge was a small tear that suggested a piece of it had remained pinned to the board when he'd ripped it down. If so, the police must have tested the thumbtack for prints, then they'd taken both the tack and the scrap with them as evidence.

I shined the flashlight at an angle and leaned down to study the surface of the workbench, confirming that the dust and hay chaff had settled to the wood over a period of time. The round void where the madman had put the cookie tin was comparatively clean. That puzzled me.

I stepped back and pondered the situation with folded arms. Staring at the places the police had dusted with graphite powder, I found myself puzzling over the pattern of dust on the bulletin board as well. Why would there be a void in the old layer of dust that matched the size of the note? It was subtle, but I could see the outline of it for sure.

Once again, I studied the photo of the note that I'd briefly held in my hands. Zooming in, I realized it didn't look like a fresh piece of paper. It was covered with visible dust, just like everything else in the room, as if the note had hung in the barn for a long time.

I straightened, my eyes wide as a possibility took hold.

Not wanting to get excited by a wrong tangent, I carefully checked the evidence again. A round void on the bench. A note-sized void on the bulletin board. Now that I thought about it, the lid of the cookie tin had been dusty. Enough for it to feel chalky, as if it had sat in place in the barn for an extended period of time. Not for days. For *months*.

Maybe the madman hadn't come to the farm in secret to leave the skeleton hand. What if he'd come to *retrieve* it?

Maybe I was wrong, and the awful surprise had been intended for me to find at some point. But as the police had studied the photos of the other cookie tins and human remains, I'd heard them saying something about "vendetta against officers" and "a lot of hate for our folks out there these days." That fit with *Raymond* being the target.

A scenario flared to life in my mind. The plan must have been to leave the surprise in a place where both the tin and the note would be in plain view. With the light shining on the bones from above, the table was the right height for an up-close level of shock. The problem was, Raymond must not have had reason to go into the tack room. With Goldy gone, he didn't work Dodge in the harness anymore. I pictured him coming and going for weeks, maybe even months, no idea there was a jarring shock waiting for him to find. Then he'd died, and I'd followed the same pattern of not looking into the tack room. Even if I had poked my head in to look around, I might not have seen the snowman cookie tin as out of place.

The skeleton hand had taken time to construct. Emotional injury had been the intended payoff, but month after month, the intruder must have grown increasingly frustrated. He'd finally decided to pick up the cookie tin and note, maybe thinking he could dust it off and leave it with some other target he wanted to harass to the maximum extent.

Instead, he'd nearly gotten himself nabbed.

It was possible the intruder was an ordinary burglar who'd stumbled onto the tin and decided to take it with him for whatever reason. But that didn't fit with his effort to grab the tin after it was knocked from his hands. I'd prevented him from securing it, so he'd fled.

From confusion and bewilderment, I felt my mind settling into a zone of hope and determination. Brumby still had some explaining to do. I was certain he'd been tipped off to possible trouble on my farm. His shock when he'd seen the bones was obvious, so it must have been a general tip without any details involving human remains.

I turned off the lights and headed back to my house a different woman from the cowering mess who'd felt shocked and slammed by the awful phone call. I used the flashlight to see where I was stepping on the driveway, not to check the black shadows under the trees.

Back inside, I sat down with my laptop and zoomed in on the photo of the ring to crop out everything except some of the surrounding grass, then I saved the photo as a jpeg and sent it to myself so I'd have it on my phone. How it could be used to solve anything, I couldn't begin to say. But I didn't want to regret not being able to show the photo to anyone who might shed light on the woman the ring had belonged to.

The caller had hoped to frighten me. Instead, he'd sparked a breakthrough that had changed how I saw the case. Could I count on being out of danger? Not completely, especially after the phone call. But the bowl metaphor the trooper had used gave me hope: he'd indicated that once the police left my farm, the awful business would exit as well.

I stretched out on the couch and closed my eyes.

14

At 8 a.m. I shoved gloves into my back pocket and headed out into the sunshine to finish the job of rescuing my berry crop from weeds. Dew had settled over the entire hillside, creating a sheen of rainbow glints on the berry plants, and enhancing the golden color of the fresh straw that my helpers had put down. Shadows were fading, and everything around me was dreamy and still, glowing like a mirage.

Raymond had written about how working in the berry field had helped settle his mind when he had a problem to sort out. I felt the power of it, retreating inwardly as I dug out a weed and pondered the theory I'd come up with last night. If Raymond had been the target, maybe it had to do with a case he'd worked on at some point.

You didn't ask the right questions. You didn't follow through. You didn't believe. You didn't care. Were the notes a complaint that justice hadn't been served? Or were they a mean-spirited taunt? Figuring out the identity of the perpetrator was key. If Detective Allen had zeroed in on a suspect based on my description of the jeans jacket, which he'd definitely reacted to, I assumed he would have presented a line-up for me to check.

What was taking so long?

Even Sue and Kate had presented me with a possible suspect, though their guess had been wrong. That was yesterday morning.

I held my breath, remembering the photos on Nadine's phone as we'd sat in almost this same spot in the berry field yesterday afternoon. I'd been too distracted to tune in on specific faces, but there had been a few men wearing jeans jackets. I was almost certain of it.

I opened my phone on my way to the house, pulled up my screenshot of Nadine's flyer, and called the number she'd written down.

"Hello," she crooned. "Starlight Lounge."

"Nadine, it's Sonny."

"How are you, hon?"

"I need to see you," I said, exiting my work clothes, and then changing into jeans and a clean shirt. "Right away if possible."

"Well, sure. I'm straightening up here at the club."

She told me the address and gave some loose directions.

With my camera bag in hand, I headed out the door. I might not learn anything new from Nadine, but then again, maybe I would. I certainly wasn't going to find any answers in the berry field.

* * *

Nadine's club was a thirty-minute drive from my house. It was on a main route, so I didn't disgrace myself by getting lost on any back roads, as had happened more times than I could count since I'd moved to Raymond's farm. It helped to be traveling during daylight hours. Once night fell, it was as if the road signs and turnoffs conspired to switch direction and twist themselves around until a person had no idea where they were.

Nadine's car was the only one in the parking lot as I pulled in. We would have hours to talk before the club opened.

She'd taken pains to uplift the façade. It took a second glance to know the building housed a strip club. A small, discrete silhouette of a busty woman was on the sign, and I noticed window film that would diminish the ability to see the activities going on within at night.

The club door was open. A bell jingled as I walked in. Nadine was humming as she wiped down the wooden bar. Wearing a tropical print leotard that clung to her curves, she'd shown up for the day's work in lipstick, mascara, and flawless blue eyeliner. How she managed to get her makeup to stay in place without creasing I couldn't imagine.

She beamed as I came in. "I wanted to catch up with you, so you saved me the trouble," she said, crossing to me and embracing me with her usual perfumed zeal. "Chuck gave me hell when I told him about our conversation yesterday. I'm sorry I got carried away."

"About the …?"

"You and the cop. I don't know what gets into me. Chuck's view is that you should give the police a wide berth from here on out. Is it true you spent the night at Joan's house and let the cops come and go on your farm? Basically do whatever they pleased?"

"I had to. For safety."

"Oh my goodness, they convinced you of that?" she said with a frown that showed deep concern on my behalf. "Well, you'd better buckle up for them to conclude you're behind whatever went on."

"But I'm not. It's obvious."

"Honey, you never know which cops are shifty until it's too late. I'll be praying for you." Nadine studied me. "You look like you need a drink."

"Just tonic water, maybe."

"Take a seat at the bar."

She shoved a glass through a compartment of ice, then used a hose contraption to fill it with sparking tonic water. "Lime?"

"No thanks."

I took a quick look around, noticing the usual sad feel of being in a bar in the light of day. Scuff marks on the floor, flaws in the ceiling, and faded paint on the walls. It was near darkness that brought an air of magic to nightclubs. Once the sun went down, beer signs and colored lights would cast a spell over the entire scene. Add alcohol to the mix, and either trouble would well up, or a sense of glory would take hold. Some patrons would grip their drinks and brood. Others would let loose.

"Here you go." Nadine pushed the glass my way, then crossed around the bar to sit down on the adjacent stool. "Out with it. What's up?"

"Can I see your phone? Your photos?"

Nadine closed her eyes with a disappointed sigh. "They've convinced you it was Kyle after all. They've brainwashed you."

"No, not at all."

"You're sure?"

"It wasn't your son. That hasn't changed. But I got to thinking, the police aren't telling me anything. No facts to ground me, or line-up of suspects. You have photos of local men on your phone. I know it's asking a lot, but I'm desperate for answers."

"You looked through my photos, remember?" she said. "When we were weeding your berry patch."

"We were scrolling fast, and daylight put a glare on the screen. I would never point to anyone if I wasn't positive."

"I believe you. I do, and I suppose we need to know if there's a bad sort amongst us." Nadine pulled her phone from her back pocket and opened it with her passcode.

"Thank you," I said. "Golly, there are a lot of photos."

"How far back do you want to look?" she said.

"I have no idea."

Nadine scrolled until she reached Christmas time when most of her patrons tended to stop in for holiday celebrations.

"The girls dress up as elves," she said. "It's very festive."

With Nadine leaning close on my right, I carefully scrolled through her library, not bothering to click on any images of the strippers, or of the bartender once I definitely ruled him out, or of any men who looked too old, too heavy, or too bald. Nadine kept things lively by pointing out men I might recognize in town.

"That's Pete, your mailman. That's Ed from down at the bank. This one, Frank, leaves the best tips. Single, in case you think he's cute."

"I can't focus on romance right now."

"Oh, honey. Never give up on love."

A half-hour later, having failed to identify the culprit, I sagged with disappointment. Seeing photos of patrons on the walls, I slipped from the stool and studied them, one by one. They were faded, grainy, and absolutely no help at all. Nadine said a few empty spaces were from pictures that had gotten knocked down during fights.

"Like this one," she said, pulling a frame with shattered glass from behind the bar. None of the men in the photo fit the bill. "You know what? Maybe the burglar was from out of town."

"He must have been," I said.

"What now?" Nadine said.

"I guess I'll go home."

"Not in this sorry state," she said. "What you need is positive activity. Nothing brings on a sense of empowerment like pole work."

"Oh, golly. No, I'm kind of a klutz."

"Don't tell me you're one of those low self-esteem types? In fact …" Nadine circled me with a raised eyebrow as she sized me up. "Athletic. Nice little tush. You'd be a superstar on the dance pole."

"That's not really … do you think so?"

"Sue and Kate learned. They love it."

"It's just … I had a scary moment with a guy. I can't talk about what happened. I don't know why I brought it up."

Nadine grasped my arm, her frown deepening as she searched my face. "A guy *tried* something? Against your will?"

"He was angry and awful. But I'm ok."

"Was it the undercover cop? Did my crazy talk cause this?"

"No, it wasn't him."

"I can see you won't tell me the details."

"I can't. It's complicated."

"All the more reason for you to get on the pole. If you really aren't inclined to give it a whirl, fine. But don't say no because you got robbed of confidence by a man. If you let that take hold, it will keep getting deeper. You'll become less and less yourself. Believe me, I know about this stuff. There isn't anything I haven't seen."

Once again, this protective mother and former hooker seemed to have a solid grasp on how to strike a balance in life. I'd taken tai chi, and ballet to a certain point, and I had a yoga routine I practiced whenever I had enough time. It felt good to flex and feel strong. But attempting the blatantly sexual style of dancing she was talking about felt alien. Flirting was beyond me. It just never clicked. "Pole work" was not my style.

"Golly, you do look miserable," Nadine said. "Poor little thing."

"It's been a tough week. Maybe later."

"Come on, I'll demonstrate."

I followed her onto the stage and stood by with folded arms. As Nadine gripped the pole and swung her legs around it in a graceful twirl, I realized I could make good use of the moment after all. I reached for my cell phone and launched the camera app, already making decisions on how and where to stand to best capture her at work.

"Oh, no." Nadine dropped lightly to the stage floor and plucked the phone from my hands. "Your talent is in taking pictures. That's all well and good, but not when you use it to hide behind and stop living your life to the fullest extent."

"I don't use it to hide."

"Just watch."

Putting my phone on the edge of the stage, Nadine leaned down and flipped a switch on a control panel. Lights suddenly spangled around us and a song with a thudding beat began blasting around us from the ceiling speakers. Seeing me wince at the volume, Nadine shook her head and turned the music down to a tolerable level.

"Here we go," Nadine said.

Once again, she gripped the pole, stepped lightly on her toes, then through some means I couldn't grasp, she was suddenly suspended by her hands, all the while twirling, her tropical floral design leotard catching the moving points of light as they strobed.

With grace and style, she dismounted.

"You try it," she said. "Shoes off. Bare feet."

"I don't get how you did it. At all."

She fussed until I complied and shed my shoes, then she took my right hand, swung it high up on the pole, and squeezed to indicate I should grip it. She patted my butt, saying I should move forward.

"I'm too distracted right now."

"Nonsense."

Nadine hollered encouragement and instructions, clapping her hands to the beat to get me to pay attention to the ambience.

"Toes, toes, toes to get the feel of it," she said. "Grip the pole up high with your inside hand. Now, in a minute you're going to put your outside hand on the pole more or less chest height. Perfect. As you step forward, hook the pole with the pretty little divot above the back of your ankle bone … what happened? You lost momentum!"

"I'm sorry. I can't sustain the twirl."

"Come on, now. You've got a brown-eyed police officer lusting after you. Brumby too, by the look of it the other day. This little tushy is as tight as a drum." She patted my butt for the fifth time. "You're nice and perky up top. Lots of men love a perky top."

"Nadine …"

"Grab that pole! Come on!"

With gritted teeth, I snagged the back of my ankle on the pole the way I'd seen her do it, all the while moving forward.

"Look graceful, for heaven's sake! You're not carrying buckets. Try again. Toes, toes, toes. You're a woodland elf, stepping through the leaves. Not a care in the world. Snag your ankle, now swing the other leg around, then tuck both legs up into a butterfly. Yes! Keep going, keep going. Guess what? You just did a fireman!"

"That's it?"

"It's a start. Try again. Grab the pole way up high. Stop thinking! Just do as I tell you. Toes, toes, toes, lean your torso away from the pole a bit to create momentum, snag the ankle, swing around, legs in a butterfly. Excellent! Let's try a move called 'Hello Boys.'"

"It's called *what?*"

"Stop the nonsense. Hold with both hands right here. Swing your legs up at the same time, then grip the pole with your thighs, legs straight out in front of you. Perfect. Cross your ankles and point your feet, real pretty. Sonny, you have crazy strength! You were born to do this! Now, reach this hand underneath so you've got one hand above and one below. Excellent. Retract into a butterfly, then legs out in a wide V."

"You want me to do a *split* up here?"

"Hence the name, 'Hello Boys.'"

"I'm out of breath …"

"You're thinking again!"

"Golly …"

"And smile! It has to look effortless."

I was sweating. It was not effortless. But against all odds, I was starting to get the hang of it and actually enjoy myself.

"Now, I know what's going to happen," Nadine said briskly. "You'll talk yourself out of coming back, so let's give you a glimpse of the future. The kind of power and confidence you could own if you'd trust what I'm saying and give it a chance."

"Is it hard?"

"You bet. I'll be here helping you. Now, grab the pole and shimmy up like you'd do at the firehouse. That's it. Swing up both legs, there you go. Ok, wrap your right leg around the pole this way, extend your left leg, foot pointed." She gently started pulling me around. "Slowly, start arching your back. Don't be scared. I got you. Arch back and down. Beautiful! Now, let go of both hands and just drape."

"Hang on by one leg? But—"

"Believe in yourself, Sonny. Come on!"

"Ok, ok."

"There you go. Excellent."

I was not confident hanging upside down with only my right leg gripping the pole, and it was dizzying to see the room turning. The bar slowly passed by, then some tables. Daylight bloomed across the room, and I heard a familiar jingle. From upside down, I assessed who'd come in. I saw a man's boots. Then his pants. His shirt. His frown.

The man in the doorway was Stable Bartlett.

My leg abruptly released.

Nadine clucked with dismay, helping me land at the bottom of the pole without cracking my head open.

"Stable Bartlett, you irritating man," she hollered. "I was making progress! You ruined everything."

"Outside, Alison," Stable said. "*Now.*"

"You can't order her around," Nadine said.

"You stay out of it. I'll be outside."

The door slammed. I looked up at Nadine.

"This is why I'm pessimistic. I have bad timing." I closed my eyes. "Of all the people who could have come in."

"Stable has never been here before. I think he tracked you down."

"How?" I said.

"I don't know, hon."

As I put on my shoes and climbed to my feet, Nadine fussed over how much progress I'd made in a short time and insisted it was a genuine accomplishment. Just remember, she told me, Stable was flesh and blood like the rest of us. He had no right to act high and mighty.

I hugged and thanked her, then I started to leave.

"Sonny, wait."

Nadine appeared to be wrestling with conflicting ideas, then she shook her head as if telling herself to keep quiet.

"Nadine, if you know something …"

"I'm trying to figure out who came at you and got you so rattled that you won't talk. It wasn't Earl, was it?"

I paused. "Everett's father?"

"I heard he got drunk after Chuck and I left your place."

"He did get drunk," I said. "But the guy who came at me was someone else. It's handled, so don't worry."

"You are having a very bad week."

"Tell me about it."

Fussing like a mother hen as she smoothed my hair, she gave me a parting hug and insisted I come back for a second lesson any time I wanted. Her compassion was so palpable that I wanted to stay a while more and soak it up. But Stable was outside, scowling and pacing in a way that seemed the embodiment of the phrase, "Fit to be tied."

"Thank you, Nadine. It was fun."

"You're welcome, hon. Come back soon."

15

I steeled myself as I left the dim sanctuary of Nadine's club, where music was still playing, and crossed to my car in the glaring sunlight. Maybe if I slipped inside and tossed a quick wave to Stable, he would take the hint and keep his disappointment to himself.

But no. As he crossed to me, his chiseled features forewarned a tempest of ire was coming my way. A vein on his forehead further announced that once again, something I had done had turned him into an example of what high blood pressure could do to a man.

"Sorry to interrupt your new vocation," he said tersely.

"Nadine was trying to cheer me up," I said.

"Her, of all people. What the hell is wrong with you?"

"Excuse me for responding to kindness."

"You do realize the severity of the case? You were told to stay out of trouble and not put yourself in front of the wrong people."

"Let's assess what I've been told. Nothing that would help me understand, so pardon me if I don't know what *not* to do."

"Enough. Where are Raymond's journals?" he demanded. "The ones he used to keep his schedule straight."

"Interesting," I said. "Your question implies that you looked for them in my house, and came up empty."

"They might be important to the case."

"Why?"

"Because I said so. Where are they?"

"In my possession." I shook my head. "I guess Nadine was right. I was naïve to let you push me out the other night."

"You were in the way."

Of your illegal search of the house, I thought.

"I'm busy, Stable. If you don't mind—"

"In fact, I do mind. A lot."

He stepped closer until he was looming over me. Beyond his immediate anger over what he'd glimpsed, his face betrayed the twitching emotion that my presence always brought to the surface. It had to do with one of the most confounding shocks of his life: Raymond's death.

"You go on and on about wanting to get to know Raymond," he said. "Somehow you've missed the obvious."

"I suppose you're going to tell me."

"I knew he had a daughter," Stable said. "That's right, I knew from the start. Comes back from Camden one day years ago, looking like he'd had a shock. He told me then and there. You were eleven, around that age. He said you looked like his sister at that age."

"For you to relate this in an angry tone—"

"Shut it, you haven't heard the relevant part," he growled. "He was all set to reach out. Told his wife, Ella, everything. But you were young, your father dead. The other father. Littlefield. A long time went by before I asked him about it again. Raymond said it was a mess. Your mother told him how you were willful, stubborn, always causing trouble. Why should he get saddled with somebody else's mess?"

"Unbelievable," I said furiously. "It doesn't occur to you that she had selfish reasons to put him off? With made-up crap?"

"Oh, it's believable. Look how you behave now."

"I'm coping pretty well, considering."

"Raymond was ashamed of you," Stable said. "Get it through your head. That's why he didn't reach out."

I'd steeled myself when he'd started hollering at me, but this hit me so hard, I felt it in my gut. "Then why did he make me his heir?"

"Guilt, some misguided notion," Stable said. "There's no doubt in my mind that he would have corrected it if he'd had the chance. Think about it. He's a man of the law. A pillar of the community. You were his worst nightmare. Spoiled, willful—"

"You've already listed my flaws."

"Oh, no," he said. "Don't start with the tears stunt."

"The tears stunt?" All the more furious, I stalked around him until he was the one staring into the sun. "Let's see how your eyes do."

"This isn't a game."

"You're damned right it isn't," I hollered, trembling from the sudden unleashing of emotions. "It's not my fault if Raymond left his farm to me. I'm not to blame for his choices. I've given you slack because I understand what it's like to grieve. But that's over with now, so you can pack up your anger and get the hell out of my way."

"Alison—"

"And no more barking my name like that!" I thundered. "My name is Sonny. Sonny Evelyn Littlefield from Newton, Massachusetts. I'm determined, impulsive, unstoppable, reckless, stupid from time to time, and I'm here to stay, so you'd best get used to it."

I turned and stalked to my car, climbed in, and slammed the door so hard it sounded like a cannon going off. *Nobody* makes me cry. It's a code. An unbroken rule. It would be a cold day in hell before I let Stable or anybody else push me to the point of tears.

The interior of the car was about ninety degrees as I gunned the engine, backed out of the lot, and pulled onto the road. I opened the window and let the wild air billow around me. What Stable had said about his conversations with Raymond billowed around me as well. Which parts were true? Any of it? All of it? My hands felt lifeless. Numb.

It wasn't as if I hadn't wondered what had gone into the decision to not reach out to me. I'd guessed part of it. Raymond's wife had been diagnosed with leukemia at some point. Not sure when. I'd figured he was in pain after she'd died. That had made sense. Waiting might have been for my benefit. At least, that's what I'd assumed.

Had I been making a fool of myself all this time?

I couldn't deny I had been a willful child. Different. Trying to cope with the sense that Donald hated me. The fear that I would be cast out. From afar, all Raymond would know was that I might be tough to handle. Hard to understand. Why bring trouble to his life?

Making me his heir was a mistake, Stable had said. A mistake he would have corrected if he'd lived.

Finally, my driveway was up ahead. Raymond's driveway. It didn't have to be my driveway anymore. I could leave. Just give up.

I'd scarcely driven past the pines on my way up the hill toward my house when a flash of light drew my gaze to the rearview mirror. A red truck was pulling in behind me. I hit the brake hard, not wanting whoever it was to think they could come uninvited. As my car skidded to a stop on the gravel, the truck skidded to a halt right behind me.

There was a pause, the driver invisible behind the glare on the truck's windshield. Then the engine shut off and I was startled to see the handsome trooper from the Corner Pocket climb out.

Shit, I thought. *Stable probably sent him.*

He looked concerned as he stepped to my window and leaned down so we were more or less eye to eye.

"I just missed your bumper," he said. "You surprised me."

"Maybe call first."

"Listen, I think I messed up the other day. I saw you talking to people, and taking risks. I figured a light approach would—"

"Great, just what I need. Another lecture."

"Are you ok? You seem—"

"I'm peachy. Dandy."

"Look—"

"Just step *back*," I hollered.

When he did so, looking alarmed, I pressed the gas more than I'd intended, thinking great, act like a menace in front of the police. I drove to the top of the hill and climbed out, trembling and feeling winded, as if I'd run all the way from the bar. I crossed to the fence and gripped the gray, weathered top rail that always left splinters in my hands. I felt desperate to pet Dodge, but he was dozing at the bottom of the hill.

My visitor couldn't take a hint. He drove up after me and closed his truck door, then I heard his footfalls stirring the grass behind me.

"Something is clearly wrong," he said. "What happened?"

I confronted his concerned gaze, his blue T-shirt, his hands poised as if he were ready to tackle me if I didn't stop looking insane.

"This is funny coming from the guy who escorted me out of my house so his buddies could rifle through my things."

"We didn't search your house. At all."

"No? You weren't on the quest to find Raymond's journals?"

"I have no idea—"

"I left voluntarily," I said furiously. "And what thanks do I get? Harassed, threatened, pushed to the brink. Here, do you want a turn stomping on my phone?" I held it out with a trembling hand. "Go on, take it. Throw it on the ground."

"What happened? Tell me."

"I don't want to do this," I managed. "I don't."

"Hey …"

He touched my arm. I pushed it away, my eyes brimming.

Shit. Damn it.

Suddenly, I was shaking and sobbing and sinking to the grass, where bees were stirring around the purple clover, and earthworms were living their simple, uncomplicated lives. Why couldn't my life be simple? Why was there always complete and utter chaos?

"Hey," he kept saying. "It's ok."

"It is *not* ok."

Furious, I tried to stand up, but collapsed back down, crying so hard I could scarcely see anything anymore. Three months of suppressed grief was coming out at the worst possible time. In front of a stranger. A man I couldn't trust. Curled in a ball, I gripped handfuls of grass and pressed them to my face, inhaling their sweet, living fragrance. Like the beautifully trimmed grass around Raymond's gravestone in the local cemetery.

Come back, I silently begged him. *Please come back. Come home and smile. Ask what's for supper. Anything. It can't be too late.*

A hand persisted in resting on my shoulder. I swung wildly against his gesture several times, and then I uncurled myself and met his sympathetic gaze with a scathing glare. I didn't need his pity.

"I told you to leave."

"If you just tell me—"

"Just go. Nobody asked you here."

Kneeling next to me, he blew out a breath. "All I know about is a thing that must have been awkward. A misunderstanding ..."

I blinked at him through tears. "What ...?"

"A deputy heard something yesterday at Joan's house. He didn't understand that it was ... you know, a consensual thing."

"He said *what?*"

"You and Brumby. He came in, thinking you needed help—"

"Oh my God."

"Look—"

"Get *out*. Just leave."

I gripped my aching, bewildered skull and cried all the harder, wondering how I could survive in a world where people like the deputy were taken at their word. Where Stable Bartlett was allowed to lash out at me as a way of channeling his grief. He had to be wrong about how my father had felt about me. It couldn't be true.

Come back, I silently begged Raymond. *Please come back. Tell me the truth. Were you ashamed of me? Was I your worst nightmare?*

"Here." A tissue was offered.

"I told you to leave."

"Look, gossip can be tough to take—"

"Stop! You idiot. You have it all wrong."

"Then set me straight," he said softly.

I closed my eyes, feeling hopeless. Tell him, and I would set off a new conflict and round of chaos. Keep it contained, and I would let a horrid liar off the hook. A sheriff's deputy. A man who thought he could get away with whatever he wanted. Just bend the truth.

The trooper's hand arrived on my shoulder again. I let it stay.

I began at the start. Tyler Bergley setting dogs loose to chase my sheep and vandalize the place in the dark of night. The deputy saying dog control was not a police matter. Kids pulling pranks wasn't either. He was angry to be up at 1 a.m. for no good reason.

"You saw him the other night," I said. "Stable yelled at him."

"I did see that. His name is Pike."

"He'll hate me all the more now."

"Just tell me. The whole thing."

It was clear from his patient expression that he was still expecting me to say how jarring it had been to be startled out of an intimate moment with Brumby in Joan's guest bedroom.

I set him straight.

My bath. Getting out of the tub. Putting on a towel. Hearing the kitchen door open. Calling out, asking who was there. Whoever it was didn't respond. I heard footfalls in the hallway. I thought it was the perpetrator coming to get me. My desperate struggle to keep the door closed. It was violent. Horrible. Getting pushed back. The hand opening the door. Slowly. The deputy's angry face. What'd he'd said. How he'd stepped on my phone. Held it out as if he was daring me to grab it. I was *naked*. Except for the towel. I couldn't breathe. No idea what to do. That's when Brumby arrived. It started to get ugly. I was scared. But Brumby said he'd recorded the whole thing. Only then did the deputy leave.

The feel of my voice getting louder and steadier as I described the incident had a centering effect. I'd stopped crying, but tears were still wet on my face as I looked past the fence toward the sheep placidly grazing down near the flickering stream.

"You'll want to believe his version, of course," I said bitterly.

"No, I can tell."

Only now did I look at his face, his gaze trained on the long view. He looked ashen. Tanned, but ashen at the same time.

"I'm so sorry," he said softly. "Not just for what happened to you. But for how I approached it. Taking him at his word."

I wiped my eyes. "Police stick together."

"Not in a case like this." He turned to me with an expression I couldn't recall ever seeing on a man's face before: anger and fierce resolve directed at someone *other* than me. "I get why you didn't report it. The position you're in. But trust me, it'll be handled the minute I leave your farm. I'm going to make sure—" He stopped short and visibly regrouped, then he said in a calmer tone, "I'll make sure it's handled correctly."

"He'll hate me all the more," I said.

"For one thing, it's procedure. We can't have a man like that wearing a uniform." He rubbed his head as if it hurt like hell. "I've seen Pike in action. I had misgivings, and did nothing about it."

"It can stay between us. I don't want to pit you or any other officer against a colleague. Your job is tough enough."

"Sonny, listen to me."

His hand returned to my shoulder, and once again I let it rest there without complaint, riveted by the way his presence created a kind of make-shift shelter around us. I decided it had to do with the intensity of his gaze, his gentle touch, and the fact that he'd used my nickname.

"Don't second guess yourself," he said. "I will handle it in such a way that you don't get hassled. There's a procedure to follow. If he comes at you again, tell me or Detective Allen, ok?"

I nodded. "I hope you're right about not getting hassled. Pike said he'd gotten a tip that I'd made a false statement. I didn't leave anything out. I have no idea what he was talking about."

"He was trying to justify what he was doing. Making it up as he went along. Nobody has doubts about your statement."

"Are you sure?"

"I'm sure, so don't worry about it."

I inhaled the warm, sunny air, then exhaled with my eyes closed, feel-ing more and more centered, more and more grounded. After getting ripped apart by Stable a half hour ago, I was surprised how fast relief was sinking through me. Talking had helped. More than I'd imagined. It was so simple. Like magic. The power of being heard.

16

On my feet again, I brushed grass from my pants and struggled to regain my composure after my vivid meltdown. A way out of the awkward aftermath arrived as Dodge woke from his nap and caught sight of me. With his usual air-shattering whinny, he pounded toward me up the pasture slope with the same enthusiasm he expressed over just about everything in life. He was a model for me to plan my thinking around for the rest of my days. I just needed time. A break in the chaos.

I reached for the whiskered muzzle that pushed toward me, Dodge's nostrils puffing as he sniffed my face and hair. He nickered softly and draped his huge head over my shoulder as I reached my arms around his neck. He bumped my back with his chin a few times as if to say, *There, there, everything is going to be ok.* His version of a hug. Or maybe he was using me to chase away flies. I found myself smiling.

The trooper patted his neck with solid landings, causing dust and hair to stir upward into the breeze. "Dodge is his name?"

"Yes."

"He's a Belgian? That's his breed?"

I nodded, finding it difficult to focus. He'd been kind and supportive on three separate occasions. I'd failed to so much as glance at the business card he'd handed me the other day. There had to be a smooth way of getting him to say his name without admitting I was a flake.

I turned to him and gave a self-conscious shrug.

"I bet that was a ride you didn't expect," I said.

"Do you need to talk more?"

"No," I assured him. "I'm good."

"The problem is, I'm still processing what you said the other day. Your history. Again, I'm sorry I overheard—"

"The PTSD thing? You need to forget I said it."

"I kind of can't," he said. "I'm familiar with the concept."

"Oh no." I searched his eyes. "You have it?"

"No. I know people. Knew someone."

"They died?"

"A while ago."

"Well, if I did ever have it, there's no lasting effect in my case."

His eyebrows twisted. "I don't think it works that way."

Once again, I found myself studying his neatly trimmed beard. I could see the lines of his face and decided I would prefer him without the beard. He would be more handsome with a clean shave. Maybe no one had told him. He didn't wear a ring. His brown eyes were very clear, with interesting flecks. I often assessed people this way in my line of work. They tended to catch on and start worrying. The trooper seemed at ease with my scrutiny, which had me relaxing a little more and deciding it was ok to refer to him as "cute guy" in my head, especially during moments like that when the angled light added nice definition to his face.

I put on a smile to convince him I'd rounded the corner. "You need to put aside what happened here as well. I'm ok."

"Are you sure? I mean ..." His gesture indicated where I'd been a short while ago, slumped in a ball and unable to speak.

"It's been building," I said. "For a few months."

"That makes sense," he said, eyeing me carefully as if not quite sure I was off the ledge. "You've had a few shocks."

I decided if he were a car instead of a man, his crankcase would be making a grinding sound from my rapid change of mood.

I said helpfully, "It sounded like you wanted to deliver another lecture about not talking to people about the case."

"A lecture? Nothing like that."

"You think I'm too soft to hear it?" I said.

"Not at all."

"Then go for it."

Something in my smile apparently convinced him that all was well. He relaxed and seemed to accept that we could turn the page.

"Ok." He shrugged off his hesitation. "Are you ready?"

"Ready."

"Five words."

"That sounds doable."

"Be careful," he said slowly. "Trust no one."

"Got it." I paused. "Isn't that six words?"

"Umm ..."

"You're right. Five words. I was going by syllables for some reason. Care-full. It's odd how the mind does that sort of thing."

"I feel I need to deliver the lecture again," he said.

"I heard you. I get it."

"Because I'm overdue for heading out. Came for my mom's birthday, then this whole thing happened ... why are we smiling?"

"We are amused, hearing you say 'mom.'"

"Can I finish this part of the speech?"

"Sorry."

"Depending on developments elsewhere—"

"You mean Canada," I guessed. "Specifically, the border."

Cute guy closed his eyes. "How ...?"

I started listing relevant details. "Plain clothes. Won't say his name. State Trooper. Speaks fluent French. There've been record illegal crossings at the Canadian border. The very sort of thing that would require someone working undercover, more or less. I'm guessing it's not a *deep* undercover gig. If it was, you'd be a lot more guarded."

"Have you mentioned it to anyone?" he said.

"No, but people around here know you."

"Yeah, it's complicated, and you're right, it's not—" He sighed. "I asked because you have ties beyond the local area."

"Not up north. Even if I did, I don't share knowledge that's better left private. We've gotten off track." I paused. "Right. I'm avoiding questions, and I have a job that will keep me occupied this week."

I told him the details.

"Chuck Brewster hired you? Ok, not good. I can't say how or why, but there's possible involvement with the case."

"How?" I said. "Why?"

"Just delay the photo shoot," he said calmly. "That's all I'm asking."

"It's a job. I need the money."

"A few months won't matter, surely."

"A few months?" Good Lord, this was not what I'd hoped to hear. "It's a moot point. I've already cashed his check."

"Chuck gave you *money?*"

"Don't make it sound criminal. It's standard procedure for commerce."

"How much?"

"Five thousand dollars."

"Good God."

He conducted a silent conversation with himself as he walked in a circle, a standard feature of my interactions with men.

"It's all arranged," I said. "I'm meeting Chuck tomorrow at his garage. I'm shooting him working on his latest car."

He turned back to me, agape. "Chuck's garage is on a hill in a heavily wooded area. The road is pitted, muddy, washed out—"

"Sounds like my driveway."

"It is *well* beyond that. Trust me."

"It's all set. Chuck is a good guy. I can tell."

"Ok. All right. Look." He cupped his hands in midair. "Picture the current situation—"

"No, no, no," I said. "Not the invisible bowl thing again."

"Invisible what …?"

"You used the same metaphor at the Corner Pocket."

"I'm trying to help you understand."

"Then enlighten me. Straight up."

His eyes closed. His hands moved. Then he just looked at me as if feeling the depth of defeat for the first time in his entire life. I found myself sympathizing with him, in a way. Athletic. Smart. Methodical. Handsome. Success would come easily to a man like this, complexities resolved with minimal fuss. In my case, none of it worked.

After a moment of silent deliberation, a look of determination arrived on his face. Something had occurred to him. An important revelation, perhaps, or another way to approach the argument.

"What?" I said.

"Just thinking."

"Are you going to tell me?"

"No."

I folded my arms, indicating I was finished talking, too.

Well, almost.

"Listen, umm …" I snapped my fingers a few times, but his name didn't magically appear in midair. "Porter."

He caught onto the problem immediately. "I gave you my card."

"I never looked at it."

"Ok." He took it in soberly. "Good to know."

"I'm sorry. I've been busy."

"I understand. Don't apologize."

"I sort of misplaced it, so …"

"You want me to give you *another* card."

"Why not just say your name?"

"You know what? Let's stick with Porter. I mean, it's my fault for putting it out there in the first place. It was habit, the undercover thing. Not knowing you. I almost reversed myself on the spot. Then it seemed easier to let it stand."

"People in town don't know you're working up north?"

"That's the assumption, but if you've figured it out …"

Cute guy looked conflicted and downtrodden. At this point, I decided I had to take pity on him, a big, grown officer of the law reduced to staring at the ground as if he couldn't recall how to walk.

"Ok, I'm curious about a few things," I ventured. "I think we had a moment at the Corner Pocket. You asked me to lunch, and expressed some interest … unless I misread your intent."

"You didn't."

"Then I'm confused. If you believed Pike's story that I had a hook-up with Brumby, I'm surprised you stopped by today."

"Actually, I didn't believe it. You were clear when you talked about Brumby. The way Pike described things didn't match up with my sense of you. I should have listened to my gut."

I nodded, recalling how he'd taken a leap of faith when he took my suitcases. My gut told me it was safe to make a similar gesture in return. I told him there'd been a development the police needed to know about. He looked alert and careful, not sure what to expect as we crossed to the house, climbed the porch steps, and stepped inside.

"I got a call at 2 a.m. There's a message on my father's answering machine." I indicated the device on the table near the couch.

"Who called?"

"Just play it."

Following the standard procedure of not touching any kind of potential evidence with ungloved hands, he pulled a pen from his pocket and used it to press the answering machine button.

I folded my arms tightly as the message played.

"You didn't ask … the right questions," the voice droned. "You didn't … follow through. You didn't … care. You didn't … *believe.*"

After the recording ended, he stood there with a frown, looking puzzled as he digested what he'd heard. He rubbed the back of his neck as if gauging how to put the call into context, or maybe wondering why I wasn't asking questions during the extended pause.

"I know about the other notes," I said. "The other skeleton parts."

He turned to me. "What …?"

"Can we step outside? After hearing that voice, I need some air."

"Detective Allen will want this tape."

"Take it."

"He'll want to collect it himself."

Once we'd stepped off the porch and reached the sunshine near his truck, I told him everything. How I'd used binoculars to look at the activity when I was supposed to be packing a bag. How I'd seen the police photos of the notes and the bones, which I assumed had been collected at other crime scenes. How I'd figured out that Raymond had been the target based on the dust patterns I found in the tack room.

"Have you told anyone else your theory?" he said.

"No, but I'm right, aren't I? It's why you used the bowl metaphor to let me know the case didn't involve me directly."

"I can't confirm or deny anything."

I sighed. "I understand."

"Anything else?"

"Right before I came home today, one of the reasons I was upset was because Stable tracked me down and told me—" I closed my eyes, debating whether I wanted to say it out loud, then I went ahead. "Raymond never reached out because he was ashamed of me."

"Stable said *what?*"

"I'll get over it. The main reason he tracked me down was because he wanted to see Raymond's journals."

"Do you think they're relevant?" he said. "Having read them?"

"So, you know about them. You figured it out."

"That along with your camera, you'd packed a lot of books, maybe like the one on the coffee table? Pretty much."

"I don't want to rush through them, and I'm not sure what kind of clues I would be looking for." I paused. "The journals are important to me. I've never told people they're anything but lists and reminders. But spur of the moment here, I want this awful business sorted out. If anyone wants to look through them, unofficially …"

"I would be happy to."

"Can you narrow down a time frame? Only take a few? I can't believe I'm even thinking of letting them out of my sight."

"I won't tell anyone. If there's an entry that has a direct bearing, I can probably attribute it to an unnamed source."

"Ok."

"They each cover a year?" he said.

"Yes."

"I think two volumes would do it."

I told him where the suitcases were stowed, and was fine letting him fetch them on his own. While he stepped into the house and disappeared for ten minutes, I sat on the porch steps in the sunshine, feeling liberated by the trust I was putting into him. I craved a reality where I got to express my opinion and confess my feelings, and a man actually listened to me. He'd shown me that it wasn't an impossible dream.

Soon, his voice neared the screen door. He was talking on his cell phone, and by the sound of it, he'd covered the latest news.

"Zero doubt," he said. "Yes, immediate action." He paused. "Yeah, I know I've extended past the date I told them." He paused and listened for a moment. "That's interesting. Good to know it wasn't a career-ending move." He chuckled. "Right. Ok."

He stepped out with two leather-bound journals. "Detective Allen is coming straight away," he said. "Do you want me to stay?"

"No need. He seems like a good guy."

"Roy is a great cop. You can trust him to be fair."

"It sounded like you got good news."

"Well …" He lightly came down the steps, then turned to face me with one foot resting on the lowest tread. "You've caught onto my delayed departure. Normally in undercover work, you don't make any waves. The thinking is to not alarm interested parties. But apparently, not showing up as planned can rattle people. They make mistakes."

"Maybe you don't have to go to the border?"

"I do have to go. Soon." He indicated the journals. "I appreciate you trusting me with these. I'll return them as soon as I can."

"The fact that both you and Stable want to see the journals confirms that I'm right about Raymond being the target."

"The trouble is, logic doesn't play a role in this sort of case," he said with an umpteenth appealing twist of his eyebrows. "There's power in who you are, Sonny. Smart. Observant. Some people admire it. Others will see it as a threat. I don't know what to make of the call you got. The warped voice quoting the notes. It's not good news."

"Thank you for being straight with me."

He smiled. "Thank you for cutting me slack."

I had the impulse to ask if we could talk about the journals over dinner later in the week. I'd asked flat out if he was interested, and he'd said yes, and then we'd moved on. It felt like a pressure point, a valve that needed to be released. A related notion was nagging at me. If only he wasn't so attractive. How was I supposed to focus?

Nadine was right, you are hopeless, I chided myself.

I buckled and looked away from his brown eyes. He took the hint and followed suit, seeming tempted to warn me about Chuck again, maybe, then changing his mind. He appeared to consider another topic. Out of the corner of my eye, I saw him rule that out, too.

I'd given him an impossible mountain to climb, and he'd only worn sneakers, jeans, and a blue T-shirt. Not suitable for tackling the chilly summit of my current shut-down demeanor.

"Well." His sneaker left the step. "Remember the five words."

Watching his athletic build in motion, I said, "I did catch a glimpse of your card. I think it said … Trooper Buttons."

"You've almost got it." He opened his truck and tossed back to me, "Au revoir, j'espere vous revoir avant trop longtemps."

"Hopefully, you're not cursing me out," I said.

He paused. "You don't speak French?"

"Not really. I just know it when I hear it."

"Ok." He smiled. "I was telling you, 'Bye.'"

"*Wait.*"

He looked startled. "Something else?"

I crossed to him and looked him in the eye. It wasn't just curiosity and attraction that had blasted away my hesitation. I felt a sudden, desperate need to acknowledge the reasons I'd trusted him.

"I'm sorry I treated you like a wall," I said.

He paused. "What?"

"The other night," I rushed on. "I almost dropped like a stone when I thought the bones belonged to Raymond. You caught me. Held me upright. I picked up on how you turned your face away so you weren't breathing down my neck. For you to know that would be helpful … it's the opposite of how the deputy behaved."

"There's no need—"

"Seriously, there is." Suddenly on point, I indicated his handsome face and awesome physique. "All of this is a distraction. It threw me off from how I normally handle things. You took over carrying my bags. You were subtle and kind. I want you to know that you made a huge difference on a really difficult night. Raymond wrote about what it was like to shoulder burdens and not get thanks for it. I can't bring him back and make it right. All I can do is live a certain way. So, please don't remember the awful part of today. Me venting at you because of Stable and the deputy. Remember this moment. Right now. How I'm saying *thank* you."

I released my grip on his arm, having not realized I'd reached out to hold him there while I put my feelings into words.

He blinked and looked away, apparently moved to the point where I saw a hint of emotion in his eyes. He was geared to take the hard hits of his job as they came along, to serve as a wall if that's what it took to prop up a woman who was starting to faint. Like Raymond, he would move on afterward with no expectation of being noticed, let alone thanked.

"You really are a surprise," he managed. "Which brings me back to what I've said here multiple times. There's no point denying that Raymond was the target. You figured it out. But honest to God, Sonny, if you're not careful, the tide could turn really fast "

"I'll be on guard. I'll rein in my perceptive powers."

"That's not possible," he said. "It's who you are."

"How could you know that?"

"How do you know to trust me?" he said.

"I don't, exactly. The other day ..."

"It crossed your mind that I might be a murderer?"

To my relief, his amused smile dispelled the idea to a passable degree. Nothing was a hundred percent in my life after finding a human skeleton hand outside my barn, but it seemed a good sign that he'd caught onto my thought at the Corner Pocket, and wasn't put off by it.

"I'm not, by the way," he clarified.

"Please tell me your name."

"Hmm." He debated the idea. "You seem drawn to mysteries. I hate to spoil the idea of you wondering about me from afar."

"It's silly to not say."

"That's how to tackle it," he said. "Your descriptions are on point. In my case, go with shady, squint-eyed, silly—"

"Annoying," I added, cracking up. "Come on."

137

"Or you could show my photo around." He closed his eyes with mock disappointment. "Right, you deleted it."

"Ok, fine. Be a mystery man."

"*Mystery* man. I'll have that sewn onto my cape."

I cracked up again and shook my head.

His gaze conveyed all kinds of complicated sentiments like, *Why do we have to meet now when I'm heading back to the Canadian border?*

I knew I was conveying the same thought because it was true. It was par for the course in my life, a possible good thing coming hand in hand with the fact that it had zero chance of liftoff.

"Take care, Sonny," he said softly.

"You, too."

I watched him climb into his truck with his phone in hand, his shoulder flexing as he spun the steering wheel and put his exit on a smooth course. He didn't seem the sort to handle the story I'd disclosed any way other than by the book. But a pain in my gut said I needed to brace myself in case I hadn't seen the last of Deputy Pike.

To recap, I'd been approached by people I'd never met, any of whom could be connected to a lunatic who played with skeleton parts, then I'd learned some pole dancing moves, shouted down Stable Bartlett in a strip club parking lot, and cried my eyes out for the first time in months in front of a trooper whose name was a new mystery to sort out.

And it was only 4 p.m. in the afternoon.

17

Hearing Detective Allen's unmarked cruiser slow down and pull into my driveway, I paused next to the pasture fence, where I'd been in the midst of capturing Gracie, who'd escaped through the rails once again. I felt my heart pick up speed as I returned the lamb to her mother, then stepped down the driveway as the detective climbed out with an unreadable expression. The next chapter of chaos was at hand.

"Miss Littlefield," he said. "How are you today?"

"It wasn't my first choice to make a complaint."

"We're there now. I understand there's a video."

I handed him the thumb drive I'd left near the kitchen door. "Can you limit the number of people who see this? I'm in a towel."

"I'll do my best to keep a lid on it."

He returned to his cruiser and was joined by another officer who climbed out of the passenger seat with a laptop in hand. They set the device on the front hood, plugged in the thumb drive, and in a minute, they leaned down and started watching Brumby's video.

Within ten seconds, I could see the detective react, putting a closed fist to his forehead as if he suddenly had a splitting headache. He'd banked on Deputy Pike's account being at least partially correct. The two officers exchanged a glance that alluded to the shitstorm the video would cause. Detective Allen returned to me looking apologetic.

"I am so sorry," he said. "Did he grab you? Touch you at all?"

"No."

"So, there was no assault. Not that it's any less awful."

I cut off the back and forth by stating my wishes: the matter removed from my life as fast as possible. I didn't need the deputy to get fired if there was a path that guaranteed a significant upgrade in his behavior. Maybe put him on probation for a while. I was told that would not be possible. The deputy had furthered his wrongdoing with lies.

On to the next reason for his visit.

I led him to the house and waited outside while he listened to the message. He stepped out with the tape sealed in a bag.

"There's bound to be another tape you can use," he said.

"I think I'll leave the machine off for now."

"I'd prefer it if you put in a new tape. That way, if any further calls come along, we can keep track of those as well."

"Any idea who made the call?"

"There's a list of possibilities. A narrow list."

"Has anyone else gotten messages like that?"

"No." He paused. "Why do you ask?"

"I just feel singled out."

"You've made a real good trooper friend," he said.

"You mean …" I paused, then ventured, "Officer Buttons?"

The detective choked back a snicker, then he turned away and devolved into a hooting round of laughing.

"I'm sorry," he managed. "I've been so keyed up from lack of sleep and all, I couldn't stop myself." He sighed and wiped his eyes. "What is it with you two, the name thing?"

"I take it that's not his name?"

The detective choked again, then reined himself in. "No, it's not."

"What is his name? This is maddening."

"I'm not going to end something that's made me laugh harder than I have in a year. You two need to work it out yourselves."

"But he's going to the Canadian border."

Detective Allen looked surprised. "He told you that?"

"I guessed it."

"Well." He reached out to shake my hand. "Raymond missed out on not getting to know you. He would be as proud as punch."

My eyes threatened to well up. "You're sure?"

"Yes ma'am."

He left me with a quick nod for a goodbye, then he returned to his cruiser. Soon, I was alone on the hill again.

* * *

Inside the house, I headed to the refrigerator, in need of a cold drink. With the door open and cool air wafting around me, I paused and frowned, seeing a business card perched on the wire shelf. I picked it up and slowly smiled as I saw the name printed on the flip side.

Trooper Daniel Bolton, Maine State Police.

I don't know why tears gathered in my eyes. His gesture was funny. Playful. Surprising. A good way to end a crazy day.

I grinned all the more when I saw another business card fastened to the wall where I had a sheet of local phone numbers, including emergency contacts. He'd drawn an arrow pointing to his name.

The next thing I knew, a treasure hunt was at hand. How he'd managed to fetch the journals and put business cards all over the place in ten minutes, I couldn't imagine. There was a card on the bathroom mirror — impossible for even a blind dummy like myself to miss — and one on the table near the dreaded answering machine.

I had an idea I'd find more, but I left it for another day.

In need of processing the events of the day on a deeper level, I Facetimed my best friend, Arlene, on the chance that she was awake at 10:30 p.m. London time. I was in luck. When she was on screen, I read from her pursed lips and stern gaze that she was upset because of my absence from our normal daily check-ins.

"Before you start spinning fibs, I know what's been going on," she said. "I texted Sue. She told me about the break-in."

For a moment, all I could do was wish she wasn't too far away to hug. With tears in my eyes, and seeing her eyes fill too, we just sat there for a moment absorbing the impossible turn our lives had taken: Arlene married, with three children, and me lagging behind. It wasn't supposed to turn out this way. Since childhood, we'd planned to have parallel lives, sharing passages, and watching our kids grow up together. Now life had delivered another blow against all those dreams. From weekly visits, we now only saw each other once a month. Arlene had added highlights to her dark, wavy hair that I didn't know about until just then. Her children were adjusting to not having their "Aunt" Sonny show up with gifts.

"I miss you so much," I said tearfully.

"Me, too. Please come to London."

"I can't. I'm sorry."

"I know, I'm being unfair." Arlene wiped her eyes. "Now, what in the hell is going on over there?"

"This is for your ears only, ok?"

It was entertaining to see Arlene's reactions as the story unfolded. Her eyes wide, her mouth agape. Hands in the air in astonishment. Leaned in with a grimace. Eyes closed in disbelief as I got to the pole dancing lesson. Total support as I said I'd kicked Stable's ass. Her head tilted with interest and she slowly smiled as I described finding the business cards.

"Wait, who is this guy again?" she said.

"Porter. The trooper from the first night."

"Send a screenshot of his card," Arlene said. "I've wanted to know who to get in touch with besides Sue and Kate if I think anything is wrong during your silences."

"He's heading out of town."

"Send it," she commanded. "*Now.*"

Describing the ordeal to my lifelong best friend was enough to lift my spirits. Arlene knew me well enough to not weigh in with what she would do if she were in my position. No lectures. No warnings. Nine times out of ten, she trusted my instincts.

Soon we moved on to her adventures in London. I smiled at her stories about their visits to museums and their day outside Buckingham Palace. She sent photos as we talked. Plates of English food. Selfies of Arlene and her husband. Her giggling children. A funny shot of her exasperated face with her in-laws in the background.

"Come join us," she said. "Leave that nonsense behind."

"I can't."

A few hours later, I locked the front door and checked all of the windows. I decided to not put a new tape in the answering machine. In fact, I unplugged Raymond's landline to ensure that I would have a decent chance of catching up on my sleep. With the knitted quilt pulled over me, the one Ella had made, I didn't recall a single dream.

I just slept.

18

I wasn't scheduled to arrive at Chuck's garage until one o'clock in the afternoon, but I had my camera bag packed and my portable lights tucked into a case next to the kitchen door shortly after the sun came up. As my cell phone rang, I was surprised to see Hollis's number come up, and even more interesting, he was reaching out via Facetime.

"Hi," I said, then paused, seeing blurry glimpses of a room swishing by, as if Hollis was on the move. "Hollis? Are you there?"

Lily's face appeared, blurred and slipped away, then appeared again. With the phone unsteady, she held up a drawing of a sheep. Then she held up a drawing of my face. It was her usual atmospheric style of rendering, and I could tell she'd come up with the concept at the picnic the other night. She'd depicted me smiling at someone on my left, highlighted by the campfire, my hair curling around my face.

In the background, I heard Hollis hollering that he couldn't find his phone. He prompted Lily to tell him if she had it, sounding impatient, and then I heard his voice getting closer.

"I knew it," he said. "Lily, come on. I'm late for work."

There was a brief struggle, then Hollis appeared. He squinted at the camera, seeming surprised to see me on the other end of the line.

"Sonny," he said. "I was just trying to call you on your landline."

"It's unplugged," I said. "What's up?"

"Well, it's a disaster, and I hope you can find a way to be understanding about it. The problem is right here."

As he turned the view to include the room he was standing in, I saw a lamb scampering past a chair. It was moving fast and issued a frightened *baah* at the top of its lungs.

"It's one of yours," Hollis said. "I'm sorry."

"One of *my* lambs? Are you sure it's from my flock?"

"Positive."

Shocked and confused, I flung open the kitchen door and tuned in on the drama I'd somehow missed: Woolberry was pacing near the fence with only one lamb gamboling after her. Her other lamb was missing.

"Hollis," I said. "How did this happen?"

He explained that at some point during the night, Earl had gotten "worried about my safety," and had made a trip to the end of my driveway to be sure there wasn't any trouble brewing that needed sorting out. Lily had slipped into the bed of his truck, as she'd done the other night to Everett, and once at the farm she'd dashed to the pasture and grabbed the lamb. Back to the truck she'd raced to stow away with the lamb under a tarp. She'd managed to hide the theft all night. It was only in the morning that Hollis had heard the lamb hollering and caught on.

"Hollis, lambs get very loud when their mother is out of sight. How in the world did Earl not hear it in the bed of the truck?"

"He had his music up loud, I guess."

And was drunk to boot, I had no doubt.

"Don't fret, the lamb is fine," Hollis assured me. "Once I'm finished at the building site I'm on this week, I'll bring the lamb to your place."

"When would that be?"

"Later today. Evening, maybe."

"It can't wait that long. It's probably starving by now."

"Everett can't do it, either," Hollis said. "He works with me."

"I'll come there."

I only half heard Hollis's directions as I scribbled them down. I mean, really. How much was one woman supposed to take?

"Text me when you're getting close," he said. "I'll dash home to make sure Lily doesn't kick up a fuss. Please don't report her, Sonny."

"I won't. I'll be there in about a half hour."

I spent the first five minutes of the drive reminding myself how grateful I'd felt when Lily gave me the drawing of Dodge. She was different in ways I didn't understand, and sheltered by Hollis. I couldn't let the chaos of my own life cloud how I handled the situation.

There is nothing like getting lost on a road in rural Maine to shoot a positive attitude all to hell. Confronted by mysterious forks and diabolical tangents that were based on logging trails from the ancient past, I was on my own when my phone signal dropped out from time to time, forcing me to course correct on the fly. It was pure bad luck that my inner workings had a penchant for putting me on dirt roads and shortcuts past ramshackle trailers that looked like the lairs of gun-toting drug smugglers.

In desperation, I answered my phone when it rang, hoping Arlene was calling to say she'd arranged a surprise that involved airlifting me out.

"Alison," a man said.

"Who is it? I'm very busy."

"It's Stable."

"Good crap on a freaking stick."

"Are you answering the phone while driving?" he said.

"My life is not up for discussionnn!" I hollered, drawing out the word to an extent that would be just cause to land a person in the loony bin. "Lose my number, Stable. Never call me again."

I tossed my phone onto the passenger seat, then with my pulse surging through my temples, I gave myself over to the twists and turns up ahead, and the crumbled, ribboned results of years of savage cold and thundering plow trucks. The faded yellow lines on the road took me through stands of pines and a stretch of open farmland, where cows grazed on a lush hillside near a collection of red barns and ancient silos. Every so often I crested a hill with a spectacular view of corn fields sprouting in neat rows, with a backdrop of white steeples perched above forests, finally ending with the blueish haze of mountains in the distance.

It was still early. I would have plenty of time to finish getting ready for my photo shoot at Chuck's garage. I smelled bursts of mown grass as the car glided down hills and I braked around curves. Every mile was connected to the next by the rush of tires on the pavement, a sound reflected back to me by occasional houses and stands of trees.

"Ok," I said. "Hollis described this fork."

And look! Perched in the weeds was a sign that confirmed it was Quaker Lane Road, the very one Hollis Oakes lived on.

I slowed as the numbers on the mailboxes fell into the range I was looking for. 823, 834, then after a field, 856. The logistics of country addresses never failed to baffle me, jumping from one number to the next with nothing in between. Finally, I saw "Oakes" on a mailbox up ahead with the number I was looking for. The mailbox next door had "Pruett" printed on the side. At the end of the short driveway was a trailer where Earl and Everett apparently lived. The place looked very dismal and run down, with a battered truck up on cinder blocks.

Hollis's two-story colonial was a cheering dwelling. The house looked a little worse for wear, but overall, Hollis kept the place in decent condition. Fresh paint. Newish windows. The red barn with white trim was picturesque with chickens clucking amidst a few neglected flower beds, and a cat sitting in the doorway, licking a front paw.

I recognized Nadine's blue sedan parked in the driveway. She stepped out of Hollis's house as I climbed out of my car.

"I just got here a few minutes ago," she said. "Hollis asked me to stop by and help. He's got a glitch at the building site, so he couldn't make it home in your time frame."

"Where is the lamb?" I said.

"Hang on, he asked me to explain what happened." Nadine pulled a half-smoked cigarette from her cleavage and set it aflame. "Trying to quit. I allow myself five puffs a day." She savored the first drag. "Why the good Lord made vices so tough to resist ..."

"Nadine, I'm in a hurry."

"Relax, honey, the lamb is fine. The whole reason this happened is because Earl heard some talk in a bar. Not *my* bar," she added with emphasis. "I won't serve him because I care about Everett. I'm helping Hollis get Earl on the straight and narrow. Anyway, Earl hears this deputy going on about you in a very troubling way."

"Oh no ... was the deputy's last name Pike?"

"That's the one. Earl stuck his oar in on your behalf and almost got clocked. The both of them were drunk. Came home, stomped around in anger a bit. Then he set off to make sure you were all right, no idea Lily had climbed into the back of his truck."

"This is a nightmare."

"Let me guess. Pike is the guy behind how rattled you seemed at my bar," Nadine said with an arched eyebrow.

"I think he's getting fired, but that isn't what I wanted."

"Honey, if he can't sort right from wrong in how to treat a woman, he shouldn't be wearing a badge."

"This business of Earl showing up at my farm can't happen again."

"I know, and Hollis does, too. He wanted me to stress that Lily isn't the one to blame. We have to let her know that what she did was wrong without making her feel scared."

"I'm totally on board with that," I said.

"Earl doesn't want Everett to end up like him, so he's trying to help his son land a good woman. He was impressed with you."

"It wasn't a good interaction from my perspective."

"Earl might not remember that part. Everett got upset with him for getting drunk again, so what does Earl do? He heads off on a well-intentioned mission that makes it worse."

"I'm starting to understand. He's using *man* logic."

Nadine smiled. "You're catching on."

"How do I convince them I'm not interested?"

"You could do worse, hon. Everett is a good kid."

I shook my head. "That's the point. He's a *kid*. With guys, four years younger can mean a significant gap on the emotional front."

"I get it."

"Plus, Earl was probably drunk. A menace on the road."

"Hollis will hide his keys if that's what it takes from now on," Nadine said, leading me up the flagstones into the house.

I stepped into the living room of cozy, lived-in furniture. The TV was on, casting the colorful light of a cartoon across the room.

Nadine put her cigarette out on a tray, then indicated I should follow her to the kitchen at the end of the hallway. I'd expected to find the lamb dashing from room to room, terrified by the way his hard little hooves slipped and skidded on the floors. Instead, it was quiet, and up ahead the kitchen light was off. As we arrived and my eyes adjusted to the dim room, I was surprised to see Lily sitting on the floor with the lamb noisily drinking milk from a baby bottle. I'd panicked over nothing.

"I brought grain," I said. "I guess you don't need it."

As Lily looked up at me, I found myself likening her expression to the way a toddler would assess an adult in the wake of a naughty moment they were hoping to get away with. No, I decided. "Naughty" seemed too harsh in tone. Lily gave away her artwork, maybe in hopes of being accepted and understood. In her gaze was a plea. I had a notion it wasn't a request to keep the lamb. Maybe she'd picked up on areas we had in common, both of us artists, and burdened with hidden challenges that made us unique. Stealing a lamb wasn't above board. She appeared to know that, but her eyes seemed to be asking if I could please understand that she was cut off from normal channels of making friends. I knelt by her side and smiled, telling her I wasn't angry, and yes, I saw her as a friend.

Lily beamed, which I took to mean my gut wasn't too far off, and then she made a quick gesture that plunged me into another revelation. I'd taken American Sign Language in college. I'd never gotten proficient, but I understood the question that Lily had posed: *All good?*

I lifted my hands, pausing to formulate a response.

"You use ASL?" I said out loud as I signed the words.

Lily impatiently indicated that Nadine should continue feeding the lamb, and then she carefully moved her hands again. I was frustrated to only catch part of it. She was either using signs and shortcuts I'd never learned, or she had resorted to making up her own symbols.

"Wait," I said as I signed the word.

I pulled out my phone, launched a search engine, and found a site that offered English to ASL translations.

"Are you hard of hearing?" I carefully signed.

Lily replied, "A l-i-t-t-l-e."

I nodded. "I understand."

Lily clutched me and rocked for a moment, making tiny whimpering sounds, then she took me off guard and grabbed at my phone. Judging by her sudden palpable determination, and remembering that she'd taken Hollis's phone, I had a feeling she wanted to keep it.

"Lily," I said, gently extracting myself from her grip. "We can put this website on Hollis's phone."

The girl pouted, but let go.

Sorry I take Pinkie, she signed.

"I like that name," I said. "From now on, I'll call him Pinkie."

This sparked the smile I'd hoped for.

I turned to Nadine. "Does Hollis use ASL with her?"

"Lily, how about you fetch a box for bringing Pinkie home?" Nadine said. "Sonny and I need to talk over a few things."

"I'm in a hurry," I reminded her.

"I don't want you to get disappointed," Nadine whispered when we were mostly out of earshot. "Here's the deal. Lily might be impaired, but she does hear us, and she can lip-read. She understands more than she lets on. She had a best friend in grade school who was deaf. I remember her tantrums when the family moved away."

"Nobody told me she was deaf. I saw no sign of it."

"Well, it's a sore subject for Lily," Nadine said. "Hollis can fill you in on the history of her fighting the idea of being handicapped. From what the folks at the school said, her tantrums pointed to further problems than hearing loss. They told Hollis to check her for autism, but the waiting list was a couple of years. He gave up."

"What about hearing aids?" I said.

"He had her fitted. When Lily realized she would be hearing things she *shouldn't* be doing with more clarity, she busted them."

I said quietly, "Does Lily talk, ever?"

"I think she tried early on and got made fun of by other children."

"She seemed eager to use ASL with me just now."

"Just be aware that she'll try to knuckle you under to use her made-up signs instead of official ones. Here's the good news. She's eighteen, and I think she's finally seeing that she'll be better off if she stops acting out. I wanted to let you know all this so you're not surprised if she gets temperamental. I haven't seen her have a major tantrum in quite a while. Maybe the hormones are finally working in her favor."

"She has exceptional talent as an artist," I said. "Maybe we can channel that in some positive directions."

"Hollis will be thrilled. You're the kind of role model he's hoped to have in her life. You're an artist, too."

"I really need to get the lamb home."

"Lily, honey—" Catching the teen hovering in the kitchen doorway to overhear us, Nadine gave me a look. "See what I mean?"

I hugged Lily to diffuse any mistrust she might feel if she'd caught onto the fact that we'd been talking about her.

"No more hiding in trucks," I said, hoping her lip reading would fill in any blanks if I got the signs wrong. "It's not safe."

Lily looked as if she'd sucked on a lemon.

"*Please*," I said, holding my hands together.

This appeared to win her over.

Once we got to my car, Nadine and I secured Pinkie in a large cardboard box with the flaps folded together.

"Hey, listen." Nadine perched next to my open window as I started my car. "I've been wanting to fix her hair. Let's tackle it together."

"I heard a rumor that there was some sort of tussle when Hollis tried to comb her hair. It's why he limps, maybe?"

"Picture him trying to comb a tangle out of your hair with his clumsy man hands. How would that go?"

"Good point. I'd love to help."

She gave me directions to the main road, and I hoped to heaven they were accurate because the lamb was bleating nonstop. Pinkie kicked and struggled against the cardboard box. It was only a matter of time before he got out. I pulled over at the fork at the end of Quaker Lane Road, got out, and cooed assurances as I tucked the flaps tighter.

Just then Hollis pulled up in his truck, with Everett in the passenger seat. They stepped out and crossed to my car.

"You got the lamb?" Hollis said.

"He's in a box. Do you have any tape?"

Hollis instructed Everett to fetch tape and tighten the seal of the box, but not to the point where the lamb didn't have air.

"I'm glad to catch you," Hollis said.

"I'm in such a hurry—"

"Hang on a second. That deputy you tangled with. Pike. I owe him because he's been tolerant with Lily a time or two. He's all upset, about to be fired from his job."

"I didn't want that. I really didn't."

"All I'm saying is, I told him he can work with me and Everett while he's sorting things out. I wanted to tell you in person so you don't think I'm disloyal. I didn't want you to be mad about it."

"Not at all."

"I figured so. Having a path to land on will help. He'll realize that contracting is less stressful than police work."

"I expect it is."

Having secured the lamb, Everett responded to my thanks with an eager smile. "I can stop by later if you want."

"Absolutely not. This afternoon, I'm meeting Chuck Brewster at his garage. I'm super busy all week."

"Chuck Brewster?" Everett demanded. "He's not trustworthy."

"Sonny is a sharp cookie," Hollis said. "She can handle herself."

"Chuck has ulterior motives," Everett said. "You know what he's like, Hollis. I can't say what's on his mind in mixed company. It's not decent."

"Come on, boy," Hollis said. "Get in the truck."

With a roll of eyes, he gave me a look of apology that said it was just a phase the young man was going through. If I was patient, Everett's interest would land elsewhere soon enough.

I hoped to heaven he was right.

19

"Raymond, I hope you truly did trust this guy," I murmured, idling at the bottom of a winding, heavily gullied dirt lane that cut steeply upward through a hillside of hemlocks, pines, maples, and just about every other kind of tree jammed together with very little space in between.

I had to ignore the voice in the back of my mind who'd watched enough horror movies to believe that dirt roads were the domain of outlaw hideouts and landing strips for alien spacecraft. I had to ignore State Trooper Daniel Bolton's warning as well.

On my right, the only indication that I'd found the correct address was a hand-painted sign that read, *If you want peace and quiet, drop dead.*

There was no time like the present to begin my assignment. Climbing out with my camera, I crouched close to the sign and took a series of shots, liking how the unique message played well with the effect I got with the wide angle of my 17-40mm lens.

I pressed onward and upward at 5 mph, gripping the steering wheel as the car lurched over craters that caused the undercarriage to scrape over bare dirt from time to time. Rain had clearly come down the steep lane in torrents many times. I was fortunate to be visiting on a clear day. From what I could tell, a wide-bodied tractor had dug into the mud after past rains, creating two deep, winding channels that did not fit the positioning of my car's tires in the slightest way. I either crawled precariously along the ridges or plunged, lopsided, into one of the channels.

As I steered to the left around a deep gully, branches shrieked and scraped along the windows, then the car dropped two feet as the rear tires slipped into the muddy hole. The tires spun madly, spraying a fan of brown water behind me. I hit the gas and lurched free.

That's when the doomsday machine thundered to life. I clutched the steering wheel and hit the brake, struck dumb by a deafening roar reverberating through the forest. It was coming from up ahead. Deafening, I decided, fell short of the level of the noise. Whatever Chuck was working on up there had enough power to vibrate the Earth off its axis.

Intrigued, I pressed onward and rounded a bend into the kind of scene my photojournalist friends would kill to know about. In front of a run-down trailer, I saw heaps of rusted car parts, warped fenders, and assorted disassembled appliances. Next to the trailer, two German Shepherds were lunging against their chains. How the dogs had heard my car approaching, I couldn't imagine. The doomsday machine was thundering and growling and revving inside a two-bay garage that appeared to have vomited more car parts at some point in time.

The noise ended abruptly, allowing me to hear the barking dogs. Their slavering excitement drew Chuck from his lair. Wiping his hands with an oily rag, he grinned and motioned for me to exit my car.

"You found me," he hollered.

"You have quite a driveway."

"What's that?" he said.

I understood that he would have hearing difficulties after hovering over the epicenter of the ghastly level of noise. Fallen pine needles that had vibrated to the edge of the roof of the garage were still dangling there, and a few jumped off as if to save their lives.

I slipped my camera bag over my shoulder and reached for my case of portable lights. Easy set-up was one of my golden rules.

"By God, I can't believe you did it!" Chuck shook my hand. "I kept expecting a call saying you were stuck."

"You wanted me to get stuck?" I demanded.

"Well, it would have been entertaining. Tomorrow, a guy I know is coming to smooth the lane with a tractor."

"So, I ruined my undercarriage for nothing?"

"You enjoy a challenge," Chuck said. "Admit it."

He wore overalls that had never, not even once, seen the inside of a washing machine, but he'd shaved for the occasion. His eyes looked keenly at everything they landed on as if he saw the potential for humor or interesting commentary everywhere. A quick word silenced the dogs, who collapsed in front of the trailer with their tongues hanging to one side. Behind them, impenetrable weeds and saplings said nature intended to annihilate Chuck's efforts to establish a yard. Maybe he couldn't mow because of the debris scattered around out there. It would take rubber boots, a jungle-caliber machete, and a quart of insect repellent to find out.

"You done sizing the place up?" Chuck said.

"Just checking the light."

"I thought you were imagining bodies out there."

I hesitated. "Not until now."

"I'm just messing with you," Chuck said with merriment in his eyes. "Come and meet my beauty, 'Wicked Pissah.'"

Inside the garage was a fascinating world of mufflers, cables, and oily engine parts that at first glance seemed a jumbled mess, but soon resolved themselves into categories. Carburetor parts here. Shocks and struts there. Ignition components in another heap. This was Chuck's version of a cluttered desk. I suspected he could find whatever he needed with no trouble at all. A workbench spanned the back of the garage. Amidst tools dangling from hooks, centerfolds of naked women lined the walls.

I tried to not react as I took in the blatant example of the very different priorities of men. Every breast was thrust forward invitingly and plumped to a staggering degree. As for the other themes on display, holy moly, where did anybody get the confidence to pose like that?

"So." I turned to Chuck with a diplomatic smile intact. "You'd mentioned wanting photos for the media. That tends to eliminate taking pictures with this wall in the frame."

"What's that?" He followed my gaze. "The place is nothing without them inspiring me from time to time. Part of my system. It's art."

I didn't want any further discussion of what kind of inspirational moments he was talking about and decided to give every last one of the spent towels, filthy chair cushions, and stained, ripped-out car seats strewn around the edge of the garage a wide berth.

"What now?" Chuck said.

"I shoot you."

"Just like that, without even knowing me."

"I'm pretty sure you deserve it."

He grinned the way I'd hoped he would. I raised my camera and framed him. *Boom.* The rest was reflex. Chuck had snapped on a few work lamps that cast a warmer light than the fluorescents along the ceiling. I adjusted my camera's white balance and shot him pondering the engine, grinning again, and reaching for a tool to snug a part into place. I knelt and waited for interesting angles and moments when his love of engines showed through. It was tricky, exhaling and stilling my hands at the right moment to keep the camera steady for the slow shutter speeds it took to capture scenes in the garage. Any blurring of his hands would hopefully be interesting. I experimented with the camera's flash a few times.

The natural light coming in was nice, but I wanted options.

"Hang on," I said. "Let me set up some lights."

He helped me with the collapsible stands, umbrellas, and reflectors.

"Prepare yourself for liftoff," he said, fishing earplugs from his pocket and snugging them into place. "I'm hitting the ignition."

"Do you have any extra plugs?"

Handed a filthy, grimy pair that had once been pink, possibly when dinosaurs had roamed the Earth, I inhaled for strength, then shoved them deeply into my ear canals. I had entered yet another realm of choices that had once seemed unimaginable.

The engine thundered to life with a violent, shuddering power I had never come close to experiencing at point-blank range. Nothing short of a lightning strike could rival the bellows of the combusting machine as Chuck tested it with a succession of revs. I started moving around the car to frame shots. Jittery vibrations coursed through my bones and reverberated in the concrete floor. My feet tingled in my shoes.

As he smiled and said something, I faced the challenge of keeping my hands steady so the photos I was taking wouldn't come up with any blur. What I aimed to capture were glimpses of what it was like to be in the spot where I was standing. The room could vibrate a little around us for all I cared, but Chuck's tanned face needed to be well-defined.

Chuck cut the power, returning me to some semblance of quiet, but with a high-pitched ringing sound in my ears that hopefully wasn't permanent. I felt a little breathless, yet I was full of amazement over the lifelike menace he'd forged out of car bodies and parts.

But holy moly, what a horrific neighbor to have in the tranquil woods of Maine. I hoped he never transferred his garage to my end of town.

* * *

During a break, Chuck offered me a bottle of soda and sat down on an old wicker couch that he'd stationed amidst the weeds near the driveway: a place for him to kick back and admire the sunset beyond the rusted fenders later on as evening rolled around.

"You gonna join me?" he said, patting the seat.

"No thanks, I'm good."

"I was surprised you came alone," Chuck said. "I usually have to do a lot more convincing to get a young woman up here." He took a swig of soda, his eyes twinkling. "Nadine told me you took a shot at pole dancing. I'd pay to see that. You're a knock-out with clothes on."

When shooting construction workers and other rough sorts of men in the past, I'd found that silence carried the highest degree of thwarting powers. Drunk, Chuck would probably be a handful. Nothing he'd said or done in the garage constituted a threat or direct innuendo, but his last few comments were pushing the limit, and it had my guard up.

Hearing a twig snap some yards away, I glanced toward the dark surrounding woods, with its understory of grape vines, shrubs, and brambles. If some kind of ugly business did start unfolding up there, I would be shredded to bits if I tried to escape into the forest.

"I have to confess something," Chuck said.

I blew out a long, fed-up-with-men breath, regretting that the photo shoot had hit a snag. I turned to face him with folded arms.

"Maybe not," he said. "You look mad already."

I said nothing.

"All right." Chuck used his soda to indicate north. "The trouble the other night at your farm? I sent Brumby there to keep an eye out."

I hesitated. "*You're* the reason he showed up that night?"

"I was in Nadine's bar and heard some talk a week or so ago. Your address, general time, etcetera. Bars are noisy. I couldn't tell what it was about, but I mentioned my concern to Brumby."

"Who was doing the talking?"

"No idea, just a voice," Chuck said. "My gaze was fixed on the stripper pole. It would have been impolite to look away from an artist at work."

"Why tell me now?"

"If I'd kept my mouth shut, maybe whoever it was would've come and gone without any fuss. At least, I assume so."

"Is there anything else I should know?"

Chuck flicked the bottle cap away. "I missed the chance to weigh in on my son's early years. I think it's why he's so messed up."

I hesitated. "Oh?"

"Nadine's son. My son. One and the same."

I resumed my assignment, liking how his quick smiles and pensive tangents were highlighted by the afternoon sunlight.

"Nadine said the paternity isn't certain," I said.

"When you meet Kyle, you'll know. He's mine."

"Is there a reason you mentioned him?"

"All Nadine and I want is somebody who's sensible on our side. You've made it clear it wasn't Kyle the other night, but for reasons unknown, the cops keep hounding Nadine for Kyle's whereabouts, which keeps him in hiding. They don't care about matching the right person with whatever crime. All that matters to them is making an arrest as soon as possible so they can head home and watch a ball game."

"That's kind of one-sided."

Chuck stood with an air of distraction. "At the farmer's market, I told you I had pictures of races you could look at. Lo and behold, a friend

158

stopped by the next day to see my clippings and pictures of local races. Took the whole lot of them to study."

This pulled me up short. I lowered my camera.

"Someone took them?" I said. "I remember you telling me a trooper had approached you about jeans jackets."

Chuck snorted. "You think I'd cooperate with him?"

"Who was it, then?"

"Somebody I trust. He'll get the facts straight. If there's a need, he'll do the right thing with the information."

I paused. "Please tell me it wasn't Brumby."

Chuck's wince confirmed my hunch.

"Unbelievable," I said.

"I was worried you'd be angry."

"Now, why would I be angry?" I said with sarcasm. "The two of you conspiring in secret, making plans without solid information, and who gets caught in the crossfire? Me."

Chuck grinned. "I heard you're the one firing rounds all over the place. You tore into Stable like nobody else has ever done."

Nadine must have told him. My argument with Stable had been loud enough for her neighbors down the road to be able to quote every word of our exchange. What concerned me the most was how fast news spread through the town, and most likely beyond. The back-and-forth going on behind the scenes was making me dizzy.

"The light is good now," I said. "Let's finish the shoot."

"Hang on. I need to show you something."

Chuck pulled a snapshot from his overalls, paused for a moment, as if debating whether or not to share it, then he handed it over.

I felt a thrill of shock as I recognized the back of a jeans jacket with cut-off sleeves. I saw the flag patch, the baseball patch, and others I remembered glimpsing the other night. The person wearing it was looking to the left and grinning as he straddled a dirt bike. I frowned at the guy's face for a long moment. He was young. It was Kyle.

"What the …?"

"Tell me," Chuck prompted.

"This is the jacket the burglar wore, but it's Kyle sitting on the dirt bike. You know I've ruled him out."

"Thank God."

Chuck exhaled with relief. This told me he wanted to know the truth, even if it ended up looking bad for his son.

"Is this Kyle's jacket?" I said.

"I think he borrowed it. Kids swap things all the time. I'm still asking around about it. The minute I can point the cops in the right direction away from my son, I'll do it in a heartbeat."

"When I first heard your son's name the other day, someone was talking about a boating incident."

"It's one of the only times Raymond and I almost came to blows. He assumed Kyle was the one driving the boat."

I frowned. "You don't think it was Kyle?"

"I picture him bragging about something he hadn't done," Chuck said. "You know how boys want to score street cred."

"This is very confusing."

"It was never investigated to the full extent. Kids in the water had all kinds of wild ideas about who was at the helm. Elvis, for all I know. I wish to hell I hadn't hollered at Raymond, though."

"Can I keep this snapshot?" I said.

Chuck eyed me carefully. "Depends on why you want it."

"I'll tell the police that this is the jacket, but it's not Kyle wearing it."

"Ok, go for it."

I wanted to get on with the photo shoot, but something nagged at me. The police had been silent for days, with zero updates indicating they were gaining ground on the most important questions. Never mind about Kyle's possible involvement. The primary issue, in my mind, was who the human bones had belonged to. If we could come up with that one answer, maybe every other aspect of the case would become clear.

"What are you thinking?" Chuck said.

"I need to show you a photo." I'd no sooner said it when I changed my mind. "I don't know. Maybe I shouldn't."

"You want answers. If I can help, I'm glad to do it."

160

Chuck had a lot of connections, and I'd uploaded the photo of the ring to my library app for this reason. With my stomach in a worried knot, I unlocked my cell phone and showed him the shot.

"What's this?" he said.

"Do you recognize that ring?"

"It's not the best picture."

"This was a bad idea."

As I reached for my phone, Chuck pulled it away and frowned at the image for a long moment. In that breathless instant, my gut said he recognized the ring. My heart thudded fast as I waited for him to respond, then his brow smoothed and he shook his head.

"A woman's ring," he said. "Pretty typical."

"It looked like you recognized it."

"Nope, doesn't look familiar." Chuck handed me the phone. "Where'd you find it? Lying around somewhere?"

"That's a long, complicated story," I said. "I can't explain, but if it is familiar, Chuck, you need to tell the police."

"It looks like a zillion I've seen."

Seeing that he was not going to budge, I pointed toward the sky. "The light is good right now. Let's head back to the garage."

"Got your earplugs?" he said.

"Right here."

I snugged them into place.

From his constant joking during our earlier session, Chuck had settled into a more introspective mood. I couldn't tell if his thoughts were on Kyle, or the photo I'd shown him, or Raymond's passing, or his relationship with Nadine. Maybe, like me, he'd reached the part of the afternoon when he was running out of gas from his earlier high spirits.

Once again, the supercharged engine of "Wicked Pissah" thundered to life with a violent, shuddering power that made me think that if I stood in the garage long enough, I would find that my sneakers had traveled sideways all on their own. I moved my portable lights with one hand and took test shots with the other. Finally, I left the lights in place and moved to different spots, capturing Chuck's frown as he "listened" to the engine and conducted mysterious tweaks that, from my perspective, had no effect on the sound. But he was sensing minute differences in the performance of the machine. I could tell from his face as he looked satisfied, then concerned, then satisfied enough to nod.

It was close to 4:00 when we called it quits. Chuck helped pack my equipment and carried the bags to my car, showing none of the lingering disorientation and shakiness that I felt as I walked on legs newly returned to the solid, non-vibrating Earth.

"I enjoyed this." Chuck gave the roof of my car a couple of parting raps as if it were a pet he admired. "See you on race day."

It was too late to realize I'd pulled into one of the sole open spaces on the property. "There's no room to turn around."

"Forward and back. You're up to it."

I proceeded with the business of surging forward, then backward, then forward, making progress by fractional degrees while rusted bits of hidden junk scraped the fenders and undercarriage of my car.

Chuck watched with his arms folded and a grin on his face.

"You should see it," he hollered. "If only I had a camera."

20

Once I'd lurched, braked, swerved, and cursed my way down Chuck's pitted, unforgiving lane, I rejoined the paved road with a new appreciation for the miracle of asphalt.

At last, I could process the latest news to hit my frazzled mind. Chuck Brewster was the reason Brumby had "happened" to show up at my house on Saturday night. Was Chuck telling the truth about not knowing who'd done the talking at the bar? Even if the information would help get Kyle off the hook, Chuck might not want to disclose any names to me.

It was sad to think that both of Kyle's parents had worried their son might have burglarized my barn. A person didn't dive for cover and stay there without good reason. Logic said Kyle was either connected to the guilty party somehow, or afraid. Possibly both.

No one, other than the police, had given any hint that they had knowledge of a crime involving human remains. The need to suppress the details helped me get through the day without drawing attention to myself, but when I was alone, the horror of my experience rushed back with dizzying force. I'd found a human skeleton hand. I'd seen beneath the living exterior of an actual person whose death had yet to be avenged.

A few miles from Chuck's lane, I pulled into a large diner that looked promising. With my camera equipment in the car, I didn't want the interior to get too hot, so I swung around toward the rear end of the parking lot and backed into a spot in the shade of some maple trees. Stepping through the door into a spacious interior, I discovered the diner was a hidden gem of delicious aromas, with hamburgers sizzling on a grill out back and workmen sitting at the counters or guffawing in the booths.

A fiftyish waitress in a delightfully retro outfit stepped briskly over to hand me a menu as I claimed a front window booth.

"I saw you smiling at the burgers," she said. "Medium, or rare?"

"Actually, I think I want a BLT and fries. And a Coke."

"Coming right up."

Once I'd visited the restroom to scrub car grime from my hands, I returned to the booth and studied the menu for future reference. Hamburger with fries. Cheeseburger with fries. Bacon cheeseburger with fries. My kind of place.

"Here you go." The waitress set an unasked-for mug of coffee on the table, then looked at me expectantly with a pen poised on her receipt pad.

"I think I ordered already," I said.

"We're talking pie, now. We're famous for it."

In truth, I had been craving pie. The restaurant had a strong showing of options: blueberry, apple, rhubarb, banana cream, lemon chiffon.

"There's always the sampler plate," the waitress said.

"That's what I want."

She eyed my slender build. "Are you sure you can handle it?"

"Absolutely."

Taking my menu, the waitress frowned toward the parking lot. "Bit of trouble unfolding out there. I saw that woman's car skid to a stop on the road when she clapped eyes on the guy in the lot, then she reversed and pulled in. Somebody's been cheating, I bet."

Leaning toward the window, I was startled to see Nadine Gilbert and State Trooper Dan Bolton in a heated exchange near his red truck. Even from a distance, I could see mud on his boots, sweat on his neck, and bits of leaves on his camouflage shirt and pants. He had the look of a man recovering from a rough haul through the woods.

Just a few miles from Chuck Brewster's garage.

I scooted to the window, so close I had to look through my own reflection as I watched Dan motion for Nadine to calm down.

"Love triangle," the waitress said. "I knew it."

"*Shh.* I need to focus on what's going on."

"Say no more." The waitress clambered into the opposite seat and joined the effort. "I'm excellent at lip reading. It's how I stay in the know."

"There's really no need—"

"The guy is staying pretty calm," she went on. "But the woman is mad as hell. She's saying, 'Why do you keep yanking on my sock?'"

"Picking on her son, maybe?"

"He's talking again. Something like, 'You need an enema.'"

"This really isn't helpful."

"Hang on, hang on … now he's saying, 'Bring a ham.'"

"'Bring him *in*,'" I corrected. "Then I'm pretty sure Dan … er, the guy out there said, 'The sooner the better.'"

"Oh, big mistake, him cutting her off to answer his cell phone, like she's on the low end of his priorities," the waitress said. "More bad news, by the look of it. He's closing his eyes and rubbing his head like it hurts. Sweet mercy, I bet there's a third woman in the mix."

"There isn't a third woman," I said.

"You keep telling yourself that, honey." She patted my hand as Nadine crossed to her car, slammed the door, and sped off toward Chuck's garage. "Well, that's it for today's drama, I guess," the waitress said. "If I were you, I'd find another love angle, if that's your fella."

"Thank you," I said tersely. "So much."

"No need. The pie will be on the house, you poor thing."

Finished with her expert translation, she bustled away to fill coffee mugs and relate the juicy details to the men sitting at the counter.

At least I'd caught the gist of the interaction, and could guess how it had come about: Nadine was on her way to see Chuck, and Dan was heading home after keeping an eye on my meeting with a person of interest in the case. My car was parked out of sight, so I figured Dan had pulled in to freshen up and eat, not knowing I was in the diner.

Maybe it was wrong to hope that he was uncomfortable after his stealth surveillance of my day, his stomach growling and his bladder about to explode. I watched him make a call, then my phone rang.

I answered with a musical, "Hello!"

165

"It's me," Dan said. "Trooper Bolton."

"Only longtime friends get to say, 'It's me.'"

"Ok, good to know."

"I have to tell you, Chuck was a perfect gentleman today," I enthused, watching Dan through the window and thinking two can play at observing someone in secret. "Whatever worries you had about him were *totally* unfounded. I hope *you* had a nice day."

Dan sighed. "You found out I was up near Chuck's place, keeping an eye out. Are you still on your way down his lane?"

"Nope," I said. "I'm almost home."

Dan gaped in alarm. "Then I estimate you're doing 80."

"Is there a reason you called?" I said.

"Has anyone named Beverly Pierce reached out to you?"

I frowned. "Beverly Pierce? No."

"If she does reach out, let me know."

"Why would Beverly Pierce want to talk to me?"

"She's the wife of a deputy who died some months ago. A friend of mine. Aaron Pierce. There's a possible link to the case." Dan paused and rubbed his head. "A local contact alerted her to the situation at your farm. I doubt she'll call. She lives in the Midwest, now."

"I don't understand," I said.

"Sonny, I'm sorry to cut this off. I have to make another call."

"I'll want an explanation eventually," I said.

As we hung up, I found the waitress hovering next to the table with an aromatic burger on a plate heaped with golden fries.

"I was right," she said, studying me. "There's a third woman."

"Ten, for all I know," I said.

She heaved a sigh. "Men, huh?"

"Leashes should be mandatory."

"And those zap collars," the waitress said.

I indicated the plate. "I ordered a BLT and a cola."

"Oh, sorry." She started to turn away, then changed her mind. "I like you, and it was my mistake. This is on the house."

"Thank you," I said.

I *loved* this place.

I focused on restoring my strength with the delicious burger, which had been cooked to perfection. As I neared the end of the feast, I saw an elderly man with an oxygen tank acknowledge my glance with a nod, his hands thick and speckled with age. A burly man at the counter stirred his coffee with a contrary note of delicacy. The cook drummed his fingers as he read the next order written on a slip. I rubbed my eyes, unable to stop looking at peoples' hands. Had the one I'd found been severed during a horrific final moment? Or was the victim already dead? There would be a slim comfort in knowing they hadn't suffered.

"All right, let's get this sorted out." With a voice that was gravelly from age, the man with the oxygen tank wheezed as he crossed to my table and sat down in the opposite seat. He looked up at the sullen teenager who'd trailed after him. "Go text yourself silly out in the truck, genius. Miss Littlefield and I have business."

The kid rolled his eyes and skulked away, happy to leave.

"Have we met?" I said.

"At Raymond's memorial service," he said.

"I think I do remember you."

"Not my name, though."

I lifted my hands. "You're right, I'm sorry."

"Doesn't matter to a man who's meeting his maker in twelve days." He signaled to the waitress. "Cup of coffee and more pie."

"You already had two slices," she said.

"Sugar's my drug of choice."

The waitress shrugged. "It's your funeral."

"Damn straight." The man turned his watery eyes back to me. "When you're my age, they park your butt in restaurants, churches, the hair salon. You hear things. Bet I can answer any question you got, starting with who the hell is Beverly." With a sage squint, he went on, "Beverly's the wife of Sheriff's Deputy Aaron Pierce. They were robbed and/or broken into a year or two ago. That was the official story, anyway. Very hush hush. Very odd. Whatever happened ended up sparking a divorce, from what I heard. Aaron took it hard and killed himself."

"Oh no … that's awful."

"Fits the picture, does it?" he said.

167

"I'm not sure. I'll have to think it over."

He rolled one hand. "I'm fading fast. What else you got?"

"Not much that makes any sense."

"What did you overhear the night of your robbery? And none of this crap about not spilling the beans to anyone," my self-appointed informant growled, wheezing from the force of his comment. "Sitting behind enemy lines with no ammo and intel is dumb."

"I didn't hear much. Just snatches, like 'out of state' and 'compare the DNA.' I think that had to do with ties to other crime scenes. There was some mention of people playing dress up."

"Dress up?" he demanded.

"With guns. That's all I overheard."

"What's the case got to do with? Drugs?"

"I don't think so."

"What's the gist of the crime, then? The basic element?"

"*Shh.* Please keep your voice down."

"Honey, I only got eleven days left."

"You said twelve."

"They're dropping fast," he said.

"All right." I sighed, then whispered, "The part I really need help with is whether or not anyone went missing unexpectedly."

"Missing person. Now we're talking." His fingers were beset by tremors as he rubbed his whiskered chin. "There's genuine missing, and there's people who don't want to be found. I can think of a dozen wives or husbands that up and left without notice."

"It does happen a lot."

"Now, playing dress up with guns … missing person. Damned if it doesn't ring a bell." After a moment, his eyes widened. "Bingo!"

I hesitated. "Seriously?"

"Some thirty years ago there was a big hoopla over a couple vanishing out of the blue. Never found. Out of state relatives made a fuss. Said the police weren't doing enough. Guess what brought the couple to Maine? One of them Revolutionary War re-enactments."

"With tents and pretend skirmishes?" I said.

"Exactly."

"What was their last name?"

"Christ, I'm not going to remember that level of detail this far down the line." Wheezing, but with a pleased grin, the old sage groaned his way out of the booth. "No need, no need," he added as I rushed to help. "By God, this is the most fun I've had in years."

"Thank you so much."

"Thank *you*. I'm up to fourteen days left now."

I smiled. "Glad to have helped."

* * *

I had roughly five minutes to enjoy the unexpected bounty of food on the table, and the information offered by the elderly man. With a forkful of apple pie halfway to my mouth, I suddenly noticed that Dan Bolton had stepped in some time ago, and was standing next to the cash register with one hand resting on the countertop, one boot casually crossed over the other, his fist resting on his belt, and his brown eyes trained on me.

I continued bringing the pie to my mouth, then slowly started chewing. I'd forgotten the notion that he was there to rest and eat. Judging from his expression, he was bent out of shape over my claim to be almost home while he stood outside just yards away. He seemed fixed on glaring at me instead of coming over. If so, that was fine with me.

No such luck.

Looking tired, Dan crossed the distance and slid into the opposite side of the booth with a drawn-out groan, then he folded his arms and regarded me for a moment. I felt I wasn't the one who needed to explain themselves, so I regarded him back. In the angled light, his pose brought definition to the muscles under his camouflage shirt. His face was more tanned than he'd been the other day at my farm, and I saw fresh bramble cuts on his forehead. There were other signs of a rough day. Bits of bark on his sleeves, and an exaggerated pulse in his neck.

"Just so you know, this isn't Canada," I said.

Dan sighed. "Why didn't you say you were in here?"

"You followed me. I was annoyed."

"Well ..." He unfolded his arms, and took up a more relaxed pose. "It wasn't just about making sure you came out in one piece. If there's anything at stake, interested parties tend to look for intel wherever they can. I figure Chuck has an angle, anyone he might talk to has an angle. I wanted to see who came and went before your visit."

"And?" I prompted.

"A guy named Everett barreled up the hill an hour or so before you arrived. Went after Chuck for asking you up there, like it was an honor thing. There was hollering, finger pointing." Seeing me close my eyes and groan, Dan said, "What's the deal?"

"I've been very clear that I'm not interested. I told his unpleasant father as well. I've barely met them, for Pete's sake."

"Well, you might want to repeat the message." Dan paused to study the plate from the burger, the pie the elderly man had left, the extra coffee, the soda, and the platter of half-eaten assorted slices of pies. "Were you entertaining a cadre of Vikings?"

"We meet this time every month to plan raids."

"Nice. Good one."

"Leaving your business cards was funny," I said. "Very ..."

He waited expectantly. "Go on, don't hold back."

"I'll stick with funny. Dan."

With a slow smile, he said, "Well, that's one success."

"How close did you get to Chuck's garage?"

"Ten yards, maybe. Too many brambles. It was close enough to not want to be you. I couldn't believe the level of noise."

"If only I'd been able to stand far away." I pulled out the filthy, grimy earplugs and set them on the table. "These sort of helped."

Dan grimaced. "I think you have an earwax problem."

"Funny. I had to borrow them from Chuck."

Just then the waitress came over with a tray. She put BLT plates in front of us, added a cola to his side of the table, then paused.

"Look, bud, I know your type, and you need to stop the nonsense," she said with a severe tone. "Any man with sense would know how your womanizing is hurting this poor girl."

170

Dan gave his full attention to her lecture, then he looked at me quizzically. "Honey? What's she saying? I would never cheat on you."

"I saw it with my own eyes, dumb-dumb," the waitress said.

"Thank you," I told her. "I can handle it from here."

"Glad to help, hon."

As the waitress left with her usual brisk demeanor of being an asset to all mankind, Dan waited for me to explain, and of course I did not.

"She's introduced our first topic," he said. "If other people are starting to notice we might have a thing, it's something to talk about."

I cracked up.

"What?" he said.

"She is the most inaccurate person on the planet."

"Ok, you've already admitted we had a moment outside the Corner Pocket. Then you said you think I'm really hot—"

"*What?*" I said. "When?"

"Bear in mind, I'm a humble police officer, trying to follow the clues. In this case, your exact words were, 'all of this is a distraction' at the same time you made a gesture in front of me indicating—"

"You're misreading what I meant."

"Whatever you say. The next thing I know, you're grabbing me as I'm trying to leave your farm—"

"I didn't *grab* you."

"You're still smiling about it," Dan pointed out.

"I'm stunned that you didn't absorb the sincere nature of what I was trying to convey. Next time I'll know better than to thank you."

"In all seriousness, I did appreciate that," Dan said earnestly.

"Are you always extremely direct?"

"I've learned the hard way that life is short," he said. "You're in motion like nothing I've ever seen, so I've had to step up my game."

"I heard a twig snap near Chuck's garage. That was you?"

"Chuck was ogling you. I could tell it put you on guard."

"Too many brambles in your way to step in, I guess."

Dan sighed with disappointment. "If you need me to demonstrate my macho abilities, I'll shred myself to bits next time."

"I doubt I'll be in that position again."

Dan pulled a skeptical face. "Given what I know so far …"

"You think you can tease me this early in the game?"

"Not to repeat myself, but given what I know so far …"

I rewarded his effort with a small smile. "Our food is getting cold."

With a shrug, he reached for his sandwich, then he sat back with an air of amazement. "Do you see what's happened here? You ordered a BLT and fries. I ordered a BLT and fries."

"What else would someone order in a diner?" I said.

"Quite a bit, apparently." Dan indicated the wreckage of plates on the table. "Plus, I went through a range of options on the menu. Meatloaf. Ham and cheese. Chili. Cheeseburger. Chicken salad."

"Ok, it's a miracle. Wow."

"There. Our first argument resolved."

As he started eating his BLT, taking big bites but somehow not making a mess, I asked myself if I wanted to mar the moment by having bits of toast, bacon, and mayo spill all over my shirt, the way they always did. No, I really did not. I pulled off the toast and started eating the ingredients separately with a fork.

On his side of the table, he picked up each and every fry and regarded it for a moment as if silently conveying to it, *I'm really sorry about this, may God have mercy on your soul.* Then he dipped it into the ketchup on his plate, and down the hatch it went.

"Listen," he said with a frown, forewarning a change to a serious topic. "I want to loop back to what happened with Pike. Are you ok?"

"I'm fine. I told you he didn't touch me."

"I know. It was a tough moment all the same."

"You saw the video?" I said.

"No. Access is tight."

Dan's brown eyes studied me for an extended moment, his expression saying I shouldn't hold back if I needed to vent. He showed genuine concern. I don't know why it surprised me.

"I've moved on, so don't worry on that front." I paused, munching on bacon, then said, "Why did you mention Beverly Pierce?"

"I doubt she'll reach out to you."

"You were concerned enough to bring it up," I said.

"Because of how she found out about the scene at your farm. Who she heard it from." Dan exhaled. "It was Pike."

"I heard Aaron and Beverly were divorced," I said carefully. "But I can imagine she doesn't want to open old wounds."

"Compassion isn't Pike's strong suit," Dan agreed. "He's showing who he is deep down. I wish we'd caught onto it sooner."

"What did he tell Beverly?"

"I don't know specifics. It was enough to upset her, and maybe that was the point. He's bent on stirring things up."

I could tell the subject was spoiling Dan's appetite. He'd mentioned being Aaron's friend. I didn't want to pry.

"While we're clearing the air, I need to tell you something."

"About?" Dan prompted.

"My conversation with Chuck regarding the case."

"Nope," Dan said, shaking his head for emphasis. "We're not getting into the case. Talking shop is the fastest way to ruin a conversation, and I don't want that. Not with you."

"Isn't it your job?"

"Every time we've met, I've been on leave. Long overdue. Put a wrinkle in my career path for a minute, but that's been sorted out."

We seemed to be taking turns folding our arms in silent protest. Half of me was thrilled to not be on the hook for telling him about my photo of the ring. The other half was sitting there thinking, now what? I didn't want to experience Detective Allen's reaction either.

With a tired groan, Dan said, "Ok, what?"

I launched my photo app and selected the image of the ring. "While I was up there today, I showed this to Chuck."

Taking my phone with a concerned frown, Dan studied the image for a moment. "That's the ... where did you get this?"

"You know I took photos outside my barn."

"You *showed* this to Chuck?" he demanded. "Why would you do that?"

"We were talking, and ... the thing is, he reacted."

Dan put my phone down, closed his eyes, and rubbed his brow. "If there was a wall, I would be banging my head. But there isn't a wall."

"I won't do it again."

"Chuck reacted?" Dan said. "How?"

"He stared at the ring for a moment. Frowning, like it was familiar. Then he claimed he didn't know who it belonged to."

"You didn't buy it," Dan said.

"No."

"Did he indicate who came to mind?"

"No."

Dan sighed. "Wait here, I need to call this in."

"Do you know who the ring belonged to?"

"How would we know?"

"Markings. Sometimes they can be looked up."

"Not always. Say the ring was stolen before anyone wore it."

"Ohhh …"

"See, more of this, ok?" Having stood, he gently gripped my shoulder. "The epiphany moment. *Before* you do something rash."

As he stepped away to call Detective Allen, I decided it was time to head home. Seeing I wanted the check, the waitress breezed over on her way to another table. I was about to pay with a twenty-dollar bill, but the total included the older man's pie, plus all the food that was supposed to be "on the house." Dan's meal was on the tab as well.

I closed my eyes. Why, Lord?

I didn't want an argument so I dug my wallet from my bag. An uncomplicated exit was worth the price.

As she took the bill to the register, I frowned at the unfamiliar spines I'd encountered in my bag as I fished out my wallet. I unzipped the side pocket. Inside was a handful of polymer figurines, no bigger than an inch high. I stared at them in my palm, theorizing they were the work of Lily Oakes. When had she slipped them into my bag?

I studied each one: an apple tree with its roots entwined through a stone wall, a farmer in overalls, three sheep on a strip of green polymer with swirls of grass and tiny flowers. Together, they seemed to be a portrait of my farm. Looking closely at the farmer, I felt a flash of gooseflesh on my arms as I realized he was holding a pipe in one hand. This was not just any man. Somehow, somewhere, Lily had met my father.

Maybe Hollis had brought her to pick strawberries at some point. I'd meant to dig through Raymond's journals for some mention of the people I'd met in the wake of the jarring incident in the barn. Now I had another reason to comb through his daily musings.

Just then, Dan returned.

"You're heading out?" he said.

"I paid the bill."

"Here, let me give you cash."

"No, it's fine," I said.

"I don't know if this will help, but if the guy you mentioned, Everett, insists on not taking a hint, you can put him off by saying you're involved."

"I guess I could use Brumby's name."

"Not a good idea."

"Who, then?"

Dan shrugged. "Me."

I'd started to inch out of the booth. Now I froze. "What …?"

"I've indicated it wouldn't be a stretch from my end," he said. "No pressure, understand? I'm just giving you a possible out with Everett if he doesn't grasp the word no. If at some point things settle down and you're good with it, who knows. About us, I mean."

"So, I would …"

"Tell him we're dating. We did just have lunch."

"And you wouldn't …"

"Assume anything? Expect anything? Of course not. Here's forty bucks. Does that cover my tab?" Dan held out two twenty-dollar bills, then waved them a little when I didn't respond. "If it's not helpful, forget the idea," Dan said. "It's totally up to you."

I'm sorry, but if a guy offers to serve as even a *fake* boyfriend, I'm immediately engaged in a quick assessment of the assets. His earnest brown eyes and nice lips. Handsome face. Chest muscles and healthy pulse. His hands looked very strong. He seemed open and honest, willing to state his feelings. Even more intriguing, he'd shown reluctance when it came to lecturing me, but who were we kidding? He would put on the pressure at some point. Not with aggressive means. That wasn't his way. He'd use humor, as he'd done with his business cards, and all kinds of other soft approaches. Nadine's scenario for getting him to disclose information could easily work the other way. Could I stonewall him after a passionate kiss and quality time? Not likely, that was for sure. Even agreeing to fake girlfriend status might come with significant risks.

"Sonny?"

"Huh …?" I nodded. "Right, thanks."

The table lurched as I went through the motions of securing my bag and sliding out of the booth like the seat had caught on fire.

"Do you need a hand?" Dan said.

"No."

"Your phone." He pointed to it on the table.

I snatched it up, and before I could stop myself, I did my best impression of an uptight old woman clutching her precious things to her chest in the presence of danger.

"See you around," Dan said with a smile.

"Yes. Can't wait."

On my speedy way out, I saw the waitress shaking her head with an expression that said I'd handled the moment all wrong.

Trust me. This *never* needs to be pointed out.

21

The turn of events in the diner had obliterated the other important development I'd intended to share with the police. The photo of Kyle. Right jeans jacket. Wrong guy. Now I would need to call Detective Allen and suffer another round of apologizing for not doing a good enough job of steering clear of the case. Who *would* be good at it right out of the gate? Pretending nothing had happened. Living with unknowns, possibly for the rest of my days.

I opened my car, tossed my bag onto the passenger's seat, and stood there for a moment, rubbing my brow. Who was I kidding? It wasn't the photo of Kyle that had me feeling flustered. What kind of cruel twist of fate had convinced Everett to confront Chuck? And why did Dan have to witness it and come up with a bold way of resolving the issue?

"Thanks a lot, Dan," I said sarcastically.

"For what?" he said behind me.

"Oh, crap."

"You didn't hear me come up?"

With a sigh, I turned to face him. "No, I didn't."

"Look, I could tell my bright idea didn't go over very well," Dan said with a disarming, puppylike twist of eyebrows.

"It's the timing and the fast pace. It threw me."

"Fast pace?" he said. "People hook up with each other based on a photo on their phones. By modern standards, we're moving at a snail's pace."

"Maybe I like a snail's pace."

"I get it. That's fine."

There was a long moment where neither one of us said anything, and neither one of us attempted to walk away. I studied the trees. He studied the vehicles in the parking lot. Which, if anyone wanted to make note of it, was the operational definition of a snail's pace.

Seeing him standing there in his camouflage shirt and pants, looking confused, I felt boiling mad. Boiling *something*, at any rate.

"Ok, here's the problem." I started listing events on my fingers. "In Costa Rica, I almost got bitten by an eyelash viper. Why? Because I lost track of taking pictures and got too close. In Canada, I almost got washed out to sea when the tide came in really fast. In Turks and Caicos, I almost got eaten by a shark. If you don't see the potential conflict here, there's no point explaining. The world is captivating and beautiful. Fish, flowers, people. The way the light shines, the way the world sounds. I'm out of control. I know this. You're in control. Great."

"Hold on," Dan said.

"No arguments. It makes no sense."

"Nothing you've said puts me off."

"Then you're a ding-a-ling."

"The fact that you're different, and special—"

"Oh, like Lily with the wild hair."

Dan looked baffled. "Who?"

"Never mind."

"*Wait.*"

As I moved to get into my car, he held me in place with both hands on my arms. A gentle grip. I could have pulled away. With his brow deeply furrowed and his brown eyes on my face, his expression moved through a range of gyrations, as if he were watching a strange phenomenon that might turn out to be highly dangerous, or possibly something good. I could hear his intakes of breath. Feel the heat rising from his chest.

I gripped his shirt and kissed him, pulling his startled face down far enough for me to plant my lips on his wonderful, expressive mouth. I pushed forward, wanting to know if what we were talking about was a bad idea, or something worth all the turmoil it would involve.

Doubt left him. We melded together, and holy moly, all the essential elements were there. He was strong, yet relaxed, taking the lead in eliminating every molecule of space between us until it was like we were in a dance we'd perfected over time. His breathing was intense at close range, deep and sexy, an indication of pistons firing at full tilt. Exploring his chest and shoulders, all those muscles I'd admired in the booth, I felt a moan rising within me, little happy sounds. And the kissing.

Oh my God.

His back slammed against my car. He swung me around, gripping my ass and making frustrated sounds in his throat. I knew exactly how he felt. We were in public. A parking lot.

As if to highlight the fact, we heard the whine of a door hinge, then the waitress's voice as she paused with a bag of trash in her hands.

"I knew it!" she said. "You two all but set the booth on fire."

Winded, with heat flooding all kinds of places that had been dormant for months, I broke away and walked in a tight circle in hopes of cooling off. Dan did the same. I tossed a quick wave to the waitress, indicating she should give us some privacy. For once, she followed through on a move that was actually helpful for a change.

When we were alone, Dan said, "What was *that?*"

"I don't know. You started it."

"Me?"

"Yes, you. In the diner." I closed my eyes and held up my hands. "That was great. Kind of awesome. But it's not the right timing."

Dan's face was in motion again as it dawned on him that a blast of encouragement was mixed in with my retreat.

"Do you need a day?" he said. "A week?"

"What does it matter? You're going to the border."

"Just so you know, you need to look up the definition of a snail's pace. Wait," Dan said as I opened my car. "We need to talk about this."

"I can't. It took me off guard."

"This is unbelievable."

"I warned you. I did."

"Hang on one minute," Dan said, gently gripping my shoulders as I started to turn away. "I agree, what just happened out here was awesome as far as I'm concerned, but it's fine to put a pause on that front if it's what you need right now. I get it. I really do."

"Ok." I blew out a breath. "Good."

Dan released me now that I didn't appear to be a direct flight risk. "Is there a short answer on why the timing is wrong?"

"Well, there's skeleton parts all over the place," I said. "I inherited a farm out of the blue, you're about to disappear to the Canadian border, I'm independent to the point where men decide they can't handle it, you're bound to dislike how I operate—"

"Ok." Dan motioned for me to stop. "No short answer. Hence, the snail's pace. Let's step off of the shifting sand, and change the subject."

"You're being very understanding."

"We're talking. This is good."

Instead of putting forth more questions and opinions, he took in a deep breath and let a pause extend between us, which was the absolute correct way to coax me off of the ledge. After a moment, I was breathing steadily too, then my functioning brain kicked in.

"What did Detective Allen say?"

"He's kind of pissed, but he'll get over it," Dan said.

"I'm sorry I showed the photo to Chuck. It's the frustration factor."

"Don't show it to anyone else, agreed?"

"Agreed."

"In the diner, I was about to tell you I found a passage in your father's journal," Dan said. "I'm not sure if it would lead to anything."

"A passage?" I said. "Linked to the case?"

"Not directly. I'll text you a screen shot of the page."

My phone dinged. I zoomed in on the photo he'd sent.

I get sad when I look at The Wolf, Raymond had written. *It brings me back to the day I found it. How Ella said it was the perfect guard for things we want to keep safe. I suppose I should tell Joan or Stable about it, just in case.*

"Does 'The Wolf' mean anything to you?" Dan said.

"It's not ringing a bell."

"Let me know if you figure it out, ok?" he said. "If it's a place where Raymond kept sensitive paperwork, it might offer some clues."

"I'll definitely look."

Dan appeared to grasp that unveiling a new mystery was the surest way to put the kibosh on where we'd landed a moment ago. He indicated it was ok for me to finish my exit, which I understood was a further glimpse into his character. Brumby would whine, beg, and plead for me to jump into the back of his truck and finish what I'd started.

Once inside my car, I opened the window and squinted at Dan. Not from the sun in my eyes. I was about to go out on a limb.

"Full honesty," I said, "when I switched gears over there, it's possible I subliminally figured it would be a crash and burn sort of moment." I shrugged. "It wasn't supposed to lead anywhere."

Dan nodded thoughtfully. "If I'm hearing you correctly," he said with an intrigued smile and a wry twist of eyebrows, "I'm happy to have disappointed you, and I hope to disappoint you again."

It was impossible to not smile in return.

Valor in the face of the unknown. That was his training, and it would have to pull him through the surprise encounter. I had no such training. I scarcely saw the road ahead on the drive home, and found myself quoting what Dan had said: "What was *that?* This is unbelievable."

Over and over. All the way home.

22

No matter how many times I drove up the hill of Raymond's farm, I felt a hint of the same mix of emotions that had taken hold the first time I'd set eyes on the place. How could I possibly own the fields, the barn, and the animals? At the same time, I felt a contrary note of familiarity. It wasn't déjà vu, or anything mystical in nature. It was a sense of enjoying the way everything had been measured out and put in place. Even the run-down barn and green color of the house appealed to the artist in me. It felt more and more like home.

Once I'd unloaded my car, I connected my camera to my laptop on the kitchen table and downloaded my photos of Chuck. Scrolling through each shot as they arrived on the screen, I was relieved to see that for the most part, I'd blurred out the centerfolds of naked women by creating a shallow depth of field. The white balance was on an acceptable scale as well. I wouldn't need to do much tweaking on that front.

Next, I looked up the obituary of Deputy Aaron Pierce. There was no mention of suicide, though it did list his death as sudden.

The story of the police incident that had preceded his death by a span of months made no mention of him being targeted by a note left with human remains. His death might explain why the police were keeping details out of the public eye. It would not be helpful to let antagonists know they could land emotional damage on such a deep level.

I searched for Revolutionary War re-enactments that had taken place thirty years ago and came up empty, then added "missing person" to the search field and tried again. There was no news story that fit the missing couple the elderly gentleman had mentioned. For all I knew, his ability to sort fact from gossip wasn't as sharp as I'd thought.

Finally, I turned to the most startling element of the day.

A half hour had passed since the incident in the parking lot. Every time I let my mind stray to the mind-blowing kiss, I started heating up. Dan and I had met in person only a handful of times, yet I had managed to rack up a number of shocking firsts in his presence. I'd cried in front of him after years of stifling tears until I was alone, then I'd trusted him with Raymond's journals after hiding their existence from my close local allies. To top it all off, I'd jumped him in a parking lot.

Arlene answered my call right away.

"I was just about to call you," she said.

"Why? What have you heard?"

"Ok, that level of paranoia will need to be explained in a minute," she said. "But first I have some interesting news."

Arlene had heard through mutual friends that my former boss down in Boston, code named Mr. Evil on my phone's contact list, was having a nervous breakdown because I'd ignored his increasingly persistent voicemails. He thought I was playing hardball, no idea the real reason I'd remained silent was that my life was imploding in fun new ways every time I turned around. Arlene prompted me to listen to his latest message while she was on the line. I pressed the play button.

"Look, Sonny," Mr. Evil said. "I admit I was a jerk. You asked for bereavement time, and I gave it, so firing you was a misunderstanding. A mistake, rather. On my part." He sighed. "I've heard you haven't gotten a new job so maybe we can come to an arrangement. Part time. Remote work. Whatever you want. Call me back, ok? I can't say name your price because we have to be realistic. But we're losing clients."

"He sounds desperate," Arlene said. "And you *will* name a price."

"Oh, yeah."

"Tell him you'll only work in Boston on certain days, certain weeks. He needs to adhere to your schedule, or else."

"I've always wanted to say 'or else' to someone."

Before Arlene could respond, I tumbled into a breathless description of my day, ending with the business in the parking lot. She wanted details. Style of kissing, and what kind of moves Dan made in return.

"It was a blur," I said. "But high marks all around."

"I'm dizzy from shock," Arlene said. "It's unprecedented, you jumping a guy like that. What happened to your trust issues?"

"Did I not just say it was a blur?" I said, wandering from room to room in search of artwork that depicted a wolf. "Dan's face is really expressive. Very disarming. Still, I don't know what came over me."

"It's your poor deprived subliminal mind taking over, and I'm all for it," Arlene said. "You need to repeat it as soon as possible."

"Only after things settle down."

"Sonny, he was right. You're going at a snail's pace. Back to the details. Nice lips, and his beard wasn't a problem?"

"Totally nice lips. His beard was soft."

"If you'd been in a room with nobody around …"

"We'd be naked right now. He'd be kissing me, and—" I closed my eyes. "It would be awesome. I need to block it out."

"Why? It sounds *great*."

"You know what I mean. My life is chaotic enough."

"Nadine was right. You are hopeless."

"There's a wide area between snails and the velociraptors we turned into out there," I said, poking my head into Raymond's bedroom, where forest green walls held rustic artwork, but nothing with a wolf theme. "In between would be better, don't you think?"

"Actually, I don't." Arlene heaved a sigh. "Now that you've got a potential prospect, I can clue you into something I've kept to myself for a while. Lance told me no more matchmaking between you and his colleagues. He's seen how they end up gutted."

I stopped my search of the rooms and gaped. "Your husband said that? About *me*? The two colleagues in question played mind games and cheated on me. They are the ones who ended things."

"Technically, they begged for a second chance," Arlene said.

"Let them trash me again? Never."

"I know, but Sonny, you're extreme on the independence front. The last guy was like, she doesn't need me in any important ways."

"And that's fair?"

"Of course not. You need a man who isn't thrown off by your strength. Understand, if he's too strong, it could go sideways pretty fast."

"Super. I can't win either way." I sighed. "Before we sign off can you connect to the field camera along my driveway? I sent you the link and password in an email."

"I already installed the app, and we're good to go."

"If I do iron out part-time work in Boston, I'll need as many friends as possible helping me keep an eye on the farm."

"I'll be glad to check the feed," Arlene said.

We signed off and exchanged heart emojis.

I stepped out of the kitchen into the twilight, crossed the driveway, and climbed through the fence rails. My animals made lazy progress toward me as I walked down the hillside to the flickering stream. Their stomachs were full from a day of grazing, but they still wanted to know if I had any grain in my pockets. I did not. They followed me anyway.

As I neared the wide ribbon of water, the splashing, bubbling torrent of its voice got closer and closer, and the air grew cooler. Chilly breezes stirred around me as I kicked off my sneakers and rolled up the cuffs of my jeans. Raymond had stationed a wide plank of wood between a flat boulder on the near side, and a matching rock on the far side. I stepped carefully into the water, aiming for a sandy section that offered firm footing. On past visits, I'd learned the hard way that while the nearby rapids offered captivating swirls, eddies, and churning foam, the rocks beneath the water were slick with algae, and too slippery to cross.

As I sat down on the plank, my feet were claimed by the icy moving water. This was one of several places on the farm that had special healing power. Tree swallows began swooping by as they gathered insects to feed their chicks in the boxes Raymond had set up around the field. I heard their beaks snapping at the floating clouds of midges above the stream. A few weeks ago, I'd watched them rocketing upward, playing with feathers in mid-air during their courtship flights. By mid-June, their chicks would fledge. It was amazing to think the swallows came and went on their migratory path like clockwork every year, flying as far south as Central America in the fall, then returning to the farm every spring.

A nicker from Dodge alerted me to Joan, Harry, and Jess crossing down the pasture slope to join me. I ducked as Harry clumsily splashed me as he clambered to the plank, almost tipping me backward into the stream when he sat down with sudden force.

"Harry, be careful," Joan chided.

"Sorry, Mom."

"Go catch minnows," she said.

With Jess helping him look for fish in the fading light, they used the nets that were always left by the water's edge.

"There's some!" Jess hollered. "No, dummy. *Here.*"

Falling into the water was not a disaster. They popped up, giggling.

As Joan settled in next to me, her cheeks were red, and her hair was floating around her face from the breezes of the stream. She rolled up her pant legs, as I had done, and sighed with contentment as her bare feet slipped into the churning water.

"I love this spot," she said.

"Me, too. I've been meaning to thank you for the picnic."

"It was fun. Long overdue."

I told her how things had gone in Chuck's garage. It was a successful shoot, despite the unseemly centerfolds of naked women, chaos of auto parts, and horrific sound of "Wicked Pissah."

"Did you have dinner?" Joan asked.

"I had ten dinners," I said.

I told her how the waitress had said the food was on the house, then she'd charged me anyway and added the meals of other people.

"Like who?" Joan said.

I filled her in on my encounters with Dan, a.k.a. "Porter," leaving out the part about kissing him in the parking lot.

"With regard to Raymond, does 'The Wolf' mean anything to you?" I ventured, using air quotes for emphasis.

"Not really."

"Can you pose the question to Stable without mentioning me?" I said.

"You make it sound like it'll be easy."

"I blasted him the other day, so I can't do it."

"There's no context to convey to him?"

"It might involve a place or detail here on the farm."

Joan shrugged. "I'll try."

"Look, Sonny!" Harry splashed toward us with a dripping net, then lost his balance and disappeared under the water for a second. He came up sputtering, but had not lost his hold on the net. Continuing onward, he slipped and disappeared again.

Joan and I laughed until our sides threatened to split.

All too soon darkness began claiming the pasture. We waited for our feet to dry before putting on our sneakers.

On the way up the hill, Joan nudged me. "Here comes trouble."

"Oh, no," I said, recognizing Brumby's truck pulling up to the house.

"He's been here a lot, lately," Joan said.

"I will never fall for him," I assured her.

"I'm glad to hear it."

Harry dashed to Brumby, and they roughhoused for a minute. It was clear that Jess felt left out. I had a feeling she had a crush on Brumby. Joan's expression as she glanced my way confirmed the notion. It was one of those phases every teenaged girl had to go through, and Brumby was not the sort to encourage her. He did have some sense.

Arriving at my house, I puzzled over a package on the porch steps.

"It ended up in the road," Joan said. "I picked it up for you."

"Why is it all mangled and open?"

"Well, Charlotte stopped by …"

Joan explained that she'd glanced out of her living room window when she'd heard a car slow to a stop in front of my mailbox.

"My attempt to shame her didn't work," Joan said. "Charlotte insists she has a right to see anything addressed to Raymond."

"She's welcome to the bills," I said. "And the tire marks?"

"She nicked the mailbox backing up, and the bag fell out. Even with me watching her she gunned the engine and drove over it. Twice."

I pulled out the enclosed two-piece bathing suit, liking the floral pattern and the flirty style of the separate short skirt. The return address told me it was a present Arlene must have sent before she'd left for her vacation. Maybe it was an enticement to join her and take advantage of the pool at the property she'd rented in London.

"Cute suit," Joan said. "I'm sure the tire marks will wash out."

"I hope so."

Soon the Dumas headed down the hill to their cozy house, laughing, teasing each other, the picture of a wonderful family.

Brumby crossed to me in clean jeans and a paisley shirt, looking freshly showered, with a damp cowlick of hair above his forehead.

"I'll spend the night, keep an eye out," he said, clomping up the porch steps in his cowboy boots as if it was already a done deal.

"No thanks, I want to be on my own tonight."

Brumby gave a dramatic roll of eyes. "You're mad because I got the photos from Chuck. There's no picture showing the jacket, but you're going to kiss me in a minute because I've got a major news flash. *Raymond* was the intended target, not you."

"I figured that out days ago. Anything else?"

Brumby fumed for a moment. "Just that the targets were all in law enforcement. That deputy, Pike, got a skull in his surprise box."

"Really?" I paused. "That's interesting."

"If hate was the motive, I can see it in Pike's case. A hothead like him would make enemies. But Raymond was fair and well-liked. The point is, maybe Pike came at you to rattle out whatever intel he could. He's got a score to settle with whoever left the cookie tin."

"Back to the jeans jacket," I said. "Chuck took out the photo we were looking for and gave it to me. He played you."

"Seriously? Sneaky bastard."

I stepped into the house, turned on the porch light, and fetched the photo showing Kyle on a motorbike. Once Brumby confirmed my assessment, I sent a screen shot of the photo to Detective Allen with the news: the image showed the right jacket, but the wrong guy.

"Maybe they'll finally broaden the search," I said.

"I can shed light on that, too. One of my clients is married to a cop. I got her to tell me a thing or two."

I hesitated, perceiving a note of conquest in his smile. "Oh my God," I said. "You didn't *sleep* with her to get the information?"

Brumby paused. "What?"

"See, 'what' is a very different word from 'no.'"

"It was just some kissing, and maybe some other stuff."

"I do not want to know the details."

"What I found out is useful and important," he insisted. "You told the police your suspicions about the Bergleys being involved. Guess who your description of the intruder sounds like?"

I spread my hands. "The *intruder*."

"There's a resemblance to Martin Bergley. Dark hair, unshaved. The cops wonder if you got mixed up about it."

"As in, it was Kyle, but my mind warped my ability to see him clearly?"

"It happens all the time, apparently."

"I'm a photographer. I know faces."

"I'm just telling you a possible reason they're not finished looking at Kyle."

"Unbelievable."

"Here's another tidbit you'll want to know about," Brumby said. "That kid, Everett? Apparently, he went to Chuck's place all hot under the collar about you being up there alone."

"I know. I heard."

"You told him you weren't interested, right?"

"I did."

"Next time he comes around, tell him we're an item."

I cracked up. After a long stretch of dateless months, I now had two fake boyfriend proposals on the table. Not a ringing endorsement of my future love life, but one could call it progress of a certain sort.

"That's not cool," Brumby said. "I'm trying to be helpful."

"I'm sorry," I managed. "The fake boyfriend slot is already taken."

"You're two-timing me?"

"We've never been involved, and you just admitted to having sex with another woman," I said. "The wife of a first responder, of all people. Don't do it again, understand? Where is your moral compass?"

"I did it to get answers for *you*. Who the hell is the guy?" Studying my face, Brumby said, "How far did he get?"

I shrugged. "We kissed. It was really great."

"You're yanking my chain."

"I'm not."

"If anything, this evens out what I did." Brumby started pacing. "I'm telling everyone you and I are together."

"I will be really angry if you spread that *giant* lie. I have a crazy couple of days ahead. I'm helping Nadine with Lily Oakes in the morning, then I'm swimming in the lake later on."

"The water will still be on the cold side."

"Raymond did it every year on the same date."

"You know the story, right? He and Ella swam this early a few times when they were in high school. Then adulthood set in," Brumby went on pointedly. "They decided it was better to sit in the sunshine instead of freezing their asses off."

"Raymond took it up again after Ella died as a tribute."

"He was a guy with all kinds of muscle weight."

"It's almost June, and it's mostly a shallow lake. Last week the water temperature was sixty-three degrees. It'll be warmer now."

"Swimming is supposed to be fun."

"Well, in this instance it's about building strength and endurance. I'll prepare myself with my yoga routine."

Brumby paused. "You do yoga? In one of those skimpy outfits?"

I sighed, wondering why I ever bothered to have a normal conversation with him. "Enough arguing. I need a good night's sleep."

I indicated it was high time he headed to his own place.

"No, sir. I'll be right here when the other guy comes for his booty call." Brumby flopped down in one of the chairs and folded his arms. "The nerve of the guy. Stepping in my game."

"You need to head home. I mean it."

"I'm not budging. A man can do what he wants."

Good God, he was stubborn and unreasonable during the most inconvenient times. It was clear that I needed to take drastic action if I wanted to have a decent sleep. I had an idea.

For ages, graphic designers had been using an industry standard chunk of electronic text that amounted to gibberish so they could show clients potential page designs. I'd seen it so many times that the gist of the nonsense words had stuck in my mind.

"Brumby, I will conjure Raymond if you don't heed me."

"I'm not falling for your scare tactics."

"Last warning," I said.

"Knock yourself out."

Trying to not smile, I tilted my head back as I faced the stars above the long view. For further effect, I held my palms facing east as well.

"Cut it out," Brumby said.

Ignoring him, I intoned in a low voice, "Lorem ipsum dolor sit amet, consectetur adipiscing elit, sed do eiusmod tempor—"

"Sonny! Quit it!"

Where was I?

"Umm, eiusmod tempor incididunt … ut labore et dolore …"

Just then, a bat flapped past us as it left the barn on its nightly rounds.

"All *right*," Brumby said. "Jesus."

"What …?" I pretended to be coming out of a trance.

"I'm going, ok?" He was already heading down the steps. "Honest to God, after all I've done on your behalf. Turns out you're insane."

"I asked you nicely. You didn't listen."

"You can deal with that bat on your own," he said.

"Do not tell people we're dating."

"Like I'd admit to dating a certified sorceress."

"Bye." I waved as Brumby slammed his truck door and headed down the driveway into the twilight. "Call first next time!"

Once inside the house, I locked the kitchen door and downstairs windows. Did I feel totally safe being alone with the crazy lunatic still on the loose? Of course not, but I didn't want Brumby there.

All the more so when Dan texted me.

All set, safe and sound? he wrote.

All set. Thanks for checking in.

Let's catch up in the morning.

Sounds good.

When my phone rang a moment later, I wondered what he'd decided to add that couldn't be addressed with another text.

"What's up?" I said.

"Miss Littlefield?" a youngish male said with the reedy, vulnerable kind of quality I'd heard in guys who were in their late teens. "I only have a minute. Mom says I can trust you."

My eyes widened. "Kyle?"

"Yeah. I'm sorry you've gotten dragged into some shit. And I'm sorry your dad is gone. Mom says you're a lot like him."

"I'm glad you called."

"If you ruled me out, why are the police still shaking the bushes so I'll fall out? It's like they're fixed on putting me away for good."

"Maybe it's because of someone you're connected to. If you tell me the gist of why you're on the run ..."

"It's complicated. I don't want to end up dead."

"I know a trooper you can trust."

"No way. You can't trust *any* of them."

"I'll talk to Nadine. Maybe—"

"This was a mistake."

"Kyle, please listen to me—"

Too late. There were shuffling sounds on the other end, as if he were on the move as he hung up, then the call ended.

The poor kid sounded terrified.

23

People laugh at my ritual of taking a dip in the lake before June arrives, Raymond had written in one of his journals. *I think half the folks in town would benefit from the first ten seconds of cold. I tried to explain it to Stable, how the chill of it makes my other senses come alive. It was Ella's idea. She showed me how the lake has a stirring scent when your nose is an inch above the surface. She said it was from pine needles. I think it's the sun, the wind, and the rain straight from heaven that makes the lake smell so alive.*

I stowed the journal, a couple of towels, a blanket, and my small underwater camera in a canvas beach bag for my trip to the lake on my way home in the afternoon.

By 7:00 a.m., my long-awaited day was all planned out.

Once I got to the Oakes residence to help Nadine untangle Lily's hair, there wouldn't be much time to catch up with Dan. Hoping he might have an update on any late-breaking developments, I called. When he picked up, there was a sleepy, half-awake quality to his hello.

"Sorry," I said. "Did I wake you?"

"It's ok. I was up late working on a bike I'm getting ready to part with. Minor tweaks. I want it to be in top shape."

I heard him inhale and drag his hand over his face, and possibly sheets shifting in the background. My body started to warm as I pictured him in briefs: blue, maybe, the modern kind.

"What kind of bike?" I said.

"I'll tell you about it later. When are you free today?"

"Not until around three."

Curious to see how he would react to my afternoon plans, I kept my morning obligations on the vague side, then told him about my pilgrimage to the lake. While I talked, I crossed into the barn to follow through on a few ideas I'd gotten overnight. One was to see if the electric fence was still working. With projects taking me from the farm for long hours, I wanted to have an extra assurance that the lambs could finally be contained.

"Visiting the lake is a great idea, Sonny," Dan said.

"Everyone else is lecturing me on how cold the water will be."

"You apparently outswam a shark. I think you can handle a Maine lake." Dan paused. "It sounds like you're multitasking."

"I'm plugging in the electric fence charger to see if it's still working," I said, sinking the end of the cord into a socket. "It's making a snapping sound. Is that normal?"

"That's how the fence works. It pulses every few seconds."

"How strong is the zap it gives?" I said, crossing to the place where the woven tape exited the barn and looped around the perimeter of the pasture along the fence posts. I touched it experimentally.

"Depends. Anywhere from 2,000 to 5,000 volts."

"It's not working. I've touched the tape three times."

"Sonny—"

There was a violent snapping sound and bolt of searing pain. My eyes crossed, and the world vibrated with blinding white light for a couple of seconds, as if I'd being struck by lightning on my fingertips, and then faxed to the scorching dunes of the Gobi desert.

"Sonny?" Dan said from somewhere below me.

Swaying, but miraculously still standing, I returned to the living and reached for my phone, which had dropped from my stunned hand to the dusty barn floor. I straightened and held it to my ear. Dan was laughing out loud, not even trying to contain his mirth.

"Go ahead, I can take it," I said.

"I tried to warn you," he managed.

I crossed to the charger and pulled out the plug. The snapping sound stopped.

"Are you ok?" Dan said.

"I'm good. Lesson learned."

"Congratulations. You completed an electrical circuit."

"Hilarious."

"Let's catch up. Rock your world at 3 p.m. How's that sound?"

I stopped in my tracks. "Umm ..."

"Rock Your World is an ice cream stand," Dan explained. "It just opened for the season. You've never been?"

"I'm new in town, remember? That's two things you can laugh about when ... oh, crap. My cousins just pulled into the driveway."

"Be brave," he said.

Always. What choice did I have?

After we hung up, I summoned my usual tolerant attitude as I stepped out of the barn to greet Charlotte Bergley's Lincoln. She climbed out in a form-fitting, short-sleeved flowered dress, which was two sizes too small for her ample figure. Her eternally unemployed brother, Martin, climbed out of the passenger seat, and Tyler, Charlotte's delinquent teenaged son, completed the ensemble of folded arms and hostile stares.

"Charlotte," I said. "How nice."

"I saw the appalling weeds in the berry patch."

"Actually, they're mostly under control."

"I depend on those berries for bean suppers. If you don't get that patch into shape, they'll never be appropriate for pies."

"On that front, we need to set up some ground rules. Raymond let you pick berries without paying. I can't afford to do that."

"We've *never* paid for berries!"

"I've done all the work, so it's my call."

"You wanted the farm. It's your job to do the work. But Tyler can pitch in later in the week. Say, thirty dollars an hour?"

I paused, having likened Tyler, her sullen, thick-headed boy, to the sort of teenager who enjoyed pushing toddlers off their bicycles and shaking soda cans to make them explode. But you know what they say. Keeping enemies close had merits.

"I'm not paying that much," I said. "As I already told you, the berries are mostly weeded. Next year we can loop back to the idea."

"So." She raised her eyebrows. "What was taken the other night?"

"Nothing. We chased the burglar away."

"By we, you of course mean Brumby Jones, the hopeless philanderer. No need to explain your iffy reasoning." Charlotte held out a hand with a tolerant smile. "I didn't come here to judge you. My only concern is to see if any heirlooms were taken."

"I think most of those ended up in your truck back in February."

"We did what any level-headed family would do, not knowing what kind of person had wrongly inherited the property."

"Well, the burglar left empty-handed."

Charlotte looked at me the way a school principal would study a naughty child. "Come now, Alison. The police were here all night, and spent a good deal of time in the barn. This is a historic property with a rich lineage of occupants."

I hesitated. "You mean cows, and …?"

"Not *cows*, for heaven's sake." With a flip of hands, she gave up questioning me and stalked into the barn. "Martin, Tyler, come along. Once we've inspected the barn, we'll get to the bottom of things."

I closed my eyes, grasping the tortured avenues her mind must have gone down in the face of all the secrecy. Buried treasure under the floor boards of the ancient building. A cache of antique coins, or maybe a golden canon with ruby-studded balls. Sure enough, I heard the staccato rhythm of her patent leather pumps moving from one end of the barn to the next. She poked her head into the tack room, saw nothing there, thankfully, and returned to the aisle where she peered toward the loft.

"I'm not leaving until I know what was taken," Charlotte said. "Because if you think you're going to collect insurance money on artifacts left here for all the years my family has owned the property, you've got another thing coming."

"There won't be an insurance claim," I assured her.

Charlotte was studying a penny she'd found, as if to estimate its value. "I've been wanting to inventory the barn, anyway."

"Looking is fine. Don't make a mess."

I capitalized on the moment by fetching the items I would need once the strawberries were ripe. First out were the hand-painted signs Raymond had used on local roads. Each one showed a giant berry with directions to the farm. Other signs were for the parking area and the weighing table. Every last sign was inspected by Charlotte.

"Fine." She motioned with her hand. "Take it away."

"Are you sure? Maybe the paint has a layer of gold leaf."

I stacked my armload at the front of the barn where I could easily fetch the items in June. I dug out the canopy Raymond had used to shade the weighing table, the folding chairs, and the berry boxes.

The one element I could count on was that the Bergleys were not accustomed to manual labor of any kind. It wasn't long before Charlotte ripped the hem of her dress, and Martin and Tyler climbed down from the hay loft covered with dust, and looking spent. They'd found a few old tools they planned to sell online. Martin said they were "highly valuable." I let them imagine they'd won a victory. Tyler remained sour faced, casting hateful glances at me as they retreated to their car and pulled away.

I rallied in the following silence. Onward. Queue next challenge.

* * *

When I got to Hollis's house, Nadine was already there, taking over the kitchen with an assortment of hair care products, makeup, curlers, and other items she'd brought for tackling Lily's hair.

I was afraid the shy girl would turn and run at the sight of the arsenal of products, but Lily seemed delighted by our attention. I signed to her that I hadn't gotten a chance to improve my facility with ASL, and warned her that some of the tangles might hurt as we combed them out.

Lily grinned.

I signaled to Nadine that I needed a private word.

"What's up, hon?" she said.

"Kyle called me last night," I whispered.

With wide eyes, Nadine gripped my arm and pulled me further to one side. "How in the world did he get your phone number?"

"I thought you gave it to him."

"Maybe Chuck did. What did Kyle say?"

"Not much. He sounded scared."

"Can I see what number he used?" Studying the caller ID information with a frown, she shook her head. "It's a different number every time. He's using burner phones."

It seemed she'd been in touch with Kyle all along.

"I was trying to tell him I wanted to come up with a plan to make him feel safe. He cut things short."

"What kind of plan did you have in mind?"

"It might be smart to find an attorney. Take steps to keep him separate from anything a friend might have done."

"You'd help Kyle?" Nadine said. "Truly?"

"Of course."

"Thank you, Sonny. You really are like Raymond."

Nadine looked distracted by my news, but soon she settled into a work rhythm. She had an easy way with Lily, joking and hugging the teen every so often. Maybe I could amend my first impression that it must have been tough for Lily to grow up being different, with a single father and a drunk who lived next door. There were gaps in her skill set, but there were bright notes as well. She'd found ways to cope.

Nadine opened one product after another and held them out for Lily to sniff. With pursed lips, the youngster shook her head over the first five products. Finally, she gave the sixth bottle a long sniff.

Yes, she signed.

"What did she say?" Nadine asked. "Show me how to do it."

I did so, and Nadine picked it up fast.

"I'm committed to learning," she said. "You've inspired me."

With Nadine issuing commands, I wrapped a thick pink towel around Lily's shoulders so her shirt would stay mostly dry, then I helped lean Lily over the kitchen sink. We used the spray attachment to wet her mop of extreme tangles with warm water.

After the shampoo was rinsed off, we added a generous dollop of cream rinse. Nadine massaged it in, and I started to grasp that she had an expert's flourish.

"Did you train as a hairstylist?" I said.

"Sure did. I preferred dancing. More money. I'm sorry, I don't mind being ogled. God made us a certain way, and he made men like to look."

"I have to say, I love your attitude."

She shrugged. "Keeps me going."

I almost teared up, seeing how pleased Lily seemed by our attentions, and was impressed by Nadine's expert detangling technique. She firmly gripped each length of hair, never letting the tugging motion of the comb reach the scalp area. It looked painless.

Hearing an alert coming from my bag, I dug out my phone and clicked on the app for the field camera I'd set up along the driveway. Clear as a bell were several photos of Stable Bartlett approaching the lens. He stopped, folded his arms, and glared at me.

"I'm not home," I cooed. "But thanks for helping me test the camera!"

Nadine chuckled as she looked over my shoulder. "A lot of men don't know how to handle a woman like you. Independent, speaks her mind. Stable's trying to apply his Stone Age views."

"Well, it won't work in my case."

Nadine kept glancing at me as she worked on the tangles. I started to perceive a tiny furrow between her eyebrows.

"I could touch up your hair," Nadine said. "Put in some layers that would give a wow effect. Maybe the trooper would like it."

"The trooper?" I said.

"Don't play with me. I've heard things."

I sighed. "Ok, I'm not sure where he and I are heading, but I've come to trust him. I want to see where it leads."

Nadine looked dismayed. "Sonny ..."

"Just listen for a minute, ok? I've come to trust you as well. You're strong and independent. We have a lot in common, so I see the potential of becoming friends. This means I need to draw a line with the two of you. I won't talk about him with you, and—"

I stopped abruptly, seeing Nadine's eyes welling up.

"I'm sorry," I rushed on. "I know you don't like him."

"Oh, honey."

Nadine put her comb aside and crossed around Lily's chair to hug me. I was startled and confused by her emotion, but I hugged her back. With a concerned whimper, Lily slipped from her chair and added her arms to the hug, as always smelling of cherry candy.

"You're the sweetest thing," Nadine managed. "To hear you say we have a lot in common. You don't know what that means to me."

"You're smart and bold," I said. "I admire you a lot."

Nadine wiped her eyes. Somehow, her mascara and eyeliner remained flawless. Whatever makeup she used had magical properties.

"You know my past," she said. "Most women treat me as such."

"Well, I'm a fan, so don't you forget it."

Nadine gently scooted Lily back to the chair and resumed her work untangling the snarls, adding as she kissed her client's cheek once again, "You're doing great, honey. Almost done."

"Is Chuck all set for the race later in the week?"

"I don't know," Nadine said. "We're not on speaking terms today."

I paused. "Can I ask why?"

"He's prone to foul moods. The timing is odd this time. When I called, he said he didn't have time for my nonsense."

"Ouch."

"That's us. Bickering, then flirting. He'll come around, probably after he wins. He'll be wanting some special Nadine time to celebrate."

I looked toward the lace curtains on the window, wondering if Chuck's bad mood had to do with the photo of the ring I'd shown him. Dan had alerted Detective Allen, so maybe Chuck had been subjected to an unwanted interview with the police when he was trying to focus on his upcoming race. My rash move had caused ripple effects everywhere.

Nadine was watching me again.

"I heard you, honey," she said. "I was the first one to see sparks between you and the trooper, so I'll stand back and let it run its course if that's what's in your heart. Just promise me you'll never completely drop your guard."

I sighed. "You have things to say. Go ahead this one time."

"Ok." Nadine paused her work with the comb. "Hollis and I used to do a crime podcast. Most of what we learned never got to the air. We didn't want to get sued. So, we hear about the poor deputy killing himself. Aaron Pierce. Then we got wind of some sort of incident at his house in the months before he died. We're thinking, why would he end his life? Promising future, and all that. Your trooper took his death really hard."

"I know they were colleagues."

"Friends since childhood," Nadine said. "From what I heard, how your trooper handled it was to get reassigned."

"Oh?" I managed.

"Now he's back. I wonder why?"

"What do you mean?"

"Oh, my goodness." Nadine sighed at my slow speed. "He's in plain clothes, so there's no official role that would be easy to figure out. What if he's got some sort of ulterior motive for hanging around? He's coming at you, for instance. Isn't that odd?"

"He's not coming *at* me. He's been kind and helpful."

"If you're sure ..."

"Maybe he got reassigned out of grief. That's how it sounds to me."

"What caused the deputy to end his life?"

"I don't really know."

"The trooper never said?"

"No. I'm not sure why he would."

"What's his interest in your burglary?"

"Maybe he's like me when it comes to work," I said. "Dedicated to the point where it's hard to let other people handle things."

I didn't think it would be kind to point out that her preconceived notions about a police officer might be the very sort of prejudice she'd faced when people learned the details of her past.

"Is there a specific reason you don't trust him?" I said.

"He's been asking around about Kyle, so naturally I'm concerned. Did you tell him about last night's phone call?"

"No, I didn't tell him," I assured her.

"Maybe you should. I'd like to know what he has to say for himself. I bet it'll help you see if he truly is a trustworthy sort."

"Then sure, I'll tell him when I get a chance."

"*Mm*," Lily prompted, scowling and clapping her hands to get our attention. She signed, *No argue. Me hair. Me me me.*

I translated for Nadine.

"Here's the good news, angel." Nadine gave Lily a peck on her cheek. "I'm finished with the detangling. Let's trim a bit."

Humming, Nadine slipped into her new role with frequent pauses to examine the effect as she clipped off long ends and sections that looked too frizzy. She focused intently as she worked, and as the haircut slowly took shape, I started to have the mad idea that maybe I would trust Nadine with my own hair one day. Every time I had found a stylist who could manage my unruly mop of curls, they got married and moved away, or had children and quit.

"Show me how to sign 'wispy bangs,'" Nadine said.

I did, and Nadine slowly posed the question.

Lily was elated by our efforts to consult her. She nodded, though I suspected she didn't know what wispy bangs meant.

Clip, clip, clip. Nadine continued to work wonders.

"Now for the blow drier," she announced.

Looking around the room, I saw some of Lily's artwork in simple frames on the walls. The cat I'd seen out front. The flowerbed. I abruptly remembered I'd wanted to thank her for the figurines she'd left in my bag. I pulled them out and set them on the table.

"Lily," I said, "I love these. Thank you."

She nodded.

I pointed to the figurine of the farmer holding a pipe. "Is this Raymond who lived at my farm? Did you know him?"

Lily darted from the chair and left the room.

Nadine shut off the blow dryer and looked at me with exasperation. "Sonny! Now it'll dry all wrong."

"I'm sorry."

Lily returned in short order, handed me a painting, then sat back down in the chair and motioned for Nadine to continue.

I studied the painting of deep blue and green shadows, bordering on black, with many specks of glowing golden light. Some tiny. Some larger. Cutting through the scene was a subtle ribbon of white flickers and reflected lights here and there.

"I know what that is," Nadine said. "Raymond used to have firefly parties in July. Hollis must have taken Lily. It was magical, Sonny. I'm not a fan of bugs, mind you, but the fireflies seemed like tiny candles. Thousands of them. In the trees, floating in the air. People were silent as they watched. It was awe inspiring."

"I missed out on so much," I said.

"Have your *own* firefly party this July."

Nadine's unstoppable optimism had a brightening effect. And there was more reason to smile as she finished with Lily's hair.

I was so astonished that I stood up. "Wow!"

"Didn't I tell you? She's gorgeous."

Handed a mirror, Lily looked confused by her reflection. She leaned forward and stared at herself, then she looked up at Nadine as if to ask, this isn't *me* in the mirror?

"It's you, baby." Nadine kissed her. "You're a knockout."

Somehow, with a brush, scissors, and a blow drier, Nadine had transformed the ratty tangles into flowing, straight, shoulder-length hair and wispy bangs that cupped Lily's heart-shaped face and huge green eyes with long, curved lashes.

"Wow," I said again. "I mean, wow."

Behind me came the sound of keys dropping to the floor. Hollis stood there in the doorway, looking as astonished as I felt.

"What on earth …?"

"We gave her a makeover," Nadine said. "Surprise!"

"My good Lord." Hollis knelt in front of his daughter. "I didn't know how to help you properly. You look like your mother."

"Don't feel bad for not having the skills," Nadine said. "I'm kicking myself for not doing this sooner. I didn't want to interfere, but with Sonny around lately, tackling the farm on her own, I've started seeing things in a new light. Outsiders can have that effect."

"They certainly can," Hollis said.

He seemed poised to touch Lily's cheek, but there was the sense that with her looking perfect, he didn't want his work-weary hands to undo the transformation.

"My good Lord," he said again. "Do you like it, honey?"

She nodded eagerly.

"Well, why wouldn't you?"

With a groan, he climbed to his feet, then he reached for his cane and attempted to straighten out a kink in his posture. "Shouldn't have lost my mind and knelt. I'll be paying for it later on."

As I helped sweep up Lily's hair from the floor, Hollis touched my arm. "Sonny, I wanted a word."

"Sure. What's up?"

"You know I hired Pike, that deputy you apparently tangled with. It's been uphill getting him to focus on building site work. Complains a lot, and he's a bit of a hothead. But I'm committed to seeing it through. I think he'll get the hang of it."

"He's lucky to have the opportunity."

"Not from his perspective. Anyway, he didn't show up this morning. Long story short, it turns out he got jumped last night."

"Jumped?"

"Apparently, he was heading home from a bar. They came at him from behind and beat him up." Hollis winced apprehensively as he looked at me. "The culprit said it was on your behalf."

"Oh no … I can't imagine who it would be."

"Brumby, maybe? He's got a history of assault."

"He does?"

"I don't think charges were ever applied."

After a moment, I shook my head. "Brumby wouldn't attack someone from behind. He'd go straight at the guy."

"Well, Pike refused to go to get x-rays. Says he's tough and can take it. I suppose he'll want a paycheck while he recovers."

"You shouldn't feel obligated."

Hollis shrugged. "We'll see how it goes." He smiled as he watched his daughter and Nadine sort through some of the products on the table. "It's still getting to me, how much Lily looks like her mother, now that she's all fixed up. I can't understand how you brushed out the tangles without Lily getting … well, the important thing is, you prevailed."

"Where is her mother now?"

"Died a long time ago." Hollis opened a drawer, fished around for a moment, then pulled out an old newspaper clipping. "Awful car crash. Down in Massachusetts."

A photo of a smashed-up vehicle was included in the article. "It says she was the passenger."

"That's right."

"Who was driving?" I said.

"Somebody she was dating, I guess. We were separated. She wanted to find herself. The coward at the wheel took off."

"Couldn't they ID him through the car?"

"No such luck. It was her car."

Here was a woman's death. I'd promised Dan that I wouldn't show the photo of the ring to anyone else. I would honor the promise, but found myself asking, "Was she wearing her ring?"

"What ring? Oh, her wedding ring? I doubt she was wearing it, the way things stood, though we never divorced."

"What kind of ring was it?"

"A simple band. All I could afford at the time." He paused. "Why do you ask? Seems an odd question."

"I go down tangents that don't make sense."

"Story of my life." Hollis chuckled. "See how tattered the clipping is? Lily won't tolerate me throwing it out. Pulls it out of the drawer and looks at it from time to time. Can't grasp why her mother would leave her with relatives. It isn't something I can explain."

"What relatives?"

"My wife took Lily from the home she knew, saying it was her place as a mother. Then she dumped Lily off with her cousins in Massachusetts and ran around."

"That must have been hard on Lily. You as well."

"After the accident, I let it go on for a while. Then I heard things. I went and brought Lily home." Hollis watched his daughter with glistening eyes. "I suppose you think I'm a pretty dim bulb. You and Nadine have made inroads where I've failed."

"Don't be hard on yourself."

"The thing is, I've got that language situation."

"Dyslexia?"

"That's it. It was years ago when the doctor said she had hearing loss. Lily drove me nuts, making up her own signs. Add my clumsy hands to

205

the picture, and even the official ones were a challenge. I gave up. Now I feel awful about it."

"Just take your time. You'll get it."

"Speaking of getting things wrong, I'm sorry Everett keeps acting like you have interest. He's a good kid, but with Earl the way he's always been, Everett's upbringing was from watching television. Families in shows. People getting married without a care. Nutty stuff that you can't expect to happen in real life."

"What the hell, Hollis?" Everett said, suddenly in the doorway. "What are you going on about? Talking like I don't have any sense."

"I'm sorry you overheard."

"Yeah, you're always sorry," Everett said, stomping in and red in the face. Stepping in the water, he slipped and almost fell. All the more furious, he shoved the chair Lily had been sitting in.

"What the hell is all this mess?"

"You calm right down," Hollis said.

"Everett," Nadine chimed in. "What's got into you?"

"What do you think? Come the weekend, Dad will be on another bender. I'm starting to feel like I'm the old man, weighed down by his shit. I can't take it anymore."

"You can because you're strong," Nadine said softly.

This helped calm him. Glancing around at us, he clapped eyes on Lily standing there looking shy, as if waiting for him to notice her.

"Who the heck ... *Lily?*"

She smiled.

"What'd you do to her?" Everett demanded. "She's all ..."

"Beautiful?" Nadine said.

"I never ... is it a trick? Makeup?"

"Nope. Just a proper haircut."

"It's got to be more than that."

"So, you approve?"

"I guess," Everett said. "I mean ... yeah, it's nice."

With Lily's hair swept from the floor and the towels stacked on the table, I made my excuses, saying I had plans for the afternoon.

On my way out, I couldn't help but pause and presume that I would not be having a problem with Everett anymore. He was staring at Lily the way young men do when they're suddenly infatuated with a potential new flame. Lily was blushing and looking shy as if her biggest dream was now being realized. Maybe this was why she'd climbed into the bed of his truck. Who knew how long she'd had a crush on him?

Nadine saw me looking dismayed. I hoped to see her reflect some knowledge that this development might not be the best thing for Lily, who seemed on the verge of stepping into a new mindset, a new phase of internal development. Given all the turmoil that came with Lily's unique qualities, any step into more of an adult footing, especially with men, had to happen at a pace that suited her. She shouldn't be rushed.

Nadine made a quick motion that said, here you are again, not letting things develop naturally. Stop worrying, her eyes said.

She was right. Who was I to judge?

24

When Joan, Harry, and Jess had first told me about their local "swimming hole," which had been maintained by the town as an informal park for generations, I'd pictured an iffy pond with snapping turtles and duckweed. But the dirt lane opened onto a grassy glade surrounded by balsam firs and pine trees. In the middle of that part of the relatively small lake, over a hundred feet from the beach was a pile of submerged boulders marked by a buoy where my neighbors staged diving contests.

With no one in sight, I ducked down in my car and changed into the two-piece bathing suit Arlene had sent as a gift. I wore it with great satisfaction, despite the tire marks that Charlotte had left across the front when she'd knocked it from my mailbox. One, I loved the flirty skirt. Two, I didn't want Charlotte to think she'd dented me.

I set my blanket and bag of towels on the grass, then I kicked off my flip-flops near the water's edge, where steps fashioned out of huge granite slabs led down into the lake. The lowest step was completely submerged. On my right was a small sandy beach.

Glints flickered across the lake under the blue sky as I paused to center myself with a short version of my yoga routine. With my hands in a prayer position, I closed my eyes, inhaled the fresh air, and tuned in on the flickering light playing against my eyelids. This brought on the sense of being in a conversation of sorts, a connection to the forces of living things that could not be explained through logic or common sense. I smiled, sending my thoughts upward into the sky, picturing Raymond and Ella smiling down at me from the clouds.

My focus had always been on poses of power, starting with the mountain pose. With my shoulders back and my hands at my sides, I inhaled deeply and faced the lake. I swept into a sequence of warrior poses, first with one knee bent and my arms straight up. As I struck each stance, I pictured reshaping my encounter with the intruder and winning the fight to the point where he hadn't escaped. Breathing quietly, strictly balanced, I felt more and more centered as I took up a succession of poses. Eagle. Horse. Dog. Dolphin. Crane. Tiger. Lion.

With a final deep breath, I stood and opened my eyes. Ice cream awaited me at three o'clock. I wanted to be dried off and reasonably pulled together before I headed out for my appointment with Dan.

Not an appointment, I decided. It was a date.

With my small underwater camera in hand in case I saw any interesting fish, I winced my way across a stretch of gravel next to the granite steps. The bottom of the lake was sandy, the water clear. With my right hand on the railing, I stepped down the granite slabs into the water's chilly grip all the way up to my thighs. It helped to picture Raymond and Ella as teenagers, giggling as they dove in head first. Then I pictured Raymond there on his own, even last spring, wanting to honor his wife.

A man in a small outboard boat in the middle of the lake looked my way and shook his head as if thinking I was crazy. He resumed the absorbing task of watching his fishing line do nothing.

The sun was hot on my bare shoulders and arms. Soon my thighs and hips began adjusting to the chill, and the notion of actually enjoying the swim seemed possible. I inhaled, pulling air deep into my lungs, then I braced myself with a countdown: one, two, *three*.

With outstretched hands, I dove straight under and survived the grip of cold by hollering underwater at the top of my lungs. With bubbles pummeling my ears and trailing behind me, I skimmed the sandy lake bottom for a few yards, then I surfaced with a gasp.

I blinked away water and smoothed my bangs, grinning from the exhilaration of casting doubts and hesitation aside. I could do anything with the right attitude. I kicked and splashed for a moment to adjust to the cold, loving how the bubbles wobbled their way upward through the water. I dog paddled for a few strokes, my arms glistening with reflected light, then I dove under and rejoined the stillness of the lake without all the hollering this time. In the distance, a boat engine clicked to life. Mostly, I was alone with the tiny bubbles escaping from my lips and the bright flashes of fish up ahead as they darted away from my approach.

I pushed myself to stay underwater as long as possible, making note of the sandy bottom and each rock I passed on my way to the pile of boulders that were marked with a buoy. I always hoped for a personal best in terms of distance, but the cold was cutting down my endurance. My heart started slamming, and I needed to take a breath.

I floated upward, releasing bubbles that I enjoyed looking through as they churned across the surface, then I burst free with a gasp.

"This is fun! Take that, skeptics."

The lake had a fresh, sweet scent. With Raymond's journal entry in mind, I treaded water with my nose an inch above the surface and inhaled deeply. The memory would stay with me forever.

My chilled toes told me it was a good idea to get my blood flowing with some brisk activity. In the spirit of the occasion, I coached myself through my recollection of proper freestyle strokes, hoping this time would be different. I would finally summon the right moves.

No such luck. Two strokes in, I was a milling, splashing maelstrom of arms and legs, yet somehow, I went absolutely nowhere. As always, my mother's voice in the back of my mind demanded to get her money back from all the swimming lessons she'd invested in during my youth. I focused on what mattered. My effort had warmed up my extremities.

The buoy was twenty feet away. I turned on my camera and checked that it was in the underwater setting. I dove downward and started plowing forward, as always mindful of keeping the camera steady to create an inviting video, rather than a wobbly mess.

Hearing the boat engine approaching, I surfaced so the driver would know I was there. Just in time. It was heading straight toward me. I waved and hollered, then I swam toward the boulders and buoy at a good clip.

Almost there, I checked to see if I'd reached a spot that was beyond his trajectory. He veered and headed toward me.

"Stupid idiot!" I hollered.

With seconds to spare, I dove underwater and pushed downward with all my strength, my heart pounding from the effort. My ears protested the pressure eight feet down. I swung my camera up to catch a clip of the boat's propeller blades churning madly above me. I would figure out how to use it for a boating safety PSA. People needed to be more aware.

Once he was past my spot, I surged upward, expelling bubbles, and then I surfaced with a gasp. The only good news was that adrenaline was making it easier to operate in the cold water. The boater had paused, probably to start fishing in a new spot.

"Hey!" I hollered. "I'm swimming here!"

The prow of the boat was facing me. I couldn't see the fisherman, which meant he might not see me. He gunned the engine and closed the distance between us fast. Maybe he hadn't heard me.

I dove downward. As he sped by dangerously close above me, I gained speed by gripping the slippery boulders, aiming for the flat, underwater stone in the center of the pile. I surfaced with a gasp, switched my camera to a daylight setting, and then started filming the idiot.

The prow was coming at me again, the engine full on. I stood, knee deep, with sheets of water shedding from my limbs and bathing suit. With an angry scowl, I held the camera in front of me and made it known that I was filming his careless spree. The boulders protected me. They would wreck his propeller if he got too close. He was too low in the boat for me to see him. He swept by and veered in a way that cast a wash of cold water at me. Was that the first moment he'd realized I wasn't a log or some other object bobbing in the water? Or was it an outright attack?

Alarmed, I lost my balance and slipped, knocking my knee against one of the boulders. I could tell it was bleeding even without looking. Raymond's description of the spot came to the rescue. My teenaged neighbors loved collecting stones and mussel shells from the bottom of the lake to toss out and challenge each other: *Can you retrieve a stone in one shot without coming up for air? How many seconds will it take?*

Looking down, I confirmed that they'd left an assortment of stones on top of the boulder. I could thank my lucky stars for the kind of eye-hand coordination that comes with years of aiming a camera at fast-moving targets, plus a secret pastime my mother would have put an end to if she'd known about it: helping a friend's younger brother hone his baseball skills during high school. With any luck, my aim was still pretty good.

With my camera gripped in my left hand and a new video rolling to catch him in the act, I picked up a smooth stone the size of my palm just as the boater swerved and came at me again. This time, I was prepared. I ducked down, turned my head away as the water struck me, then I stood up, aimed, and sent the rock hurtling his way with the hardest throw I'd ever mustered. It didn't strike him, as hoped. But it struck his engine.

It sputtered and threatened to quit. I reached for another stone, stood, and aimed. The rock all but whistled as it cut through the air as he bent over the laboring engine. It struck him on his back. I heard him curse. I picked up another stone and whipped it forward with my best impression of a major league throw. It struck him on the back of his neck.

"*Shit*," he hollered.

The boat swung away, the engine laboring.

I'd done it. I'd driven him off.

My pulse was pounding in my limbs. It helped keep me warm for the moment. I waited to make sure he truly was retreating before I ventured into open water. Then I realized I'd dropped my camera.

"Crap!"

I could see it four feet below me, settled between two boulders. I had to reach for it carefully, or it would tumble away into twelve feet of water. I inhaled, then dove downward with my eyes wide open in the half-clear water. I gripped the camera strap, tugged, and it released.

Fading in strength as I surfaced, I decided I needed to warm up before I attempted the swim back to the beach. Raymond had done this one year when the water was unusually cold, standing on the center rock and rubbing life back into his limbs so he didn't overtax himself.

Once again, water cascaded from my bathing suit as I stood. I had the good luck of getting a stretch of sunshine as the clouds tumbled by overhead. I attached the camera to my bathing suit strap to have my hands free.

Staring in the direction the attacker had fled, I rubbed my arms and made note of landmarks so I could figure out where the boat might be tied up. I slapped my legs, which were an angry shade of red. I took this as a good sign. It would be time to panic if they turned white.

I wasn't warm by any stretch, but clouds now obscured the sun, and my heart had stopped slamming. To keep an eye out for the boat, I decided to swim back to the beach above the surface. With the camera in hand, I growled as I rejoined the cold lake. My limbs were stiff, making my sad swimming style all the more ungainly.

"Miserable, selfish, rotten, *jerk*," I seethed, plowing forward through the water. "This was supposed to be a sacred event! I had it planned out for months. The day, late afternoon. You *ruined* it!"

Forty feet from the rocks, gasping for air, I paused and wiped water from my eyes as I caught a split-second glimpse of a man on the beach diving into the water, fully clothed. He churned toward me at top speed like an Olympic athlete.

Was it the crazy boater coming to finish me off?

With a moan, I plowed back toward the boulders, hoping I could get there and secure a stone before he reached me. He was loaded with unspent energy, and operating from warmth. My feet and hands felt like ice, and my heart was exploding.

Gasping, terrified, I yelped as his hand slipped past my shoulder, then he regrouped and got a good grip on the back of my bathing suit.

"*Uhhhh ...*"

I kicked backward and caught one of his legs.

He cursed and grabbed me again.

"*Sonny*. What the hell?"

Sinking, struggling, I swiveled and was shocked to see it was Dan.

"How," I gasped, "Are you ...?"

"Come on."

He looped one arm around my torso and started hauling me backward through the water. It gave me a minute to catch my breath. He was cursing, impatient to get the job done, which was not the kind of attitude one needs during a rescue attempt.

I'd driven off the boater. I'd almost made it back on my own. He was treating me like an incompetent, helpless victim.

With a burst of motion, I escaped from his arm.

"I can get back … on my own."

Wet and angry, he sputtered, "I can do it faster!"

As he reached for me, I dove downward, kicking hard and scooping with my hands to complete the journey my preferred way. Dan hollered above me, swimming with efficient speed and easily keeping up with my underwater journey. I drove myself onward until my lungs threatened to explode, and then I reached the shallow beach area.

I lurched above the surface, inhaling in gasps, grateful to feel my feet connect with the sandy lake bottom. I staggered, tripped, plunged underwater, and staggered again. Dan gripped my elbow, plus the back of my bathing suit, and "helped" me forward, which had all the appeal of being dragged forward like a piece of luggage.

"Let go," I managed.

"Are you sure?"

"Yes, I'm sure!"

I staggered, my pulse thrumming. While I squashed through the shallows, feeling like a pulpy mess, he emerged like some kind of majestic rendition of Poseidon, with droplets flashing in his hair and water cascading from the muscles under his shirt.

"What the hell, Sonny?" he demanded.

"Give me a second," I gasped.

With my pulse pounding in every artery, every vein, I reached my blanket and grabbed my towel. The textured terry cloth helped bring life back into my icy skin as I stared toward the spectral glints and lapping wavelets where I might be floating if the boater had caught me off guard. Knocked senseless by the hull, I would have gulped in water, an easy target for him to speed past again and slice me to bits with the propeller.

No, I realized. Propeller blades would cause a whole lot of damage. Maybe the awful boater had meant to trap me in the middle of the lake, hoping hypothermia would sap my strength until I couldn't make it to the shore. It would look as if I'd drowned on my own.

Dan was asking questions as he rubbed warmth into my icy hands. I didn't hear what he was saying. Telling him about the boater would spark the need for crime scene tape and officers looking for evidence and a fresh round of complexities in my life. Questions. Chaos. Scrutiny. Criticism. Stable Bartlett would show up. I was certain of it.

"I can't survive another crime scene," I murmured.

Dan paused abruptly. "What?"

"I'm fine."

"You don't look fine."

"I will be. Just give me a second."

25

Slowly, I focused on Dan, who was still in rescue mode. He settled me to the grass, pushed my towel aside, and took hold of my right leg.

"*Excuse* me," I protested.

"You've got a scrape. Not too bad."

I followed his frown to a raw spot on my knee. Startled by the sting of the antiseptic he applied to the abrasion, I yanked my leg from his grasp.

"Sorry," he said. "The label says it's a non-hurt variety."

He offered the bottle for my inspection, as if that were the most important thing to clear up. Then he tossed it aside with an air of having too many questions to know where to start.

"Oh, do let me go first," I said. "What are you doing here?"

Dan started to respond, then his gaze snagged on my bathing suit.

"Are those tire marks?" he said.

"Yes, my cousin knocked the suit out of my mailbox, so—back to my question. What are you doing here?"

"You were late. We were supposed to meet at three."

"What time is it now?" I said.

"Three forty-five."

I gaped. "I'm sorry, I had no idea …"

"What happened out there?" Dan said. "You were yelling, and didn't seem to hear me call over to you. Who were you hollering at?"

"Help me to my feet. I need to walk around."

Dan gripped my hand and steadied me as I climbed onto shaky legs. It was only now that I understood how far I'd pushed myself out in the water. Limping to help blood flow into my chilled feet, I wilted internally. Instead of invigorating myself with a swim in order to tackle my photo shoot at the race in two days, I'd worn myself to the bone.

Shivering, I took over the job of rubbing life into my hands.

"Sonny, you're strong and athletic," Dan said. "You wouldn't have a problem for no reason. I need to know what went on here."

I was too cold and rattled to devise a way to alert him about the boat attack without sparking an entire crime scene investigation.

"Sonny?" Dan prompted.

"Just so you know, I had a great swim until—" I regrouped. "I was on my way back when you dove into the water. I hadn't a clue it was you."

"You were struggling. I saw you."

"I was cold. Speaking of which, I need to head home."

"Hey, *hey*." Dan's hand snagged my arm as I headed toward my car. "Why did you say you can't survive another crime scene?"

"I didn't say that."

"Yes, you did. When you first came out."

"Maybe you misheard me."

A reprieve from his astute gaze came in the form of his ringing phone. He apologized and stepped away to take the call.

I pressed the power button of my camera and watched the video I'd taken from eight feet deep with the propeller blades chopping a swath of chaotic bubbles overhead. The next video showed the boat surging toward me, with the driver sitting too low for me to see him. The engine growled as he swerved to create a wake, and then I hollered something as a plume of water struck the lens with a burst of sound.

"What's that?" Dan said, suddenly behind me.

I shut off the camera. "Just checking a video."

"I heard a boat over the speaker."

"It was from last summer."

"I heard you hollering. You sounded upset."

"That was … we were horsing around."

217

Dan studied me. "Who?"

"Joan. And Harry and Jess."

Dan didn't look chilled at all. He looked tanned, handsome, and alert, and very much like the smartest police officer on the planet.

"You're saying you knew Joan, Harry, and Jess last summer," he said carefully. "*Before* you inherited the farm?"

"I meant it's a video of Arlene's family. My best friend."

Dan was not buying any of it. I had to escape ASAP.

"I need to head home," I said. "I'm wet, and cold—"

"Sonny." Dan snagged my arm. "Please talk to me. What's going on?"

"You're being ridiculous."

"Was it your cousins 'horsing around?'" he said with air quotes. "I've looked into the record of harassment. I can picture them throwing your camera out into deep water so you had to go get it."

"I think it's my turn to be asking questions. You've been to my farm. You've seen me cry. You've looked through my photos. All I know is that you're a trooper. There's an imbalance in our … thing."

Looking annoyingly reasonable, Dan accepted the change of subject and spread his hands. "If it'll help, what do you want to know?"

"Tell me about Aaron."

This threw him, but only for a moment. "Aaron was my best friend growing up. I assume you know how he died. It hit me really hard."

"Were you angry about it?"

"Shock, anger, denial, guilt." Dan motioned with one hand. "All the stages, all the time for a while. Now there's acceptance."

"I'm worried you're making it sound like a list."

"It's not a list. But it is contained, more or less."

"You forgot isolation."

Looking impatient, Dan stepped away a few paces, then he exhaled as he stared across the lake with a pensive frown. An epiphany of some sort was going on. I could tell by the way tension was leaving his shoulders. When he turned back to me, his eyes reflected the sense that I'd brought on some sort of soulful moment he hadn't expected.

"Yeah," he said. "It's why I took the post up north."

"I've pieced together that Aaron was on the receiving end of one of the awful surprises," I said softly. "It's why you're invested in the case."

"That's part of it. Where is this coming from?"

I didn't want to mention Nadine's dark conclusions. The important thing was, Dan's explanation fit what I'd arrived at on my own.

"It's natural to want to know about an important event in your life," I said. "Balance is a key element of friendships."

"Sonny, come on. What happened out there today?"

"Please let it go."

"Which means yes, something did happen."

Dan frowned at his watch as if the need to dash to the lake for a potential rescue had come at an inconvenient time.

"Well, pardon me for keeping you for five whole minutes to hear a few details about your life," I said crossly, wishing I wasn't shivering from head to toe, my skin so clammy that it cut the power of my indignation by half. "You clearly have better things to do."

Dan looked at the ground on his left, then his right. "Am I not standing here after coming to your aid? Maybe I'm hallucinating."

"You looked at your watch."

"Because if your cousins were here, they'll be long gone by now."

I motioned toward his truck. "It's ok if you need to leave. You're a guy, so work is your main area of interest."

For the third time, Dan gently snagged my arm and held me in place. "I know you're stalling, but to your point, I've told you several times, in all kinds of ways, that part of the reason I'm still in the area is because of you. If that spells a lack of interest—"

"I guess not."

"You *guess* not."

"I can't have this conversation while I'm freezing." I crossed to my car and opened the door. "I need to change into dry clothes."

"Not here?" Dan said.

"Yes, here. I'm freezing, and it's your fault."

"You're the one who went swimming in sixty-four-degree water."

"You kept me here beyond my limits."

As I dug through my car for the spare clothes I always brought for unplanned photo shoots, I felt frustrated and angry. Fed up with all the attacks I kept having to handle every five minutes.

Cursing under his breath, Dan snatched my blanket from the ground and arrived in time to hold it up so I wasn't stripping off my top in front of any cars that passed by on the road. He said nothing as he waited, but out of the corner of my eye, I saw him expressing his irritation with eye rolls, silent comments, and a general lack of buy-in for what I was doing. I'd told him we weren't suited for each other. Here was the proof.

"I didn't take you for a prude," I said.

Dan's jaw dropped. "I'm a *what?*"

"You heard me." My jeans and shirt stuck a little as I pulled them on over my damp skin, but it felt good to have shed the dripping wet bathing suit. "There are accommodations for showering outdoors in the nude all over the place. I've done it many times. In Hawaii, and Costa Rica. You need to get around more."

"Are you done?" he demanded.

"Not quite." I zipped up my jeans, put on my shoes, pulled on my blue hoodie, and took my time adjusting the sleeves above my wrists. "Now I'm done."

Dan roughly folded the blanket, glaring at me as if I'd crossed a line that nobody in his experience had dared to approach. Then his expression indicated he'd landed on a way to get over it.

"You know what?" he said. "I agree. It sucks being wet and cold."

Watching him cross to his truck and wrench open the door, I realized he was taking the childish route of blowing off steam by making the same extreme choice I had made. He dug around behind the seat and pulled out a fresh pair of jeans and a different shirt.

"Now who's being a nut?" I said. "You're a police officer."

"Hold the blanket up, if you can't handle it," Dan said.

"Nope. You're on your own."

I followed him and folded my arms as he stripped off his shirt, revealing a holy mackerel kind of chest and arm muscles that had grown pink from the cold. Dan reached for the top button on his jeans. The zipper went down. He wasn't bluffing. He was going for it.

"All *right*." I grabbed the blanket and held it up with my arms outstretched. "People say I'm stubborn."

On the other side of the blanket, there were reflective fenders and gleaming windows and a rearview mirror that made it very difficult to not invade his privacy. I did my best.

Tossing his drenched jeans into the truck, Dan muttered a stream of commentary that included liberal use of the f-word, Costa Rica, people calling him a prude, and things I couldn't quite hear. The good thing was, we would emerge from the double dare warm and dry, thanks to our preparedness. The bad thing was, neither one of us would be looking back on the moment as a high note in terms of personal growth.

Dan zipped up, grabbed the blanket, then he tossed it aside and pulled me into a kiss. Sudden. Intense. Thrilling.

I closed my eyes and responded to his wonderful, expressive lips. Soft and gentle. Then playful. Then very sexy. He was taking me on a ride, and showing me who was in charge: how dare I call *him* a prude. We melded together, moving, turning until we bumped into his truck, his arms around me, and my hands exploring his back, the way his muscles flexed. I felt his heart beating, and heat rising from his chest. I started making breathy moans, and his kiss agreed that things were going really well.

Like a master chef preparing bread dough for the oven, Dan set about relaxing me, shaping me against him until I was completely pliable and willing to assume any kind of position he wanted next. I was starting to warm up and feel like it was time to toss the blanket on the ground and rip his shirt off, but the sound of a passing car pulled me from the thought, and the next thing I knew, guilt was creeping into the back of my mind. We would never rise to the demands of a meaningful connection if I held things back, starting with the boater.

With a groan, I leaned away and looked at him.

Then I noticed we weren't alone.

Dan turned and followed my gaze to an elderly man who was standing next to a hatchback. Maybe we'd been out of view at first, then apparently, when he'd clapped eyes on us, he'd frozen in place with his eyes wide from a sense of not knowing how to handle the situation, his fishing pole and tackle box suspended in his hands.

"Afternoon, Dan," the man said.

"Hey, Mr. Wheeler."

"You got her resuscitated all right?"

Dan cracked a smile. "I think so."

The man approached with a grin as Dan and I pulled apart in order to conduct a civilized introduction. I told him who I was.

"I know all about you," Mr. Wheeler said. "You're Raymond's girl."

"I am."

"I've got his flies right here in my tackle box. Whatever he did, Raymond wanted to get it right. Kind of like this one." He indicated Dan. "A bit on the wild side early on. Good at sports as well as books. FYI, he's got a stubborn streak."

"He used to be the principal at the high school," Dan explained.

"Well, I can see you two have business to sort out," Mr. Wheeler said. "I'll be down on the steps seeing if the trout are biting."

Once we were alone again, Dan returned his hands to my shoulders and pulled me close. Not steamy close, as he'd done before. Respectably close. He raised his eyebrows.

"You were about to confess something," he said.

I had to admit. He was good.

"First, I hate being rescued," I said. "I really do."

"You equate being rescued with being weak. I get it."

"And before we move on, we're two for two on the kissing front. You know what I mean. Sudden. Awesome. I need to know a few things. Like, are you a Brumby sort of guy, or—?"

"I'm not a player, if that's your concern," Dan said. "For me, a strong connection needs to happen first." He motioned between our foreheads. "Ask me to explain it, and I can't."

"It still might be a fluke. A response to the drama of the moment."

"Do you feel calm now?" Dan said.

"Sure, but—"

Gently pulled into a third round of unanticipated kissing, I found myself relaxing against his chest without hesitation, those strong hands of his traveling all over the place, and his lips assuring me that this was no dream, it was a reality I could bank on any time he reached for me, or I reached for him. Gently released a moment later, I wobbled a little as I resumed the job of balancing my weight without his assistance.

Once again, Dan raised his eyebrows. "Three for three?"

"I guess so."

He cracked up. "I'll take it. Look, I'm just as thrown as you are on this thing between us happening out of the blue. It's got me struggling as I try to hit the right tone. Like earlier. I'm sorry if I got it wrong when I asked what went on here today."

"No, I get where you're coming from."

"So …?"

"Right. The videos."

I retrieved my camera, pressed the power button, and handed it to Dan. I could tell he expected to see Martin Bergley or some other minor menace in my life causing trouble during my swim. As the first video played, showing the propeller churning above the spot where I'd taken refuge, Dan looked at me with an expression of horror.

"Why would you not want to report *this?*"

"Focus on the other videos. They show how I coped."

"Who was it?" Dan said. "Can you ID them?"

"One guy. I didn't see his face."

After he watched the videos, Dan went on a journey of processing the moment, walking in a circle with all kinds of silent curses and other indications that understanding my unique cross-section of traits was going to take a team of scientists to sort out.

"He's long gone now," Dan said severely.

I pointed. "The boat went straight over there."

"Who knew you were coming here today?"

"Everybody."

I explained how I'd divulged my plan to the people who'd shown up to weed my strawberry patch, and how the boat was on the lake before I'd arrived. I'd heard the engine engage while I was underwater.

"Why would someone come after me?"

"You're more transparent than you realize," Dan said. "I'm an open kind of guy, so I don't mind being assessed. Other people will see you as a threat. Your camera will be needed as evidence. It might be a while before

223

you get it back." Dan looked up and signaled to a guy on a motorcycle pulling into the parking area. "I'll be right back."

In less than a minute, Dan returned with one of the two journals that he'd borrowed, and a bag from a local restaurant.

"When I took the call earlier, I asked a friend to bring food since you looked cold," he said. "Burger, fries, chocolate shake."

"Thank you," I said. "You're done reading this journal?"

"That one, yes. After what happened here today ..." He leafed through the volume, reversed to a page, then handed me the journal. "You should read this July entry from a few years ago."

"Nice motorcycle. Is he a colleague?"

"He's a trooper," Dan agreed.

"I can't believe today got ruined. It was supposed to be uplifting."

"I know, Sonny," Dan said softly, giving my shoulders a bolstering squeeze. "Give me five minutes to get a team out on the lake to look for the boat, then I need to ask for a huge favor."

I groaned. "Can't the camera serve as my statement?"

"Eat the burger. Read the passage."

In my car, which was blissfully warm from sitting in the sun for a few hours, I wolfed down the food as I read the entry Dan had indicated. It was about Kyle Gilbert's spree in a speedboat.

He could have killed those kids in the swimming area, Raymond had written. *I flipped the motor out of the water and said, do you see these awful blades? How fast they go? Think what they might have done! Kyle smirked, his usual go-to routine. I felt bad for the kid early on, seeing what a struggle it was to be faulted for elements of his life he had no control over. Nadine's lifestyle. Couldn't organize his thoughts or bear to wait his turn. Sure, it's a condition. Nadine refuses to believe it's something he needs to work on.*

Next thing I know, Chuck Brewster is in my face saying who did I think I was, hollering at the boy for horsing around. Chuck has a mean right hook. I didn't want to mar the day with a fist fight. He's been a friend all these years, but I don't know about Chuck anymore.

I understood that Dan wanted me to read it because the threat of injury by boat was similar to what I'd experienced that day. I had to admit, his notion was possible, but what sense did it make? Why would Kyle call me one day, and try to kill me the next?

"Sonny?" Dan said, returning to my car.

"Can I go now?"

"Come on out."

I allowed him to reach in and gently extract me from my car. It seemed only polite to say our goodbye face to face, but I was distracted by the lack of a red truck in the parking lot. Only Mr. Wheeler's hatchback, my car, and the motorcycle remained.

"Did somebody take your truck?" I said.

"The trooper who brought the food. I'll explain all that in a minute." Dan scrutinized me. "Are you ok after that attack?"

"Three rocks, three direct hits. That's the takeaway."

"You looked really rattled at first."

"Then I bounced back. I know it's hard to grasp how I operate—"

"No, we're good." Dan sighed and rubbed his neck. "You were right when I looked at my watch a while ago. Partly, anyway. I had a thing scheduled for five o'clock. I was concerned I would be late. I'm sorry. I'm multitasking. I haven't been at my best."

"You're babbling a little …"

"Remember me saying I was here for my mother's birthday?" Dan rushed on. "I gave her a book she'd wanted, a bouquet of flowers. She only wanted one thing." He motioned toward the motorcycle. "She's hated the idea of me having it from the start. Asked me to sell it."

I paused. "That's *your* bike?"

"It belonged to Aaron. He left it to me when he died."

I focused on Dan's brown eyes. "Oh …"

"Riding his bike was all I did on my off hours when it first happened. There's a risk with bikes. I was distracted, upset. I pushed my luck a few times. My folks rode my case about it to the point where I decided it was best to head out. I took the border gig. Now, I've come up with a positive way to part with the bike and move forward."

"By agreeing to sell it?"

"Money won't change hands." Dan opened his phone and showed me a shot of his friend, Aaron, looking heartbreakingly happy in that moment, grinning as he straddled the motorcycle. "There's a list of troopers and deputies who want to own the bike for a while. Ride it in Aaron's memory. Like I said, a positive move."

"That's wonderful. A great idea."

I paused and waited for a moment, seeing that Dan was struggling, his hands moving as if to formulate one of those bowl metaphors he liked to use. In the end, he sighed and gave up.

"I told you how surprising you are," he managed. "Earlier, you pegged my year with lightning speed. Drilled right down to the isolation issue. This afternoon was supposed to be my last ride on the bike. After you and I got ice cream." Dan indicated the two leather jackets resting on the seat of the Kawasaki. "I'm asking you to join me. Partly because my sense is you need a break from the chaos. A chance to unwind, but here's the thing. I need to explain the rest of the context in case it seems ..." He paused and rubbed his brow. "You lost Raymond. I don't know what that's been like for you. Your errand here today ... I get the sense you picture him watching you from afar. From heaven, that sort of thing."

"Totally," I said. "It's how I get by."

"I've had the same thing going on. With Aaron. I got to thinking, with handing the bike down the line to others, it has to be done right. *Shit.*" Dan walked away a few paces, cursing under his breath, with emotion in his eyes. "I'm sorry. Give me a second."

"Dan, it's ok. I understand how hard this will be."

"That's good because the rest sounds nutty."

"It doesn't. Not to me."

"Hence, why I'm asking you to ride with me. I need to set the right tone for moving on. I need to turn the corner. To not live with the dark vibe. You're so positive, Sonny. Full of light and hope as you look out on the world. I need to borrow some of that in case there's any merit in Aaron keeping tabs. It wasn't great for him in the end. Things went to shit, and he gave up. I need to let him know that it's ok for *him* to move on, too."

"I get it, Dan. Let's go. I'm in."

"Thank you," he said softly.

From not disclosing any details about his private world, he'd leaped into the ozone layer of sharing an important chapter of his life. I could see in his gaze that he believed I would *help* with the healing process. I was floored. Downright stunned.

In a somber tone, with touching emotional pauses, Dan explained that he'd help Aaron rebuild the classic Kawasaki over a span of years. He shrugged on the leather jacket he'd worn in my kitchen the night of the break-in. It had belonged to Aaron. He presented me with his own leather jacket, complete with the beaten-up look of having survived hail storms, lightning strikes, landslides, and other kinds of wear and tear.

I zipped up the jacket that was way too long in the sleeves, and roomy to an extravagant degree, then I adjusted the helmet he handed to me.

"Ready?" Dan said.

"Ready."

26

I'd ridden behind a man on a motorcycle a few times, so the sensation of hugging Dan's chest on a powerful machine was not new to me. It was a unique moment where I could straddle a man, up close and personal, in plain view out in public. I could pass the Pope's motorcade, and my behavior wouldn't be seen as the least bit inappropriate.

With a helmet on, there was a bit of an alien element to my view of the world passing by, but it didn't diminish my awareness of how Dan had attempted to keep in touch with his departed friend through his bike. Smooth and effortless as it shifted up and down gears, surging forward on straight stretches, and easing around curves on wooded lanes, the stirring, ever-present growl of the Kawasaki had me thinking it was almost like experiencing Aaron's voice joining us on the ride. I could picture Dan wanting to continue on and on through familiar haunts of the past, unable to face the empty silence after he shut off the engine.

Once Dan felt me relax into the rhythm of taking curves, he surged forward with more of a commanding approach. Having been instructed to keep my arms around his waist for stability and safety reasons, I was happy to comply, enjoying the wind blustering against my visor, shoulders, and legs. I tuned in on the subtle movements of his arms when he used the throttle or the clutch, then almost in the same instant, the slight flexing of his left thigh as he shifted up or down gears. Every now and then he glided to a stop at a crossroad and balanced the bike with both feet. The engine dropped down to a rhythmic growl, a quiet rumble of power. Dan turned and checked in to see if I was still with the program.

I nodded and gave his chest a squeeze.

At Rock Your World, we tasted different samples of ice cream and frozen yogurt until the girl behind the counter started to look huffy and irritated, especially when we finally picked chocolate.

As we ate at a picnic table, I was happy to see Dan in a much brighter mood. He pointed to the cars lined up behind us.

"Parking lots seem to be your sweet spot for romance. Too many people here, I guess."

"You're the one who turned up the heat at the lake," I said.

"You stripped off your clothes right in front of me."

"There was a blanket. It was all very proper."

Dan stood, crossed around the table, then sat close to me and confided in a near whisper, "The thing is, I have really good peripheral vision."

"I do, too. So there."

"My ice cream is melting *really* fast," Dan said.

"Then stop causing trouble."

"Right, you claim to be a snail. I'm not buying it."

"What happened to the solemn mood?"

Dan blew out a breath. "Thanks for bringing it back."

"I'm sorry. I'm not sure how to—" Seeing him crack a smile, I nudged him hard. "What is wrong with you? It's not funny to toy with people."

"With you, it's hilarious, and you give it right back. Now, the entire ride here, it was clear what you wanted. Let's give it a whirl."

I gaped. "I beg your pardon?"

"Learning to shift gears on the bike. Where did *your* mind go?" Clearly enjoying the back and forth, Dan straddled the bench and motioned for me to face him and do the same. "Come on. Hands out like you're on the bike and ready to roll."

I had to admit, I'd flexed my hands as he'd shifted up and down gears, curious to know how it would feel to operate the motorcycle.

"Your right hand operates the throttle and the front brake," Dan said. "Right foot is the back brake. Left hand operates the clutch. Left foot controls the gears. First gear press down, the rest lift the gear up. Start in neutral. Ready?"

"Not really."

"It'll get easier. Let's start with the clutch."

Dan described a friction zone where the clutch was slowly released, an action that would transfer power to the rear wheel. In first gear, the imaginary bike would move forward without any need to use the throttle. Next, he said to gently apply the front brake.

"Why am I stopping already?" I said.

"You're getting a feel for balancing the bike," he explained.

"If I *were* to keep going …"

"You're moving your wrist the wrong way," Dan said. "Rolling the throttle toward the front is easing down in speed, rolling back is how you'd pick up speed."

"This is harder than learning pole dancing."

Dan paused. "Please explain."

"I told you I'm taking lessons."

"You were fibbing," he said.

I smiled. "Well, I'm giving it a try now."

"See?" Dan flipped his hands. "This is not snail behavior. At *all*."

The lesson came to a pause as Dan got a text about the search for the boat. He'd no sooner stepped away to make a call when I saw Earl heading toward me from the ice cream stand. I lurched from the table and crossed the picnic area to intercept him, desperate to send him packing. I wasn't about to let anything ruin Dan's afternoon.

"I thought that was you," Earl said, looking sober and sounding almost normal for the first time since I'd met him. "What the hell are you doing?"

"I'm having ice cream."

"With a biker? I saw who you're with."

"You look good, Earl. It's nice to see you sober."

"I mostly don't touch liquor on weekdays," he said. "I work hard, and so does Everett. He deserves better than how you're acting here."

"Earl, I *never* encouraged Everett," I said. "Not once. It's a moot point because your son has moved on. He has a new love interest."

"Since when?"

"This morning. Talk to him."

"Until I hear it from Everett, I need to make sure you stay in one piece." Earl reached for my arm. "I'll bring you home."

I pulled away. "Ok, I'm done being polite about this. I am not keen on your son. At all. I don't need your help. Don't come to my farm uninvited. Just get your ice cream, then head home."

"What do I tell Everett?"

"He won't care. Now back off. I mean it."

I all but flexed the way a fierce badass would do to convey an air of menace on the subject of being disobeyed. He paused, looking startled, then seeing Dan on his way toward us, Earl made a fed-up motion with his hands, then stepped away.

"What was that about?" Dan demanded.

"It's Earl, Everett's father."

Scowling, Dan said, "I'll talk to him."

"No." I gripped his arm. "I handled it. This time, I was rude."

"What's your connection to these people?"

I groaned. "I didn't want to mar the afternoon."

"Sit." Dan pointed. "Explain."

With him studying me intently, I began at the farmer's market, where I'd essentially met Everett and Earl for the first time, then I gave a quick summary of my conversations with Nadine because it was high time I told Dan that Kyle had called me.

"The call was brief," I said. "Kyle sounded scared."

As I sent the contact information from the call to Dan's phone, he said, "Why didn't you tell me earlier?"

"You said you didn't want to discuss the case with me."

He closed his eyes. "Yeah, I did."

"I'm sorry. Crazy you, seeing me as a source of light."

Dan focused on me, and his scowl began to smooth. "Sonny ..." He snagged the back of my jeans and scooted me closer across the bench, which made me laugh, then he draped his arm around my shoulders. "Do you know my takeaway from this moment? Nadine has been hammering at you to not trust me, but here you are, letting me pull you closer. A day or two ago, you would have popped up like a Champagne cork."

"What if you'd given me a splinter just now?"

"No, no, I won't be baited into proposing any kind of hands-on assistance. I live by a strict code." Dan paused. "I would hold up a mirror so you could do the extraction yourself. In fact, *please* tell me you have a splinter in your ass …"

"This has gone completely sideways," I said, wiping my eyes from laughing. "I'm supposed to be cheering *you* up."

"We help each other. That's how it works." His arm tightened around me for a moment, then he studied me. "Now, tell me about this pole dancing thing. It's a joke, right?"

"It turns out I'm a natural at it. I learned a move called 'Hello Boys.'"

"*Shit.*" Dan rubbed his eyes. "I walked right into that."

I couldn't help but smile as he turned a little pink. Yup, he was right about my unconvincing performance in the slow lane. He had dimples under his beard when he smiled a certain way. It had me veering wildly and blurting things.

"I practice yoga and tai chi on a regular basis," I said. "Those skills seem to mesh with pole work. But you saw how I swim. My coordination isn't a hundred percent."

"That's because you were exhausted and cold."

I confessed the truth. With his memory of what he'd witnessed at the lake fresh in his mind, he tried very hard to keep a straight face.

"I'm sorry," Dan said when I folded my arms and arched an eyebrow. "I blame whoever taught you. What I caught onto was … don't hit me, ok? You have noodle arms."

I cracked up, despite my best effort to scowl.

"Look." Dan leaned forward and lifted his right elbow. "Picture your arm at forty-five degrees. Fingers together, but relaxed. Reach for a spot in the water further from your head than you've been doing. That one element will make a difference."

"I guess."

"Here you are again. You *guess.*"

"I'm supposed to believe your every word?"

Dan smiled. "When have I steered you wrong?"

Kiss Your Strawberries Goodbye

"The jury is still out," I said. "By the way, I haven't figured out the wolf reference. I've searched the house, and I asked Joan."

"Keep it in mind. I'm sure you'll get there."

It was six o'clock when we returned to the lake. Dan stowed the extra helmet and the jacket he'd given me to use. It was clear that he would be heading out for a solo last ride on his way home. I waited next to my car, not surprised to see his mood back in the somber range as he attempted to fashion a parting for the unusual day.

"Thank you for the ride," I said. "I'll never forget it."

Dan studied me. "You were attacked out there. Are you really ok?"

"In my shoes, would you need coddling?"

"I suppose I wouldn't."

He pulled me into a comfortable hug, with his arms encircling me and my hands resting against the small of his back. We stayed there for a moment, showing that we could relax together and let our quiet breathing and steady pulses do the talking for once. I'd figured the serious occasion would rule out a parting kiss, but I was wrong. He leaned back and looked at me, then he kissed me with a soft brush of lips, the way couples do when it's an ordinary, everyday event to acknowledge a bond.

"Mm," he murmured. "Chocolate."

"You had chocolate ice cream, too."

"I guess so."

"You *guess* so." I paused as our inside joke didn't turn his concerned frown into a smile. "You don't seem to be letting go."

"Somebody went after you today," he said. "Your house is isolated. The idea of you being up there on your own ..."

"You know I can handle myself." I gently pulled away from his embrace. "Remember, three rocks, three direct hits."

With the lake casting glints behind him, and the golden, angled rays bringing soulful depth to his brown eyes, Dan wrestled with the understanding that I needed to call my own shots.

"I'll check in tomorrow," he finally said. "Call if you need anything."

"You too."

I climbed into my car and followed Dan out of the parking lot. On Aaron's restored Kawasaki, he gave a quick wave as he turned right.

233

I turned left.

I alternated between smiling at the funny things he'd said, then agonizing over his friend's tragic, untimely death.

Wasn't it just like life to deliver a few swift kicks in the pants to unhinge my coping skills, followed by the introduction of a man whose mix of complexities I couldn't have dreamed up in a million years.

* * *

"No, no, *no*," I moaned, jarred awake in the dark living room as Raymond's landline phone began ringing at 1:15 a.m. This was what I got for following Detective Allen's wishes and plugging it back in with a new tape in the answering machine. I'd figured that after getting the cold shoulder for multiple days and nights, with no pick up on my end of the line, the awful caller would have given up that angle of harassment.

Once again, I'd figured wrong.

With a groan, I pushed up onto one elbow. I'd prepared myself to hear the warped voice over the answering machine again. It would be unsettling, but not the shock it had been the first time.

There was a pause after Raymond's recorded prompt and following beep. Instead of a machine-generated recitation of the handwritten notes, a clear, smooth, voice sounded over the answering machine's speaker. It was a familiar voice. It was my father's voice.

"Hey, it's Raymond. We need to talk. Call me."

Click.

I froze on the couch, vibrating from shock after all. I stared at the winking red light that indicated a new message had been left. Just because I'd never met Raymond didn't mean I didn't recognize his voice. I'd seen videos his friends had captured of him over the years. And there was his recorded prompt addressing callers that I'd just heard.

He'd sounded normal. He'd sounded *alive*.

Slowly, I slipped from the couch, then I stood there in the darkness for a long moment, shaking, and wondering if I were in a nightmare. It wasn't a nightmare. I felt my blood pounding through my limbs and landing against the floor through my bare feet.

I caught sight of my reflection in the window. Transparent, nearly invisible. I looked ghostly. Less real than the voice I'd just heard.

I yelped as the phone rang again.

Seized by the fear that someone might be watching me, enjoying how I'd reacted to the call, I stepped closer to the wall. I heard Raymond's recorded prompt for the second time, saying he wasn't in, and that whoever was calling should leave a message. The tape engaged.

"It's Raymond," he said so clearly that I staggered a few steps, wanting to follow the impulse to pick up and beg him to keep talking, to please be real. "I wanted to let you know I'll be out of town for a while. We'll touch base when I'm back."

Click.

With a shaking hand, I reached for my cell phone to call for support, and accidentally knocked it to the floor because I couldn't take my gaze from the winking red light. My shin collided into the coffee table. I tumbled to my knees, grabbed my phone, and crawled to a spot where moonlight helped me see the screen. As my cell phone winked on, bathing my hands and face with light, I couldn't decide who to call at 1:25 a.m. Not Joan. If she heard the messages, her shock and anguish would be worse than mine. I didn't want to bother Dan. Or should I?

The phone rang.

I shuddered from the jarring noise of it, then scrambled away and crouched in the darkness against the wall. It wasn't my father on the other end of the line. It was a madman. A murderer. I needed to focus. To resist the shock that he was trying to inflict. I needed to breathe.

"It's Raymond," he said, clear as a bell. "I've got tickets for the game on Sunday. I hope you can join me. Give me a call."

"Oh my God," I moaned.

Click.

I closed my eyes, vibrating, unable to move. If I pulled out the plug, the caller would know I'd heard the messages. He would know that he'd landed a punch. How long would he keep this up? There had to be an end to it at some point.

I curled in a ball, moaning as the phone rang again, filling the room with jarring noise. The recorded prompt played Raymond's voice, inviting the caller to torture me some more.

The tape engaged for the fourth time.

"It was a place of mist and darkness," Raymond said softly, as if he were reciting a poem. "Of whispers and shadows. Even on a clear night, moonlight never penetrated the gloom."

I held my breath, shaking as I stared at the machine.

"When he woke, he couldn't remember how he'd gotten there," Raymond softly went on. "How he'd come to that place under the dark trees. He looked down at his hands. They felt chilled and numb. Pieces started coming back to him. The coffin. The mourners. Then he knew. He was there, in the graveyard, because he was dead."

With a feral scream, I scrambled to the phone and yanked the cord from the outlet, then I retreated and sat with my back against the wall and my arms wrapped around my knees. Whoever had called had reduced me to a state of quaking, senseless idiocy. If he burst in at that moment, he could easily catch me. And kill me.

I'd only pulled the phone line from the outlet, so the answering machine's red light winked on like an evil eye as I sat in the shadows against the wall. Detective Allen said I was the only one getting horrid calls in the dark of night. I was the madman's plaything.

Why would Raymond have said those things? What kind of horrific moment in time had made him foretell his own death in a soft, clear voice?

As long as I was breathing, I was coping. In the morning, I would figure out what to do. Who to tell, if anyone. What good had it done to report every blasted shock that I'd gone through that week? I was worse off than when the nightmare had started.

27

"You're acting really weird," Brumby said for the fifth time.

I said nothing, furious with myself for letting the Bergleys upend the barn yesterday morning. Where Raymond had arranged the hay bales in the loft in neat stacks that offered plenty of airflow, Martin and Tyler had created a messy pile that would apparently be a fire hazard during the summer months. Harry and Jess had discovered it while they were in the barn brushing Dodge. Joan had left me a voicemail about it. She'd enlisted Brumby's help. He'd arrived at four o'clock.

Hot, sweaty, and covered with prickly bits of hay chaff, I focused on stacking the last of the bales the way Brumby had shown me. With the loft door open, sunlight gave us plenty of light to work in, and a constant warm breeze stirred through the nearby trees and brought some semblance of relief as we gripped the baling twine that bound each fifty-pound rectangle of timothy and clover, then lifted the heavy load into place. Even with gloves on, I was starting to feel the burn of the baling twine on my fingers. Brumby had paused often to wipe his face and grumble about dust and chaff getting into his eyes. Some time ago, he'd started pausing to stare at me as I worked like an automaton.

"*Sonny*," he prompted.

"I'm sorry. I had a bad night."

He gripped my arm. "Tell me."

"I got a crank call. It woke me up."

"It must've been bad to put you in this mood."

"Let's finish. I'm shooting the race tomorrow."

At some point during the night, I'd conked out, curled in a ball on the floor. I'd woken with a headache. Climbed to my feet. Crossed to the bathroom and splashed water on my face. What I'd figured out was that most of the messages must have been left on someone's voicemail in the past. That's how they'd sounded. The most likely recipient would be a close contact, like family. Tyler Bergley was my best guess.

If so, I'd let a teenaged jerk reduce me to a catatonic state.

First thing that morning, I'd gone to the racetrack and stared around in a half daze. I'd assessed angles. Determined how sunlight and clouds would affect the scene. When the track photographer had asked what I was doing there, I'd coldly stared at him.

"I'm shooting the race tomorrow."

"Why?"

"Chuck Brewster hired me. He's a family friend."

"I always cover Chuck."

"It's just this once. Now get out of my way."

I'd come home. I'd gulped down a sandwich and thanked Brumby for showing up to help at four o'clock, though he was still miffed by the way I'd sent him packing the other night. Now, at last, we were finished stacking the hay. It had taken an hour and a half. The Bergleys were a problem I needed to sort out. I couldn't keep cutting them slack.

Brumby had made a call during our work. Apparently, he'd reached out to Joan. She arrived as we climbed down the loft ladder.

"Hey," she said brightly. "I came to help."

"We're done," Brumby said. "Except for this cardboard cutout of Sonny I've been dealing with. She got a crank call last night."

"*Shh*," I hissed, bumping his arm to shut him up.

"What kind of crank call?" Joan demanded.

"Don't listen to him, it's not a big deal."

"It's ok to ask for support."

"I'm sorry I'm not in the best mood. I'm just tired."

"I'll make a snack," she said. "You're probably famished."

"There's no need," I said.

"I don't mind. I'm hungry, too."

As she headed to my house, I glared at Brumby. Then I sighed and squeezed his arm with appreciation because he'd shown up for me on a day when he'd been booked from morning until night. I needed to direct my anger at the right people from now on.

"Come on, tell me about the call," he said.

"It was Raymond."

"It was *what?*"

"They used his voicemails. You need to keep it to yourself. I can't let the caller know it freaked me out."

Brumby looked relieved to see me easing out of the cardboard cutout phase. He brushed chaff from his jeans, then he decided his discomfort was to the point where he needed to strip off his shirt and give it a good shake. His quick smile said I was welcome to ogle the muscles under his T-shirt. I shook my head. He never quit.

We turned to the sudden clatter of my kitchen door banging open. Joan staggered out, lost her footing coming down the steps, then tumbled to her hands and knees on the grass.

"Joan!"

I rushed to her side and attempted to help her up. She didn't budge, her face pale and her lips drained of color. With her eyes squeezed shut and tears on her cheeks, she started to heave a little, then she firmly pursed her lips together and stopped herself.

"Oh my God," I said. "You listened to the messages."

She tightly nodded.

"I didn't want you to hear them."

"Shouldn't have … it's horrible …"

"Come inside."

"Not with those … those ..."

"Just breathe," I said. "It's ok."

"I thought up the ghost story," she tearfully whispered. "I wrote it for a Halloween party at the grange hall a few years ago. Raymond … he wanted to give the kids a scare."

Of course. A haunted house with rooms decked out with fake cobwebs and bowls filled with peeled grapes that felt like eyeballs.

"Oh, Joan. I'm so sorry."

"I need to go home." She allowed us to help her to her feet, then she swayed as she looked at me. "Who would do that?"

"I don't know."

"You told the police?"

"Not yet."

"*Why?* If you had told them, maybe I wouldn't have ..."

"I didn't want the caller to know he'd freaked me out."

"I think Joan is right, you need to call it in," Brumby said.

Brumby helped her into the passenger seat of his truck. I started to climb in too, but Joan waved me off, saying the shock had sparked the beginnings of a migraine. She needed to rest.

I knew the feeling, but my day was not over yet.

* * *

As I showered and changed into clean clothes, I debated who to contact. Dan had been dealing with issues of his own yesterday, and I didn't want to give him another chance to see that my life had devolved into the proverbial circles of hell. On the other hand, it seemed a minor incident for the detective to handle. I called Dan.

His truck pulled in at seven o'clock. He climbed out in jeans and a short-sleeved shirt with a dark gray pattern that looked like weathered wood. I waited on the porch while he listened to the recordings. I saw the message machine tape in his hand as he stepped out and joined me, his expression grim. This time, he wasn't leaving the tape for Detective Allen to pick up later on. Dan could tell I wanted it gone.

"I wasn't going to report it," I said. "Then Joan listened to the messages. It shook her up. She insisted I let you know."

"We'll need to look into the Bergleys."

I nodded. "I'm ok with that. Any news on the boat?"

"Divers found it in the area you indicated," Dan said. "The hull was damaged so it would sink. It's at the lab now."

"So, another waiting game."

"I'm afraid so." With a look of concern, Dan stood close and used his shoulder to give me a gentle bump. "I can tell the call shook you up, too. How about I stay on your couch tonight?"

"That's not necessary."

"Sonny …"

"I have the race tomorrow, so …"

I hoped a shrug would convey my inability to put my feelings into words. Joining him on the motorcycle had deepened our connection, but given his departure in the wings, there was a major downside. Dan turned to the twilight and rested his hands on the railing, drumming his fingers in a steady rhythm. Thinking, pondering possibilities.

"Have you always had a beard?" I said.

He glanced at me with a quick smile. "I've seen you studying it. You're not a fan."

"I wouldn't go that far. I assume it's a part of the northern border gig."

"That was the idea."

In the fading light, Dan gave up drumming his fingers and turned to face me. His brown eyes studied me for a moment.

"I have something really serious to talk about," he said softly.

"Oh?"

"I'll just come out with it," he said.

"Sure, go ahead."

"My colleagues are calling me Officer Buttons."

I cracked up. "That's not fair, building me up for bad news."

In truth, I was grateful he'd come up with the best way to turn the corner. Laughing was my favored lane. He'd figured it out.

"It *is* bad news," Dan insisted. "I'm hearing every known cop joke along those lines. Officer Push My Buttons. Why is Officer Buttons depressed? Because somebody pushed him too far. What did the trooper say to his belly button? You're under a vest."

His woeful delivery had me laughing all the more. "I've been lifting hay bales all afternoon. Show some mercy."

"It's been hurtful," Dan said. "Really hurtful."

"Ok, it's my turn," I said. "What's with the cocoa butter?"

He winced. "Oh, that."

"Yes, that. I can't figure it out."

"Well, I sent my parents to Hawaii for their anniversary last fall. The border gig didn't sit well with them. I wanted to make it up to them. Two weeks. Three islands. They were so thrilled to be there, they started sending gifts. Books, coconut shell art, shirts. This one, in fact." He indicated the wood pattern of the shirt. "One box had a rough transit. I didn't know they'd packed honey, cocoa butter, and barbecue sauce in it. I had to change vehicles to head for Canada. The box sat in my truck on the seat for a few months. Freezing, thawing ..."

"Uh oh."

"I wiped down the seat. I'll step up my approach."

"Leave it, maybe," I said. "Go with it."

Dan smiled. "Yeah?"

"I'm still stuck on two weeks in Hawaii. It must have cost a fortune."

He shrugged. "It's my parents. Only the best."

"So, the border gig."

"It's still in the wings." Dan winced and scrubbed a hand through his hair. "I'm expected back on Monday."

I nodded and folded my arms against the chill evening air. I dreaded the night to come, but there was no point in delaying his departure. I needed to be sharp for the race.

"Thanks for coming," I managed.

"I can stay," he said. "On the couch."

"The thing is, there will be tomorrow night, and the next night, and the night after that. Thanks for offering, but I have to face reality."

"Sonny ..."

"Spend time with your parents."

I was facing the night, his truck sitting there in the gloom. Not sure if it was best to stand there and watch him drive away, or step into the house and listen to the crunch of the truck tires receding down the gravel lane. My eyes threatened to well up. I gritted my teeth the way Joan had done when she'd lost control of herself at the bottom of the steps. Women who lived in rural towns, and had to face life on their own, had to be tough.

"You've shut down on me again," Dan said.

"It's not hard to figure out."

"What can I do to help?" he said.

Change time and space. Bring Raymond back. Meet me someplace simple. A beach. A crowded plaza. Anywhere but here. Anywhere but now.

What I actually said was, "If you include the parking lot at the diner as a separate instance … it sort of was, in a way … this is only the sixth or seventh time we've met in person."

"You know what's crazy?" Dan said. "Every one of those days has so much weight. I've never known anything like it. I've come away full of what you've said. How you looked. How you smiled. We've met a hundred times, Sonny. That's how it feels to me."

"I guess it's the same for me …"

"Let's go inside." He rubbed my shoulder. "You look cold."

"It's better out here."

Dan sighed heavily, then he stepped behind me and rested his right hand on the railing beside me, and his left hand on the railing to my left. Hugging me in a way, with my back warmed by his chest, his soft beard against my ear. It reminded me of the trick he'd done with the suitcases, slipping the weight of them easily from my hands.

If I turned, I could kiss him. I didn't dare.

"Is this ok?" he said.

I nodded.

"You don't have to do it all alone," he said softly in my ear. "I want to fast forward. So much. The case resolved. Me back in town. I want you safe. That's all I care about. You don't have to give anything up. Independence, sharks, eyelash vipers."

I refused to laugh.

"Sonny …"

"You're leaving. So, it's not fair."

"I know."

"Maybe someday," I whispered.

Dan sighed, and the feel of his breath on my neck made me shiver. It was a hint of what could be, and he knew it. He leaned closer. Waiting, hoping. His hands flexed on the railing, and I guessed he was tempted to turn me around and make me try to put him off while looking him in the eye. He knew I would buckle. But all he did was exhale, and it was torture. I couldn't help but shiver every time he breathed.

He was right. Looking back on the week with a sense of waking from a dream, I suddenly realized that every talk we'd had, every flirtation, every argument, every glance, every smile had spilled knowledge and feelings around me like an ocean wave. That's what made what he was asking impossible. When he left on Monday, all that energy would pull away like a retreating tide. Then what? Even with our rapid rise to the present moment, we'd only met a handful of times. He might change his mind. Never come back. Then I'd have two missing men in my life to feel wretched about for the rest of my days.

However warm his chest felt against my back, the night was cooling down, and it had me tightening the fold of my arms. I felt him give way a little, and knew he'd taken the move to be my final word. It was just as well. We were getting nowhere.

"This is impossible," he said.

"I'm sorry," I whispered.

Clearly torn, he balked at leaving and gripped the railing. "We've both lost people. We know the downside of thinking time will be on our side. We have a connection, Sonny. It's special, and it's real. I see you embrace it. Then you back away. I'm trying to understand."

"It would take days to explain why I need to know I can survive on my own when trouble hits the fan," I managed. "It's the absolute first thing I learned in life. It wasn't great back home in Newton, like people imagine. Donald knew I wasn't his daughter."

Dan paused. "How did he handle it?"

"You don't want to know."

"I *do* want to know." Dan exhaled. "You have the race tomorrow. Let's spend the next day together. I'll take you to the coast. We'll have dinner and talk and fill in some of the blanks."

I nodded, knowing that agreeing to the possibility was my best bet for helping him break away from the current standoff. I felt it happen. He relaxed and pulled away, just a fraction.

"Call me *any* time tonight if you need support," he said.

"I will. Thank you for coming."

"Sonny ..."

"Dan, please. This isn't helping."

"I know." He sighed a final time. "Ok."

Cool air claimed my back as he stepped away. He paused at the top of the porch steps, debating, then again at the bottom of the steps. But the decision had been made: I would watch him drive away, because I really couldn't move. He stopped next to his truck, looking as miserable as I felt, then he shook his head and climbed in.

The headlights blazed on. The taillights flared. With my arms still folded, I lifted my fingers as a quick wave.

Once his truck was on the road, surging away, I blew out a breath and stepped into my house. With my back against the closed door, I sobbed and sank down until I was sitting on the floor. Shaken and torn, just like last night, but even more wretched, unable to believe my luck.

Wiping my eyes, I regarded the plaid couch along the far wall, and congratulated myself for making the right choice. However indifferent I'd felt having Brumby spend the night on those soft cushions, I wouldn't have lasted five minutes of letting Dan get a decent night's rest. I would have thrown caution to the wind. Invited more chaos into my life. It would be glorious. Mind blowing. I could feel it in my soul.

Then the bottom would drop out because three days later he would disappear up north. The fewer memories he left, the better.

28

It was only a matter of time before Sue and Kate called and wanted to know why I'd paused my normal routine of stopping by the store every few days. I needed snacks to bring to the racetrack, so I headed to the Corner Pocket on my way to complete my assignment with Chuck.

I stepped into the delicious aromas of brewing coffee and fresh pastries, pausing for a moment to let my eyes adjust to the cozy light, and also to brace myself for any questions they'd come up with.

Once Kate caught sight of me, she signaled to her partner that their most sought-after quarry had arrived. She motioned for me to join them at one of the tables up front. I smiled and headed over.

"I can only stay a minute," I said. "I want to get to the racetrack on the early side. I'm sorry. I'm in a rush."

"We know," Sue said, handing me a bag of goodies. "Here you go, iced tea and all your favorite snacks, on the house."

"You didn't have to do this."

"Nonsense," Sue said. "We are baffled by the silence surrounding your break-in. We've rarely ever seen such a clamp down."

"Oh …?"

"We get it. You can't talk. But we're not comfortable letting all kinds of unknowns come at you left and right. In case it's helpful, we've compiled dossiers of everyone who is new to you. Stats. Known associates. Photos. We'll keep asking around, of course."

"Coming!" Kate said to a man signaling that he needed to check out. "Sonny, stop in after the race. We'll catch up then."

"Thank you for all this."

They hugged me, then they were off to the cash register.

I tucked the dossiers into my bag. Life had been kicking me in the pants lately, but friends like Sue, Kate, and Joan made up for it.

* * *

Tumbling clouds cast slow-moving shadows across the Jackson Speedway as I joined the crowd of fans arriving at 4:00 p.m. During my scouting visit yesterday, I'd learned that any photo I took from the grandstand would be marred by the safety partitions separating the crowd from the track. I used my 17-40mm lens for some ambience shots as a pre-race event blasted to life. Even with new ear plugs in place, I was appalled by the *vroom, vroom* of engine noise of the cars hurtling around the track.

Chuck had forgotten to send me a pass allowing me access to restricted areas. Following directions to the lot where racers where unloading their cars, I saw that Chuck's attention was trained on the Mustang he'd nicknamed "Wicked Pissah" as it was rolled from a truck bed. With a dark blue chassis embellished with flames, the car appeared to grin at fans who'd gathered behind a mesh fence to watch.

Chuck's face was attentive as he inspected his supercharged Mustang and readied himself for a grueling haul around the track. I took a range of shots, then as I knelt too close to the front fender, a member of Chuck's pit crew approached and motioned me away.

"You're not authorized to be here," he said.

"I'm with Chuck. He hired me."

"Well, you're un-hired now."

Looking past the clueless man, I caught Chuck's eye and hollered, "I need a pass to get into restricted areas."

"I'm sorry, Sonny. No more pictures."

I paused, not sure I'd heard him correctly. "What?"

"You're done. Go home."

"Done? What happened?"

"I'll explain later." Chuck signaled to a security guard and hitched a thumb my way. "Escort her up to the stands."

"Wait, *wait*," I said, protesting and pausing, but losing the battle as the guy scooted me away from the restricted entrance lot, then ushered me all the way to steps that flanked the rows of seats.

"Stay up here," he said.

"I don't believe this!"

"Believe it," he said. "Don't cross that line."

Staring at the yellow line at the bottom of the steps that he'd pointed to, I gaped as Chuck Brewster, now in the distance, resumed his pre-race business without the slightest look of apology.

"What the *hell?*" I said.

Was he angry that I'd told the police about showing him the photo of the ring, and interviews had followed at an inconvenient time? If so, he could have called and let me know I didn't need to schlep my equipment to the track, and waste hours of my time.

Fuming, I decided I had come to shoot the race. I would shoot the race. Maybe sell photos to other drivers, especially if Chuck lost.

I took out my earplugs during lulls in the action to hear the echoing announcements that gave the speedway a carnival atmosphere. Floodlights ringed the racetrack like the points of a crown, and the delicious aromas of hot dogs and other foods hung in the air.

Here and there as I explored the track, groups of men were exchanging views on sticky tires, radical camshafts, and ass-kicking horsepower. Every detail of the sport was meant to spark an adrenaline surge, from the loud challenges of the drivers revving their engines to the vibrant colors of their vehicles. The logos of sponsors were emblazoned on fenders, doors, and just about every other free space on the cars.

Squeezing my way past onlookers near the edges of the stands, I photographed the track from different angles. At one point I caught sight of a blue baseball cap melting into the crowd above me. I was certain I'd seen the same hat a few minutes ago in another spot.

The thought of being watched by someone with an ulterior agenda made me go from feeling irritated to boiling mad. I shouldered my bag and headed to a relatively clear section of an upper deck where I could survey the crowd above and below me. I needed the element of surprise on my side. I couldn't let them know I was on the lookout.

I'd no sooner settled in place when a heavyset man laden with nachos and a sloshing cup of beer sat down next to me.

"This is my favorite spot," he said.

And by that, it seemed he meant the exact portion of the bleacher that I had taken. He bumped into me on his way down, apologized, then gulped some of his beer and wiped his mouth.

"I'm a photographer," I said, grabbing my bag and sliding to my left. "I need elbow room, so I'm moving down a bit."

"Oh, sorry," he said. "Are you here alone?"

"No, my boyfriend is here somewhere."

"Checking out the cars, I bet."

"Probably."

"These stock car engines are amazing," he said loudly over the noise. "Up to 800 horsepower, if you can believe it. People think some fancy turbochargers are behind the bursts of speed. No, ma'am. I'm not a total expert, but I've heard it's got to do with radical ignition systems and cylinder walls that can handle the heat and pressure."

I looked heavenward, dying inside as his lecture droned on. What was it about car engines that made men weak in the knees? I had a solid grasp of the workings of a camera, but I would rather stomp on my own toes than stand around and describe the details to anyone. Just tell me which buttons access critical functions. I'm good to go.

My phone dinged from an incoming text. Seeing Everett's name on the caller ID, I groaned, thinking it really was not my day.

I clicked on the text and frowned. He'd sent a photo. I zoomed in and was surprised to see an image of myself sitting there in the bleachers, looking heavenward, as I'd done a moment ago. I swiveled to my left, and saw Lily Oakes smiling at me from thirty feet away.

"There's a friend," I said, leaving the racing fan in the dust. I stepped upward through the seats and sat down.

"Who are you here with?" I said as I signed.

Everett, she signed. *We are on a date.*

I worked hard to keep from letting my smile reflect my concern over this bit of news. She didn't seem to notice.

"Where is he?" I asked.

Getting food.

I nodded. "Is that his phone?"

She nodded.

"Does he know you have it?" I said, tilting my head playfully.

No, she signed with a guilty smile, then she dug a hairbrush from her bag, which was similar to the cloth bag I carried.

I wondered if she was copying my style a bit.

Lily conveyed with dismay that her hair had lost some of its smoothness and luster. This was the problem with haircuts. However miraculous the effects when the process was executed by an expert stylist, things often started going downhill the next day. With careful strokes, I smoothed the sections of Lily's hair that were starting to frizz. I would need a product to do the job properly, but brushing helped.

A booming announcement said a pre-race form of motorcycle mayhem was about to start. I winced through the *vroom, vroom, vroom* of the first thunderous laps, and found myself thinking maybe I wasn't too downcast about not being on the track. Ensconced in flame-retardant jumpsuits, the motorcyclists steeply banked around turns. It was a miracle they stayed upright. I figured the crowd would be riveted by the threat of bodily harm, but many of the spectators were chatting or eating a snack.

Lily's hand slid toward me across the bleacher, leaving two pink balls of polymer on the seat between us. When I looked confused, she tucked her hair behind her ear. With her face and neck in view, I saw a blue bud of clay in her right ear.

"Oh," I said. "Thank you."

Fleeting risks. Tiny steps. That was how a friendship with Lily would unfold. I took the bits of polymer and snugged them into my ears. They muffled the noise as well as the official earplugs.

I gave Lily a thumbs up.

"The noise bothers you?" I asked in time with signs.

She fluttered her hands near her ears. I took this to mean the vibrations created discomfort to a certain degree.

With her head bent and her hands turned to the left so I couldn't see what she was doing, Lily fashioned bits of clay into commentaries on the strange goings on at the race. First came a depiction of a young woman below us with spiked pink hair, then a face with a frown and pinched nose to indicate the smell of exhaust fumes in the air.

I pulled out my camera and took a shot of a Chihuahua with tufted ears peering out of a woman's flowered handbag. Lily giggled and clapped her hands. A moment later, a figurine of a chicken-shaped cloud slipped toward me across the seat. I photographed a man wearing one of those hats with attached cups and a straw and showed it to her.

Lily either ran out of inspiration, or out of clay. She stuck out her lower lip, then brightened as she regarded my phone.

Music? she signed.

I'd been sensing that she was tired of living within the confines of being different and misunderstood. Envious of Everett's freedom, coming and going as he pleased, she'd taken to stowing away in his truck to explore the world. Who knew how long she'd been trying to find out what life could be like if she were perceived as "normal?"

The makeover seemed to have kicked her quest into overdrive, and she was looking toward me for help and advice. She was on some sort of date with Everett. Who knew what he expected from it. Her new request felt all-important. A crushing weight.

Show me songs, she insisted.

"Well ..."

Opening my streaming app, I wondered what would be a good choice to share with her. As I looked through the titles, I had to admit they tended to be about love gone wrong or needing to get through impossible moments. Some were a little frisky.

Thankfully, I had an entire empowerment playlist.

A lull in the noise down on the track allowed us a moment to take out the clay ear protectors. I attached my corded earbuds to my phone and handed them to Lily. Given her awakening interest in Everett, I resorted to an old classic, "You Don't Own Me" by Lesley Gore.

As Lily stared at the lyrics scrolling by on my phone, I tweaked the volume until she indicated it was a good setting. She didn't wait for me to select the next song. She reached for my phone and studied the list, seeming fascinated by the implications in their titles.

As I gently pried it from her hands, I saw Everett approaching with hotdogs and sodas tucked into a cardboard tray. I groaned, seeing Pike, the awful deputy, looming behind him wearing sunglasses with reflective lenses and a T-shirt showing a cartoon figure vomiting.

"What the hell are you doing here?" Pike said.

Hoping for a speedy exit, I gave Lily a look of apology as I reached for my earbuds and tucked them into my pocket.

"Well?" Pike demanded.

"I'm here for the race, like everybody else."

"And happened to end up where I'm sitting?"

"I had no idea you were here." I stood and acknowledged Everett, who looked unhappy. "Enjoy the race. See you later."

"Oh, no," Pike said. "You're going to explain."

Everett put his hand in front of the hothead. "Leave it alone. Like Hollis says, you need to move on."

Pike wrenched his arm away. "How about you focus on your nutjob girlfriend before she starts going postal?"

"That's *enough*," Everett hollered.

"I'll handle this," I said. "It's my problem to sort out."

"You're damned right it's your problem," Pike said. "You followed me here thinking you could drop more shit on me."

"I have zero interest in you," I said. "Ze-ro."

"Then why did you send some goon after me?" He pulled down his sunglasses a few inches, revealing a black eye. "Bastard hit me from behind and said, 'This is for Sonny.'"

"I don't know anybody who would do that."

"Well, guess what?" Pike said, breathing his beer breath in my face. "I've got some ideas on next steps because you're still getting away with lying. How about you and me have a private chat?"

Just then, his cell phone rang. He scowled at the contact information, then answered the call. "Who's this?"

Pike raised a hand to stop me as I tried to slip past him, then he paused for a second, his mouth agape as he listened to the caller. He started to speak, then snapped his mouth shut. The call only lasted ten seconds. Pike's expression was not pleased as he hung up.

Before he left, he hissed in my ear, "This is just a pause. Your luck is about to run out, and you're too dumb to know it."

Once he was heading away, Lily gave me a sideways hug, looking confused by the confrontation. *All ok?* she signed.

I hugged her in return. "I'm fine."

"I wonder who called him," Everett said. "I don't think even Hollis would've shut him down that fast."

"I'm sorry," I said. "I know you work with him."

"I was an idiot for letting him talk me into meeting him here," Everett said. "He's guzzling beer, and picking fights with people at the food stand. How did he ever get a job with the police?"

"I'm not sure Lily likes the noise here."

"Hollis said it was ok to take a day off, but it doesn't feel right." He turned and slowly signed to Lily. "Head home?"

She smiled and nodded.

"Everett!" I gripped his arm. "Are you learning ASL for Lily?"

"She asked me to. I'm not the brightest bulb with it."

"You did great! You'll pick it up fast."

As they waved goodbye and headed away, I was further heartened to see how Everett protectively put his hand on Lily's back to help steer her through the crowd. Maybe I'd been an idiot thinking he was too unsophisticated to handle a change in their relationship.

I could use some pointers myself, I silently called after them.

I sat down and studied the snacks Sue and Kate had given me. Granola bars. Blueberry cookies. I pulled out a package of mixed nuts, paused, then grabbed the dossiers they'd created, showing photos of the people who'd come into my sphere in the aftermath of the "burglary."

Right on top was Chuck Brewster's page.

"Stupid race driver," I muttered, flipping it face down on the seat.

One by one, I angrily went through the other pages.

"Miserable drunk, decent son, cheating wife." *Flip.*

"Stripper, delinquent son, half-brother." *Flip.*

"Father, artist daughter, deceased wife." *Flip.*

"Asshole deputy, logger uncle who is also an asshole." *Flip.*

I paused, grabbed the sheets I'd just put down, and stared at Nadine Gilbert's page. Photos of her associates included Chuck, Kyle, and another man. Blood drained from my head. I slowly stood.

The man looked to be in his early thirties. Dark hair. Stubble. In the photo he was smiling with one arm draped around Nadine. The caption listed him as her half-brother, his name Samuel Perth.

He was the intruder who'd knocked me down.

"What the *hell?*" I hollered so loudly that people ten feet away looked alarmed. "It was Nadine's *brother?*"

29

I felt completely thrown for a moment, trying to sort out who to contact. People were milling around, choosing seats, making it difficult to focus. One man stepped forward, then stood perfectly still while everyone else bumped into him on their way from one place to another.

I focused on him. In jeans and a plaid shirt, it was the man I'd just identified on Nadine's information page. Her half-brother, whom she'd never mentioned. Sue and Kate had added that he lived in Massachusetts. Nadine was his only local contact that they could find. The half siblings had been estranged for a while, no mention of why.

"Wait!" He held up both hands. "There are things you need to know. Give me a chance. Not here, though. It's too crowded."

"Nadine played me," I said. "All week."

"Come with me, ok? Let me—"

Samuel's eyes widened as something behind me caught his attention. He cursed and dove away into the crowd.

"Coming behind you!" Dan hollered, almost colliding into me as he rushed after Nadine's half-brother. In the blue baseball hat that I'd seen melting into the crowd several times, he pivoted for a split second and said, "In case I lose him, stay here so I can find you!"

The two men disappeared into the crowd so fast I could scarcely process what had happened. I stepped forward, trying to see where they were heading, but aside from a few yelps of irritation and shifts of position from people who were apparently getting knocked aside by the chase, I couldn't continue following where they'd gone.

"Shit!" I hollered.

I turned and collided into Nadine. She gripped my arms with a look of apology, and the same level of shock that I'd seen in her brother's face when he'd clapped eyes on Dan.

"Sonny, I'm sorry," Nadine said. "Let me explain."

"I can't believe it. You lied to me all this time."

"I had to. Please listen. I can explain."

"Of all people. My God, do you have any idea what I've been through trying to figure this out all week? Even before it happened my world fell apart because of lies. I can't believe this."

"I'm sorry, Sonny. I really am."

"Oh my God … you curated your photos when I came to the bar the other day, didn't you?" I said. "You deleted any with your half-brother in them. All the while, you acted like my friend, saying I should learn pole dancing and loosen up. And I fell for it."

"Sonny … Kyle is dead."

This pulled me up short. I focused on her face. For once, she didn't reflect a breezy attitude. She looked anguished, but for all I knew it was because her brother had just made a mistake and might be in handcuffs by the end of the day.

"Kyle is *what?*" I said.

"I've known for some time. Sam, my brother, vowed to help me find out who did it. You need to hear me. I need your help."

"What makes you think Kyle is …?"

"He should have reached out long before now." Nadine paused and looked toward the crowd where her brother and Dan had rushed away. "How in the hell did that trooper escape our notice? We checked faces for a half hour. Did you know he was here?"

"No, but he's followed me before."

"That doesn't worry you?" she said.

"Of course it worries me!" I shouted. "Now will you please explain what is going on? Are you serious about Kyle? That he's …?"

"When he didn't come home for ages, I started upending stuff in his bedroom. Here." Nadine shoved a stained metal badge of some sort into my hands. "I found this in Kyle's closet in a box of awful things. Bones, crazy notes, stuff from the Civil War."

"Bones ...?"

"The skeleton hand Sam dropped outside your barn. Kyle made it. He wanted to get back at the police. Even Raymond. I know Kyle was wrong half the time, but he has ADD. And he's just a kid. But that didn't matter. One of the cops took revenge. They—"

"*No*," I interrupted. "I told you the other day, Kyle called me, Nadine. And guess what? The next day a boater tried to mow me down while I was swimming in the lake."

Nadine looked baffled. "You were attacked? By a boater?"

"Yes, and the police think it was Kyle."

"This is a nightmare," she said.

"We agree on that. Again, I talked to Kyle."

"That was one of his friends. I asked him to do it, thinking you'd tell the trooper and it would cause him to act in a way that outed what he'd done. Or he'd pass the tip along. Stirring the pot has been my only means of getting answers. Wait—" Nadine gripped my arm. "Where was the trooper the day you were attacked at the lake?"

"He was ... he helped me after it happened."

"He was *there*? Jesus, Sonny."

"For the last time, he's a good guy," I insisted.

"His friend killed himself because of Kyle's pranks. I know you don't want to hear it, but he took revenge. Now he's going to kill my brother."

"That's not going to happen." I gripped my head, praying to heaven that I was right. "What proof do you have that Kyle is ...?"

"He would have been in touch if he was alive," Nadine said. "There's been no word from him from as far back as last year."

I sat down. "This is crazy."

"Listen, I had a bad feeling Kyle had left an awful surprise for Raymond. He left notes about it. I wondered if it got overlooked, so I asked Sam to get it before you got scared out of your mind. Him coming to your farm was from good intentions, Sonny. Chuck heard half the story, and warned Brumby to keep an eye out. Everything went to shit. But guess who showed up that night? Your trooper friend."

"I feel sick."

"Sam wore Kyle's jacket in the spirit of getting justice. You described it to the police, so they were all the more bent on tracking down Kyle. They *knew* he was behind the pranks. We're almost there, Sonny. Help us bring down Kyle's killer. I'm begging you."

I stared at the filthy badge in my hand. "What is this?"

"It's a Civil War badge. I found it with the bones. I think Kyle must have come across an old crypt that wasn't locked. He figured the bones were old, the people long dead. He's not a monster, Sonny. He's just a confused kid with a chip on his shoulder."

"I can't believe you found human bones in your son's bedroom closet, and didn't tell the police."

"When they're responsible? I wanted to see if I could rattle the truth out of them, so I kept my suspicions to myself. Hollis talked to somebody anyway. He didn't mention the bones, of course. Just alerted them that Kyle hadn't come home for a while. They said it was part of the pattern for delinquents to hide when they're in trouble."

"Maybe he *is* still hiding."

"No, Sonny." Nadine looked miserable. "Kyle loves attention. To be the life of the party all day every day. But he's been silent."

Staring at the tarnished badge in my hand, I realized I'd been put onto the wrong path when it came to looking up people who'd gone missing in the area thirty odd years ago.

"The old guy in the diner said Revolutionary War events …"

"What?"

"Nothing, you might be right about the crypt. That makes more sense." I closed my eyes. "You need to tell Detective Allen what you've told me. And you need to hand over the evidence."

"Can't we wait a bit longer? You've made inroads with that trooper. Isn't there some way to get him to talk? Say what he knows?"

"No, I can't do that."

"You think he loves you?" she demanded. "I'm sorry to break the news. Love at first sight ends the second a guy pulls his zipper up."

"We never went that far …"

"Sonny, please." Nadine's hands were chilly as she gripped mine, and her long nails dug in a little. "I need to know what happened to my son. Once they have the bones and other stuff, they'll shut down even tighter. We might never learn the truth."

"You lied to me," I said. "How can I know if you're not still holding back? I mean, what's Chuck's involvement?"

"Same as mine. Finding Kyle."

"He knows about the bones? The pranks?"

"He does now," she said. "I told him a few days ago after Sam's attempt to get the cookie tin went wrong at your farm."

"Chuck knew when I was at his garage. Unbelievable."

I thought back to the night Brumby had come to my house uninvited. I'd accepted it, no idea there was a chain of people pushing an agenda that involved trying to manipulate me, or scare me into disclosing some tip that would help them learn what they wanted to know. Dan had been right. Be careful. Trust no one. I couldn't imagine he had anything to do with Kyle's disappearance. I'd looked in his eyes. Kissed him. Whether he was as trustworthy as I'd imagined during those moments, or he turned out to be deeply flawed, I had a feeling I would find out soon.

Nadine was ashen as she looked toward the racetrack area, desperate to catch a glimpse of her brother. I was searching the crowd myself for the blue baseball hat Dan was wearing. It was a huge place, and they'd left nearly ten minutes ago.

"Let's head down to the track," I said.

"Wait, here's one of Chuck's crew coming up."

Out of breath, the man said, "Where the hell is Chuck?"

"How should I know?" Nadine said.

"He got a call. Said he'd be back in five. He's got to get down there. What the hell is he thinking, taking a call at race time?"

My stomach clenched. Dan had dashed after Nadine's brother with no back-up. What if Chuck's absence had to do with trying to protect Sam from getting arrested? How far would these people go to protect themselves? If only they'd come clean from the start. Their lies and maneuvering had amplified the situation to the point where somebody might panic and make a move they couldn't take back.

I had to find Dan, or Chuck, or Nadine's brother, or all three of them.

"Where are the places Chuck would go?" I said.

"I don't know," the pit crew guy said. "Men's room. Food area. Parking lot. Stands all around. I'll take the men's rooms."

"I'll check the stands and the food areas," Nadine said.

That left the parking lot.

It wasn't ideal to end the conversation with Nadine before I'd gotten a better handle on whether or not her claims about Kyle were the truth. Unlike Dan, I had no authority to hold her in place. What I did do was put the Civil War badge into my bag. I would give it to Dan, or Detective Allen, whoever I ran into first.

After the three of us had dashed in different directions, I found it impossible to move with speed through the milling crowd without sparking trouble. People whirled and chided me at every turn.

"Watch it!" a man said. "I'm carrying drinks!"

"Sorry!"

"What happened?" another said. "Did I miss a crash?"

"No time to explain."

"Talk about rude!"

"My bad," I said. "Coming through."

In frustration, I pulled out my camera with its telephoto lens attached. With my heart beating fast, I could scarcely hold the camera steady as I scanned the stands. I saw no sign of Dan.

Vroom-g-g-g, vroom-g-g-g, vroom, engines down on the track blasted, sending an earthquake through the pavement.

"If they would *stop* that infernal noise," I said.

The only person having a worse night was Chuck's pit crew guy.

"This is freaking me out," he said, joining me near an entrance. "If it's an emergency, he would get word to us. Something's got to be wrong."

"Where is Chuck's vehicle?"

The crew guy led the way to an area of the parking lot that had been designated for staff and race participants. Above the din, I heard a loud *pop* somewhere nearby that sent a shock wave through my system. Was that a backfire? Or a gunshot?

"Where did that come from?" I hollered.

I paused as an announcement echoed from the speakers making light of the fact that the notorious racer was taking his sweet time getting to the starting line. Would he please leave whatever pretty lady he was flirting with and get in his car? Applause and cheers erupted across the speedway. Everyone was having a grand time.

"Here," the crew guy said, crossing around the flatbed that had carried "Wicked Pissah" to the race. "Empty, like I figured."

With a pounding heart, I dashed between other trucks. Looking, searching. The setting sun cast amber rays across the area as we rounded a trailer and saw Chuck Brewster sprawled on his back. Zipped into his racing attire, with his right hand clutching his chest, he looked astonished as he stared at the crimson clouds.

"Oh no," I said.

"Holy shit. Is he drunk?"

"Get help!"

"Why is he covered in oil?"

"It's not oil!" I knelt next to the racer and gripped his hand. "He's bleeding. Are you listening? You need to call for help!"

The man hovered there another second with a disbelieving stare, then he dashed toward the grandstand and racetrack hollering and waving his arms to attract attention, for all the good it did. The din of revved-up race cars consumed every other sound.

Holding Chuck's hand, I dug my phone out of my pocket, dialed 911, and pressed the receiver to my ear in hopes of hearing the dispatcher when they picked up. All I heard was a click and an unintelligible drone.

"Please listen carefully," I hollered. "A man has either been stabbed or shot. It's Chuck Brewster. I'm near the parking area of the Jackson Speedway. Send an ambulance and the police. Call Detective Roy Allen. Tell them to hurry!"

Chuck's fingers tightened on my hand, a crushing grip that I would normally want to pull away from. I set my phone aside without disconnecting in case it would help the police hone in on our location, and rested a hand on Chuck's shoulder.

"Help is on the way," I said.

"Fucked up …"

"Who would come after you? I don't understand."

"Jhhh s' call," he wheezed, then he shoved a phone at me. I took it from him, but without the passcode I couldn't open it.

"I called the police," I said. "And an ambulance."

He looked anguished. I wasn't understanding him. As a shiver raked through him, I saw the pit crew guy near the entrance hollering his news to a security guard, not nearly fast enough.

"Na … deen … find Kyle …"

"Just hold my hand. Help is on the way."

Chuck's anguished gaze begged me to do anything but sit there saying ridiculous things. I clambered down and dropped to my stomach on the pavement. With his calloused hand gripped in mine, and my face so close to his that I could see his pulse moving in his neck and smell the aftershave on his jaw, I spoke in a furious tone.

"You listen to me, Chuck Brewster. I have questions about Raymond and that blasted ring and a hundred other things. You were born to race cars, so you'd better buckle up and focus on getting through this, do you understand?"

"Nee t' get … Khhyle." Chuck squeezed his eyes shut, then his gaze focused on me again. "S' gone … keep forgetting …"

"Just rest. EMTs are on their way."

"Shit …"

"Don't let go," I said tearfully. "Keep gripping my hand." I could feel his strength draining, his lips smiling and his eyes taking on a dreamy look. "I'm sorry to be yelling, but you need to focus on what I'm saying! I mean it! Don't you dare quit on me!"

"See'm soon … ol' fish'n hole …"

"If you're talking about ditching Nadine for someone in heaven, don't you *dare*," I hollered. "That's no way to treat a lady."

I was desperate to hold his attention with jokes, metaphors, anything that would dispel the awful specter of life fading from his eyes. A unique soul was in there. A personality. A loving father and genius with cars. It couldn't just vanish. Not in front of me.

"Hurry, for God's sake, he's fading in strength," I said as the track EMTs arrived with a clatter of equipment. "He's bleeding. Can't someone shut off those *engines?*"

"We've got him. Come away."

"I'm keeping him going."

"Let go."

Reluctantly, I grasped the hand an EMT offered, climbed to my feet, and gave them room to work. Security personnel blocked my view, except for glimpses of Chuck's blank stare and limp reactions as his gear was stripped off. Medics darted past me in all directions, crowding around where only a moment ago I had been the only one to help. Now, in the fading light, I was tripped over, cursed at, and in the way.

But I couldn't move. Not for a long while. Whisps of smoke drifted below the clouds as the engines finally silenced. A hushed murmur stirred through the crowd. The news was spreading fast.

Chuck Brewster was gone.

* * *

However angry I'd been with Nadine a short while ago, I felt nothing but sympathy as she tried in vain to get past the security guards and reach Chuck. I'd learned that he'd been shot at close range. I watched Nadine react as her glimpses of the hopeless scene sank in. Gripping her head with both hands, she asked over and over again what had happened. Who would have shot him? What had gone wrong?

I couldn't tell her. I didn't know.

"He got a call," she said. "That's what pulled him away."

I looked at Chuck's phone in my hand. Nadine followed my gaze, recognized the device, and grabbed it from me.

"The police will want to see it," I said.

"I know the passcode. It's all ones."

I should have guessed. Number one all the way.

"What the hell?" Nadine said.

Leaning toward her, I saw the ID for the last call Chuck had received. It wasn't a long name. Not difficult for me to see. It was Kyle.

"Nadine," I said. "For God's sake."

"It can't have been him."

"No wonder Chuck left the race track."

"I know. It's the one call he'd take. But it makes no sense."

My gaze took in an approaching group of officers. In the lead was Dan ushering Nadine's handcuffed brother forward.

"You're not *pinning* this on me," Sam hollered, letting his weight be a drag, his shoulders pulling against the restraints.

Dan paused. Patient, unmoved by the struggling of his prisoner. Once the fight left Sam, Dan began ushering him forward again.

"Where'd you get him?" one of the troopers asked.

"Near the exit," Dan said.

"Did he have the weapon on him?"

"No. We need to organize a search."

"People saw him arguing with Chuck near the track a few hours ago," a trooper said. "Seemed pretty heated."

Dan looked down at Chuck for a long moment. In his frown, I saw a note of weariness. Unlike me, he'd probably seen death of many kinds, from many ways, and it never got easier to absorb.

When I turned to check on Nadine, she was gone.

I closed my eyes, thinking, *I really suck at this crime scene business.*

A half hour later, the detective in charge of the scene seemed to agree. He was astonished when I reached the part of my statement when I said I'd let Nadine grab Chuck's phone, and shortly afterward, I'd stood by while she slipped away. What was I supposed to do? I mean, really? I'd just held a man's hand as he'd taken his last breath.

Score one more point for the liars behind the whole mess.

Zero for me.

30

With my arms folded against the chill evening air, I watched Dan talking with the other officers. He motioned toward the direction he'd come from, saying that Nadine's brother was unarmed when Dan had caught up to him near an entrance. Having been seen arguing with Chuck, Sam was the prime suspect in the shooting. There were dozens of trash barrels and other places where he could have ditched his weapon.

Seeing me standing there, Dan crossed to me, in a hurry because he needed to be a part of the search for the missing handgun.

"You gave your statement, so it's ok to head home," he said. "I'm sorry about Chuck. I know you liked him."

"Why would Nadine's brother kill him?"

"I don't know. Head home, ok?" As he gave my arm a squeeze, he frowned as I pulled away. "Sonny, I'm sorry to be in a hurry—"

"Pike was beaten up. He confronted me about it. I don't think it was you, but I wouldn't mind hearing you say it."

"Of course it wasn't me," Dan said. "It's not how I operate. I did call him and tell him to step away when you were up in the stands."

"You didn't have to do that. I was handling it."

"It was escalating. I didn't want it to interfere with ..."

I raised my eyebrows. "Your surveillance of me?"

"You're getting the spirit of it wrong," he said. "Was it ideal to shadow you today? No. But you wanted freedom to work. I had a gut feeling about the people involved. I've been telling you from the start. Look at the results. We got one of the main links in the case."

"Nadine thinks her son is dead. She told me it was Kyle who made the skeleton parts. He wanted to lash out at the police. Even Raymond. She thinks someone got angry about it. Enough to …"

"You *promised* to not delve into the case," Dan said. "What happened to being on board with the five-word warning?"

"What if she's right? That he's dead?"

"Sonny." Dan flipped his hands, looking exasperated. "Nadine will say anything to get her son off the hook. She lied to you all week. And if I understand things correctly, the last call Chuck got was from Kyle. It's in your statement. I know the implication is awful—"

"There are ways to clone a phone number, aren't there? If someone did go after Kyle, the guilty party might have his phone."

"Or, Kyle made the call."

"I know," I said. "I *know*." I paused, then fished through my bag for the Civil War badge Nadine had handed over. "Before I forget, I was talking to this older guy in the diner—"

"Sonny, I need to get moving."

"I just … it's in here somewhere."

"Hang on."

Dan signaled to his colleagues that he needed another minute.

"Look," he said. "I know it's a rush to follow your curiosity. I admire it in all other instances, seeing where it leads you on the creative front. But we have the guy who broke into your barn in custody. Your role in the case is officially over. This right here is the line."

Dan motioned sideways with an expression that said if I crossed beyond the line regarding the case, his opinion of me would plummet. This was a world apart from how he'd looked and sounded last night. It was obvious he was pumped from catching Nadine's brother, one of the elements he would need to head back to the Canadian border with a sense of making his extra time in town worth the delay. I don't know why I was shocked by the sudden shift of his priorities and tone. This was the price of trusting a man. Believing what he said during an intimate moment in the dark of night. The wind always shifted against me. Always.

I stopped looking for the badge. "Got it."

"We can talk later," Dan said. "Tomorrow, ok?"

"Go find the weapon. I know it's important."

I lingered long enough to watch the paramedics finish gathering the blood-stained dressings left on the pavement from their futile efforts to save Chuck. Then I shouldered my bag, and headed home.

* * *

The night closed around my car as I drove down the wooded lane. For the umpteenth time, I thought about the handwritten notes. *You didn't ask the right questions. You didn't believe. You didn't follow through. You didn't care.* If Nadine was right and Kyle was dead, there would be an unsettling truth to the notes he'd written in the spirit of harassing the police. If he was alive, and possibly involved with the death of his own father, the notes would fall into the category of too sad to believe.

It had taken five minutes to come up with two words that described what I needed to do next. Hard reset. I didn't want to watch the local news and find out that there were videos sent in from fans showing me kneeling over Chuck's lifeless eyes. And I didn't want Dan to stop by and say anything that made me feel like a meddling idiot.

Arriving at my driveway, I climbed out to gather the mail. As if she'd been waiting for me, Joan stepped from her porch and walked across the road to join me in the darkness next to my idling car.

"You've heard?" I said. "About Chuck?"

Joan nodded. "It's horrible."

"Nadine's brother was taken into custody. He was the one who broke into Raymond's barn. The police think he shot Chuck."

"You don't look convinced."

"There are so many things to sort out."

"I know the feeling."

I studied her tight, angry expression. "I know you're upset from hearing the messages. I should have erased them."

"It's not that," Joan said.

"What is it, then?"

"Well, I found out that a deputy came into my house and all but assaulted you. Why didn't you tell me?"

I closed my eyes and pushed my frizzing bangs away from my forehead with a very long, very labored, and very tired inward groan. I should have told Joan the moment the police had gotten involved.

"What if my kids had run into him?" she said. "Plus, you apparently delayed reporting it. You left the threat out there."

"Brumby and I—"

"Oh, Brumby helped make the decision. Great."

"He stopped the deputy. This might not make sense to you, but I didn't want the police stomping all over your house. And it's a big deal to make an accusation against a member of the police."

"It's jarring to find out days later."

"I'm sorry. If I could reverse time—"

"You don't have children, so maybe you don't understand," Joan said. "It terrifies me to think how it could have escalated."

In the back of my mind, Dan's numbing words repeated over and over again. *This right here is the line ... this right here is the line ...*

"Well?" Joan demanded.

"It was selfish. And wrong." Tearing up, I said, "I decided on the way home that I'm driving to Boston as soon as I pack. Moving here without a plan was misguided. I'm going to start from scratch."

Joan looked shocked. "What about the berry field?"

"Harry and Jess said they helped Raymond with the 'you-pick' operation. If you're ok with it, they want to help again this year. The berry money can go to their college fund. I mean it, Joan. Raymond had a bond with them, and with you. Not with me. So, whatever happens, if I sell the farm ... I'll make sure the people who mattered to him get the benefit. I'll be working full time, so I won't need the money."

"Sonny, this is ..."

"I'll call later. I have to go."

"*Stop.*"

"This *is* my way of stopping, Joan. Nadine tricked me all week. I've managed to alienate Dan in record time. Now Chuck Brewster is never coming back," I whispered. "And it's all my fault."

I could scarcely walk from a sudden rush of emotion. The farm. The animals I'd come to love. It had been a foolish notion to think I was up to the task of filling the deep void that Raymond's death had left.

I drove up the hill and reversed so I could throw things into the cargo area without delay. It was all I could do to not break down as Dodge bellowed his usual greeting. The sheep lined up at the fence, expecting the attention I usually lavished on them. Trembling, with my teeth clenched, I turned my back to them and climbed the porch steps.

My camera gear was in the car, so there wasn't much to pack. I hadn't sublet my apartment in Boston. I had plenty of clothes there.

I turned off the light, then paused to see who was calling when my phone rang. It was Sue. She and Kate could help with my exit.

"Sonny?" she said. "Joan just called."

"I can't talk," I managed. "I need someone to take care of Dodge and the sheep. To live here full time. A caretaker. I don't want any of them to be sold, or … I don't trust Charlotte to care about them, so you need to promise that nobody will harm them."

"Sonny, just pause for a second, ok?"

I stifled a sob. "Promise you'll help. Please."

"Kate and I will live there if that's what it takes. If you need to sort things out in Boston, that's fine. But wait until morning."

"Joan has a spare key."

"Sonny—"

"I can't, Sue. I have to go."

I hung up and tossed my phone into my bag. I paused for one last time in Raymond's pipe-smelling kitchen. From the start, it had been a place of darkness, shadows, questions, and pain.

I opened the door, my eyes brimming, and caught a glimpse of a man-shaped shadow with a mask that showed only his eyes. His fist shot out and struck me in the face. Yelping in pain, seeing stars, I clutched my nose and staggered backward, felt my own blood in my hands.

Tripping, collapsing to the floor, I rolled and clambered toward the kitchen table, but he was like a bull charging in, sweeping the chairs aside as if they were nothing. Noise exploded in the room, my legs milling against his efforts to grab them, then one of his hands gripped the back of my shirt. My collar became a strangling force, my eyes wide and my sneakers slipping on the floor as he dragged me to the door.

I braced my feet on the frame. Kicked. Scrambled to the table again, his hands on my legs and hauling me backward.

I inhaled to scream, but in the same instant a strap swung over my head and I felt it connect with my throat and pull hard. Choking as I grappled with it, afraid I would black out, I went limp and heard him growling in a horrible voice behind me.

"I heard what you said on the phone. If you don't quit fighting, I will kill every one of your animals. Your neighbor, too."

I recognized his voice. It was Earl.

"Understand?" he hollered.

I nodded tightly.

"Grab your keys. Nothing else."

Held in check like an animal on a harsh leash, I groped for my purse, which had fallen to the floor, and stared at my phone, trying to figure out a way to bring it with me. He jerked on the strap and told me to hurry up. I picked up my keys.

"Get up. Out the door."

With shaking hands, I did as he told me, then I staggered awkwardly down the steps and paused next to my car. He opened the driver's door and shoved me in. There was a moment when I imagined I could gun the engine and race away down the slope, but he was in the back seat before I could put the keys in the ignition. The strap returned around my neck. He said start the car. I tried to. It stalled. I couldn't get it to work.

I paused, knowing it was crazy to let him abduct me. *Would* he kill Joan? My animals? Or was it a bluff? I couldn't take the risk. I would pivot at some point, not go down without a fight, but only when we were far away from the farm.

"Come *on*," he bellowed.

As I tried again and the engine kicked on, I had one tiny shot at alerting a friend to my peril without Earl knowing about it. Slowly, I drove down the driveway and made several exaggerated brakes as I passed the trail camera. It was 10 p.m., and fully dark along the slope. With his head covered by a black hood, it wouldn't be obvious that someone was in the back seat. Plus, Arlene was in a completely different time zone. Five hours ahead. What chance did I have that she would be awake at 3 a.m., and inclined to check my trail camera's alert on her phone? But I had to cling to at least one shred of hope.

"Get going," he said. "Turn left."

A half mile down the road, he cursed, apparently uncomfortable with the mask covering his sweating face. He ripped it off. Then he ripped black nitrile gloves from his hands. I hadn't realized he'd been wearing them. I looked in the rearview mirror to confirm that it was Earl. A look of desperation made him ugly, his eyes bloodshot and watery. I saw my own wide eyes as well in the mirror, and blood drying under my nose.

A notion hit me like a brick. The police had Nadine's brother in custody for the death of Chuck Brewster.

I had a bad feeling they'd arrested the wrong man.

And they didn't know it.

31

I could feel Earl's agitation through the length of webbing, or whatever it was he'd looped around my throat. He was controlling me like a puppet, jerking the strap every time he hollered where to turn, or if I was driving too fast, or too slow.

Up ahead, beyond some bends, a strange light began blooming upward into the night sky. Blue lights. Police lights.

"Shit," he hollered. "Lights off."

"But I—"

Coughing, jerked into silence, I fumbled for the headlight control, then gasped and gripped the webbing. The car began to slow.

"Faster!"

"Can't—"

"Turn in here. *Now!*"

With the tension on the strap eased enough for me to use both hands on the steering wheel, I turned into the wooded lane he'd indicated. With jerks and prompts, he instructed me onward, then ordered me to shut off the car. He was looking backward toward the road, which caused his tight grip on the strap to loosen. Not enough to feel I could pull it out of his hands. Any mistake I made might be the end of me.

The inside of the car was a dark, contained theater for our gasping breaths. Soon another sound obliterated all else — the rush and gunned-engine bluster of a vehicle approaching at top speed. It passed with a whoosh behind us, blazing down the road at 80 or 90 miles per hour. In the rearview mirror, I caught a flash of a red fender. A truck.

I closed my eyes. It was Dan.

"No siren," he said. "Shit."

"It means they know something happened."

"How? Never mind, back to the road. Keep the lights off."

"Listen—"

"Get going! Now!"

Once I'd backed onto the road and glimpsed the dismal sight of Dan's flashing lights retreating into the night, I took a stand.

"You need to ease up with the strap," I said.

"Shut up."

"I almost blacked out. I will cooperate."

"Then do it. Up there, take a right."

Even with the tension on the strap eased, the next fifteen minutes were a hell of catching glimpses of his desperate eyes and dark scowl in the rearview mirror, and smelling his cigarette breath sawing in and out of his horrid lungs. Turning as instructed with robotic moves, with the headlights back on, I started recognizing the landmarks we passed. It was the route I'd traveled to fetch the lamb and to help Nadine with Lily's makeover. Did Earl not understand it was the wrong move to head to his own house? If they caught onto who had taken me, the police might even be there waiting for us when we arrived.

My flicker of hope faded as I realized Dan had been heading to my farm. Unraveling what had happened to me would take time. He would find my phone. My bag. Blood from my nose. I hoped to heaven he would assess every item, fast, picture all the people who'd approached me in recent days, and figure out where to look.

"Turn here," Earl instructed me.

My hope faded a little more because we were a mile or so from his house. Once again, my car entered a pitted dirt lane overshadowed by undergrowth and trees. A recent logging trail, but flat, and not nearly as rough as Chuck's lane. Looking ahead, I desperately searched for a spot where I could get the car stuck, and one presented itself. I swerved the steering wheel slightly, then again, not wanting the move to seem obvious, then the right side of the car dipped suddenly. I gunned the engine, hoping it would sink the tires deeper. With him cursing behind me over the noise of the car, I saw leaves and dirt spraying behind us.

"Stupid asshole," he said.

"I'm sorry. I'm not good on dirt roads."

"Goddamned women drivers!"

"Let me try backing up."

I reversed fast before he could argue and lurched a few feet toward the road, thinking if it was visible to passing cars, someone — maybe even the police — would stop to investigate. But I'd done too good a job of getting the tires stuck. The car wasn't going anywhere.

"Shit," he hollered. "Get out."

Shaking, I opened the door, scanning the dark woods for the best avenue of escape. Then what? Would he try to chase me down or slip away and follow through on his threats later on? I decided for now, running was not an option. I'd succeeded in getting the car stuck. Now I needed a plan I could execute fast, without warning, to bring him down.

"You got any aspirin?" he demanded.

"What …?" I realized he was sober for the first time since I'd met him. His head must be slamming if he hadn't had a drink for a while.

"Well?" he said.

"I think so. In my car."

"Get it."

From the back of his waistband, he produced a gun. I groaned. Whatever plan I came up with had to be airtight and foolproof.

I opened the passenger door and fished through the glove compartment. Inside was a bottle of a mix of over-the-counter pain medications. Wanting to appear helpful in the wild hope that he would relax out of his frenzy, I eased two aspirin onto my palm.

"Here."

"I'll need more than that."

"Four. Any more and your stomach will hurt."

He gulped them down and chewed. A fleck of aspirin ended up on his lower lip, stuck there by spittle. He motioned me forward with the gun.

The thick darkness under the trees allowed me an excuse to walk slowly. Behind me, he tripped and cursed a few times. At one point I fell and made a drama of twisting my leg, wincing, and gripping my ankle, all the while watching his reaction carefully.

"Get up!" he thundered.

"Ok." Once on my feet, I said, "Can I lean on you?"

"No."

"It hurts."

"Tough. Move."

Second by second, minute by minute, I stalled every chance I got. Soon I realized he was assisting my goal by lagging behind and clutching his stomach. Aspirin to the rescue. He staggered a few paces, then pitched forward, gripped by dry heaves.

"Let me help—"

He swung the gun my way. "Get back."

"I'm trying to help."

"I'm not stupid. You remind me of my wife."

I held my breath, seized by a question I'd been too overwhelmed to finish answering. Why had he abducted me? Why now?

"You killed Chuck, didn't you?" I said.

"Doesn't matter."

I think it does to him.

Earl heaved again, then he knelt for a while, wiping his mouth, cursing, heaving miserably. I shifted, poised to move, but the crackle of leaves had him wildly aiming the gun my way. I couldn't escape. Not yet. I passed the time by counting, second by second, grateful for every last one as my tally reached sixty. I counted five minutes. Six.

Finally, he stood and motioned me on.

As I walked, I plowed through what I knew. Ever since I'd found Chuck at the track, I'd been worried that it had to do with showing him the photo of the ring. Earl's wife had left him years ago. If her ring was the one that was left with the skeleton hand …

I stopped in my tracks.

"Who left the cookie tin? And the bones?"

"What?" he said, then he looked around himself. He crossed to a tree to stare at a metal disk, then he searched the undergrowth.

I looked from one dark tree to the next as well. At first, I didn't see much out of the ordinary. But twenty or thirty yards away I could make out what looked like the crumbled remains of a building. It had to be very old, nothing more than a pile of stones.

"What is this place?" I said.

"Right there." He pointed. "My two-timing wife."

Gooseflesh claimed my arms as I stared at the leafy area. If I had continued walking forward, even two yards, I would have stepped on his wife's secret, unmarked grave.

"Shit, now what?" he said.

At the sound of footfalls approaching, he waved for me to stand behind him as if having a mental breakdown that involved protecting me from potential harm.

"Earl?" Hollis called out. "Is that you?"

"How'd you know I was here?"

"Trail camera. What the hell are you up to?"

"I'm solving a problem."

As Hollis stepped into view with a flashlight in one hand, my heart thudded from the need to alert him to Earl's gun without startling the desperate murderer.

Leaves crunched as I took a step. Earl swung the gun toward me.

"Earl!" Hollis said. "Have you lost your mind?"

"I shot Chuck. He's dead because *she* showed him Mary's ring and the damned fool recognized it. I don't know how, but he did."

"*You* shot Chuck?" Hollis said.

"He confronted me. Threatened me. Talked nonsense about getting Kyle off the hook. Are you listening? He figured out I killed Mary."

"You're a damned fool. Honest to God."

"Well, I'm not the only one, am I?" Earl said.

"Stop waving the gun around."

"You know, I'm thinking I might kill two birds with one stone."

"So, now you're threatening me? Jesus Christ, Earl." Hollis stepped forward. "I have been carrying your sorry ass for twenty years."

I cringed, thinking, *Don't provoke the madman.*

"I can't take this anymore," Earl said. "It's eating me alive."

Hollis shook his head. "I knew it would come to an awful pass like this. I tried to keep you on the straight and narrow. For Everett's sake, at the least. He deserves a good life."

"What do we do?" Earl said.

Hollis closed his eyes, as if praying for a miracle, then he swung a shotgun up and shot Earl in the chest.

Shocked by the sudden blast, the awful sound of Earl's groan as he fell backward, I staggered a little, then fell to my knees, as if I'd been the one who was shot. Earl landed four feet away, his thrashing movements casting oak and maple leaves into the air.

"Shit," Hollis said.

"Why?" I managed. "Why did you …?"

I stared in horror as Hollis knelt and covered Earl's mouth and nose with both hands. The injured man thrashed and kicked out all the more, choking, groaning.

"Hollis!" I gripped his shoulders. "*Stop.*"

"He was going to shoot you."

Seeing the handgun a few feet away, I picked it up and tossed it toward the crumbled building so Earl couldn't grab it.

"I threw his gun," I said. "He can't reach it."

Hollis clenched his teeth as he leaned his weight into the business of suffocating Earl. I gripped his shoulders and pulled backward.

"Hollis! Don't!"

Within seconds, the thrashing stopped.

"Jesus," Hollis said, sitting back on his heels. "Shit."

"You killed him!"

"He's just passed out."

I pointed to Earl's open eyes. "That is a death stare!"

"All right, settle down."

"Settle down? Call 911."

"My phone …" Hollis frantically searched his pockets, then searched again, finally cursing under his breath. "*Damn* that girl."

"Lily has it?"

"Of course she has it, because I was in a rush." Climbing to his feet, Hollis angrily kicked Earl's body a few times. "Stupid, stupid man."

"What the hell, Hollis?"

"All right, Ms. Curious." Hollis swung the shotgun toward me, then sat down on a boulder. "Park it over there. I need to catch my breath."

Mouth open, eyes wide, I slowly sank down and knelt in the leaves, rather than sat as instructed. I wasn't saved. Not in the least.

It was now going to get worse.

32

Hollis slipped a cartridge into the empty chamber of the shotgun. As he caught his breath from rushing through the forest and killing Earl, he pulled a cloth handkerchief from his pocket and wiped sweat from his face. I found it jarring to see him using an accessory that I'd always connected with a more genteel period of time in the past.

"Where is your cane?" I said.

"Left it back there. Don't worry, I'll find it."

"You move pretty well without it."

"I stopped needing it some months back, but it suited me to get sympathy from folks." Hollis sighed heavily. "This is the problem with you, Sonny. Smart as hell. Observant. Look where it's landed you. I liked you from the get-go. But you've managed to undo decades of careful upkeep of a delicate situation. You're my worst nightmare."

"I still can't grasp why you killed Earl."

"It was helping him cover up his crime that put me on the wrong path," Hollis said. "Once you see a sinful death up close, there's no going back. I got used to it, I guess."

"You helped him bury his wife out here?"

"He was a wreck that night, all shook up, coming to me and asking what he should do. Everett was four years old. No other relatives." Hollis shrugged. "He had her wrapped in plastic so it wasn't too awful to help bring her out with my ATV."

I looked away, trying to not show my revulsion.

"Look here. I threw these out years ago," Hollis said, tossing folded papers my way. "I should've known Lily would fish them out of the trash. She pulled them out of hiding today."

Rescuing the sheets from the leaves, I recognized the thickness and texture of watercolor paper. Tattered edges and signs of wear told me they were old, and possibly had been unfolded many times, then put back into a secret hiding place. In the darkness, I couldn't see colors accurately, but each of the sheets appeared to be a furiously scribbled tale of terror. Knives dripping with blood. Skies with boiling, dark clouds and lightning bolts that sparked fires below. One showed the silhouette of a monster in a bright doorway at the top of faintly lit stairs.

"Oh my god," I murmured. "What did you do to her?"

"*Do* to her?" Hollis said. "I saved her. You've seen Lily's work these days, full of light and wonder. That's thanks to me. I encouraged her. Made her feel special. I come in the house today. Instead of cartoons on the TV, she's got songs blasting. I asked what the hell is going on. Lily scribbled a note saying it's Sonny's empowerment playlist."

"What are these drawings about?"

"What the hell …?" Hollis said, peering into the night.

Following his gaze, I heard footfalls approaching. I held my breath, terrified that it was Dan, and he would get shot.

"Stop!" I yelled. "He has a—"

There was a swift, dark motion on my right, then stars and pain obliterated my vision as Hollis struck me across the cheek so hard that I nearly blacked out. I fell to the leaves, my nose bleeding again. Dizzy, almost nauseated, I pushed up from the damp undergrowth with shaking hands and gingerly touched my burning, aching face.

"Hollis!" Nadine was yelling as she crashed toward us from the direction of the crumbled dwelling twenty yards away. "Hollis!"

"Nadine? What are you doing here?"

"Lily Facetimed me. She was frantic. I drove to your house and she got across that you were in trouble, and needed help. I was right behind her in the forest when we heard a gunshot, then ... good God, Sonny?"

"Come over here," Hollis prompted.

"Is that Earl?" Nadine stared at his body. "What happened?"

"He kidnapped Sonny. Where is Lily?" Hollis demanded.

"You're not going to convince her to come closer if you keep yelling," Nadine said. "She was over there by the stone pile a second ago."

"Lily!" Hollis called out. "You know what I've said about you being out and about at night. You head home, do you hear me?"

"I think I hear her heading home," Nadine said. "Makes sense now that she's heard your voice and knows you're ok. She's obsessed with looking in the mirror and brushing her hair. She and Everett had their first date today, can you imagine?"

"So, you're not curious about Earl lying there," Hollis said.

"I assume he's drunk, right?"

"Just sit down next to Sonny."

"Why? I don't understand."

Hollis raised the shotgun. "Just *do* it."

Nadine sat next to me without further fuss, keeping her eye on Hollis as he fixed his attention on the area where Lily might be hiding.

Once his back was turned, I whispered, "Nadine—"

"*Shh,*" she prompted. "Help is on the way. I have a plan. When I say the time is right, your job is to take Lily away."

I stared at her, scarcely recognizing the stripper I'd come to know during the past week. Her face was scrubbed free of makeup, her hair in a tight ponytail, and the long, bedazzled nails she usually wore were gone. She gave me a nod, her eyes flinty.

She'd come to wage war on Hollis Oakes.

"Hey," Hollis demanded. "What are you doing?"

"I'm looking at this poor girl," Nadine said. "Did Earl do this damage to her face? Horrid drunk. I never imagined—"

"You're not fooling anyone," Hollis said.

"Fooling?"

"*Stop* the dumb act. I'm not in the mood."

Nadine shifted as if poised to spring if the need arose.

"What have you figured out?" Hollis prompted.

Nadine looked dismayed that the surprise element of her plan had been dashed to pieces, but she lifted her chin as if to indicate she wasn't afraid of Hollis's attitude, or his shotgun.

"Chuck left me a note," she said. "When Sonny showed him a photo of a ring, he had a good idea it belonged to Earl's wife. There's a short list of ways a ring goes missing from a woman's hand. I assume Chuck confronted Earl, and it went wrong."

"You're sitting on her," Hollis said. "Earl's wife."

"Jesus Christ, Hollis."

I nudged Nadine, desperate to convey that it wasn't a good idea to provoke him. Hollis was distracted, keeping an eye on us one second, then peering into the darkness the next. He still looked winded from killing Earl. I couldn't tell if his tears were an indication that even a murderer could possess something akin to a conscience.

"I can't believe it came to this," he muttered, wiping his eyes. "Earl gone. It happened so fast, after all these years. I can't believe he's gone."

"You shot him?" Nadine said. "In cold blood?"

I groaned internally and nudged her again.

"Cold blood." Hollis snorted, wiping his nose. "I don't know why that line ever took hold. There's nothing cold about blood when it comes out. Why did you have to fix Lily's hair?" he demanded. "I almost lost it when I saw her."

"Why?" Nadine said.

"Shut up," he said. "Just be quiet." After a pause, he sighed and held out his hand. "Give it here."

"What?" Nadine said.

"Your phone."

"I don't have it."

Hollis fired the shotgun toward my right. Nadine and I yelped. I could tell she was having to give up another piece of her plan.

"Give it *here*," he said. "Toss it."

Nadine slowly pulled the phone from her pocket and tossed it to him.

Touching the screen, Hollis chuckled. "Making a recording. I heard about this trick. It's how Sonny nailed Pike for his visit."

He set the phone on a boulder and smashed it with a rock. The screen flickered with light, as if registering its demise, then went black.

Hollis demanded my phone. I told him Earl had come at me so fast and unexpectedly that my purse, my phone, and everything except my keys were at my house. Instructed to prove it, I had to turn out my pockets, unzip my pants, then lift my shirt.

Hollis reloaded the empty chamber of the shotgun, then he raised his jacket to one side, showing a hidden shoulder holster with a gun, and a lot of extra rounds.

"I'm sorry to destroy your pluck," he said, "but you need to understand. There's zero chance of you walking away. Zero."

"You're ok with killing women?" Nadine demanded.

"This is a spooky place for me," Hollis said. "Shadows and ghosts. Terrible stuff. I never come here without being loaded for bear. And I was right to do so, because … I'm sorry Nadine, but Kyle found this place some months ago. Maybe you figured it out already."

"Sick asshole," she seethed, with tears streaming down her face. "All this time, you had me believing the police killed him. Acted like you cared about Kyle. You're a sick, horrid, fuck."

"That I am."

"Don't you dare gloat!"

"I'm not gloating. And you're still alive, aren't you? Every time I need to make a course correction, it's hard. Like Earl said. It eats at me."

I gripped Nadine's hand to offer my sympathy, and to urge her one more time to please, please not provoke him.

She nodded, and thankfully, he didn't seem to see it.

"If Earl hadn't killed his wife, who knows how things would've turned out over the long haul," Hollis said. "But I helped him, and that uncorked something. It's jarring to get away with a crime. It's like money in the bank. Dark money. It tempts you on."

Hollis wiped his eyes.

"Months go by, a year. Then this couple shows up. Said they heard they could camp for free out here. An adventure. They'd finished up being in one of those war reenactment events in the area, and wanted to extend the fun of it. My God, the wife was beautiful. Strawberry blonde hair. Green eyes. Not the coloring I usually go for. I like blue eyes. Like yours, Sonny. But she was full figured, I guess from having a child. I let them pitch their tent and have their fun. I came out here and watched them at night. Listened in. A day comes when the husband heads out for supplies. So, I took a shot. Went to the tent and indicated how I admired her spirit. She looked scared. That hurt. The thought of it came on fast. I couldn't figure out how to—" Hollis made hand motions, as if indicating his level of effort in not devolving into being a monster.

"It was not my best moment," he said. "It wasn't enjoyable, truth be told. A lot of work holding a woman down who's not … well, the way she'd been with her husband. The screams had to be stopped. She sounded like an animal. I had no idea she was deaf. Not at first. The husband had to be dealt with once he got back from shopping. That was a whole other nightmare. Luckily, I had Earl to help. He owed me."

"*Jesus*," Nadine said. "Do you hear yourself?"

I blanched, once again obsessed with not drawing his attention to us, however nauseating it was to listen to his vile recollections.

"Where is Kyle?" Nadine sobbed. "Where is my son?"

"I'm sorry," Hollis said. "You won't believe it, but I am sorry about Kyle. I liked the boy. I thought he had promise, but he went and found the place where we'd buried the couple and Earl's wife. I see you reacting," he said with rising anger. "Let it be known I did the right thing with the couple's child. I brought her home. Kept her safe."

"Oh no," I whispered, catching onto another point where I'd let the elderly man in the diner steer me wrong. The married couple he'd remembered hearing about hadn't disappeared thirty years ago.

It must have been more like sixteen.

"I named her Lily," he said. "Made her my own. You've said yourself she's gifted. A rare talent with art. That's thanks to me."

"Why did you have to take Kyle?" Nadine moaned. "My baby."

"Some animal or other dug around in here. Plus, winters can stir up the ground over time. Kyle saw their old war costumes and figured they'd been long dead. From Civil War times, I guess. I'm sorry Nadine, but his dark side came out. He hatched a plan to torment the police who'd hassled him. He took the bones. Cleaned them ..."

As he talked, Hollis rubbed his shotgun barrel with his handkerchief. If he touched the wrong part, we'd end up like Earl.

"My work with volunteer fire and rescue put me at one of the crime scenes where somebody had left a scary surprise for an officer. Everybody was saying where the hell would somebody dig up human remains? I got a bad feeling about it, and knew I had to act fast. My trail cameras only showed deer for so long I'd stopped checking them. But I went home and checked the feed. Sure enough, there was Kyle returning to the area multiple times. I caught him at it one night. I'm sorry. He had to go."

"Is he here?" Nadine sobbed.

"Over there, I think," Hollis said.

Nadine's plan seemed to have buckled, and so had her defiant attitude. She was doubled over with grief, clutching at the leaves as if she wanted to dig up her son and hug him.

"I sent Everett to your farm, Sonny, when a call about trouble came over the scanner," he said. "Kyle had blurted that Raymond was on his target list. I couldn't tell Everett why he should go, of course. With Lily hiding in his truck, it was a near disaster. Pike was my next avenue. I could've kept tabs on the case through him, but he went and got himself fired. I was so mad I clocked him outside his favorite bar. Had his pants unzipped, pissing on bushes instead of using the men's room. I used your name to keep his anger stoked. If I'd had more time to steer him, I think he'd have helped me get rid of you, if need be."

"Good God," I murmured.

"Earl mucked up the chance to pin Sonny's demise on Kyle." Hollis waved one hand. "Stole a boat, waited for you to arrive at the lake. But apparently, you have skill with a rock. Like I said, Earl was a problem from the start. His drunk, irresponsible ways."

I held my breath, seeing Lily appear from the woods behind Hollis, moving carefully, silently. Seeing her fierce gaze, I had a split second to recalibrate the signs her wild hair had helped to hide. Instead of shy, she was wary. Instead of impish, she was smart. Stowing away in Everett's truck wasn't a sign of a child who refused to grow up. They were trial runs at breaking free. Who knew how old she'd been when she'd realized she had to stay under the radar of Hollis and Earl. Men who were liars, and didn't know the first thing about love.

In the same split second, the staccato thunder of a helicopter could be heard in the distance behind us, and it sounded as if a herd of deer were crashing toward us through the forest. Hollis lurched to his feet, keeping the shotgun trained in our direction.

"Did you call the cops?" he demanded.

With a look of determination, Lily lifted a long-handled shovel and clipped him hard across the back of his head. Nadine grabbed my arm and hauled me upward.

"Go, go, go," she hollered. "Get Lily away!"

Like an agile fox, Lily jumped over a log and gripped my hand. The force of it jerked me sideways, but I recovered fast. I felt winded from terror, clenching my teeth from the effort of lifting my legs in a hell-bent dash, half expecting a blast to come from behind us and rip us apart. I tripped, cursed, then pushed on, gripping Lily's hand.

Seeing bright, moving lights spangle through the dark forest up ahead, I felt hope for the first time that night. I didn't see officers, but rather their geared-up shadows lengthening toward us. Far ahead of them, closing in on us, was a lone figure looking as if he were attempting to win the Heisman Trophy, hurdling logs and all else in his path. It was an effort so extreme his breathing was audible across the entire forest.

I risked a quick turn and realized Nadine was nowhere to be seen.

I came to a stop, breathing hard. "Nadine?"

Lily gripped my hand, urging me onward. I pulled away and started running back to help Nadine. She wasn't thinking straight, out of her mind with grief.

A gunshot rang out up ahead.

"No!" I screamed, running faster. "Nadine!"

The flashlight Hollis had brought with him showed glimpses of Nadine grappling with Hollis over the shotgun, and Everett rolling on the ground clutching his leg. Good God, he was a part of the plan? And it wasn't going well. The shotgun blasted again. It pushed Nadine off balance. Hollis tossed the gun to the side and reached for his holster.

"Get up!" I shrieked. "Roll!"

Nadine kicked out, and Hollis fell backward, spraying pistol fire into the air. He clambered to his knees and began shooting in all directions. *Pop-pop-pop. Pop-pop-pop-pop.*

I was about to holler again when a thudding tumult of snapping sticks and scattering leaves came from behind me. I felt a rush of movement, then I seemed to have four legs as I was scooped off my feet by an arm that locked around my waist. I caught a glimpse of Dan's determined face as I pitched forward onto my stomach amidst the leaves.

I scrambled, desperate to help Nadine and Everett, but Dan was clambering along with me, cursing under his breath, then I was pinned down by his inescapable weight.

I struggled against him, furious.

"Head down!" Dan hollered in my ear, "Head down!"

His arms shifted and I felt a new weight settle over my head, something that blocked out all but a few slivers of light and smelled of synthetic fibers. A ballistic vest, I figured out, improvised to cover my head and neck. Over the sound of our combined labored breathing, I heard more gun blasts echoing through the forest, and strange zipping sounds, then a few thwapping sounds. Bullets, I realized, hitting rocks and trees.

I struggled, unable to bear the thought of Dan taking a hit on my behalf. Chuck was dead. Maybe Nadine. Everett, too. Enough was enough. Desperate to transport myself to anywhere but that horrible scene in the forest, I attempted to free myself.

Dan's muscles flexed, redoubling their effort to pin me down. My right leg dug into the leaves. He clamped down on it with a boot. My left leg stirred. His left boot pushed it into the leaves.

Moaning, weeping, I listened to the rain of gunshots and the police talk squawking over a radio he'd brought. The ground around us registered the thudding drumbeats of helicopter blades above us, and a blast of wind sent leaves spraying everywhere.

There was very little air in the protective tent Dan had created. Every time I exhaled, it got harder to refill my lungs. My brain heard everything, but it was all very distant, too outrageous to be real.

"Drop the weapon," a voice above us boomed.

More shots rang out, then a single, echoing gun blast split the night, and it seemed a very different kind of weapon than Hollis had been using. There was a moment where I didn't hear shots anymore, only the thudding helicopter blades, the snatches of police talk, and Dan exhaling in my ear with a whispered "Jesus," then, "Holy crap."

33

Unintelligible codes squawked over Dan's radio for a long moment, then came a clear statement: "It's done. He's down."

Dan exhaled, his breath palpable on my neck, then he lifted his weight from my back and rolled away. The sudden influx of cool night air in my lungs had my eyelids fluttering like moths. Hands gently rolled me over, and I was blinking up at Dan. He looked as if he'd been thrown into a pond and pulled out dripping wet. He was sweating from his run through the forest, I realized, visibly shaking as he looked down at me. He stared at my face, from my bloody nose to my bruised cheek.

"Oh my God, Sonny ..."

I lurched up into a sitting position. "Where is Nadine?"

"She's fine." Dan steadied me and gently tried to turn my face toward him. "Sonny, is anything broken?"

"*Everything* is broken. I was going to Boston. I was all packed. Joan is mad at me. Everything is a mess."

"Joan is not mad at you," Dan said.

"How did this happen? I don't ... Earl's gun is over there. I tossed it away. Then Hollis showed up."

"Sonny—"

"It's ok if you need to go find the gun." Pushing his hands away, I searched the forest. "Nadine!" I hollered. "Nadine!"

"Right here, hon," she said, stepping over sticks on her way through the shadows to join us. She knelt by my side, her eyes red from crying, but shining with triumph as well. "We got the asshole. You, me, and Lily. Three women." Nadine focused on my nose. "Give her a cloth, for heaven's sake! Did anybody not think to help her clean up?"

Prompted by her lecture, multiple officers who'd arrived, plus Dan, quickly searched their many pockets. One guy had a bottle of water. It was offered with a package of tissues. Nadine took them and gently wiped my cheeks, under my nose, and my chin.

"Lily," I said. "Where's Lily?"

"She's over there with Everett. He's a mess, seeing his father dead, and learning his mom was murdered," Nadine said.

Too dazed to hear what Dan was asking me as he gently touched my shoulder, I saw Everett crying, stretched out on the ground with EMTs working on his leg wound, and Lily holding his hand. Their path forward would be tough. They would face challenges most people never knew, but the turmoil of their early lives had instilled strength and unique coping skills. I had a feeling they would be ok.

"Sonny?" Nadine prompted.

I focused on her. "How did you survive?"

"I keep telling you the benefits of pole dancing."

With brimming eyes, she gave up trying to crack a joke. I hugged her with tears streaming down my face, unable to express my gratitude for her heroic effort to save me. In the days to come, I would be there for her as she faced heartbreaking funerals. Instead of helping Chuck update his social media accounts, all I could do now was pull his photos together for a memorial service. Chuck grinning. Tuning his hot rod. I would make sure everyone knew the man who'd been cut down before his time.

It would take a while for the other victims to be exhumed. Kyle, cut off from the chance to own up to his awful deeds and redeem himself. Lily and Everett had been left with scattered bones to mourn over. How had Hollis described that area of the forest? A place of shadows, ghosts, and terrible stuff. He'd been right about that much.

Blinking, tearful, I realized that Dan was in a hell of his own. There were tears in his eyes as he looked away from us into the dark forest, but he refused to let them take hold, his jaw firm and his mouth in a fierce line. Nadine reached out and gripped his hand, as if to convey that she saw him for who he was now, a solid cop and a good guy.

Sniffling, wiping away our tears, Nadine and I held each other at arm's length with wide-eyed looks that conveyed our astonishment to be alive. Like people who'd gotten out of a war zone, we would probably share a moment like this whenever we met for all time to come.

"I need to go," she finally said. "I'm not done venting."

As she stood, two officers gently redirected her toward the police lights and vehicles arriving beyond the woods. She resisted for a moment, then she hollered over their shoulders as she was led to safety.

"Who's got zero chance now, Hollis? You killed my son and lied about it all this time! Had me thinking the police did it!" She broke down and cried, her voice fading as she got further and further away. "Lying asshole. It's not right that he had a quick end."

"Your turn," Dan said softly. "I know I screwed up."

I focused on him, realizing I'd left him to imagine that I'd blocked him out for the past few minutes out of anger.

"What?" I managed.

"We had the wrong guy. I'm trying to calculate how mad you are at me to want to break free during a hail of bullets."

"I did that because you were risking your life. It was scary and awful. Never do it again, do you understand?"

I gripped his vest and hugged him tightly with my eyes closed. That only made it easier to relive my memory of him running toward me while Hollis fired pistol rounds in every direction. Dan collapsed against me with his arms pulling me close, shaking as he gave into the emotion he'd been holding in check. With his beard against my neck, he choked and cried, whispering over and over again that he was sorry.

I tried to say the same to him, but my throat was clamped in a vice as sobs wrenched through me. I couldn't catch my breath. Footfalls stirred the leaves as officers gave us some privacy.

We stayed there for a long moment, hugging each other, breathing in desperate, uneven gasps. My throat began to unclench. I whispered assurances that I was ok. It took a while for the truth of it to sink in. I could tell he was having trouble pushing back the horrific scenarios that had dominated his thinking as he'd rushed to the scene.

Pulling away from each other, we wiped our eyes. I asked Dan how on earth he'd put the right picture together so fast.

"Joan wanted to apologize to you," he managed. "She saw you driving down your lane. It didn't seem normal, how you handled your car. She saw a guy behind you as you drove by. She raced to your house and saw a mess, signs of a fight. Things exploded from there."

"Did Earl leave his car near my farm?"

"He hitchhiked. First to the race, then to your house. Nadine reached out to me. It came together fast, figuring out the ring belonged to Earl's wife, and where she might be buried. I told her to not approach the area. She refused to listen. Her concession was to have her phone line open the whole time. Lily called me from Hollis's phone, so we had a backup for sound at the scene. That's how I knew—" Dan closed his eyes. "I heard Hollis say your chances were zero. The SWAT team needed a minute to gear up. I didn't think we had a minute."

"You took a huge risk."

"I didn't think we had a minute," he repeated. "I had to approach slowly at first to not tip him off. Then—" He paused, seeing an EMT coming toward us. "I'll tell you the rest later."

With Dan's help, I climbed to my wobbly legs and discovered that I'd sprained my right ankle. I was repositioned to a log that offered a more comfortable place to sit than the damp ground.

"Sorry it took a while," the EMT said, covering my shoulders with a blanket, and then shining a penlight in each of my eyes.

"Is Everett ok?" I said.

"Shot in the leg. He'll recover."

He assessed me for injuries, gently examining my throat, touching my face, and checking my pulse. I struggled to stay calm.

"Now for the hard part," the EMT said. "I should take a look at your nose. You're not going to like it."

"My nose …?"

"Are you ready?" he said.

"No …"

Even though his fingers were gentle as they felt my nose, I winced from the pain and hollered for him to stop.

"That woke her up," he said. "I don't think it's broken."

"Is a stretcher on the way?" Dan asked.

"A minute out."

"No," I said. "I want to walk."

"Your ankle is sprained," Dan said. "And it's a long way."

"I'll lean on a stick."

Dan sighed. "Sonny—"

"I just escaped being murdered. I get a say."

"It's fine if you need a minute to catch your breath," the EMT said, adding amiably as he pulled out his phone, "Dan and I go way back. In high school, we were on the ski team. I tried to top his speed, but never could. This is him right here."

I squinted at the photo of Dan, which appeared to have been taken during a race. "Oh, that's unfortunate," I said.

Dan choked back a snicker.

"I didn't mean your ability," I quickly went on. "I mean, look at you skiing. All tucked in, very fast. I was talking about the way the photo was taken. The exposure is all wrong, the snow too gray."

"I took the picture," the EMT said.

"Oh ... sorry."

He peered at the screen. "The snow isn't gray."

"It is. Your mind is telling you it's white."

"How do I fix it?"

"It's easy. Your phone is different, but ... crap, where did it go?"

"I think you deleted it."

A smile tugged at the corners of Dan's mouth, but he'd been watching me intently during the entire exchange. I suspected there was no need to tell him that I'd embraced the moment of distraction for a very good reason, but I spelled out how I felt all the same.

"Once I'm hauled out, I'll be asked to make a statement. I'm not ready. Not even close. Can't I just go get my car?"

"Your car needs to be processed," Dan said gently.

"Good God."

Dan signaled for the EMT to give us some space.

The definition of "space" was anything ranging from ten feet to ten yards of shadowed forest as officers came and went. Dan reached for my hand and held it between his strong, warm palms, rubbing life back into my fingers when he found them to be chilled.

Focusing on his face, I was crushed to see that he seemed poised to raise a difficult subject. I guessed what it was.

"Sonny …"

"I get it," I said. "You're glad I'm alive. Hence all the hugging. But we're past the line by a million miles."

"The line …?"

I recreated the back-and-forth motion he'd made at the racetrack indicating that if I crossed it, our "thing" would be over.

"Sonny, I'm the one who crossed the line," he said. "I knew it a minute later. By then, you were heading to your car."

"Oh."

"The thing is—"

"I don't want to make a statement," I insisted. "If I relate the details out loud, I'll have to go through it again." I grasped his hand, desperate to make him understand. "I'm numb right now. It may not be healthy, but I prefer it to letting the feelings take hold. Is there any way I can just go home? Delay the statement, like, for a month?"

Dan joined me on the log, adding his warmth to the comfort zone I'd created under the blanket. His troubled gaze said he didn't want to hear the details any more than I wanted to relate them.

"I saw you," I whispered.

"Where?"

"On the road. You—" I closed my eyes. "This is what I'm talking about. I don't have the energy to edit things as I go along."

"You can't edit what happened. Why would you?" Dan paused. "Are you saying you saw my truck? Tonight?"

"I'm sorry. I shouldn't have said."

"Where?"

"I saw flashing lights. Earl made me pull into a dirt lane and shut off the car. I knew it was you. He made me just sit there."

Dan said not to worry about telling him, then he rubbed my back as if to remind me in a real and tangible way, *We're here now, you made it past that awful moment.* But I felt him shaking again.

"I was miserable about the need to head north on Monday," he finally said. "Now it's exponentially worse."

"I can't be the reason you make a career change."

Dan paused, debating. Now he was the one holding back.

"What?" I said. "Tell me."

"I heard Hollis," he managed. "Rushed out here. And a miracle happened. There you were, running toward me. I'd grabbed a second ballistic vest on the hope that I'd have time to give it to you. Put it on you and get you out. I'm like, I can do this. Save her. Just bring on more steam. Then you stopped. You started running the other way."

I couldn't bear his suffering gaze. "I'm sorry …"

"I get why you did it, but I can't undo those seconds. They're in a loop in my head. And it's been, what? Less than an hour?"

"It's too much. I told you this would happen."

"Sonny, I'm *not* trying to push you away." Dan looked at me intently. "Forget how I sounded at the track. It was from my concern for your safety. I wanted you out of the nightmare. We're back to the benefits of the snail's pace. You have things to process. I have things to process. I'm worried that if we try to work through the fallout when we're still getting to know each other, there's a chance we'll implode."

"I guess the boat attack was a mini version of that," I said. "I didn't want more chaos, so I was evasive."

"And I was impatient. Sonny, you went through multiple crazy things in a short span of days with no chance to process any of it. If you want me here, that's flat-out what will happen. You need to be straight with me about what you need because—"

"You can't derail your job because of me. End of discussion."

"You say that, but …" He studied me for a moment. "You need to understand, I would be up north for at least a few months. I wouldn't be able to call or text anybody. It's that sort of deal."

"I know. I get it."

"If that is the path we agree to land on ... just, during the silence, don't picture me enjoying myself. I'm going to question it. Second guess. It's going to be a tough haul."

"It's ok to have a beer," I said. "Maybe watch TV."

He nodded. "You, too."

"I'll be busy growing old doing farm chores."

"You need to make your statement, Sonny," Dan said. "I watched you when you were describing the incident with Pike. You got more and more grounded as you told the story. This will be the same deal. Somehow, you beat the odds. You even dodged flying bullets. I know this because I have a giant gash in the back of my ballistic vest."

"Oh no ..."

"Just surface damage. No harm done."

"Are you sure you have to go to the border?" I whispered.

"My heart says no. My gut says yes."

"I guess so."

Dan cracked up, and the burst of emotion brought tears to his brown eyes. "Unbelievable. You *guess* so."

"I'm nothing, if not consistent."

He indicated the officers bringing gear to the scene. "This isn't what I'd planned for our third fake date."

"There've been three?"

"Right. I guess it's our second fake date."

"You saved my butt," I said. "When I lost my mind."

"Let's keep that in mind when I screw up again." He nodded toward the outside world. "Are you ready?"

"Will Stable be there?"

"Most likely. I heard you pounded him into the ground in Nadine's parking lot. I'm more worried about him than I am about you." He offered a hand, gently pulling me to my feet so I could clamber onto the waiting stretcher with dignity. "Don't forget your cape."

"It's a blanket."

"Not on you. It's a cape." Once I was installed on the stretcher with my arms folded in irritation at the need to be hauled out, Dan motioned officers and other personnel out of our path. "This woman is a certified sorceress, so don't make any wrong moves."

"You heard about that?" I said.

"Brumby is apparently talking about it nonstop."

"He's mad because I already have a fake boyfriend."

Dan paused. "Just so we're clear ..."

"It's you. Dummy."

"Hmm," he murmured. "Je sauve la vie d'une femme, elle me traite d'idiot. Je suppose qu'elle a raison, donc ça va."

"All of which means?"

Dan squeezed my hand. "I said, 'Yes, dear.'"

"How do you say, 'That's annoying?'"

"C'est ennuyeux."

"C'est ennuyeux," I repeated. "Clearly, that one will come in handy."

"Oui."

I smiled, deciding if he was going to insist on calling in the cavalry and saving my butt, I would let him have the last word.

Just this once.

34

Joan and I were on my porch in forest green rocking chairs that had been battered by countless summers and freezing winters until their wooden seats threatened to leave splinters if one didn't pay attention to how she rocked. With glasses of iced tea on the round table between us, we basked in the sunshine and the first real heat of June.

Joan indicated the book on my lap. "What's that?"

"A present from Dan."

Before heading to the Canadian border, Dan had given me a blank volume that was identical to the ones Raymond had used. On the front, Dan had added a label that said, *Life on the Farm, Continued,* and told me I should start writing down my thoughts.

I'd picked it up a dozen times, but never found the right frame of mind to express myself, nor could I decide which stories to impart.

"I haven't seen him in a while," Joan said.

"He's up north. Border work."

When I didn't elaborate, Joan sighed. "Did you hear Nadine might sell the strip club? She's talking about adopting Lily."

"I heard."

"She's on the verge of signing a book deal. It might be a movie." When I said nothing, Joan said, "You'd be in it. Is that ok with you?"

"She'd come up with a way of not mentioning me directly."

"But if she makes a lot of money …"

"I said I don't need any. She says she'll insist."

"That would be nice." Joan paused. "Back to Dan, did I ever tell you what went on that night? When we found out you were abducted?"

This pulled me out of my half-doze. "No."

Looking thrilled to have gotten my attention, she said, "There's a future with him, right? It's pretty clear he felt that way."

"Why?"

"Well. Sue, Kate, and I were in your kitchen. He all but takes the door off the hinges on his way in, and I think he almost vomited when he saw your blood on the floor. Then he dumps the contents of your bag on the table, grabs the pages of people you'd met, and slaps them down side by side. We were all yelling at him, asking why anyone would kidnap you, and he turns to us with that police officer voice thing, and hollers, 'Stop talking. *Now.*' He plants his hands on the table and stares at the sheets, the Civil War badge, everything. In two seconds flat he hammered the table and uttered an expletive I won't repeat."

"He figured it out," I said.

"Enough to blaze off and all but empty the gravel on your driveway as he left. Typical man. Wouldn't tell us what he'd figured out."

I nodded, though I knew very well that State Trooper Daniel Bolton was anything but a typical man. There was no way of knowing if our flirtations would lead to anything solid once he was back from his assignment, whenever that might be. I'd learned to not count on anything until there was zero room for doubt. There were moments of optimism. Moments of anger, where I would glare at my phone even though he'd said there would be no texts or phone calls. And moments where I would remember, so clearly, how his voice sounded, or how he'd looked when he'd smiled. How it felt when we'd kissed. Even in my banged-up state, I'd refused to settle for a quick parting hug. It was tough. Intense. Emotional.

I rarely allowed myself to think about that. There were too many other memories that threatened to break me.

"You know what I can't figure out?" Joan said. "How Hollis got people to believe Lily was his daughter. Didn't his neighbors suspect anything when he suddenly had a child? I know his wife died out of state. Maybe that's a factor."

"I think so."

"You never write in that journal," Joan said.

"It's hard. The pages are so pristine."

"Write about this moment."

"I have a notion. I'm working on it."

"Eat the strawberry, for heaven's sake." Joan indicated the bright red berry that sat on the table between us on one of Raymond's pie plates. "There are a zillion others in the field, just as ripe."

"But this one is the first," I said.

I know you can't murder a berry, but that's what it felt like every time I picked it up and tried to take a bite. I would get there eventually.

For now, I knew how to start the journal. Not with my own thoughts. I needed to begin with Raymond. A dark day. How it all began.

I picked up my pencil, and started to write:

On a frigid morning last February, Raymond French sat down at his kitchen table with a cup of coffee and two pieces of cinnamon toast, wanting to fortify himself against the cold before he went out to clear ice from his roof, and tend his flock of sheep. Wind threw sleet against the windows as Raymond ate, and sipped, and read an article in Coast & Candle Magazine about the effects of climate change. Shaking his head over the state of affairs in the larger world beyond his quiet, thirty-acre farm in the town of Gracious, Maine, he dabbed one finger against the plate, licked off the cinnamon he'd collected, then tipped the magazine to dump scattered crumbs into a neat pile on the tabletop.

He planned to finish cleaning up later on.

He set his reading glasses next to his plate, put on his heavy boots, buttoned up his parka, and walked out the door. Fighting his way through deep snow drifts in the pre-dawn darkness, he set up a ladder next to the house to reach the ice dam and started climbing. Minutes passed. Maybe a half hour. Nobody knows the exact timing. Whether he'd finished the task, or had just started. He slipped. Fell. Took his final breath. Doctors say he didn't suffer.

The things he'd left on the table remained untouched for days, waiting for someone to come along and piece together his last moments on Earth.

That someone turned out to be me, the daughter he never got a chance to acknowledge, let alone meet. I believe he made me his sole heir on the blind hope that my mother would agree to tell me about him one day, not imagining he would die in his forty-ninth year. All I know for certain is that I'm left to start at the end of his life, and work my way backward.

About the Author

People have described Nina DeGraff's writing as funny, suspenseful, and very real. During her travels to jungles, coral reefs, and other destinations in search of adventure, Nina's practical side endeavors to maintain control. The rest of her is a plucky photographer with a ridiculous amount of optimism, and a fascination for the unknown. It seemed natural to wrap her unique real-life experiences into a mystery series.

Her Sonny Littlefield novels are based on the years she and her husband raised sheep and horses on a small organic farm in rural Maine. In writing the series, she draws heavily on her own brushes with disaster, moments when she pressed her luck too far, even the time she brought a tip to the police and ended up helping them solve a crime.

Nina loves photographing animals and scenes that she can use in her art. At the same time, she pays close attention to atmospheric details that enable her to bring a sense of realism to her writing.

Her albums of nature audio tracks are available through Spotify, Apple Music, and other streaming services. Examples of her photos and videos are on her website, www.ninadegraff.com. She blends her photography and graphic design skills to create a range of fabric products, which are available through Spoonflower and her Etsy shop.

Made in the USA
Monee, IL
26 September 2024

66232357R00174